ARCANA
by Scott Michael Stenwick

ARCANA

by Scott Michael Stenwick

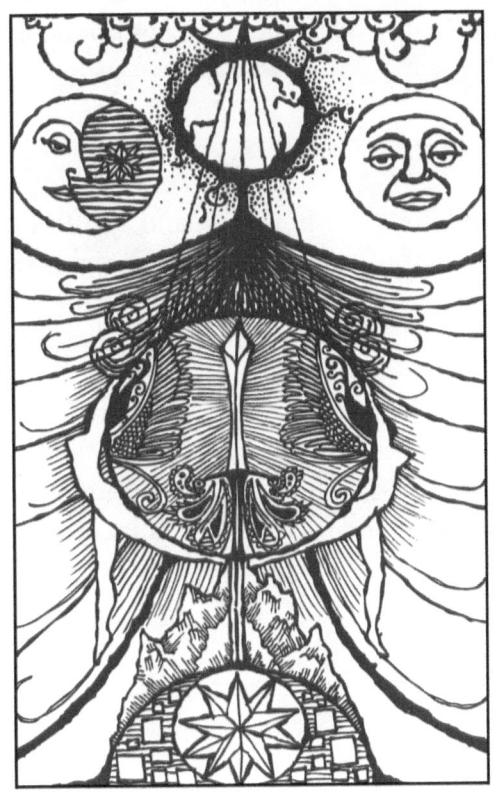

PENDRAIG PUBLISHING, Los Angeles

Pendraig Publishing, Sunland, CA 91040
© 2009 Scott Michael Stenwick. All rights reserved.
Published 2009
Printed in the United states of America

ISBN: 978-0-9843302-5-6

For Maurine, with love.

00. Prelude
Ain – Nothing

A chilling wind shook the forest, rattling the dry leaves that still clung to the swaying limbs of dormant oaks, as the dark procession traversed a lonely trail in the dead of night. The thirteen figures clad in full black robes took no notice of the cold, intent as they were upon their task. Some carried the ancient implements of magick described by medieval Inquisitors and occultists alike - the ritual dagger for tracing infernal shapes or letting blood, the cup for purification, the censor for consecration, the scourge for punishing disobedient spirits. Others simply trudged empty-handed, working their way through the brush where the trail was overgrown and warding off the encroaching branches that seemed to part effortlessly for the first figure in the line, only to snap sharply back into position as the second approached.

As the trees began to thin, the leader of the procession pointed across the clearing to a low hill. "There," he said in a voice as gentle as it was commanding. "I have already prepared the place." The others nodded, continuing their hike out of the wooded area and up the sloping bank to the hill's summit which basked in the light of the full moon overhead. A perfect ring of stones lined the top of the hill, and in the exact center of the enclosed area sat a large flat-topped granite boulder. The procession silently formed into a rough circle around the central stone and began the work of positioning eleven black candles around the perimeter.

The leader pointed to one of the candles. "Slide that one two inches to the left... yes, like that." His face was a combination of features that perhaps could be described as average in the extreme, with medium-length brown hair and medium blue eyes, almost too ordinary to be credible, but as the candle was moved to its proper position the malevolent grin that flickered momentarily across his face offered a glimpse behind the forgettable mask. His voice remained soft and unshakeable. "Now we are ready."

The woman bearing the cup stepped forth from the circle. She filled the silver chalice with brackish water poured from a small vial, and then walked to each of the four cardinal directions in turn, beginning in the east and moving counterclockwise. At each quarter, she traced a circle with the chalice and spoke the words of purification. "By the salt of earth and the water of the great sea, I purify this place of working." Upon completing her walk of the perimeter, she stepped up to the boulder, which served as a natural altar, and held the cup aloft, tracing an inverted pentagram in the air. "In the name of Typhon, lord of the seas and the deep earth, I purify by water." She then poured the contents of the cup upon the altar and stepped back into the circle.

As she returned to her place, the man carrying the large brass censor stepped forward. He poured incense upon the burning charcoal, and as the smoke billowed forth he likewise walked to each quarter beginning in the east, but proceeding clockwise and tracing a cross in the air with the censor as he spoke the lines of consecration. "By the air and fire that make sweet the world, I consecrate this place of working. " As the woman had done, he completed his walk of the perimeter and then, before the altar, held the censor aloft and used it to trace an inverted pentagram in the air. "In the name of Set, lord of the sun and the boundless sky, I consecrate by fire." He then placed the censor in the center of the altar and returned to his place as the smoke rose invitingly to the heavens.

As the rest of the figures stood silently, the leader closed his eyes and drew a deep breath slowly and evenly, inhaling energy almost tangible from the earth and sky. His features faded into placid concentration, absolute serenity become one with the convergence of cosmic forces. Then, abruptly, he extended his right hand toward the central altar stone with his fingers spread wide, and spoke a discordant incantation. "*Yolcam ialprg!*" Obediently, the candles set around the circle flashed and flared to life, causing several members of the circle to react with visible starts. "Now the chant," he ordered, his voice forceful but still low and quiet, as his followers stood silent and transfixed by the sudden conjuration of fire.

Finally, their voices rose slowly in unison, the chant resonant and somber.

> *We celebrate the powers of night,*
> *That which vanquishes the light,*
> *This night, Dark One, hear our call*
> *And stand before us all.*

As they repeated the chant it become louder and more insistent, the sound merging into a backdrop over which the leader raised his arms skyward and spoke, his voice now penetrating and resonant. "Coronzon, lord of chaos, lord of entropy, lord of dispersion, mighty dragon of death, *telocvovim*, I, Balzador, summon thee from the infernal abyss! Come forth and stand before us, your adoring servants! *Coronzon, zacare ca od zamran, odo cicle qaa, zorge lap zirdo noco Vovin, hoath drilp!*" The smoke from the censor curled up into a vortex of whirling fumes upon the altar, bringing with it a cacophony of chaotic sound and muffled light that somehow completely failed to fill the circle with anything but silent darkness. "Now the sacrifice," he said softly, "to bring the Dark One into full manifestation."

"What sacrifice?" asked the woman who had performed the purification, caught off guard. She spoke in a near-whisper, not wanting to disturb the aura of fearsome power that now filled the circle. "You said nothing of…"

The malevolent grin returned. "You," he replied succinctly, extending his right hand as he had done when lighting the candles. "*Yolcam teloch!*"

Like marionettes cut loose from their strings, the woman and her eleven compatriots slumped to the ground, leaving Balzador standing alone amidst his broken human toys. He watched expectantly as his magical sight revealed shimmering luminance radiating momentarily from the twelve bodies before being swept

9

up into the vortex above the altar, which grew in intensity until it towered at least thirty feet into the air like a whirling tornado formed from the stuff of shadows. In its center, space itself rippled like fabric and then tore in two. From this hole between worlds stepped a being wreathed in blackness that the moonlight was unable to penetrate, a figure vaguely humanoid but shifting constantly in the grip of continuous change, decay, and recombination of myriad forms. Around it, the smell of the air turned from that of the sweet and cloying incense to the suffocating stench of decomposition. "So it *is* you," growled a voice hastily constructed from the chaotic noise itself. "I expected a pretender."

"It is, my lord," replied Balzador, throwing back his hood. His face twisted and changed, its new shape remaining vaguely humanoid but marked by the horns and pointed features of a legendary devil.

"Do you summon me now to beg for death?" demanded Coronzon, the Dark Lord. A low chuckle rippled through across the circle as the smoke within curled into nightmare shapes poised to strike.

"No!" Balzador countered quickly, holding the aerial phantoms at bay with a tight gesture of his hand and a forced incantation. "*Adrpan lonshi telochvovim.*" The shapes slowly weakened and began to dissolve, unable to approach their intended prey.

"Then what?" pressed the Dark Lord impatiently.

Balzador took a deep breath. "I have summoned you to ask for my freedom."

The clouds shrouding the altar darkened with rage. "Never!" the cacophony struck the protection spell like a hammer hurled in anger. "You dared to challenge my throne. You will never again be allowed to threaten it!"

"Perhaps. But I have a deal that I believe will interest you."

Coronzon's voice was a contemptuous sneer. "You can offer me nothing. Your impertinence exceeds all bounds!" The phantoms swirled more forcefully, gaining strength, their hatred hanging in the air like leaden fumes.

Balzador's brow furrowed as his concentration intensified. His protection spell was still working, but he knew that it would only hold for so long. He spoke quickly. "I can offer you a weapon that will ensure victory over the Archons in this universe, and perhaps countless others. Do you expect me to believe that such a thing doesn't interest you?"

The air suddenly stood immediately silent, the shadows considering. After what seemed like a timeless interval for the protection spell to endure, the Dark Lord finally spoke. "No," said the voice slowly. "I know your trickery all too well. You lack the power. You are an exile. You are separated from the source of infernal light and the Archons will not have one of your kind. There is no other force great enough in this universe or another to aid or oppose me."

"You are incorrect," countered Balzador swiftly, his spell beginning to fail. "My research has discovered such a force – a power not yet slaved to the will of the Archons or your own. The humans call it magick. It is a kind of energy unlike anything found in the Abyss, for it is a neutral force formed from the interaction of order and entropy. I believe that it can be harnessed and controlled, much as you harnessed the principle of dispersion Aeons ago. If I can do this, I will become a being of great power. But I cannot do so as an exile on this plane. That is why I have called you here."

"You are a fool if the humans have convinced you of such nonsense, and you must think me a fool to expect me to believe. Have you called me here merely to explain a fruitless plan that can bear no possible outcome?"

"No," repeated Balzador, more emphatically. "I have called you here to offer you an alliance in exchange for my freedom." The protection spell collapsed as he spoke, but as he prepared to cast another, the swirling air held its ground, the phantoms now awaiting the orders of their dark master.

"Explain," commanded Coronzon.

"I've been trying to do just that. As the humans say, I want to make a deal. The deal is this: should I manage to collect and focus the energy called magick, I will pledge my own powers to your side against the Archons in exchange for the freedom that I have long sought. Together we will be strong enough to defeat the Archons and drive them first from this world, and then from this universe entirely. With the balance of power shifted in our favor, we should prevail. Otherwise, I suspect that your forces will remain immobilized by what I assume to be the current stalemate."

The air settled as the phantoms receded, and stillness settled over the hill. "It is so," admitted Coronzon. "As was true in your time, the Archons remain evenly matched with my own minions in countless battles across the multiverse. An ally of significant power could help to turn them back. But you betrayed my trust once. I will not simply free you on the basis of your word that this power exists."

"Oh, I'm not asking you to do so. Naturally, this deal is contingent upon my success. You have nothing to lose. And are you so filled with disbelief that you would risk my offering the same deal to the Archons?"

The sound rose, the air twisted, the phantoms returned, poised for battle. "You would join forces with our sworn enemies?" demanded Coronzon furiously.

"Only if you won't help me. I've been a prisoner on this world for centuries, jumping from body to body as these pathetic creatures age and die. I'm ready to go home, and what better way than to return as a conqueror? I will seek the Archons, if that is what I must do, but I am making the offer to you first."

Again, the convulsing air fell away. "Then I will accept." From the human-shaped fog of darkness, a black, clawed hand rose. "By my Throne I swear to you, that should you master the power of magick and pledge unto me your eternal support in the war against the Archons, I will grant you your freedom. Is that enough? I have already remained here too long to go unnoticed."

"It is," replied Balzador. "Now go in peace. We will meet again soon. *Adrpan comselah madriax.* " He raised his left hand in a gesture of dismissal, and as he did so the figure of Coronzon faded. The spinning vortex of smoke and sacrificed souls slowly wound down into wisps of cloud that hung over the top of the hill and dispersed in the soft night breeze.

As the Dark Lord departed, Balzador's features resumed their nondescript form. He removed his robe and tossed it into the circle of corpses, revealing a button-down heavy flannel shirt and jeans, and then turned and strode down the hill with effortless grace. He faced a daunting task – collecting and focusing the magical energy of an entire world in exchange for the freedom that had eluded him for millennia.

But he knew exactly where to begin.

0. The Fool

The Spirit of Aethyr
The Element of Air

Spring had come to the city of Minneapolis, an annual event of a significance not nearly so appreciated in parts of the country free from Minnesota's arctic winters. The snow that had blanketed the city for the previous five months was gone, melted into runny slush and mud underfoot. It was a relatively warm Friday night, and the fashionable clubs and restaurants of the warehouse district were packed in an exuberant celebration of the end of an unusually cold and nasty season.

The slick black Pontiac GTO was a classic from 1965, in perfect condition and, judging by the low scoop on top of the hood, modified for racing. The car's engine growled menacingly as it maneuvered into a parking space left oddly vacant in front of Morpheus, the Twin Cities' most popular restaurant and nightclub. Michael Niemand stepped out of the car, locked the door, and traced a quick sigil over the vehicle with his right index finger. He was relatively short and stocky with long black hair and stormy blue-gray eyes, and was dressed impeccably in a black button-down shirt and slacks. Around his neck on a silver chain hung a small silver unicursal hexagram that picked up the glow of the street lamps. He walked down the sidewalk to the high arch that served as the main entrance to the club.

Recognizing him immediately, the doorman gestured him inside. "Is she here yet?" asked Michael, already knowing the answer but asking for the sake of appearances and on the off chance that his magical senses might be wrong.

The doorman nodded.

"Does she look upset?"

"Well, with that one it's kind of hard to tell," replied the doorman with an uncertain shrug, "but I get the feeling she isn't too happy about something."

Michael let out a dejected sigh. "Thanks," he said with a forced smile, offering his usual generous tip. As he crossed the huge foyer to the restaurant entrance, he cleared his mind and checked his magical defenses, even though he was unsure they would do him much good. Elspeth's strength as a magician was surpassed only by her ability to fly into rages and use her powers indiscriminately on anyone who happened to be in her way, and he had a feeling that tonight that person would be him.

He saw her as soon as he entered the restaurant, sitting at a table off to the side of the room in the stiff, controlled posture that usually marked extreme anger or resentment. Her face was cold and expressionless, though that was nothing unusual, and even without any visible facial expression her beauty had an unearthly, almost magical quality to it, an outward mark of the shining power that filled the core of her being like molten sunlight. Fashion-model tall and slim, with long, straight black hair, she could have graced the cover of many magazines if she had any desire to do so. Of course, her obsession had always been magick, not physical beauty, but it seemed that somehow she had managed to achieve mastery of both — at least when she was able to hold on to her ephemeral cool.

As Elspeth spotted him, her silver-blue eyes flashed accusingly in the dim light.

Resigned to his fate, Michael crossed the expansive room and seated himself at the table. "Look," he began, "I know you're upset about this, but…"

Her voice was low and contained as she cut him off. "This goes beyond 'upset', Michael. Well beyond. In fact, I'm amazed that I'm even sitting here talking to you. I just want to know one thing — how did you do it? What on earth could you have promised Jonas and the others?"

"Absolutely nothing," he replied, amazed at the question. "Are you so convinced of my inferiority that you can't even accept that maybe, just maybe, I could be a better magician than you are? At least, by the criteria of the Inner Order?"

16

She shook her head dismissively. "No. I will never accept that. You know I'm stronger."

"Yes I do," he agreed. "But has it never occurred to you that strength alone isn't what the study of magick is about? Your problem isn't me and it isn't the politics of the Guild. It's you. You're so full of that great, legendary strength that you've become lazy and undisciplined."

Her eyes flared sharply. "You're a fine one to talk about laziness. I'm not the one putting lessons on hold because of a job that means nothing in the context of what is really important. Unlike you, I do nothing but work at developing my abilities and you know it."

"I suppose that was a cheap shot," he admitted. "I know that you work hard – but maybe you've lost your way. Magick isn't just about being able to produce effects. It's about evolution, moving forward instead of stagnating. It's about achieving an awareness of the fundamental nature of things." He braced himself, reviewing in his mind the speech he had practiced since his initiation into the Inner Order of the Guild. He knew that the moment he agreed to take the next step in his magical career, events were set in motion that led inevitably to this night. He had thought that after reviewing what he would say countless times, he was resigned to his fate, but still, actually saying the words was surprisingly difficult. "But I'm not going to lecture you," he continued finally. "We've had this discussion before and I know you won't listen. I knew that we were through the moment I was asked into the Inner Order, because you're so conceited that I knew you would never accept my attainment of a higher grade than yours. What was I supposed to do? Refuse? You would never turn down an initiation and neither would I. And part of me is just fed up with the whole thing – playing to your ego, trying to appease your fragile sense of self, and all this nonsense that I have to put up with to keep you around. That's why you wanted to meet me here, right? To dump me?"

An ironic smile twisted across Elspeth's lips. "You've always been perceptive."

17

Michael sighed, more relieved than anything else at her apparent calm. "Good. Does that mean I can leave now? It's really too late for dinner, and I assume that you'd rather I not stick around."

Elspeth's expression darkened. "That's it? That's all you have to say?"

Here we go, thought Michael. To his magical senses the air around her shifted and crackled with destructive force. "Yes," he replied. "That's all I have to say. It's all I really *can* say. I care about you and I'm sorry things didn't work out, but that's just the way life goes. Sometimes these things happen."

"Are you saying you're glad to be rid of me?" she demanded fiercely, rising suddenly to her feet.

"Of course not!" he shot back. "I…"

Not listening, she continued furiously. "After everything I've done for you? You bastard!"

Michael stood up, but remained silent, profoundly thankful that regular people were unable to see magical forms and perceived nothing more than a quarreling couple. He knew that nothing he could say would prevent what was coming and quickly reinforced the magical defenses he had set up before departing for the evening. *Invoking elemental hexagrams, invoking Saturn hexagram, sigils of the intelligence and spirit of Saturn…*

Calm washed over Elspeth, but it was the calm of concentration rather than acceptance or even resignation. "Here's a little present for you. Drop dead." She raised her right hand, and in a voice like unsheathed steel intoned a simple incantation, backed by what felt like all the power in the known universe. "*Yolcam drilp!*"

Elspeth stormed out of the club as the magical attack shook the club like a thunderclap, throwing Michael back into his seat. Despite the black spots that momentarily threatened his vision, he managed to maintain his defenses fairly well. Some of the energy had made it through and would probably cling to him as a low-level curse for days, but somehow he had managed to block the

18

brunt of an attack that only a few days ago would probably have sent him to the Emergency Room. With a detached curiosity, he examined the remains of his invisible defensive circle, wondering to what extent his new rank had helped him. He had guessed prior to his initiation that the higher-ranking Adepts drew on each other's strength to some extent, and now it did feel like behind his considerable individual powers stood the long line of mystics and seekers that comprised the Guild's history. The realization that his powers were indeed much stronger than before was exhilarating.

As he pondered his initiation and its significance, a premonition suddenly coursed through his mind. *Fire, heat, pain…* And suddenly it occurred to him that Elspeth was sloppy. She had not just cursed him – she had cursed the whole area. It also occurred to him that building codes notwithstanding, the space occupied by Morpheus was in a very old warehouse.

He was running for the door when the club exploded in flames.

For Michael, the next several hours were jumbled and confused. He had been thrown through the plate glass window next to the door in the initial blast, landing on the hood of somebody's BMW parked in front of the club. With the luck that tended to follow most mages and despite Elspeth's curse, he had been hurled almost twenty feet and sustained only minor cuts and bruises. He was knocked unconscious as he landed, and as he came to a few minutes later he saw that the building had become an inferno. A crowd of people dressed mostly in stylish club wear stood on the other side of the street watching firefighters desperately battle the blaze and paramedics offer treatment to what survivors they could find.

He pulled himself to his feet, visualizing the layout of the building as best he could. He extended his senses to fill the warehouse, scanning it level by level. The heat in the basement was the worst, and he could feel the weak points in the structure where the curse had taken hold. A gas line had broken somewhere inside the immense, ancient furnace, and was still spewing fire and heat that kept the flames going upstairs. He visualized a circle of stasis around the pipe and willed the fire to die, chanting once more to himself the names of the various intelligence and spirit attributed to Saturn.

Something shifted inside the building and the flames began to subside.

The warehouse still burned, but now the firefighters were getting it under control. Somehow the gas was no longer spewing from the pipe to feed the fire and for the most part the warehouse was built out of concrete, brick, and other fireproof materials. Without the gas, there was little to burn besides the furniture and the wooden studs that backed the finished interior walls.

He then extended his awareness to see if anyone was still alive inside the building. He sensed a fair number of people, though thankfully not as many as he feared might have been inside. It was still early in the evening and the club had not been even close to full. One by one, he focused on each survivor whose mind he could reach, laying circles of protection and healing spells on them to keep them alive long enough to be reached by the paramedics, after which he cast wards against infection and internal bleeding on his own injuries. He did not feel the immediate disruption of his bodily energies that accompanied most truly severe wounds, but after the sheer amount of ritual work he had performed his senses were not nearly as sharp. As a paramedic suddenly noticed him standing next to the building and gestured for him to cross the street to safety Michael did so, sitting down on the sidewalk to watch the remaining rescue efforts. He was tired and hurt, but he felt obligated to stay.

In a way, the blast was his fault. He was not as responsible as Elspeth, of course, but he had known what was likely to happen that night and maybe he could have constructed better defenses that would have protected the building around him. Maybe they could have met somewhere else that was less public, or even in some neutral temple space where they could have thrown spells at each other with impunity – someplace where there would be no risk of violating the rules of the Guild.

We do not act in anger. We do not harm innocent bystanders.

Those rules and many others had been drilled into him since his initiation into the Guild as a teenager. Acting in anger was a rule that Elspeth often broke, which he suspected was why he had been invited to join the inner order before she was. She had never harmed a bystander, though, and had certainly never killed one. As his mind had wandered through the burning club he had seen that a number of people there were dead, and the official position of the Guild leadership was that for such a comprehensive violation the only possible penalty was death – that is, unless the explosion was ruled an accident by the Supreme Council. Even though the Guild had not executed a member in almost two hundred years, to his knowledge nothing of comparable magnitude had ever transpired in the history of the organization and he suspected that some members of the leadership would want to set an example.

It surprised him under the circumstances that he genuinely felt bad for Elspeth. Whether or not she showed it he knew that she had not intended to curse the whole building and would feel terrible once she found out what happened. Being called before the Supreme Council with her life on the line would make the whole situation that much worse. Despite the scene at the club he really did care about her, and always had – he had just become sick of her immature self-centered antics. He had never understood how someone that gifted and talented could take such incredible aptitude for granted. Maybe it had something to do with the fact that she had been raised from birth to be a mage and as a result had never known anything else.

As the paramedics pulled the last of the survivors from the building, he walked back across the street to his car, which unlike the others parked in front of the building was almost completely untouched by the flame and ash. He unmade his sigil and got into the GTO, starting it up and pulling out of his parking space. He had to make a U-turn because the road in front of the club was still blocked by the fire trucks and ambulances, but he was still out of downtown Minneapolis in a few minutes, cruising east along the main artery connecting the Twin Cities metropolitan area, Interstate 94.

As he passed Snelling Avenue on his way into Saint Paul, the other half of the Twin Cities, his dashboard suddenly lit up like a Christmas tree and the big V8 engine shuddered to a halt. *The curse*, he told himself with an exasperated sigh. He had depleted most of his magical energy helping with the fire, and there was not enough power left to stave off the lingering effects that had made it through his defenses. He coasted onto the shoulder of the freeway and stopped there, turning on his hazard lights and taking his cell phone out of his pocket. He cast a sigil over it before he dialed the number, just in case.

The phone on the other end was picked up immediately. "Hey, Michael," said a bouncy, girlish voice. "Nice fireworks."

"Hi Roach. So you know already?"

"Jonas clued me in. Nice work stopping the fire and helping out, by the way."

"Did you see what happened? I know my spell worked, but I'm not sure how. I was busy paying attention to the survivors."

"A big piece of the furnace fell right on top of the gas line and crimped it off. Million to one shot, but that's just how these things work." Her voice softened, fear showing through her superficial perky demeanor. "Was it really Elspeth? Jonas didn't know."

"Who else do you know besides your sister who could blow up a building with magick? Yeah, it was her."

The phone was dead for what seemed like a long time. "Are they going to kill her?" she asked finally, her voice soft and apprehensive.

"I don't know," he replied. "I'm pretty sure she didn't mean to do what she did, so I hope not. At least, that's what I'll be telling the Inner Order council. I think maybe this will be enough of a shock to her that she'll grow up a bit and get more of a head on her shoulders. Or something."

22

"I just hope the rest of the Inner Order sees it that way. I'd hate to lose her even if we don't get along so well… anyway," she said too quickly, the bouncy lilt returning but now sounding even more forced, "did you just call to shoot the shit or is something up?"

"Yeah, my Pontiac died on the freeway. I think it's just what's left of the curse, but after tonight I'm totally wiped out. I'm going to take a cab home. Can you tow it in and take a look at it tomorrow? It's just east of the Snelling exit on Interstate 94."

"Sure. Maybe I can put in few more upgrades too. I got some groovy parts in this week."

"As long as it doesn't take too long. I need it to get to work on Monday."

"Okay, I promise I won't haul it up to the Brainerd speedway over the weekend," she said playfully. "You know, that car is really fast. My racer is faster, but not much. I can have the tow truck out there in a couple hours. Get some sleep – you sound exhausted."

"That won't be difficult. I'll talk to you tomorrow."

After calling for the cab, Michael dialed Jonas Votan, his instructor and one of the two local members of the Guild's Supreme Council. Jonas knew both him and Elspeth extremely well, and might be willing to support her once he knew all the facts. Like Rochelle, Jonas picked up immediately. "Hello, Michael," he said in a somber voice. Even without caller ID, mages generally knew who was on the phone. Michael did not remember if Jonas had the service or not.

"Hi Jonas. Rochelle told me you watched tonight's action."

"Some of it. What happened? I felt an enormous draw of energy that could only be someone extremely strong casting a powerful spell, and by the time I could get to my scrying crystal the building was burning. You did well to stop the fire and help the survivors. You have good presence of mind, which is one of the reasons I recommended you for the grade of Adept." He paused for a moment, as though trying to decide what to say, and

23

finally continued in a more somber tone. "That being said, I see no polite way to broach the subject so I will get right to the point. Did Elspeth start the fire?"

"Sort of," replied Michael, hedging. "She threw a curse at me that I mostly blocked, but the building got hit. The fire wasn't her intent. I think the furnace must have been defective in some way, since usually you don't see that sort of destruction with a regular curse."

"Right now I am only interested in the events themselves," said Jonas with curt formality. "So she did start the fire. Are you unharmed?"

"For the most part. I had a premonition before the place blew up and almost made it out."

"Almost?"

"I was thrown through a window about ten feet from the door. I'm fine," he added quickly. "Anyway, I'm mostly calling to get some idea of what the Guild's position is concerning Elspeth. Rochelle is really scared and I don't know what to think. I mean, we all know the rules about misuse of our powers and so forth and the penalty for something like this, but is that ever a sentence that gets carried out?" He paused for a moment, steeling his thoughts with the discipline of his magical training, and then asked the question directly. "I mean, is the Guild really going to have her killed?"

Jonas was quiet on the other end. As Michael was about to ask again, he finally spoke, his voice tinged with sadness. "That is a matter for the Supreme Council to decide. You are right that the sentence of death has not been carried out in generations, but then we have not been faced with a situation like this one since the late Renaissance."

"That's not an answer," pressed Michael. "You're on the Supreme Council and you're her instructor as well as mine. Am I wrong in thinking that your opinion will be the one that carries the most weight with the others?"

"No, you are not," replied the older mage with a sigh. "I will tell you this. There was a time when I believed that Elspeth could learn to harness her power and her emotions and become the greatest mage in our history. I never expected something like this to happen. Now I wonder if we overreached in engineering the Sprengel bloodline, blinded by our pursuit of magical perfection. I also see that the sages of old were wrong - power and wisdom are not two sides of the same coin. Maybe the human mind just lacks the capacity to handle her level of strength, and her instability will only worsen. If so, it may be time to bring the experiment to a close and cut our losses."

"Do you mean what I think you mean?" demanded Michael, incredulous. "You're talking about a human being. Someone you've known since she was born. Your best friend's granddaughter! You really are going to recommend her execution?"

"When pressed on the question, I doubt it," admitted the older mage. "But my emotional involvement may be distorting my judgment. Perhaps for the good of us all I should work to overcome my natural reaction. If power welded into flesh inevitably corrupts the mind, she may worsen. Do you believe that is a risk we should take?"

"I just can't believe you're saying this. You, of all people? To even consider the possibility…"

"As an initiate of the Inner Order you should not be so surprised," countered Jonas harshly. "You know that our policy exists for a good reason. We cannot harbor within our midst those who would carelessly use their powers in such a way that our presence would be revealed to the world, or in such a way that the innocent are harmed. As you know, the Guild's presence was revealed in Europe during the Renaissance, and it caused a panic that resulted in many of our people being jailed and executed. People died tonight. We must police our own, since no one else can. Or would you have the world overrun by mages who scatter their destructive spells with impunity?"

"Look, I know she didn't mean to blow up the place," insisted Michael. "The building must have been below code or something. I've seen her cast that exact curse before at my house, among other places, and while it can take weeks to banish properly the house is still standing. The furnace must have been ready to blow. My house has gas heat too, and it never has."

"You will testify to that effect before the Supreme Council? You were, after all, the only other mage present."

"Of course," answered Michael immediately.

Jonas' voice softened, sounding relieved. "Perhaps, then, they will find the circumstances extenuating. Elspeth is among the most powerful of us, and naturally she is potentially of great value if she can be trained to use her powers responsibly. Another consideration is that even with the combined power of the Council we may have trouble destroying her, and if she were to escape us, she could join another group who would protect her for the power she would bring them. That's not all, either," he added thoughtfully.

"What do you mean?" asked Michael, confused.

Jonas chose his words carefully. "There is something very wrong going on in the area. Two nights ago I sensed a dark power of incredible proportion enter this world. It didn't stay for very long, but it was here. The signature used for summoning matches that of none of our own mages. Then, in the newspaper yesterday, I saw that twelve bodies were found in southern Minnesota on one of the bluffs outside Rochester. They were dressed in robes, carrying ritual implements, and no cause of death was apparent. The papers are railing against 'Satanic' crime again, just like back in the early nineties. Of course they do not understand the nature of real demonic forces, but there is a power on the move that deals in chaos and entropy. I will meditate on this. It may be that regardless of what transpired tonight we would be wise to spare Elspeth so that she can aid us in the days to come. If my worst fears are confirmed, I suspect her power may be needed very badly. Thank you for explaining the situation."

The cab arrived a few minutes later and dropped Michael off at his large Victorian home on Lake Como, which he had spent years painstakingly restoring and updating. As he crossed from the foyer into the living room, he collapsed onto the sofa. He felt shredded, as through the power he had expended would never return. Elspeth's curse still hovered in the air around him, but he was not worried about the house; after years of ritual work on the premises it was mostly immune to magical effects and as he had told Jonas, it had not exploded the last time he and Elspeth had a fight. After awhile, he pulled himself up off the sofa and trudged up the ornately carved staircase that led from the first to the second level, and then up another flight to the renovated attic that served as his bedroom, skipping his usual nightly banishings and invocations. Now he just needed rest.

As he drifted off to sleep, Jonas' comments came back to him. A dark power, he had said, dealing in chaos and entropy. Jonas had referred to his worst fears. In all his years of study, Michael had never seen his instructor afraid of anything. Something told him that this was important, something that needed to be looked into immediately. But at that moment he lacked the strength to deal with the simplest divination, and it was all he could do to shut off the light before he fell asleep.

I. The Magician
The Magus of Power
The Planet Mercury

Elspeth was still awake. She obsessively paced the length of the enormous parlor of the Sprengel family mansion, a vast Kenwood estate that had been owned by her parents before their untimely deaths. A roaring fire burned within the ornate hearth, reminiscent of the scene only a few hours before at Morpheus, and on the expansive flat-screen television above the hearth a CNN reporter was explaining the mechanics of the blaze over footage of the inferno at its height. The room's dark paneling, carved in a style popular among the very wealthy over a hundred years ago, intensified the shadows cast by the flickering firelight and cast a heavy gloom over the cavernous chamber that even the bright liquid crystal display was unable to illuminate.

Finally, desperately, she stopped, throwing up her hands in frustration. "What am I going to do?" she demanded.

The man who lounged on one of the room's Victorian sofas looked like he would comfortable at any trendy Ivy League school. His fashionable pastel clothing looked expensive despite its casual appearance, and its cut showed off a painstakingly well-developed physique. His blond hair was carefully styled, and while his walnut brown eyes showed a glimmer of concern, it was quickly overcome by aristocratic disdain. "Don't worry about it," he said dismissively. "What can they do to you?"

"Jim, they can kill me! That's what they can do!" she exclaimed.

Jim only shrugged. "Over a twit like Michael? You're better off without him. Anyway, why would they care?"

"It's not about Michael, stupid. It's about the club. They'll know the explosion was caused by magick, even if that wasn't my intent. They'll know it was my magick because they can detect things like that!" Her voice strained with exasperation that barely masked her unbridled fear. "You have no idea how serious this is

29

to them!"

He either shrugged off the insult or just did not care. "I can't believe it's so serious that they would really want you dead," he replied, his tone still condescending and unconcerned. "You're making a big deal out of nothing."

"Believe it," she said gravely. "They'll kill me without a second thought. Those are the rules."

"Even if they wanted to, how could they?" he asked skeptically. "You're rich. You can protect yourself. Go to the police or something. Or hire bodyguards."

"You don't understand the Guild," she countered fiercely. "They're powerful mages! The police would never be able to find anything amiss and their spells can just brush past bodyguards. My money can't protect me from them."

"But you're powerful, too, right? How many of them could just blow up a building? Even if they come after you with magick, can't you fight them? You're always telling me how you're the best and the brightest in the Guild."

She shook her head. "Not against all of them. They can combine their powers so that..."

The doorbell suddenly rang, its old-fashioned metallic chime echoing through the vast house. With a start, Elspeth turned to face the door with apprehension in her eyes.

"Are you expecting anyone tonight?" Jim asked, rising to his feet protectively.

"No... but it couldn't be them," she replied, calming herself. "Not yet. There are procedures that have to be followed – if nothing else a hearing before the Supreme Council – and they take time." She walked across the room and through the long entry hall to the main door, a hand-carved slab of oak set into a stone archway. She opened the door hesitantly, not knowing what to expect.

"Elspeth Sprengel," said the excruciatingly ordinary man at the door, a statement rather than a question.

"Can I help you?" she demanded coldly, her eyes flashing

impatiently.

The man smiled, his too-average features suddenly animating. "Yes, I believe so." As Jim stepped into the entry hall, the man added, "but I must speak with you alone. May I come in?"

Normally she would have just sent him away, but there was something strange about his aura that she was unable to place. Whatever it was, it piqued her curiosity. "Sure," she said, stepping aside and allowing him to enter the house. "But if you're selling something, you had best take your business elsewhere."

"I am not a salesman," he replied in reassuring tones. "Is there a room where we can speak privately?"

"My study. It's this way." As she directed the man down the corridor that led from the entry hall to the wing of the house opposite the parlor, she gestured for Jim to stay put.

The wide corridor ran the length of the house and connected most of the rooms on the first level. It was lined with statues and paintings from various periods that seemed to glare at her and the stranger as they traversed its length to the room at the far end. Once in the study, a much smaller room than the parlor lined with tall bookshelves that almost reached the high ceiling, she closed the door and seated herself behind her desk, a mahogany antique covered in the faces of gargoyles and woodland sprites. The man had already sat down in one of the leather-upholstered chairs opposite the overbearing baroque masterpiece. "So now we're alone," she said, matter-of-factly. "What do you want?"

"To help you," replied the man, "and myself, naturally, but as is the case with all honest people that goes without saying. My true name is not that of this human vessel, which is what you will find on my driver's license and Social Security card, but Balzador. An occultist of your caliber has surely heard of me."

Elspeth rolled her eyes. *He's a nut*, she told herself. *Why tonight, of all nights?* Paranoia followed – *how did he find out I'm a mage?* "Of course I have. You lost the great battle for the Abyss. I suppose you've written a book or something? Let me guess –

Llewelyn wouldn't publish it because it was too dark and scary."

The man's grin widened. "So you don't believe me?"

"I believe that you probably think you're the demon Balzador, and that on some psychic level you may even identify with that particular entity. But I don't believe you're a demon in the flesh, standing here and talking to me like a person, even if your aura is pretty weird. That sort of thing just doesn't happen. Demons are discarnate - that means they don't manifest as physical forms."

"Oh, I haven't," replied Balzador. "In one sense I have possessed this body, in that it once had a human soul and it now no longer does. In another, though, this body is indeed mine. After the abortive war that shook the pillars of the Abyss, I was banished to your material world, forced to jump from body to body as each human lifespan expired. I have been here for over a thousand years, living countless lives. But I have finally found a way home, and it starts with you."

"You're crazy," she said curtly, "and don't even think about asking for money. Now I'm very busy tonight and..."

Balzador looked at her quizzically. "Can a crazy person do this?" he asked, feigned innocence in his voice. His features shifted, undergoing the demonic transformation that mocked his everyman looks. "How about this?" He held out his hand, and a ball of shimmering foxfire materialized above it. It floated slowly upward towards the high ceiling and then burst into a wicked explosion of flames that showered the room with sparks before going out completely. He then returned his gaze to meet Elspeth's widening eyes.

Despite the pyrotechnics, there was no smoke, residue, or smell of any kind. The fire alarm in the study had not gone off either, but the effect was not an illusion – a few of the sparks had left tiny pinpoint scorch marks on the surface of the desk. Elspeth stared at Balzador with a mix of disbelief and apprehension as the room fell uncomfortably silent for what seemed like a long time. The demon's grin was subdued as he regarded her with his inhuman eyes, daring her to speak.

"How did you do that?" she asked meekly. It had been a long time since she had seen a magical effect that she was unable to perform herself, let alone one she could not even figure out how to do. He had conjured physical fire – she had seen it with her normal sight rather than her magical vision. Jonas had told her long ago that doing so was impossible without a strong source of nearby heat that could be shaped and manipulated. No magician could just pull energy out of the air – it always had to come from somewhere.

"I'm a demon," he explained with a shrug, his features shifting back to normal. "Humans have to work hard to reach the core of magical energy that resides inside their own bodies. My awareness of this host is broader, so I can just do it. Also, my magical strength is at least partially a matter of my demonic nature, not just an accident of genetics and upbringing. It is well in excess of anything a human is ever likely to achieve, even you."

She leaned back in her chair, still not fully convinced. Pyrotechnics *was* a specialized area of stage magic, even if she had felt a surge of magical energy when the effect went off. "So if you're that much more powerful than a human, why do you need my help, if that's indeed what you want?"

"Your Guild is in possession of the only complete version of the grimoire of Dr. John Dee, called <u>Liber Iadnamad</u>, the book of undefiled knowledge. In order to return to the realms from whence I came, it is necessary that I acquire a copy of it. Within the book is encoded a specific rite that will allow me to return to my rightful place and defeat Coronzon for control of the Abyss."

"How does that help me?" she asked, confused. "So you're the Lord of the Abyss instead of Coronzon. From where I'm sitting nothing changes."

"Yes," agreed the demon, "but would you rather be dead? After your little episode tonight, you know as well as I do that you have become a liability to your Guild. Even if they allow you to live they will never allow you into their inner circle of initiates. When

I become the Lord of the Abyss it will be my prerogative to grant powers of whatever sort to those who I deem my allies. You could be one of them. I could protect you."

"How?" she demanded.

"You are familiar with the crossing of the Abyss, and the type of guardians that are likely to block your ascent and cast you back into the material world?" he asked casually, already knowing the answer.

"Of course," she replied. "That's the ordeal that confers the grade of Master of the Temple and entry into the Supreme Order. Most magicians fail and collapse into insanity."

"So," mused the demon with just a hint of contempt, "few members of your Guild have succeeded in crossing, then?"

"Very few," she admitted. "Maybe one or two of the oldest members on the Supreme Council, like my grandfather or Jonas. It isn't discussed, but I've heard things here and there and you only need to be an Adept to serve on the Council. That's probably because true Masters are so rare."

"As Lord of the Abyss I will have the power to sweep the guardians aside and allow you – and only you – to cross without difficulty." He paused for a moment, allowing her to consider the ramifications of such an offer. He then continued, "As a Master of the Temple, you will be immune to the petty magical attacks of the Inner Order. That should be enough to ensure your survival – and your cooperation."

Her eyes widened as she realized that here was indeed a way to escape the wrath of the Guild. "And in exchange for this, you just want me to steal a copy of <u>Liber Iadnamad</u>? I don't have a copy of it myself, if that's what you were hoping."

The demon nodded. "It need not be stolen, merely copied – I only require the information it contains. You may obtain that copy in whatever manner you choose."

"And I suppose there's a reason you can't do it yourself?" she asked warily.

His expression darkened. "Yes. Despite my powers over

the native magical abilities of my host body, being a demon also confers certain weaknesses. Specifically, I am more susceptible than any human to the kinds of magical wards that undoubtedly guard every available copy of the book. As a human with superior magical abilities, you should be able to neutralize them, at least long enough to get the book to me. Once I perform the necessary rites, I will conquer the Abyss and your newfound grade will permanently overcome the power of those defenses. Any long-term effects from them will thus become irrelevant."

"I suppose it could work," she said thoughtfully.

"It will, but only if I have your loyalty. I can protect you from the others once the power is mine. Do we have a deal?"

Part of her hated the idea of betraying the Guild. After her parents' death they had raised her, taught her, and been her only friends and companions. *But they betrayed you*, she told herself. Michael had never been her equal and he knew it as well as she did, but he was the one they chose to elevate. *They're going to kill you*, she added, *not for a willful act but because of a mistake*. She had not meant to harm anyone in the club – not even Michael, really. She just needed a strong curse to blast through his defenses and affect him at all. Otherwise he would have just laughed in her face. Not only that, but his shielding spells had probably deflected part of the curse into the furnace. But she was still the one who was going to be blamed. She rose to her feet. "Why not?" she said finally. "As you say, what choice do I have, really?"

Balzador's smile returned. "Excellent. How long will it take you to obtain the book?"

"It could take a little time," she admitted. "I need to find out where one is kept. Ideally, I would rather make a copy of one the existing volumes, since it will be missed almost immediately, and that will take longer than stealing it. How can I contact you?"

A plain white business card appeared in the demon's hand. It bore a phone number with no other text. "You can reach me at this number. If you value your life I recommend that you move quickly, before the Guild can call down its judgment upon you."

She took the card and added it to the thick Rolodex that sat on the desk, and then led Balzador out of the study and back down the hall to the main door. Jim was still waiting in the foyer with a concerned look on his face. He started to ask a question, but another gesture from Elspeth held him silent. She showed the demon out, locked the door, and then turned back to Jim.

"What was that all about?" he asked.

Elspeth's face was now relaxed. "I think I've found a way out of this mess. Have you ever performed a magical ritual?"

Jim looked taken aback. "Not really," he said quickly. "I mean, I've done some psychic readings and things like that, but never any of the sort of stuff that you're into."

"Well, you can assist. Come with me."

Doggishly, he followed as she walked the length of the entry hall to a set of carved oak double doors. She took a large, old-fashioned key that hung on a silver chain around her neck and fitted it into the lock on the doors, which slid open silently. "This is my temple," she explained, "the center of all my magical work. It was originally built as a ballroom, but my parents used it as a temple for years before I was born." As Jim lingered at the threshold, Elspeth stepped into the room and turned on the light, an enormous chandelier of fine crystal that scattered slivers of brightness in all directions. The chamber itself was immense, almost forty feet square, which was accentuated by its almost total lack of furniture. The molded white plaster ceiling rose in a high dome, almost twenty-five feet above the floor at its center, contrasting with the walls, which were covered in the same dark paneling found in the parlor.

Elspeth crossed the polished white marble floor to a large engraved magick circle over twenty feet in diameter, with Jim following nervously. At the center of the circle stood a tall altar table adorned with arcane letters and symbols, and upon the table sat the standard magical implements - the wand, dagger, chalice, and pantacle - that represented the four ancient elements. She opened a cabinet that was set into the base of the altar, and from

36

it removed another dagger, larger than the ceremonial *athame* and sharpened to a deadly edge. The polished ebony hilt glinted in the diffuse light from above.

"What are you going to do?" he asked softly, as though he was fearful of speaking aloud.

"I'm going to build a weapon that can kill a demon," she replied in her usual conversational tone. "It's complicated to explain, but that man who just dropped by isn't really a man at all. He's a powerful demon who was exiled here over a thousand years ago, and he has a plan to take over the Abyss, his original home."

"He convinced you of this?" Jim's voice remained lowered.

Elspeth nodded.

"And you're going to kill him?"

"Not necessarily," she replied. "But I don't think trusting him is such a good idea. First, I'm going to help him, and if remains true to his word he will survive."

"Why help a demon?" Now Jim looked really confused. "What does that do for you?"

"Well, once he's taken over the Abyss, he'll allow me to cross it without difficulty. That's the most perilous ordeal of all in ritual magick, but if I succeed I will become a Master of the Temple – I'll bypass the Inner Order altogether. It will make me far too powerful for them to destroy."

"That sounds really dangerous. If this crossing, or whatever it is, is as difficult as you make it sound, you may not succeed, even with outside help."

"Well, it is dangerous," she admitted, "but unfortunately, doing nothing is just as dangerous. This way I have a chance. If Balzador fails to conquer the Abyss, I'm dead one way or the other."

"No, you're not!" he argued, his voice rising. "You don't have to do this. We could hide from your Guild or something. We could just run for it. Aren't there other mages in the world who would be willing to help? Yours can't be the only group."

Elspeth shook her head. "They're the only really powerful one. They have access to a grimoire called <u>Liber Iadnamad</u>, the final book of ritual magick written by Dr. John Dee while he was studying at the court of Rudolph the Second in Germany. We have the only deciphered copies, made from the original volume presented by Dee himself to his successor as Guildmaster in the early seventeenth century," she explained. "Have you ever heard of something called the Voynich manuscript?"

"No. Should I have?"

"Not necessarily. It's just that some of our scholars believe that document might be a version of it, or at least related to it. The system of cryptography it uses is so complicated that even our scholars, who are very familiar with Renaissance cryptography, can't decipher any of the script. Dee was one of the only mathematicians of the sixteenth century capable of devising that sort of encryption. Also, the document can be traced to the court of Rudolph the Second around the time Dee was studying there. Besides <u>Liber Iadnamad</u> itself, I can't think of anything else that would merit such extreme protection. At any rate, nobody else has access to it, and the magick it contains is just about the most powerful system anyone has ever come up with."

"Haven't books of Dee's diaries been published, though?" he asked. "You mentioned that once," he added.

"Sure. They cover a lot of the material, but they don't include detailed descriptions of how the magick is used. Different magical orders have created their own systems of working with it, but <u>Liber Iadnamad</u> is different. Dee did put some of the earlier workings into a grimoire called the <u>Heptarchia Mystica</u>, which is powerful in its own right, but <u>Liber Iadnamad</u> includes revisions to the <u>Heptarchia</u> as well as a key to the rest of his magical system. The original system is far more powerful than any of the derivative ones that have surfaced over the last couple of centuries."

"Do you have a copy of it?" he asked nonchalantly, lamely trying to hide his interest.

Elspeth scowled, not noticing. "No. But Michael does. A

copy of the grimoire is presented to everyone who's initiated into the Inner Order. I'll need to copy one of the existing volumes, and Michael's is probably the best choice. It's new and he hasn't had it long enough to formulate any complex defenses against theft."

"So you're going to steal the book?"

"Only for as long as it takes to make a copy," she replied. "It would be missed. According to the demon, that will be sufficient. But this comes first. There's a small refrigerator over by the door. Could you bring me the vial of Holy Water? It's on the bottom shelf. Everything should be labeled."

He began to walk across the room, and paused at the edge of the circle.

"It's okay to cross it now," she reassured him. "I haven't started the rite."

Obediently, he continued across the room to the small refrigerator and opened it, staring dubiously at its contents. "Is the stuff on the top shelf really goat's blood?" he asked as he retrieved the crystal vial labeled "Holy Water" in Elspeth's neat handwriting.

"Of course," she replied as Jim crossed back into the circle. "Why would I mislabel it? Some of the rituals I study call for blood, and the blood of a goat works particularly well. It probably has something to do with the Saturn being the ruler of Capricorn. Most rituals involving blood involve Saturn energy."

"Is there a reason you refrigerate water?" he asked. "I mean, I can see why you would want to keep blood cold, but water doesn't decay."

"From a magical standpoint, it kind of does," she explained. "Holy Water has been modified by a magical ceremony so that it acts as what we call a fluid condenser - a substance that holds magical energy. The Holy Water we use isn't quite pure, either. It has a little bit of chamomile tincture added to it, because for some reason that improves its effectiveness at holding energy. I refrigerate it because it seems like cold things hold their properties longer, even water."

He nodded studiously. "So how do you use all this to build a weapon to kill a demon?"

"First I set the wards. Do you see that circle there?" She pointed to a smaller circle about large enough for one person to the west of the altar within the large circle that enclosed the center of the room.

He nodded.

"Sit there and don't move out until I tell you to. Hold these and give them to me when I ask for them." She handed him the vial of Holy Water and another from the cabinet under the altar labeled as Oil of Abramelin.

Elspeth stood to the west of the altar, facing east. She relaxed, clearing her mind, and the magical energy that burned inside her like a column of radiance began to flow. She raised her right hand high in the air and brought it down to her forehead. "*Ateh*," she intoned, her voice rising to a pitch and volume that echoed in the vast temple. She then lowered her hand to her breast. "*Malkuth*." Touching her right shoulder, she intoned "*ve Geburah*," and then touching her left shoulder, "*ve Gedulah*." Finally, she clasped her hands over her heart and intoned "*le Olahm, Amen*."

Stepping to the left of the altar, she advanced to the east and proceeded deosil, or clockwise, around the circle, tracing at each of the four cardinal directions huge banishing pentagrams in the air, which to her magical sight glowed with scintillating flames. Pointing to the center of each figure, she loudly intoned the appropriate God-name for each of the four directions – *Yahweh* in the east, *Adonai* in the south, *Ehieh* in the west, and *Agla* in the north. She continued on to the east, completing the circle, and then returned to the west of the altar and extended her hands to form a cross. Aligning herself with the cross of the elements that she could now feel encompassing the material world, she called upon the four Archangels who would stand guard over the circle during the ritual.

Before me Raphael,
Behind me Gabriel,
On my right hand Michael,
And on my left hand Auriel.
For about me flames the pentagram,
And in the column stands the six-rayed star.

Standing straight and lowering her arms at her sides, she relaxed more deeply. To her magical sight, ghostly figures of the Archangels now stood at each quarter, strengthening the pentagrams that warded the circle. The figures formed a cube that extended to the outer perimeter of the circle, with pentagrams at the four sides and hexagrams at the top and bottom. As the figures solidified fully, she repeated the opening of the ritual to connect the extended energy field back to her own center, ending with *Amen.*

She then began the macrocosmic rite, the ritual of the hexagram that would link her sealed circle to the physical world.

Virgo, Isis, mighty mother,
Scorpio, Apophis, destroyer,
Sol, Osiris, slain and risen.
Isis, Apophis, Osiris.
IAO.

She extended her arms to form a cross, saying "The Sign of Osiris Slain." She then raised one arm, forming an approximation of the letter L, saying "The Sign of the Mourning of Isis." She raised both arms and held them apart to approximate the letter V as she said "The Sign of Apophis and Typhon," and finally she crossed her arms over her chest like an Egyptian mummy forming the letter X, saying "The Sign of Osiris risen." She breathed deeply, letting the energy flow resonate and synchronize with the world around her, and as she extended her arms to form a cross and then replaced them across her chest, she intoned "*L. V. X. -*

41

Lux, the light of the cross." Her magical sight now showed a hazy hemisphere intersecting the boundaries of the circle, still warded by the flaming pentagrams and Archangels. Without moving from her position at the altar, she traced the invoking hexagram of the appropriate element to each of the four directions, loudly intoning *Ararita* for each of the figures. The hazy, indeterminate energy solidified and stabilized, becoming as tangible as smoky glass. As with the pentagram ritual, she concluded the rite by repeating the opening statements and signs.

"The wards are set," Elspeth said finally. "Now for the dagger." She took the vials of Holy Water and oil from Jim and set them next to the weapon upon the altar. Wetting her index finger with the water, she traced the entire length of the weapon as she intoned the first incantation. "*Yolcam lonshi pir!*" She then did the same with the Oil of Abramelin, intoning the second. "*Yolcam ialprg Iaida!*" Holding the weapon between her hands, she began to breathe slowly and deeply, placing magical energy into the blade to empower it as the embodiment of her will and intention. She kept it up until the blade felt like it could hold no more, then set it upon the altar and turned to Jim.

"Is that it?" he asked softly.

"No. The weapon is now purified and consecrated, so it will hold the final enchantment. You can stand up and move around now if you want to watch more closely. Just don't cross the outer circle."

Jim rose to his feet and stepped over to where Elspeth stood at the altar, watching her movements and gestures with intent interest.

"To get the energy to flow in the right direction – that is, out of the demon and into me - I need to put Saturn energy on the tip and Jupiter energy on the hilt," she explained. "In really simple terms, Saturn is contraction and Jupiter is expansion, and the two together in that configuration create a gradient of force tilted in favor of the dagger's wielder. That way, when I strike the demon its energy will be drained to nothing and I'll acquire some of its power."

Raising her voice, she intoned in weird and haunting syllables the first of the forty-eight Enochian calls, communicated to John Dee and Edward Kelly, passed down through <u>Liber Iadnamad</u>, and related to her in fragments as a member of the Outer Order. As always when using it in ritual, her impression of the Call was twofold – a sense of incredible and overwhelming power, which she used to enhance her ritual effects, but also a sense of mysterious and hidden forces whose nature she barely understood. In her idle moments she had often wondered if the Adepts of the Inner Order also felt that sense of confusion and disorientation, or if, having been taught the true nature of the Calls, they therefore understood.

As the echoes of the Call faded around her, Elspeth held the dagger aloft in both hands point up, and keeping it vertical traced a hexagram that to her magical sight hung in the air like liquid shadow. In its midst, she traced the symbol of Saturn and called upon the planet's King and Prince. *"Bnapsen od Brorges, yolcam lonshi tox! Zacare ca od zamran, odo cicle qaa, zorge, lap zirdo noco Mad, hoath Iaida!"* She then turned the dagger point downward and traced another hexagram that shone with shimmering blue light. Tracing the symbol of Jupiter in the center, she called upon the King and Prince of that planet. *"Bynepor od Butmono, yolcam lonshi tox! Zacare ca od zamran, odo cicle qaa, zorge, lap zirdo noco Mad, hoath Iaida!"* Finally, she set the dagger upon the altar, its point facing east, held both her hands above it, and sealed in the enchantment. *"Ugeg, lap noan nazpsad cors ta ge oq manin Iaidon!"* Reaching out with her mind, she felt the presence of the weapon as a tangible force upon the altar, its essence pressing against her consciousness like that of a living thing rather than that of a cold steel blade. Taking a sheath from the cabinet below the altar table, she inserted the dagger into it and clipped the sheath onto her belt. "It is done," she said finally.

"So I can cross the circle?" asked Jim.

"Not quite. I need to banish first." She repeated the first two rituals, but in reverse order with banishing hexagrams and invoking pentagrams, calling the energy she had used to sustain the magical field back into herself. As she did so, the sphere of energy that marked the boundary of the circle weakened, shimmered chaotically, and finally sank back into the earth.

They left the temple and rested in the parlor. Elspeth was tired, as the making of the dagger was an advanced operation and she had put as much of her power into the weapon as she could manage. It still hung on her belt, and every so often she touched the hilt, as though assuring herself that it was still there. "Now I'm sleepy," she said softly as she reclined on the sofa.

"You do look really drained," observed Jim. "Did the ritual take all that energy out of you?"

"Sort of," she replied. "Magical energy comes from everything around us, but it requires some percentage of the overall power raised to direct and focus it, and that comes from the magician. It's as difficult as hard manual labor in terms of fatigue, though it affects the mind rather than the body."

Jim continued apprehensively. "I certainly don't mean to question your judgment, but can I ask you a question?"

"Sure," she replied with a yawn.

"Making the dagger so that it will transfer the demon's power to you seems kind of elaborate. Why not just make something that will kill it, rather than dump its energy into you?"

She was quiet for a while, considering. "I could do that," she admitted, "but the energy drain is more likely to work because he will probably have really good defenses against outright disruption - at least, I would if I were a demon. Also, his powers are pretty amazing and I wouldn't mind having a few of them for myself. Keep in mind, also, that this is all theoretical since he might keep his word. It's just good to have an option in case he goes back on it."

"I suppose that makes sense."

Elspeth stretched like a cat about to curl up for its afternoon nap. "You know, I think you should go. I'm not going to be any fun tonight. On the good side, I'm tired enough to sleep without worrying about the Guild, but sleeping is all I'm going to do."

"Okay," said Jim. "I'll go. By the way, just out of curiosity, do you have to use the dagger or can someone else?"

She shrugged. "Any magician could use it, but that's not an issue. It's not leaving my sight."

"Well, good night, then," he said with a bright smile. He gave her a parting kiss and let himself out. The enormous wooden door slammed shut behind him ominously.

With a great deal of effort, Elspeth picked herself up off the sofa and ascended the huge carved staircase to her bedroom on the second floor. One hand still tightly wrapped around the dagger, she fell asleep as soon as her head hit the pillow.

II. The Priestess

The Priestess of the Silver Star
The Moon

The trees all around Samantha Davis seemed to pulse with energy that gathered somewhere ahead of her along the narrow and overgrown trail – magical energy, but completely unlike the human magick that flowed in her veins. It was night, and the sky above her dark and moonless, though somehow she was still able to see where she was going. *Where was she going?*

She saw that she was dressed in one of her black wool ritual robes, and in her hand she carried a dagger. The weapon wasn't hers - she knew that. Not only was it very expensive and well-made, much nicer than any of her own ritual implements, it also throbbed in her hand with a wild, alien energy that hurt if she paid too much attention to it. No matter how much it hurt, though, she understood that she could not put it down. It was too important.

Up ahead of her she heard sounds, maybe voices, coming from far off. She quickened her pace despite the branches and leaves that snapped at her face and body and tangled in her long, unbound brown hair. She could hear that she was getting closer to the voices, and she knew that was where she needed to be. A hill, she thought, with an outdoor circle like the ones she had read about witches using to raise power in medieval times – an outer perimeter encircling a central altar stone. She knew that she had never seen it, but the awareness of its form somehow came to her from the edge of her consciousness.

As the trail broke out of the dense forest, fear gripped her heart, a palpable physical reaction to the scene before her - a high treeless hill rising out of the forest, its summit illuminated by a vortex of magick the likes of which she had never seen outside science fiction films. Like a spinning inverted cone of pure light that extended into the clouds and beyond, it stood upon what she knew was the altar stone in a holocaust of blazing brightness. All the

47

energy was flowing here – from the woods, the countryside, maybe even the whole world. She tried to cast a simple concealment spell to hide her from being observed, but the energy she summoned was torn from her grasp by a force that felt like a driving wind of unbelievable intensity.

Her magick was gone. She realized at that moment what the thing on the hill above her was. It was collecting power, drawing it from everywhere like a gigantic whirlpool and putting it… *where?* Like her uncanny awareness of the form of the circle atop the hill, it came to her that the dagger had the power to stop this thing, whatever it was, and it needed to be stopped. That was what she had come here to do. She began to climb the hill, her bare hands and feet digging into the soft grass and the cool, wet dirt beneath, and suddenly a strangely nondescript man stood before her. She tried to dodge past him, tried to reach the maelstrom that screamed above her, but he made a simple gesture and she was hurled to the bottom of the hill by magical force.

As she dragged herself to her feet, the man approached. Like her he was dressed in a black robe, and like her he was ringed with the bright aura of a mage, but something about him seemed wrong, as though he were only vaguely human. He raised his right hand ominously as he intoned something in a voice shaped from what sounded like random noise and contemptuously met her gaze.

In his eyes blazed the kaleidoscopic light of the whirling column above…

Samantha was jolted awake by the ringing of the phone on the night table next to her bed. Groggily, she groped for the receiver. "Hello?" she said, pressing it to her ear and brushing her thick hair from her bleary hazel eyes. She glanced at the clock next to the phone, and through her blurry vision saw that it was 7:30 in the morning. She also realized she was still trembling from the dream.

"Do what thou wilt shall be the whole of the Law," said a

stern, familiar voice on the other end, that of the woman who had been her magical teacher for many years.

Her body involuntarily straightened as the fog of sleep lifted from her mind. "Love is the law, love under will," she replied, the proper response to the traditional Thelemic greeting. "You never call me this early, Daria. What's going on?"

"Did I wake you?" asked Samantha's instructor, sounding more surprised than anything else. "Sunrise was over an hour ago. I thought you would be up by now."

"After I do my morning rituals, I go back to bed unless I have to get up for work," she explained. "I was never much of a morning person. It's okay, though."

"Are you sure? You sound... I don't know. Agitated, perhaps."

Samantha shook her head. "It's not you. I had a dream... I haven't dreamed like that in a long time." Her heart was still racing. Since beginning her magical training with Daria seven years ago, her dreams had mostly subsided and lost much of their original intensity as she worked through the misguided conditioning of her youth.

"Well, the matter I need to discuss with you is rather urgent," she said apologetically. "We believe that another magical order of considerable power is operating in the Twin Cities area, and we have identified one of its members. The Council and I met late last night and they have come to a resolution that you are the ideal person to make contact and find out what this order is trying to accomplish."

The man in the dream? "Any particular reason?" she asked, trying to keep her voice steady.

"Several, actually," she replied. "You are one of the higher-ranked initiates in the area, which means you are more likely to understand any complex questions of magick theory that may arise. You are also the same age as this individual, which is not the case with most of the other initiates of your rank or higher. The Council thinks that this should more easily facilitate communication between the two of you, and will make meeting in an apparently chance manner more plausible. Most importantly, you are the one initiate who more than anyone else has persisted in your demands that we attempt to move beyond magical theory and into the practical realm. We believe that is precisely what this order has done. Their skills at practical magick are far beyond our own, and as such, your prior studies of it will give you a wider knowledge base than just about anyone else we could choose."

Like summoning a giant storm of living magick, or binding the powers of a rival? Maybe throwing someone down a hill without laying a hand on them? "How far beyond are we talking about here?" she asked hesitantly. The emotional impact of the dream was starting to subside, leaving her feeling silly for being bothered by a nightmare like a ten-year-old. *If that's all it was...*

"You will hear on the news today that Morpheus, a downtown nightclub, was destroyed by an explosion yesterday evening. That explosion was caused by magick," she said apprehensively, "though not by any ritual technique with which we are familiar. The magick itself feels like Enochian, but focused and directed by different means than those that we teach. Are you are interested in accepting the assignment?"

"Of course, Daria," she replied, hiding her apprehensiveness. She had never in her life turned down an assignment from the governing council of her order and she was not about to start now. "Who's the member you've identified?"

"His name is Michael Niemand. I've emailed you photos and other information, including some of the news footage of the club from last night."

"He destroyed the club?" she asked quizzically.

"We don't know. There was a big surge of magical energy right before the club exploded, and by the time anyone could scry the place it was already burning. All we know is that he was on the scene working powerful magick. That doesn't mean that he caused the explosion, but he might have."

Samantha's eyes lit up. "That's amazing!" she said quickly,

her lingering fear giving way to fascination. "You would have to have some way of doing a conversion to physical energy and some source of fuel…"

"Wait." Daria interrupted her student's train of thought, weighing her words carefully. "While as your instructor it falls to me to communicate the wishes of the Council, and despite the fact that I have relayed the relevant information to you as I was directed, it is my recommendation to you that you refuse this assignment. As you know, the Council cannot compel you to take it."

"Why should I do that?" she demanded, taken aback. "If the Council thinks it's so important…"

"The members of the Council are not volunteering to actually do it," she broke in curtly. "They're essentially volunteering you. This situation is potentially very dangerous, and at the moment none of us have any idea what you might be getting yourself into. We don't focus on practical magick because it can easily unbalance an otherwise sane mind, and Michael Niemand could be an outright lunatic. This assignment is more a request than a directive, and you can refuse it. Don't feel that you have to do this, and don't do it just because you are interested in learning new techniques."

Samantha relaxed and cleared her mind, tracing the source of her interest and motivation as Daria had taught her. She brushed past the fear lingering from the dream, past her images of the small child who had always done as she was told, and beyond even her own tendency to offer help when it was needed. Beyond lay a universe of glittering potential, and feeling the course of her own will, she knew that she was being pulled into its midst. "I have to admit, being exposed to such new techniques is tempting, but that's not the only reason I'm interested. I've always been willing to help out our order in whatever way I can, and I also would really like to exchange ideas with someone from a completely different school. As much as I enjoy working with you, Daria, I think that my own ritual work would really be helped by some new ideas – you know, a fresh perspective. In the last few years I've felt – oh, I don't know – limited, I suppose. Like something is missing from

51

my training that I just can't place. My powers have always kept me safe. I know that isn't true for everyone, but you know what I'm talking about, how things just kind of work out for me in unusual ways."

"True," she admitted. "Your powers have always seemed to bring you peace and stability, even luck. Still, this is probably a greater danger than anything you've previously encountered. You don't know your limitations in this area, and that is always a precarious situation to be in."

"I feel like it's my will," she insisted. "I think I'll be safe."

Her instructor let out a long sigh. "If you are truly committed to doing this, you know I won't forbid you to do it against the will of the Council. I wish you the best of luck, and I sincerely hope your powers will continue to keep you safe. But please be careful."

"I will, I promise. I'll talk to you soon." She hung up the phone and tried to lie down again, but her mind was racing too quickly for her to fall back asleep – not from the dream, which by now had mostly faded from her memory, but from the realization that somewhere there were mages who studied the kind of magick she had always wanted to work. Her training had given her the ability to stop her thoughts, but doing so led to quiet contemplation rather than sleep. All her life she had felt like the primitive spells that she had worked as a child and even the rigorous, methodical ritual work of her order only comprised pieces of a greater whole that remained hidden from her. Perhaps now she would finally be given a chance to complete that puzzle.

Her curiosity getting the better of her, Samantha fumbled for her glasses on the night table and walked across the bedroom to her computer. Her apartment was a spacious one-bedroom, but it had only a bedroom, a large living and dining room, a kitchenette, and a bathroom. The living room doubled as a temple, leaving the bedroom to serve as the computer room. Her order taught that too many electronic devices could disturb a temple space, though she had never noticed an effect and wasn't sure if that was really true. Opening up her email, she downloaded the message from Daria. It had several attachments, one of which was a media file. She double-clicked on the attachment and the video began to play, showing the warehouse that held the Morpheus nightclub engulfed in flames. The fire was vast, sweeping over the building like a shroud of heat and light, consuming the old structure. It was all the more frightening to watch because she often went out dancing at Morpheus on Friday nights, and it was really only luck on her part that she had not been there for the blast. The resolution of the file wasn't very good, probably because it had been captured from network television, but she thought she could make out a figure standing too close to the flames, making gestures reminiscent of a magical ritual. She could not be sure, but it seemed like as he completed the gestures and disappeared from view the flames began to noticeably subside. *Michael Niemand*, she said to herself. *Not creating the fire, stopping it.*

She opened the other attached files and took a look at the information her order had managed to assemble on Niemand's background. Like her, he was twenty-nine years old. He worked as a software engineer for a large consulting company in downtown Saint Paul, only a few blocks from the insurance company where she worked as a support technician. He lived next to Como Park, right on the lake, in one of Saint Paul's more affluent neighborhoods, and had lived there for several years. He had no criminal record and there was no information in the files about his family or associates. She stared at the photo, which had been taken on the downtown skyway. It was not a particularly good picture, but it was good enough to show her that he looked nothing like the man in the dream. He also did not openly present any aspect of the counter-culture look that characterized most of the mages she had met, except for his long hair, which was tied back in a neat ponytail. Otherwise he looked like a typical corporate drone - black suit, conservative tie, white shirt, and expensive leather shoes. *But he was a mage, and by all indications a powerful one*, she told herself as she memorized the photo as best she could. The man in the dream had been nondescript too.

As she absorbed the information, she planned her strategy. The easiest thing to do was probably to somehow run into him over lunch on a weekday. Since it was Saturday, she decided to wait until Monday and see if she could figure out when he usually took his lunch break. Then she could arrange to meet him apparently by chance. The plan had the problem that mages were often strangely aware of their surroundings, and if his spiritual self saw her as a threat he might be able to avoid her completely for weeks. Still, while she could not be sure of the intentions of her order, she knew her own mind. Like Niemand, she was a seeker after the structure and nature of magick and the universe itself, and she hoped that the superior intuition that she figured he had to possess would tell him that.

Since she was already awake, she got up and traversed the narrow corridor that led into the living room. Like most of the mages she had ever met, she had an extensive magical library, large enough to cover an entire wall of the room. The wall of bookshelves contained volumes representing the entire curriculum of her order and a smattering of books describing the other traditions she had studied at one time or another – Voudon, Asatru, Taoism, and many more. Like most Thelemites, those who followed the teachings of the founder of her magical order, the British mystic and poet Aleister Crowley, Samantha was a hopeless bibliophile. It was that particular tendency that led to the old joke:

"What do you get a Thelemite who has everything? A bookshelf!"

A smiled danced across her face as the thought crossed her mind, widening as it occurred to her that she could use another set of shelves herself.

She took her copy of Crowley's Magick: Book 4 down from the top shelf and perused the section titled *Magick in Theory and Practice*. Despite her order's insistence that Crowley was mostly interested in mysticism rather than practical magick, which was to some extent true, he had written extensively on the subject of actual physical effects and claimed to have accomplished many of them. In his <u>Confessions</u> he wrote that he had performed a few magical feats that she had never been able to do, such as summoning visible light, and his extensive writings covered many more possible magical "powers," such as summoning flame and levitation. In theory, it was very clear how such things could be done, and as far as she or her teacher could ascertain, her understanding of those techniques was accurate. It was the practice leading to material results that had always eluded her, which suited Daria just fine. Her instructor was of the opinion that practical magick was far inferior to mysticism practiced for the sole purpose of wisdom and spiritual development. Samantha was not sure if Daria had ever succeeded at producing physical effects, but since she was clearly shaken by the idea that a building could be destroyed by magick perhaps she had not, at least to such an impressive degree. Maybe that was why the Council was so interested in tracking down Michael Niemand.

Her mind drifted back to Daria's comment that the magick felt like Enochian. The Enochian system of magick was originally created by John Dee, a British magician, and Edward Kelley, a psychic, based upon their communications with beings who called themselves angels. Crowley had considered himself the reincarnation of Edward Kelley and had made fairly extensive use of Enochian magick, writing at one point that he had always wanted to publish an updated and accurate account of the system. What he had published consisted of a brief synopsis of Golden Dawn techniques, which Samantha personally thought flew in the face of some of the original material she had read, and his own account of his experiences working with the Enochian angels, a brilliant mystical work entitled <u>The Vision and the Voice</u>. Based on what she had gathered from Daria, while that book was extremely valuable to anyone hoping to explore the Enochian universe itself, it contained little information concerning practical techniques or even answers to basic questions, such as the correct pronunciation of the words that made up the Angelic language in which the Enochian conjurations were written.

The problem was not so much that the original Dee and Kelley material was unavailable or incomprehensible, but there was a lot of it and very little was organized or explained. Samantha had some of the published excerpts from Dee's diaries, but with the exception of a grimoire called the Heptarchia Mystica the various revelations they contained were not assembled together in any logical order. There were no rituals or accounts of rituals – presumably, Dee had done *something* to summon the angels into his crystal shewstone through which they spoke to Kelley, but no text of any sort explaining those rituals existed save the mention of certain prayers that they included. All of it needed a framework, or key of some kind, to be truly useful, and many magical orders since Dee's time had developed their own. Crowley used the version developed by the Hermetic Order of the Golden Dawn, which was the order in which he had originally studied magick. Her order used the same system, since it was part of Crowley's teachings. Nobody she had ever talked to had any idea what the real key might originally have been.

Did anyone? How about Michael Niemand? Could his order have the solution?

Replacing Book 4 on the shelf, she opened up the cabinet that served as her altar table and took out her deck of Tarot cards. She used Crowley's Thoth deck, ostensibly on the grounds that the Kabalistic attributions of each card were more correct than those of the more popular Rider-Waite but also because she really liked the deco-style artwork. Sitting down on the floor, she cleared her mind and then filled it with all the attributes she was aware of concerning her current situation – Michael Niemand, the Council, Daria, the explosion at Morpheus, her quest for the secrets of practical magick. Then she shuffled the deck three times, cut it, and lay out ten cards in the classic Celtic Cross spread. For herself, in the center, she drew the Priestess, which happened a lot – it was the card for which she had always felt the closest affinity. She saw this as a good sign, since usually when she drew the Priestess as a significator, it meant that the direction in which she was moving was in harmony with her will.

She drew a second card, and placed it across the first. The Seven of Swords, titled Futility. Was the reading telling her that her mission was futile? In the crossing position, she doubted that interpretation. More likely, it represented her own feelings toward the teachings of her Order. She knew that the training she had received was not futile in any sense of the word, but it was also true that lately she had felt much more frustrated in her practices by the continuing sense that something was missing from them that was preventing her from achieving her full potential.

For the next three positions, Past, Present, and Possible Future, she drew Art, the Eight of Swords, titled Interference, and the Four of Pentacles, titled Power. Art was called Temperance in older Tarot decks and it was the card that represented the perfection of the self, which she interpreted as referring to the magical training that she had undergone for many years. Interference perhaps referred to whatever was blocking her powers from developing fully, and the Power card offered the possibility of overcoming her limitations. Swords were the suit of Air, representing the intellect, while Pentacles were the suit of Earth, symbolizing the physical body and material world. She had felt for a long time that her Order certainly did lean toward intellectualizing magick instead of actually practicing it, and maybe that was the root of her problem.

For the sixth position, Immediate Future, she drew The Magus. The Magus represented a magician, and a highly skilled one at that. She thought it likely that given her current situation, the card referred to an actual worker of magick, though in truth it was attributed to the planet Mercury and thus could refer to anyone accomplished in a technical or intellectually demanding field. She suspected that it meant she would in fact meet Michael Niemand soon, but she couldn't be sure. The card could also be referring to Daria, whom she would contact soon regardless of the outcome of her mission.

For the seventh and eight positions, Querant and Environment, she drew the Seven of Wands, titled Valor, and the Ten of Wands, titled Oppression. The suit of Wands was attributed to Fire, representing will. It had not occurred to her to think of her actions in terms of valor or courage, but it was true that she was following her will into a situation that from the sound of it truly frightened her instructor, a more accomplished magician than she. Crowley's description of the card was that it described a situation similar to that found in a military operation where discipline has broken down, leaving only the qualities and strengths of individual soldiers to carry the day. Was her assignment really more dangerous than it felt? Maybe that was the point being made by the Ten of Wands. *But oppression by what?* She felt that the direction of her training had limited her, but not in an oppressive way. Was Michael Niemand looking to in some way enslave or dominate her? Was his order? Or was there some other force at work that she had not yet conceptualized?

For the ninth position, Hopes and Fears, she drew the Five of Cups, titled Disappointment. That one, at least, was on the mark. While she saw the possibility that practical magick could open up a new world of learning to her, she also feared that she would in some way be unable to take advantage of that opportunity, or that once she saw it for what it was, she would realize that it had not been worth pursuing. Maybe it took some kind of inborn ability, as she had always suspected from her research, that she did not possess. She hoped, as she sought greater learning, that it would prove to be enlightening and not a worthless waste of time and energy.

Finally, for the tenth and last position, Final Resolution, she drew The Devil, one of the most difficult cards in the deck to interpret. It was attributed to the zodiac sign Capricorn, cardinal earth, and could represent pragmatism or practicality. It could also represent obsession with the material world, or an opposing force on the spiritual plane such as an actual demon or devil. In addition, it could represent being bound or contained in some way, which resonated eerily with the Ten of Wands in the Environment position. It was also possible that the card could represent what Crowley called a "black brother," about the closest thing to the embodiment of evil in his cosmology, a magician who has rejected spiritual attainment in favor of self-glorification. Was this her destiny, or Michael Niemand's? Was her search for the secrets of practical magick a step down the wrong path that would eventually lead to her undoing? Or did the card symbolize someone else entirely, like the magician who had really destroyed the Morpheus nightclub? From the reading she could not be sure.

Since she had found that multiple readings on the same subject were usually completely useless, she put the cards away and began her daily meditations. She would meet Michael Niemand soon enough, and hopefully he would be able to answer some of the questions raised by her reading. Until then, she would simply let them rest.

III. The Empress

The Daughter of the Mighty Ones
The Planet Venus

It was a frustrated Samantha Davis who returned home from work the following Monday. She had spent her lunch break roaming the skyways around Michael's building to no avail, and had concluded that either eating lunch must not be something he did every day, his schedule was completely unlike that of other people, or his heightened spiritual awareness somehow allowed him to avoid her entirely. The result was that her assignment was going to be tougher than she thought. She dropped her bag in its usual place in the living room and sat down wearily on her overstuffed sofa, trying to figure out what she wanted to do with the rest of her evening. Maybe this exact situation was what the cards had really meant by Futility.

In the end, she decided to go shopping. She took a bus from her downtown Minneapolis apartment across the river to the University of Minnesota campus, getting off at the block adjacent to the epicenter of the Twin Cities' occult community, Magus Books. The popular occult shop occupied a storefront in Dinkytown, a commercial area that had grown up around the University, and unlike its competitors, Magus carried a truly amazing assortment of books on real ritual magick instead of a stale collection of titles on Wicca, herbalism, lucky candle magic, and little else. She had patronized the store for years, from the time when it was a small out-of-the-way shop in the back of the building across the street, but somehow it seemed that whenever she went there, the place always had something new and interesting to offer.

As she looked up from browsing through several of the latest Crowley editions, she was shocked to see Michael Niemand walk into the store.

At first she didn't recognize him, dressed as he was in a simple black shirt and slacks under a long tan trench coat. She noted that a silver unicursal hexagram, one of the holy symbols of

61

Thelema, hung on a thin silver chain around his neck. She was also somewhat surprised at how short he was – only a few inches taller than her own five feet four inches. In the photo he looked taller. She shifted her attention to her magical sight and noted that he had one of the strangest auras she had ever seen. At first, it looked like nothing at all, but then her sight deepened and she was able to see past what she realized was a complex set of magical wards that prevented most low-power psychics and newbie magicians from noticing anything unusual about the energy that surrounded him. Past the wards, his power was almost blinding.

"Hello, Roger," he said, waving to the proprietor of the store, a tall and distinguished English gentleman who seemed to know all there was to know about obscure volumes of occult lore.

"Well, hello there," replied Roger. "Your copy of the <u>Sworn Book of Honorius</u> just came in this morning. I also still have that new edition of Dee's <u>Five Books of Mystery</u> that I called you about."

Michael smiled. "Wonderful. I'll take both of them today."

"So I take it you've been working more with the Enochian system," said Roger as he began writing up the receipt.

"Absolutely. I've gotten some pretty interesting results," replied Michael. "It's powerful stuff."

"That it is. Are you still working with the original material, then, rather than Crowley or the Golden Dawn?" Roger possessed an attribute very useful to the proprietor of an occult bookstore – he knew something about almost every aspect of magical practice, especially in the ceremonial field.

"Well, mostly. I do use Crowley's <u>Vision and the Voice</u> as a source, though – most of that material is closer to the original revelation than a lot of the material that the Golden Dawn added to the system."

As Samantha was trying to figure out the best way into the conversation, Roger suddenly waved her over. *How was it that he always seemed to intervene in the most convenient way possible?* The obvious answer was that he had studied magick *somewhere,* probably before he came to America, but his interests and mannerisms gave her little insight. Neither did his aura, which looked bright but not immediately overpowering. Wherever he had learned it, his enhanced intuition always seemed to save her trouble. It was not just her, either – Daria, also a regular at the store, said the exact same thing.

"Have you met Samantha?" Roger was saying to Michael as she walked across the shop to the counter. "She's into Crowley and studies some Enochian. Samantha, this is Michael."

"Hi," he said with a polite but superficial smile. "No, I'm pretty sure we haven't met. It's very nice to meet you." For just a moment what looked like it might be flicker of recognition, not of her precisely but of something else, crossed his face, but it was gone before Samantha could be sure. "So what about Crowley interests you the most?" he asked quickly, a practiced line that she suspected he used often when meeting other occultists.

Samantha replied honestly, without subterfuge. "His whole philosophy, really. I became a Thelemite years ago because it just seemed like the most logical conclusion if you accept the tenets of Renaissance Hermeticism." Opening up immediately to counter Michael's polite veneer made perfect sense, she reasoned, since if he were truly as powerful as she suspected, hiding things from him would be pointless anyway.

"That's an interesting perspective," he replied thoughtfully. "I'm a Hermetic myself. I don't really consider myself a Thelemite or an adherent to any particular religious path, but you see the two worldviews as related?"

"Well, sure," she replied quickly. "If you're a Hermetic, you believe in perfecting yourself so that you can become akin to divinity, however you perceive it. If that potential is there, it means that we are at least partially divine. So the key to becoming divine ourselves is developing that part of us that is in touch with divinity in the macrocosmic universe."

63

"That certainly seems reasonable," he admitted. "So that's what you think Crowley was saying? I've studied some of his work, but nothing besides <u>The Vision and the Voice</u> in any great detail."

"Well, I've studied just about everything he ever wrote, and the only difference between what I just told you and Thelema is terminology," she explained. "We call the divine part of human beings either the True Will or the Holy Guardian Angel, depending on the context, and work toward union with it. But it's really all about self-actualization on all levels – the elevation of that which is human to that which is divine. It's all very Hermetic."

"I'll have to read more of it, then," he said, still polite but detached. "You find Crowley's philosophy useful in your own practices, and in your daily life, then? How so?"

She shrugged. "Words aren't the best way to talk about something as experiential as mysticism, but I suppose it can't hurt to try. My whole life, I've always made an effort to be as true to myself as possible and separate outside conditioning from real volition. I didn't realize it when I was younger, of course – I just thought I was being more independent-minded than most people are comfortable with. But when I really started looking closely and honestly at myself and realized that I really wanted to practice magick, it kind of all fell into place and made sense. Thelema just kind of solidified it for me – for all my supposed independence, a lot of what I was doing was being reactive, rather than active, and I figured out that just about every time I found myself having problems, it was because of some pretty useless cultural programming that for some reason I hadn't managed to shake. " She could tell that he was momentarily surprised by her candidness, but he regained his easygoing manner so quickly that it was hard to be sure. Still, now she thought she saw something besides detached dismissal in his eyes.

"Do you study on your own, then, or work with a group?" he asked, his wariness rising, but remaining well hidden beneath a mask of conversational amiability.

What the hell, Samantha told herself. While there was not

64

anything technically wrong with admitting her affiliation, in some contexts it was considered bad form. "I'm with the A∴A∴," she replied. "My lineage is one of the ones that traces itself back to Karl Germer, Crowley's immediate successor as head of both A∴A∴ and Ordo Templi Orientis. Of course, since my group conforms to Crowley's original design of the order, I only know my own instructor on a personal basis, so much of the time I work alone."

"How far have you advanced, if I may ask?"

"Adeptus Minor. I understand I'm one of the few in this part of the country," she replied. "How about you?"

"How about some dinner?" he asked abruptly. In a lower voice, he added with a slight smile, "I'd like to continue this conversation, but in a less conspicuous location. Do you mind?"

"Not at all," she replied, wondering if his order required such discretion. It obviously was not completely secret, or he would already be out the door. "Where?"

"How about the Loring Pasta Bar?" he suggested as he paid Roger and picked up his two books off the counter. "It's just up the street. Have you ever eaten there?"

"No. I've heard it's kind of expensive. Is it good?"

"It's usually excellent. The atmosphere is great — you almost have to see it to believe it — and I'll buy."

She returned his smile. "Lead the way, then."

They stepped out onto the mostly empty sidewalk and crossed the street, dodging the busy traffic that plagued the whole Dinkytown area during the week. Like the previous two days, the weather was unseasonably warm and the setting sun shone down on the muddy streets from a clear sky. Jumping the puddles on the opposite side of the road, Michael led her down half a block to the next intersection and turned the corner, where the entrance to the restaurant stood invitingly amidst high windows bright with the lights that were just coming on.

The Loring Pasta Bar proved to be a two-story building with an open and airy floor plan. The upper level was a sort of loft or balcony that overlooked the first floor, and in the center of the space the ceiling rose all the way to the roof of the building, giving the whole room the illusion of being much larger than it actually was. The building had formerly housed a drugstore of all things, and Samantha noted the stained glass windows that still read DRUGS along the exterior wall facing University Avenue. The building had been completely remodeled into its current configuration, which featured a lot of exposed brickwork and soft lighting. Michael led her up a flight of stairs to a relatively out-of-the-way table overlooking the restaurant and ordered dinner.

"I'll start off by apologizing for my attitude at the store," he began uncertainly. "I hope that I didn't come off as too condescending – I'm just rather used to running into complete flakes when I'm shopping for anything related to magick and being detached and aloof gets rid of them."

"Understood," replied Samantha, immediately recognizing the kind of situations he was trying to avoid. "That's maybe a trick I should learn."

He smiled, relieved. "It does come in handy, though sometimes it turns people off who have interesting things to say."

"So does that mean you think I have interesting things to say, then?" she asked teasingly, returning his smile with an oblique grin.

"I hope so. Now let's see - you were asking me about my magical affiliations," he continued, returning to their previous conversation. "I was recently admitted to the grade of Adept in my own order, which has a similar structure to your A∴A∴. I believe that should make us the same rank, since in my order we advance from Portal to Adept. Portal is the equivalent of Dominus Limnus in the A∴A∴, as I recall."

She nodded. "Does your order have a name?"

"We just call it the Guild," he replied with a shrug. "Our leadership isn't particularly thrilled with the exotic names some of the groups out there throw around like confetti. I mean, how many Ancient, Justified, and Exalted Rosicrucian or Golden Dawn

Assemblies can there possibly be?"

She laughed. "Too many! Especially when they spend all their time arguing on the Internet."

"And they're always stealing from each other, or at least that's what their leaders keep trying to claim," he added, remembering some of the chat room exchanges that seemed to happen on a regular basis. "Actually, we were the first Rosicrucians, in seventeenth century France, and when some yahoo started publicizing our existence it started a panic."

"You're serious?" She had read about the Rosicrucian scare in France. In the early seventeenth century, handbills had been posted all over Paris that claimed to expose a powerful and ancient magical order whose members possessed godlike supernatural powers. The handbills had triggered mass hysteria among the residents of the city, who feared that these great and powerful magicians were walking invisibly among them stirring up discord. Most historians considered the whole thing an elaborate hoax. "Or is that just group folklore or something, like claiming Wicca is forty thousand years old?"

"As far as I know it's for real. It's what I was always taught, and we have documentation that looks pretty convincing. John Dee founded our order in Germany during his tenure at the court of Rudolph the Second. After Dee's death in 1608 the leadership got a little messy, with several of the high-ranking members vying for control, but eventually a new Guildmaster emerged who was backed by most of the membership and the Order expanded into France. The Rosicrucian scare can probably be traced to somebody supporting one of the losing factions, but whether they just talked too freely about the group or actively publicized it we don't really know."

"So you're a lot older than the turn of the century groups, like the Theosophical Society and the Golden Dawn," she mused. "But how can that be when your grade structure is as similar to that of the modern groups as you say it is? Most of that goes right back to the Golden Dawn."

"They're part of our lineage, sort of a spin-off." he explained. "My ex-girlfriend, who's a generational Guild mage, is descended from Anna Sprengel, Mathers and Wescott's contact in Germany who gave them the original charter for the Golden Dawn in England. The lineage is messy there too, because Anna died soon after that and the Guildmaster who replaced her had very different views about expanding the order beyond continental Europe."

"'Fraulein Anna Sprengel' was a hoax, though," she argued. "We have court documents and letters…"

"Written by Mathers to discredit his rival Wescott, yes," pointed out Michael. "As near as we can figure it, Anna was dead and Mathers already knew that the new Guild leadership would deny everything – we know that in the midst of the breakup of the Golden Dawn he tried to get support from the Guild in France and was politely told not to contact them again. In the wake of that, the court cases and so forth suggest that he thought he could establish himself as the head of a completely new lineage by denying ties to my order. Mind you, by the time that happened, he was starting to lose his grip on reality and the later order he founded never went anywhere. He might have been another casualty of the Abyss, which is really too bad because at one time he was an extremely talented magician. We use versions of his Pentagram and Hexagram rituals to this day – they're better banishing and invoking rituals than the ones we had at the time, which were sloppier and more archaic. We integrated them a few years after Crowley published them in The Equinox."

"Yeah, older isn't necessarily better," she agreed. "I've always been amazed by groups that claim they're the true ancient rite of whatever, as though being behind the times was some kind of a virtue. The old grimoires from before the Renaissance are really pretty sad in most cases - like calling lots of 'Oh God, you're so big…' kind of stuff that goes on for twenty minutes a 'conjuration.' I get better results with the modern forms every time."

He grinned mischievously. "Mention that around some magicians and they'll practically bite your head off, though usually they're the ones who don't really understand how magick works. Crowley said it himself – magick should be a progressive science. It should change, evolve, and improve over time."

She nodded affirmatively. "That's a sentiment I wish my own group would take to heart. Don't get me wrong, I like Crowley's work, but it seems like my superiors sometimes get all wrapped up in what Crowley did, whether or not it works well. Crowley was cautious about doing practical magick, so it doesn't really even get taught. It doesn't help that there are so many stories out there about practical magick gone bad, even though I think most of the ones I've heard have been exaggerated or even completely false."

"Well, what good is magick if you can't use it for anything?" He held up his hand and grinned as she was about to reply. "I know, I know, spiritual development. That's true, but material things sometimes get in the way of spiritual progress and it's good to have tools to deal with those situations. But then, I'm a Taurus – a pragmatist to the core."

She laughed. "Why am I not surprised?"

"Because you're perceptive," he replied immediately, and as far as she could tell, honestly. *Apparently I have something interesting to say after all*, she thought to herself.

Their waitress, a willowy dark-haired girl dressed in what passed for the latest campus fashion, arrived with the food moments later. Michael just picked up his sandwich and took a bite, but Samantha set the plate in front of her and concentrated for a moment before eating.

"What was that?" he asked, feeling just a touch of moving magical energy.

"Saying Will," she replied. "I take it your order doesn't teach it."

"I guess not. I'm not familiar with it."

"We say it before eating. It helps keep us mindful of our direction in life," she explained. "What you do is say to yourself

69

that it is your will to eat and drink, that your body may be fortified thereby, that you may accomplish the Great Work. It helps to cultivating an attitude of mindfulness in everything."

"Nice. Does it work?"

"Of course," she replied, taken aback for a moment. "You have to ask? My order teaches a lot of regular practices. Without them it's pretty easy to get lazy about the work and then you never get anywhere."

"So long as you're not obsessively driven," he countered. "I've seen that problem, too, and it leads to all sorts of different problems – like the random destruction of perfectly innocent bystanders."

Samantha tried to look shocked, which was easier than she expected. She *was* shocked, not by the information itself, but by the nonchalant manner of its delivery. "What… what are you talking about?" she asked quickly.

"Morpheus. You didn't hear? It was in the paper yesterday. 'Gas leak destroys nightclub' or something like that. That was my aforementioned ex-girlfriend Elspeth Sprengel, who happens to be obsessively driven and is also one of the most dangerous mages I've ever met. She can do a fire evocation that will light a candle across a room, or throw a Saturn curse at you that will make everything around you quit working right for weeks. Or, of course, throw that same curse at an old building that makes the vulnerable part fail at *just that second*, so it will explode around a tedious and annoying ex-boyfriend."

"You must be joking," she countered weakly as her eyes widened. "Nobody is that powerful."

"Normally, you would be right, and I am being a bit flippant, but Elspeth is something of an aberration. She also is the best counterexample I can think of regarding mystical attainment conferring magical ability. She's probably the most powerful mage in our history, even allowing for the mythical tales of the Renaissance. She's inbred, of course, like a lot of the mages in the Guild, and the Sprengel bloodline has been one of the strongest for centuries – but her level of realization is nothing out of the ordinary, at least so far."

"Inbred?" she must have sounded shocked, judging from his expression. *Could her theory of genetic aptitude be correct?* For someone like Michael was describing to even exist, it would almost have to be.

"Yes," he replied quickly. "I know, it sounds like some kind of Nazi experimentation, but it's nothing like that. Over the years, as I understand it, we've worked toward producing more powerful offspring by encouraging other powerful mages to marry and initiate their children into the Guild to build the next generation of mages. Nobody is coerced into doing anything, but over time the order's bias tends to concentrate the bloodlines. This has been going on for centuries, and the result is Elspeth – in some ways a complete disappointment."

Samantha shook her head, confused. "What do you mean a disappointment? I would do anything to be that good!"

"Would you?" he asked, staring at her quizzically for a moment. She wasn't sure because of the precise control he seemed to be able to exert over his magical abilities, but she thought he might also be reading something else in her aura.

"What?" she asked quickly.

"Trust me, you wouldn't. Elspeth is a disappointment not because of her level of power, which is about where the best case scenario for our program would place it, but because her level of power has had curiously little positive effect on her personality and awareness of the universe."

"How is that possible? I've always found that as I've gained magical ability my mind becomes more integrated, not less. Haven't you found the same thing?"

"Yes, and so have most of the other members of our order. That's what's so scary about it. According to my teacher Jonas, who's a lot older than I am, high magical ability was supposed to make those who possessed it better and more enlightened people. The research notes that we have from the early part of the last century back it up as well. But then Elspeth came along and contradicted everything we thought we knew."

"Do you know what the genes are that control magical ability?" she asked quickly, her biology training kicking in.

"They think so. About ten years before I was born, the Guild leadership scanned the genetics of every member using magical vision combined with a series of divinations, and concluded that the genes were already concentrated to the point where they expected to see truly superior magicians emerge in my generation. Elspeth appears to have reached that threshold in terms of power. It's written all over her body – she's almost supernaturally beautiful and at the same time kind of alien looking, like a Tolkien Elf. She *is* very intelligent and gifted, but the same time she's cold and calculating about everything and probably the most arrogant human being you will ever meet. It's like in developing her powers she neglected everything else because her powers made everything else irrelevant"

Samantha shook her head. "That's a little Freudian for my tastes. Besides, I've seen similar things happen with cross-dominance in both rats and pigeons, not to mention show dogs. My parents used to breed them when I was growing up. I mean, it's not the same, but…" she trailed off a bit as it hit her that she was talking about another human being, and here she was comparing them to laboratory animals.

"What?" asked Michael emphatically. "Please go on. What have you observed?"

"Well, keeping in mind that a human being is a lot different from a dog, sometimes you think that you have a genetic cluster that confers a whole set of traits, but the along comes one individual that blows your whole model. I'm imagining that for something like magick it would have to be incredibly complex or there would be a lot more magicians running around making trouble. Sometimes even if you've got the gene cluster, one apparently unrelated gene can drop out and all of a sudden it doesn't work the way it used to. Not only that, your order was working this out with divination, not

72

real gene sequencing, right?"

"Unfortunately," he replied. "About half the research we have was conducted before we even knew the structure of DNA. Divination was all we had – but you're right, maybe drawing a conclusion about the whole program from one example is premature. And I could be twisting the situation around in my mind more than I should. I mean, some of this could be my own bitterness about her launching an attempt on my life the day before yesterday, but I think it's fair to say that a sane, well-adjusted person doesn't throw a curse that blows up an entire building just because they're upset at the person with whom they're having dinner."

"Your program must have missed something. Maybe her power could be so strong that it warps her judgment. Let's say that magical aptitude is based on heightened brain function. That's logical, right?"

"As a matter of fact, that is part of how we think it works."

"At some point, then, you could get an effect like mania, where the heightened firing rates start to bleed over into mild psychosis. Most manics are delusional, but drop their brain function down just a touch with the right medication and they suddenly become very intelligent and lucid. How about her family life? Was she raised by messed up parents or something?"

"Not exactly. But I thought you weren't a fan of Freud."

"Oh, I'm not. Psychoanalysis is silly and not at all scientific. I do believe in behaviorism, though, and significant trauma can leave behind some nasty conditioning loops."

"Significant trauma, you say? That sounds about right."

"What happened to her?"

"Her parents died when she was twelve, and after that she was raised by her grandfather, the current head of the Guild. I understand her parents were murdered, and she might have seen it happen. She won't talk about it and neither will anyone else, and I'm not sure why. I think that's where it started, though."

"That would mess up any kid," Samantha agreed, "mage

73

or not."

"And her power complicates the whole thing. Mental illness or trauma is something we're usually pretty good at healing magically, but she doesn't think she has a problem in the first place and anyone trying to work magick on her would have to overcome her defenses, which isn't likely to happen."

"So she's so far gone that she doesn't realize blowing up a building is a bad thing?"

"Well, she's never produced an effect that dramatic before, so I don't know," he admitted. "She doesn't seem to mind with casting curses on various people around her, just because she feels like it. It's like she thinks she's entitled to do so because of her level of ability."

"How do you mean?"

"Well, I've always gotten the impression that she believes that her power comes primarily from what she *is* rather than what she *does*, that she has this great destiny or something. Who knows? She could be right. Maybe she is a prophet or something and magical aptitude is really a gift from the gods rather than a matter of genetics. I just can't help thinking that if that were the case, she would be a very different person than she is."

"You'd think so," Samantha remarked, "but then I suppose a lot of the Biblical prophets were kind of messed up, calling on God to smite people and stuff." Noting his bemused grin, she added, "Yes, I've read the Bible. God doesn't come off very well."

He laughed heartily. "And that's why you're a Thelemite, right?"

She returned a chuckle. "Among other reasons."

As Michael finished his sandwich, he gazed somewhat oddly at Samantha. She suddenly felt like he might be reading her again.

"What?" she asked. "Do I have mustard on my face or something?"

"No, nothing like that, he replied, shaking his head. "I just have the strangest feeling that our running into each other was somehow planned or orchestrated, and not by Roger. Maybe I'm just being paranoid, but my intuition about things is usually right. Were you looking for me? I know I wasn't looking for you, though I'm glad we ran into each other."

She was quiet for a long time. So he'd figured it out after all. She wondered if that was what he had been trying to read from her aura. "Well, sort of," she hedged finally.

"You can tell me, you know. I'm not going to blow up the restaurant or anything."

Her anxiety collapsed into laughter. "Promise?" she asked facetiously.

"You have my word as an Adept of the Inner Order," he replied with feigned grandiosity. "Now tell me, please. It's really okay."

"Well, my instructor told me about the Morpheus thing, and some of our mages saw you in a scrying crystal on the scene. They're scared to death of practical mages running around making trouble, and they were afraid that you and your order were dangerous. They asked me if I would find you and figure out whether or not that was the case. I hung around the skyways over in Saint Paul on my lunch hour but eventually gave up."

He shrugged. "I never waste an hour on lunch. I eat at my desk."

"Well, that would explain it. I need a break in the middle of the day myself."

"So do you work in Saint Paul?"

She nodded. "I'm a support technician at Travelers Insurance over by Landmark Center, and phone work can be really draining. Anyway, I wasn't actually looking for you tonight at Magus – that was just a coincidence."

He smiled again. "Don't bet on it with Roger. I still don't know what order he studied with, but from a few comments here and there I think it was one of the Golden Dawn lineages. Whatever the case, he's quite good, and he manages to partially shield his aura rather than shutting it down. I still haven't mastered that trick."

"So you're not angry?" It suddenly occurred to her that if he was, there was really very little she could do against such a powerful practical magician, even if he had promised not to blast the building – he could still go ahead and blast her. Banishings, maybe, if they would even work. *How is it that I can study magick for almost ten years without learning anything that would help me fend off a real magical attack?*

But he just shook his head and smiled again. "Why would I be? You may not realize this, but I don't have that many friends and my life is very busy. Between work and studying magick there isn't much time for a social life. Making friends at work is a big risk if the focus of your life is something that most people consider evil, as I'm sure you're aware. I know people in the Guild, but that's a pretty small group and I don't relate well to a lot of them. My life experience is really different."

"How so?"

"Well, the Guild is mostly made up of people from what they call the 'great families' – the Votans, the Sprengels, the Palmers, and so forth. Some of those families have produced magicians for more than ten generations. The Niemands are *not* a great family – my parents are ordinary people, and while there have been a few occultists here and there in my family tree, I'm the first that the Guild took notice of. As a matter of fact, the name Niemand literally means 'nobody' in German. I essentially inherited my aptitude by accident rather than from one of their carefully maintained bloodlines. That makes me very different. I first ran into Guild representatives when I was sixteen – they sensed that my powers had developed to the point where their system of magick would work for me, and sought me out. My parents are very Christian, and they forbade me from studying occultism, but it became kind of an obsession. You probably went through something similar – most people with power do."

"Well, sure. My family never really got it, but when you

don't have that sort of insatiable curiosity and interest, it doesn't matter much what other people think. My folks still think I'm a new age flake, but at least they're pretty liberal and tolerate me. How about yours?"

He sighed, and a look that conveyed both sadness and disappointment crossed his face. "They disowned me and threw me out of the house when I turned eighteen because they thought I was possessed by Satan," he said slowly. "That was when I joined the Guild. They trained me as a magician, put me through school, and then Jonas got me my first programming job. He's been more of a father to me than anyone I'm actually related to." As Samantha's eyes widened, his voice softened. "It's okay, really. There was a time when I didn't like talking about it, but now it's just the way things are and I deal with it. It was years ago. They just aren't a part of my life anymore. Just never let anyone tell you that fundamentalism is harmless – it's probably the greatest destructive force people have ever conceived."

"I really am sorry," she said quickly. "I didn't know."

"It's okay," he repeated reassuringly. "I don't say things I don't mean. I know directness is not very Minnesotan of me, but I like it a lot better than and of the alternatives." She nodded, and he continued. "Anyway, most of the great families are also independently wealthy, which I suppose you would expect when you have centuries of powerful magick at work, and I'm not, which is why I'm one of the few people in the Guild with a regular job. That gives me a totally different perspective right there."

"I can see that," she replied immediately. Being born into a comfortable and stable life that allowed her to pursue her studies and still survive would certainly have been preferable to being forced to divide her time between a job, a social life, and magick. Michael had to do that too, in the face of a peer group that could not even comprehend that sort of pressure.

"So at any rate, it really is nice to have someone go out of their way to be interested in me, even if their apparent motivations could be interpreted as somewhat suspect," he replied. "I don't sense much duplicity from you anyway, so I doubt you're a danger. Neither is your order, if they don't work much practical magick. They probably don't even have the ability to do so. But you do."

"What?" Her jaw visibly dropped and her eyes widened.

"I can tell by looking at your aura. I noticed it when I met you at Magus, though of course there are people with the ability who have never trained or developed it. I apologize for staring, but I've checked it a couple more times as we've been talking and not only is the ability present in you, but it's pretty well developed." He paused, letting the statement sink in as best he could. "You've known for years, haven't you, but your training is missing something, right?"

"How... how did you know that?"

His eyes lit up with recognition. "Because we all go through it. I felt it years ago, too, as a teenager studying on my own. Your power needs to express itself, and it will. I was lucky – I was noticed by an order that sought me out. But you still did as well as you could. Your A∴A∴ instructor may have problems with practical techniques, but Crowley's training syllabus is still better and more rigorous than that used by just about any of the other groups out there. I don't doubt that you would make a reasonable Guild magician with a few well-placed corrections to your practices.

"But I thought you said that they found people when they were teenagers if they were powerful enough," she countered. "Nobody ever contacted me."

"They may have missed you," he replied. "I suspect that happens a lot, despite assertions to the contrary by some of the members of the Inner Order. They look for a specific type of strength that reaches a high level of power really early, because otherwise there would be too many people to check. Maybe your powers developed more slowly than mine. Maybe they're different enough that a Guild representative noticed you but wasn't sure how you would turn out. Nobody is perfect, and sometimes politics play a role in selection. But I can find out from Jonas. Would you be interested in studying with us? Even if the Guild doesn't want you as a member, I would be happy to work with you and as an initiate of the Inner Order I'm allowed to have students."

"Aren't you afraid your techniques will be misused or something?"

He shook his head again. "I don't sense anything like that from you, so no. Besides, practical magick is really not that dangerous to teach simply because so few people can do it. Just about anyone will find magick useful as a psychological technique, but without the right combination of genetics and training our 'secret techniques' consist of pointing at things, shouting nonsense words, and hoping something will happen to them. That's a hard technique to misuse – it just looks silly for the most part."

She giggled as she visualized the image. "You might run the risk of being committed, but yeah, I suppose it would be pretty pointless to practice it. But don't you think there might be another... what's her name... Elspeth? out there who is really powerful and just lacks the technique to be dangerous?"

"I doubt it. No offense, but I can sense her across a crowded room and you're just not that powerful. We never would have missed somebody like that, unless they were covered with a cloaking spell or something from birth. You should know how that works – I would guess that the senior members of your order do it all the time, 'listening' to the magical energy of the world and trying to make sense of it."

"Daria always says there's a lot of noise, and it's hard to sort out. She had an easy time with the Morpheus thing because it was big and really close - she lives out in Minnetonka. But she's pretty sure she misses a lot."

"Your technique is limited by distance, not area?" His eyes lit up. "That's very interesting. Your order might be doing it differently, then. That would be something to study."

"Why, if yours works better?"

"Because every technique has its strengths and weaknesses. It may be that I can learn more about my own abilities by studying how the members of your order are taught to use theirs. That's one of the reasons you're interested in me, right?" he asked. "Or did I misread that?"

"Do you always do this?" she replied, a little defensively. "It's unnerving."

He smiled reassuringly. "Only with other mages. Regular people get too freaked out. It also doesn't work nearly as well on regular people because their thoughts are too jumbled and there's no internal coherence. If you'd like me to stop I certainly can do that as well."

"No, it's okay. I'm just not used to it. I don't really socialize with magicians. Daria is my teacher, and she's the only other one I know."

"Well, let me talk with Jonas about having you work with us. I'm seeing him tomorrow night. We have to talk with the Guild leadership about the Morpheus incident, and it really doesn't promise to be much fun. Suffice it to say the Guild doesn't take kindly to comprehensive abuses of operant magick, especially when lives are lost as a result."

"I suppose not," said Samantha quietly. "What will they do?"

"I don't know, and for that matter it isn't something we discuss with people outside the Inner Order, let alone outside the Guild. There's a reason that this kind of thing is rare and I'll leave it at that. Actually, I need to get going soon. It's been nice chatting but I have a lot more ritual practice to do tonight and by the time I'm done it will already be past my bedtime. But I'll be in touch and I'll contact you soon."

"Okay, well, it was good to meet you and I hope we can get together again."

"Absolutely. Do you have a PDA or cell phone, by any chance?"

"Sure." She fished around in her purse and pulled out a small leather case that she flipped open.

Michael took a similar device from his pocket and pointed it at her. "Here's my contact information," he said as he tapped the screen. "Do you have yours set up?"

"Sure. Just a sec," she replied, tapping the screen to accept Michael's information. She then beamed hers over and waited for him to tap his screen in turn. "Ah, the joy of technology."

"Yeah. Now I can tell people we've interfaced," he added with a grin. "I'll call you later this week and let you know what I hear from Jonas." Dropping a couple of bills on the table to cover the meal, he added, "I need to be going, but have a nice rest of the evening. I really enjoyed meeting you."

"Good night yourself," she replied returning his wide smile. As he walked down the stairs she looked through the business card information he had beamed over. It included phone, fax, mobile, email – every sort of information an enterprising computer geek would assemble in the name of efficiency. He listed his title as Software Engineer, and there was no reference to magick anywhere. Of course, he probably also gave the same information out to business contacts and coworkers.

Samantha found herself amazed that Michael was willing to talk to the Guild about her studying with him. Most of the magical orders that she had investigated were very closed and guarded their secrets jealously. Even the A∴A∴ would not admit anyone as a member until they had spent a year as a probationer and proved their value to the group and their seriousness as a student. How was the Guild different? Or was some other factor coming into play, like the aptitude that supposedly showed in her aura?

She rummaged through her purse some more, took out her cell phone, and dialed Daria.

"Do what thou wilt shall be the whole of the Law," said Daria as she picked up the phone without even a hello, her usual practice. Samantha had always wondered how many telemarketers just hung up at that point. She also wondered if any of them bothered to consider the implications of that simple phrase, or if they just dismissed it as nutty. Most Thelemites cringed at the thought of doing a job as soulless as telemarketing.

"Love is the Law, love under will," she replied. "Daria, I

81

just had dinner with Michael Niemand."

"That was fast," she commented, sounding genuinely impressed. "How did you find him?"

"Sheer luck."

"Typical," she remarked playfully. "At least for you."

"At any rate," she continued, "I got some information on his order, if you're ready to take it down."

"Absolutely."

"The group is called the Guild. Apparently, they were the group Mathers and Wescott contacted in Germany when they formed the original Golden Dawn."

"Really? I thought that Mathers and Wescott made that up."

"So did I, but whether it's group folklore or not, Michael believes it. He says the group dates to the late sixteenth century and was founded by John Dee when he was in Germany. I'm thinking their magick might be based on the missing Dee grimoire that should follow the <u>Heptarchia</u>, but that's just a guess on my part since you said that their magick felt like Enochian. He also claims that after Dee's death they were the group that triggered the Rosicrucian scare in France. If it's true, they're older than any of the groups we've dealt with."

"It may very well not be, though. It remains to be seen how accurate their claims are."

"Michael claims that I can study with the group if I want. I was very surprised – most orders are pretty tight with their secrets."

"Interesting. Either they really are open with their information or they want to keep you where they can watch you more closely. I assume you are interested in doing so, as you indicated in our prior conversation?"

"Well, of course! This could give our order a whole new set of techniques. And it feels like the right thing for me to do spiritually. Will you allow me to pursue it?"

Her instructor chuckled. "I doubt I could stop you. I would

recommend keeping up your A∴A∴ practices as well, though. Some of our techniques slip without daily use, as you know. As I said before, I hope you will be cautious and exercise sound judgment, but if you can learn something new our order will profit as well. Is that everything?"

"So far. But I'll keep you posted."

"Excellent. I trust I'll hear from you soon, then."

Samantha closed up the cell phone and stashed it back in her purse, along with the PDA, then put on her coat and hoisted her purse up onto her shoulder. She then headed back to Magus Books.

Roger was still there, sorting some of the rare books behind the counter. "Back so soon?" he asked with a playful grin. "How was dinner?"

"Most intriguing," she replied. "What do you have on the Dee diaries?"

"Let me see – I've got a couple Dee biographies, several more technical books on Golden Dawn Enochian, the new <u>Vision and the Voice</u>... but you've got that don't you? I have a couple more unusual pieces, like this one." He took a very tall hardbound book, black with gold print on the cover, from behind the counter.

As she was well aware, unusual meant expensive in Roger's vernacular. Usually "unusual" pieces were rare and out of print. They were also often very attractive editions, like this one.

"This," he explained, "is the Magickal Childe facsimile edition of <u>A True and Faithful Relation of What Passed for Many Years Between Dr. John Dee and Some Spirits</u>. The original was first published in 1652 by a very religious man named Meric Causaubon, who wanted to show everyone in England how evil John Dee was. After all, he 'trafficked with devils' and so forth. Despite the pious and rambling forward, it includes most of the material that went into the modern Enochian systems, and this is the best edition I've seen on the mass market. It's been out of print for quite a few years, so it's hard to find."

"I see that," she replied, noting the price. Still, she had paid more for some of her rare Crowley books, and she had a hunch that she needed to get familiar with Dee and his magical works if she was going to learn anything from the Guild. "But I'll take it. I'm a bibliophile to the end."

"That's the spirit," he added mischievously. "So, I take it you and Michael hit it off, then." He totaled up her receipt and put the book in a paper bag along with a couple of the purple bookmarks bearing the name of the store that he passed out to all his customers.

She grinned sheepishly as she dug in her purse for her wallet. "Am I really that transparent?"

"Not usually," he replied, "but most people are transparent to a trained eye."

"I'll keep that in mind," she said as she set a substantial handful of cash down on the counter.

"You do that," he said, his tone suddenly more serious as he counted out her change. "You never know who might be watching."

"I think I'm starting to understand that," she agreed, taking the bag. "You take care."

Roger's smile was back. "You too. And come again!"

IV. The Emperor
Sun of the Morning, chief among the Mighty
The Sign Aries

The cold evening breeze wound its way past the upscale mansions that lined Saint Paul's historic Summit Avenue, rattling the leaves of ancient trees and setting off the atmospheric jingling of antique wind chimes. A hundred years ago the street had been home to the elite of the largest and most prosperous city in all of Minnesota, including railroad barons and shipping magnates who had made their fortunes trading with the cities further south along the Mississippi River. Many of their expansive homes no longer existed, having eventually been torn down after falling into disrepair, while others had been subdivided into upscale condominiums, breaking up the elegant architectural designs of the original builders. Still, a few remained in their original grand states.

The mansion owned by Aleric Sprengel, Elspeth's grandfather and reigning Guildmaster, was one of these. The hulking stone fortress had originally been built for a successful businessman whose company had collapsed in the stock market crash of 1929, forcing him to sell to the young Sprengel heir. Aleric had owned it ever since, and its magnificent ballroom had been converted long ago to serve as the Guild's main temple for group workings. The energy of those years of magical rites hung over the place like a sparkling shroud of light, giving the building a spiritual brightness completely at odds with its dark and foreboding appearance. Despite the fact that few passersby had any real spiritual acuity, the dissonance of the place seemed to give most of them the willies.

Jonas Votan's white Mercedes sedan pulled into the mansion's long driveway. Jonas, a thin silver-haired man, sat at the wheel dressed in his usual white button-down shirt and dark slacks. Michael sat beside him, silent, steeling himself for their meeting with the Guildmaster, while Jonas' face bore its usual serene expression, his turquoise-blue eyes dancing with curiosity and interest. Michael had always wondered how Jonas could manage to keep calm and upbeat regardless of the situation, and had asked about it once shortly after beginning his magical studies. The older mage had simply replied that it was more pleasant and effective than the other alternatives, which was a response that made perfect sense – except, of course, that Michael's own strong emotions rarely behaved in such a rational or sensible manner.

"It is vitally important that we present the situation regarding Elspeth clearly," Jonas instructed as he stopped the car at the end of the long driveway. "I agree with you that there are several key mitigating circumstances, and I think Aleric will, too. He will most likely be biased in favor of his granddaughter unless he feels forced to treat her harshly so as to appear impartial and avoid embarrassment or loss of face. We need to present the facts in an accurate manner that he will not interpret as a challenge or a threat."

"I know," replied Michael, shaking his head. The task sounded to him like a virtual impossibility. "That's why I asked you to come. You've always been better at this sort of thing than I am. I've never been able to think on my feet very well."

Jonas smiled, not with amusement but recognition of a longstanding discussion. "And I have on many occasions explained to you why that is the case. You try to control your emotions in stressful situations, as though that will somehow help your position. Cultivate perspective. When you finally are able to step back from your feelings and recognize them for what they are, it will become clear to you that such control is generally counterproductive. In any case, our task for tonight is not to put any sort of 'spin' on the events that transpired, but report the truth. That should prove a simple task."

"If you say so," said Michael with an unconvinced shrug. His training had taught him that simple and easy were two completely different things.

"So you have met Samantha," said Jonas, changing the

subject abruptly as the car stopped in the driveway.

"What?" replied Michael, caught completely off guard.

"Samantha Davis. The young woman you had dinner with last night."

"How did you know that?" asked Michael "I wasn't working any magick, so you couldn't have tracked me that way. Were you just watching me on principle?"

"Of course not," replied Jonas with a wry grin. "I was watching her."

"Why? Is she a threat?"

"I doubt it. But I have followed her magical career with some interest. We can discuss it later, but I think you will find it an intriguing story."

Michael knew better than to press his teacher, so he just got out of the car, wondering how many other things could be going on in the Guild that were beyond his knowledge.

The two mages began the long walk up to the house, Jonas in his conventional business-casual and Michael in his gothic finest, black from head to toe. Aleric was an excellent landscaper, with a real eye for harmony and detail that never ceased to amaze Michael no matter how many times he visited the Guildmaster. As they walked up the winding stone path they passed clusters of freshly planted flowers that looked up to greet them with a kaleidoscope of festive colors. Aleric grew them in his greenhouse starting in early February so that they could be planted outdoors as soon as the weather turned, and as a result the display was already in full bloom. In stark contrast, the front steps of the house loomed beyond the path, leading up to an immense porch lined with pillars and an ornate double door carved from dark wood. A brass knocker in the shape of a medieval gargoyle, darkened with age, hung from the door, completing the air of gothic foreboding that hung over the place. Michael usually liked the décor as he considered himself something of a Goth at heart, but tonight it just struck him as a bad omen.

It was Jonas who reached for the knocker, which made

a deep booming sound on the solid old wood. A young man in his early twenties who Michael recognized as Eric Palmer, one of Aleric's students, opened the door. Dressed as he was in dark, semi-formal attire he looked somber and serious, but with his bleached blond hair, pale blue eyes, and shallow boyish good looks he had always reminded Michael of a California surfer abandoned in the frozen wastes of Minnesota. As Eric recognized the two visitors, he bowed his head to each of them in turn. "Master Jonas. Adept Michael," he said formally. "You are expected. Please follow me."

Eric led them through the opulent foyer and down the main hallway to the living room, a vast chamber with high ceilings furnished with antiques from a dizzying collection of different periods. Aleric was sitting at one of his roll-top desks off to the side of the room talking to Rochelle, who Michael had not expected to see tonight. Completely ruining the fairy-tale ambience of the room, she stood next to the desk dressed in a dirty t-shirt and jeans holding a socket wrench. There was a smudge of grease on her face and a smear of it in her short dark hair, and she was being very careful not to touch anything. "Grandfather, did I or did I not tell you to avoid Jaguars like the plague?" she was saying in the tongue-in-cheek ranting tone that she always used when criticizing automobile preferences. "This is the third time this month I've been over here tuning the blasted thing!" She smiled and waved as she saw Michael and Jonas walk into the room. "Hi Jonas. Hi Michael."

"Did you ward it this time?" asked Aleric. "That might help," he added facetiously. The Guildmaster was dressed in a casual sweater and slacks. He was younger than Jonas, but only by a few years. His hair had turned completely white, but like Elspeth, he was tall and thin with eyes that gleamed an unearthly silver-blue.

"Yes, I warded the bloody thing!" exclaimed Rochelle with a laugh. "Though you could probably put up a better one."

"Don't be so sure," replied the Guildmaster, more seriously. "Your affinity with machines amazes me sometimes. I'm sorry if the car is being troublesome," he added, the lilt creeping back into his voice, "but the XJS is just so *pretty*."

Rochelle threw up her hands in mock disgust. "That's what they always say!" Now it was her grandfather's turn to chuckle. "So Michael," she said, suddenly turning her attention to him, "how's the GTO running?"

Michael grinned. "Faster than ever, Roach. I have to be careful now if somebody's in front of me at a stoplight. The thing's a rocket. What did you do to it?"

Rochelle returned his grin. "My secret," she replied playfully. "And now I'm guessing I have to get going. You guys have a lot to discuss and I told yet *another* friend I'd take a look at their car tonight. You know, if I ever decide to charge all of you deadbeats, I'll make myself a fortune. I'll talk to you later."

"Good night," said Michael as she carefully navigated around the room's expensive furniture and headed out the back door. At a gesture from the Guildmaster, Eric nodded and also left the room, closing the heavy sliding door that led into the main hall behind him.

Aleric stood up to greet them. "Jonas," he said simply, nodding respectfully. "It's good to see you. You too, of course, Michael. I don't believe that I've had a chance to congratulate you on your elevation to the Inner Order."

Even Michael thought well enough on his feet to realize that bringing up Elspeth's reaction to his elevation was a bad plan. "Thank you," he replied, keeping his sarcastic comments to himself.

Aleric smiled. "Please sit down. I know we have a lot to discuss."

"Have you spoken with Rochelle?" asked Jonas carefully.

The Guildmaster nodded. "I have, though she wasn't present when the event in question took place. She was able to determine the type of curse used by examining your car, Michael, and it appears that the spell used was indeed a generic 'bad-luck' type curse cast in anger rather than a spell designed to deliberately destroy the building. Since this is the case, we will be performing some divinations that will tell us more about the nature of the magick and the scope of its power. We have verified that Elspeth was in fact the caster, as you reported, but we are awaiting further information. Since you are the other magician who was involved, I need your opinion. Is Elspeth dangerous to the rest of the Guild?"

Michael thought long and hard, reviewing what he believed to be possible scenarios. "In the right situation, I think she could be," he said carefully, "but such situations are not likely to come up. Elspeth is jealous and fearful, which is kind of ironic considering that she's one of the most powerful human beings on the planet. If she feels cornered, she lashes out with as much power as she can manage, which is a lot. I get the feeling that rather than working on her own personal issues she hides behind her aptitude. Most of us have to clear our minds to work magick successfully. For Elspeth, that's never been a problem – her spells just work. It allows her to increase her abilities without developing wisdom or control."

"Aleric and I have long suspected as such," agreed Jonas. "As you know, I have tried to train her to use her powers more wisely, but apparently my teaching has not been enough."

"Michael," asked Aleric, "Do you believe that Elspeth could learn from this situation?"

"I think so," he replied thoughtfully. "It's really one of the first times that she's been confronted with just how powerful she is. Elspeth is obsessed with being the best, but her desire to succeed is motivated by a fear of inadequacy on her part. I don't know exactly what she experienced as a child, but I suspect it was pretty bad."

"Well, you know about her parents, of course, at least in part. As you are now a member of the Inner Order, I am free to discuss the matter with you further. We believe an assassin working for the CIA's magick office, an organization that we do not discuss with any who are outside the Inner Order, murdered them. Incidentally, that was the event that led to us listening for magick most of the time. We believe that the government does have its own mages, operating out of a supposed psychiatric organization called the Johnston Institute and funded as a black project on the federal budget."

"Why would the government kill Elspeth's parents?"

"To keep another Elspeth from being born, of course. Her level of power might have represented a new step in human evolution, and if they couldn't have her on their side, they didn't want her on ours either."

"Wasn't Rochelle born at that point, too?"

"They feared her, too, but probably with less reason. She's a strong mage, but she's no Elspeth. That odd affinity with machines seems to be her most supernatural gift, and while impressive in and of itself, it is not raw amplified power that impacts everything she touches."

"Does Elspeth know why her parents were killed?" asked Michael.

"Probably," replied Aleric. "She was twelve years old, and she was there. After killing her parents, the assassin also tried to take a shot at her, but the gun jammed, even with warded lead bullets and a cloaking spell over the mechanism. That was why they fled the scene without killing her or Rochelle. Elspeth is psychic enough to figure out that her parents died because of her, and that is likely where her fear and insecurity originated. Also, she may feel pressured, as though great things are expected of her, which of course they are. All that, and the ensuing sense of guilt and responsibility, combines to produce her personality and her erratic behavior. The real question, then, is what do we do about it? In the old days the Supreme Council would have called for her death, as you know, and that may still happen. Obviously, she's my granddaughter and I love her a great deal, but beyond that I fear we can ill afford to deprive ourselves of her power in light of other events."

"What other events?" asked Michael. His thoughts drifted back to the conversation with his instructor that night. "Jonas, you said something about that the night of the explosion. Something about a dark power entering the world?"

"Yes," replied Jonas with a nod. "Since then I have made other inquiries, all of which have come to no avail. Scrying and divination reveal nothing concerning what I am now certain was some sort of ritual sacrifice used to call a being from beyond this universe. It was not Elspeth, because she was studying with Aleric and myself on the night in question, and more to the point, that particular technique is not taught by our order. It is a form of demonology that uses the souls of the dead as a medium through which a discarnate being can materialize. We do not teach it for several reasons, but the most practical of them is that the souls have to be present in order to work as a medium, and thus the only way to use the technique effectively is to kill a victim or victims on the spot during the ritual."

"So, say, a ghost wouldn't work?" Michael was fascinated by the theory behind magical techniques, even ones he would never use. "Like if you performed your ritual in a haunted building?"

Jonas thought for a moment. "That's hard to say. I am not that familiar with the technique myself. However, as you know real ghosts are rare. Spirits usually remain on this plane for about three days and then pass on to the next. Whether or not the soul could be used during that period, I cannot be certain. I do know, however, that demonologists teach that souls sacrificed on the spot are required."

"Could it be the magick office, then?" asked Michael. "If they killed Elspeth's parents, they probably wouldn't have a problem killing bystanders of whatever sort. With the resources of the government behind them, they probably have information on just about every available school of magick."

"True," admitted Jonas, "but there is really no reason for them to do so that I can imagine. I also do not see why they would need twelve victims. Such a large number would only be required to summon the most powerful entities of the Abyss, maybe even Coronzon himself. To a true mage, that is foolishness. Such entities are the embodiment of dispersion and confusion – the antithesis of will. I have another theory, though – I think we may be dealing with demonic possession."

"Like in those exorcist movies?" asked Michael, nonplussed. "Is that real? I always thought that the Catholic Church exorcised people with mental illnesses that they didn't understand."

"Possession has been documented in the history of the Guild," admitted Aleric, "and even among mages in two cases, though those both happened in the nineteenth century. I took a look through the archives after we spoke last, Jonas, and according to the documentation we have, two mages engaged in a magical battle with rivals from another order had a spell cast upon them that bound demons into their flesh. The demons then sought to turn our magical techniques against their sworn enemies, the Archons, but were defeated by the combined power of the Guild."

"Does possession change the signature of a mage?" asked Jonas. "Did they record anything about that?"

Aleric nodded, taking a manila folder from one of the shelves inside the desk. "It is all here," he said, handing the folder to Jonas. "I don't know if it will be of use to you, but if you detect anything with a similar signature, be sure to keep me apprised of the situation. One of the issues we will have to consider concerning Elspeth is how we hope to stand against both demons and the possible machinations of the magick office if the decision is made to eliminate one of our most powerful members. Killing her, as I am sure you are aware, is not a simple matter of throwing a curse and letting it work. She will naturally fight back with all the power she cans summon meaning all-out war, and we might conceivably lose other mages in the attempt. I will not be part of a spell intended to destroy my own granddaughter, and I am the strongest of the mages you could call upon. I see in your thoughts that you have both come here with the intent of protecting her, so I know that you have mixed feelings that might get in the way of using your respective powers effectively. The same is true of Rochelle, another of our powerful young members. Eric, not knowing her well, could probably do it, but his strength is not up to the task, even with halfhearted assistance from the two of you. It would require an action of the Supreme Council, and even then it could fail. I think we all are in agreement that this is a poor option. However, there is the matter of convincing the other members of the Council."

"We are surrounded by potential enemies," agreed Jonas. "A war would weaken us to a degree that is unacceptable. But is there another option? The Supreme Council must be informed and a formal trial must be held."

"They will be arriving in a week," replied Aleric. "I spoke with Roslyn this afternoon, and we agreed that a special meeting of the Supreme Council will be held here at that time. At issue will be Elspeth's violation of Guild law. And yes, they may not see it in the same light as we do. They will see her as a threat to the Guild and its stability, and they will wish to set a precedent. Some of them believe that we have become too forgiving with our members when they intervene in the world at all, let alone bring about destruction. Tell me, Michael, do you truly bear her no ill will?"

"No," he replied. "I really don't, and it surprises me a little. If anything, I'm disappointed. I just would like to see her grow up. It's sad, because we all know that she could be the best of us. But she needs to let go of her past and get on with her life."

"Well said," remarked Jonas. "I believe that I can teach her, Aleric. Perhaps I am mistaken, but I believe that this situation has highlighted the inadequacies of her teaching. I think that now I can steer her in the proper direction. Will you let me try?"

"Of course I will," agreed the Guildmaster. "As for the Supreme Council, though, I cannot say. Be prepared to make a convincing argument to that effect, because I suspect one will be needed to spare Elspeth's life."

"I will," replied Jonas. "And I will see what I can divine concerning the magick of demons. I hope that in another week, I will have some results."

"Is there anything else we need to discuss?" asked Aleric. "We appear to be in agreement, as I had hoped."

"As did we," replied Jonas. "No, I believe that is

everything."

Aleric smiled. "Then I will bid you good night." He traced something in the air and few moments later Eric opened the sliding door leading to the foyer. The young mage led Jonas and Michael to the front door, his demeanor still quiet and serious.

They walked down the path to the driveway, Michael uttering a sigh of relief.

"That went well," commented Jonas. "Of course, there is the Council to convince, but I suspect I can do that. You seem somewhat relieved, but still a bit on edge. Does the meeting of the Supreme Council trouble you? It should not, you know. They are mages like myself, and their wisdom is great. It may be a close vote, but I think it will resolve in our favor."

"You mean to say you're not bothered by the possibility of demon magick, then? Up until tonight I didn't even believe it existed in any meaningful or dangerous form."

"It is a possibility only. If as a teacher I may offer you a piece of advice, only invest your emotional energy in actualities, not possibilities. It is difficult to do, but a useful exercise."

"I keep trying, Jonas," he replied with a rueful grin. "Maybe I'll manage to do it one of these days. I keep hoping."

As the white Mercedes left Aleric's driveway, Michael turned to his teacher. "So what were you saying before about Samantha?" he asked. "Only you would pique my curiosity going into a situation like that."

A smile crept across Jonas' face. "It distracted you from your anxiety, did it not? This goes back eighteen years. At that time, there were two children outside the great families who we began watching, born with magical ability far beyond that of normal people. You know enough about how our families are interconnected – inbred, to use a crude colloquialism – and you have studied biology. From time to time new blood needs to enter into any gene pool to ward off problematic genetic traits that are invariably concentrated along with genetic advantages. We were looking for an outsider of sufficient power to initiate, and we found two – you and Samantha Davis. That was why I moved here from the East Coast, to train you, Samantha, or both of you, depending upon the wishes of the council. Aleric and I favored contacting both of you, but the vote went against us and it was decided that only one of you would be approached. You were approached first because you are male and the bloodline that most needed tempering was Sprengel with two daughters, but had you refused, we would have gone to her next. It was hoped that you would become involved with either Elspeth or Rochelle and your offspring would reinvigorate the Sprengel bloodline, which has become rather concentrated in the last two generations."

"It almost worked, too," commented Michael. "I mean there was a time when I really did love Elspeth, and in a way I still do. She's just so *damaged* and unstable. I assume you know that she's been involved with this guy Jim for a while now – how does that fit into your plans? He's not a magician."

"Ah, yes. James Warwick. Do not be so sure," replied Jonas. "He certainly does not have a degree of talent on par with Elspeth, yourself, or Samantha – I would have sensed that, and I have met him – but I think it is likely that he has some level of power. The reason that our attention to bloodlines requires as little effort as it does is because magicians tend to be attracted to other magicians. We inherently seek out our own kind as prospective mates, a trait that most humans and I suppose most creatures share. I would be surprised to find a powerful magician like Elspeth attracted to someone with no power at all."

"I suppose that's true, though it never really occurred to me as such. Jim is really kind of a putz, to use another crude colloquialism. I've always seen him as a rich, elitist snob, though of course that could just be jealousy on my part. He tells people he's psychic, though most of the things I've seen him do are cheap tricks. I sometimes think Elspeth went for him because he puts up with a lot of her abuse, and for all that he's a snob, he lets her feel superior all she wants. He doesn't strike me as mage material, though I guess I could be wrong."

"As could we all," agreed Jonas.

"Rochelle and I have always been friends," continued Michael, "but there was never quite the same spark there between us as there was between me and Elspeth. Do you think that has to do with their relative levels of ability?"

"Maybe. There are of course other factors, like personality, common interests and so forth, but from what I have seen over the years aptitude is usually a factor."

"So you're saying that Samantha could have been a Guild initiate, too?" asked Michael.

"You tell me," said Jonas. "You sensed her power, didn't you? The two of you are fairly evenly matched, except for your training. Hers is reasonably good, you understand, but it is not up to the level at which we teach in the practical arena. Or did you offer to train her based on the quality of her smile?"

Michael had never gotten used to the way in which Jonas just knew things, despite years of experiencing it firsthand. As Jonas mentioned earlier, he had watched the entire scene through one of his crystals, which he could tune like a television. "Of course not. I was going to ask you, but I guess you already know. *Would* you be willing to train her, given the original vote? I could do some of it myself, but you're far better."

"Probably. Several of the members of the Council who opposed initiating her are now dead, hardliners who felt that the bloodlines should be diluted as little as possible. I think it is clear now that you and Elspeth will not work out as we had hoped and Rochelle is currently involved with Eric, Aleric's student. That's not ideal, but assuming that union continues it will be satisfactory, since Palmer and Sprengel are fairly divergent families. Given those factors, I do not see any reason to keep Samantha out. I also suspect, as do you, that she has already covered much of our training program. At any rate, I would like to meet her and judge for myself. Would you be willing to arrange it? Say, tomorrow evening?"

"Sure. I'm looking forward to it already."

"As am I, Michael. I've always been curious how our training might interact with another system. Now I get to find out."

"So you're not worried, then?" asked Michael. "I don't sense anything from her, but it's always possible she could become another Elspeth. We have no idea how dysfunctional she could be once we begin looking into her mind. It sounds like she had a fairly normal upbringing, but that's not always a good thing."

"Do you believe that this is likely, having spent time in her presence?"

"Well, no, but you never know what sort of trauma she could have lurking in her childhood."

"I do," said Jonas, "almost none."

"You've been watching her all this time?"

"Not only watching – helping her along. You will find, once you get to know her better, that she considers herself extremely lucky – situations simply work out for her in unexpected ways. Suffice it to say that it is not precisely luck."

"You've intervened?"

"As needed," replied Jonas. "Her luck can be attributed to the very techniques in which you have been trained. As you know, Michael, I am stubborn. The vote went against me, but it was important to keep her waiting in the wings, so to speak, in case she was ever needed. That meant protecting her psyche from damage and trauma, so that she would be clear enough to learn our system quickly. I of course had to start during her teen years so there were a few issues from when she was a small child that I was unable to control, but seeing her aura shift over the years she seems to have addressed most of those in the course of her training. You have seen the results, and I think you will agree that I chose wisely. She has become very effective as a mage, even without direct training from us."

"So you engineered the whole thing?"

"Not entirely. Her order decided to seek you out without my intervention. I was planning on contacting her in two possible cases – if the demon magick I may have sensed turned out to be a real threat, or if Elspeth were killed. Obviously, those are still both unknowns. The A∴A∴ saved me the trouble of making that decision. Their leadership clearly has some wisdom and insight at its disposal as well."

Michael shook his head. "Unbelievable. Though you'd think I'd be used to it by now."

As he got out of the car in front of his house on Lake Como and walked up the steps to the front porch. The waning moon still shone brightly over the lake, and the wind rustled the leaves of the ancient poplars that lined its banks. So Samantha was going to be an Initiate. He saw the possibility of a bright future opening before him, marred of course by the uncertainty of Elspeth's fate, the CIA's magick office, demon magick, and the possible involvement of denizens of the Abyss. As he unlocked the front door and stepped into the dark foyer of the empty house, he was reminded of the apocryphal ancient Chinese curse: "May you live in interesting times."

V. The Hierophant

The Magus of the Eternal
The Sign Taurus

"Good evening, Samantha. I am Jonas Votan." Jonas stood in the foyer of his home in St. Paul's Merriam Park neighborhood, a large Victorian house that was spacious and well-restored, but far less impressive than the Guildmaster's mansion. The front foyer, more properly a vestibule, boasted carved paneling and a sweeping, curved stairway that led to the upper level, all in red oak and mahogany. The chandelier, a sculpted Chinese brass piece shrouded in bits of lead crystal, cast a sparkling luminance over the entire scene.

Samantha stepped forward and shook his hand. "It's an honor to meet you. Michael tells me that you're his teacher?" It was only then that the aura of the place hit her. The energy of the space had a spiritual brightness to it that she had not expected, a kind of warm vitality. It occurred to her that perhaps this was simply an extension of Jonas' own demeanor, magnified by years of ritual performed in the space. She knew Michael's house dated back to the end of the nineteenth century, and wondered if magicians had a preference for older homes. That was certainly what she would buy, if she had a choice in the matter.

Jonas nodded. "Since his entry into the Guild years ago." He paused, glancing at Michael as though waiting for him to speak, but then continued. "Did Michael tell you that I was almost yours as well?"

Michael shook his head as he closed the door behind him.

"What do you mean?" asked Samantha, confused.

"That would be no, then," said Jonas with a mild grin. He gestured to the living room, adjacent to the foyer by way of a sliding door to his right. "Come and have a seat."

She and Michael sat down on the long sofa that lined one wall, while Jonas seated himself in his usual overstuffed chair. The furniture was a very modern style, somewhat at odds with the traditional architecture of the place, but she noted that as far as she could tell it appeared to be made from natural materials real leather in the case of the overstuffed chair and some sort of linen fiber in the case of the sofa. She had learned early on in her magical career about the metaphysical deadness of plastic and its derivatives, and clearly she was not the only one.

"As I was saying," continued Jonas, "you were a candidate for admission into the Guild a long time ago. Your ability is unusual, as is Michael's, and from time to time we initiate outsiders – did Michael tell you about the great families?"

Samantha nodded.

"Good," he replied. "So you understand how our Guild families work. Do you find it strange? Many people do."

"Well, I was brought up with the idea that breeding humans for a specific trait is immoral, if that's what you mean," she said carefully. "But what you're doing is different than coercing people into breeding. And from the little I've been told, it's necessary, isn't it? Your magical system really only works for people of very high ability, right?"

"Yes. And the modern world only makes that part of the equation more difficult," he explained. "Modern education has helped us in many ways. We used to have to train people in basics like math and science before moving on to metaphysics, but now there are schools that do a better job, whatever you might think of the American educational system. However, the rise of scientific materialism has also taught people a worldview entirely hostile to magick in any form. Many people born with superior magical ability repress it, or channel it other ways. Some become doctors, for example, and think their cleverness is responsible for unusually high cure rates for terrible diseases, or play extreme sports without ever getting a scratch, thinking themselves 'just lucky.' Modern people are brought up to think of the spiritual world as something silly and imaginary."

"And people who think there's something to the spiritual world are usually religious nuts," added Michael. "I've had more than my fill of that growing up. Rather than thinking we're deluded and stupid, they think we're evil. Or even if they don't accept the fundamentalist line, they think that using our abilities is somehow 'cheating.'"

"I've heard that one a lot," she replied, recognizing the attitude at once. "That's like saying a pro athlete is cheating by using heightened physical ability, or saying that smart people are cheating on the job by making good decisions."

"Well put," remarked Jonas. "What people see is that magick is unfair. So is any other kind of heightened aptitude, of course, and there is a great deal of prejudice in most societies against those who are gifted in whatever way."

"When we went to school, 'brain' was an insult," added Michael with a bit of a smirk. "I could never figure that one out, but then, maybe the answer is just that bullies are stupid. No revelation there."

Samantha laughed out loud. "I remember that. It never made any sense to me either."

"It does when you realize that most people are jealous of those they secretly consider their betters," explained Jonas. "They hate the rich, the intelligent, the beautiful, and the list goes on. But magick goes even further. Children's stories are full of magical themes that go back centuries, as in the case of literary works like Grimm's Fairy Tales. As children grow up, that world is taken away from them. They are forced to accept that magick is something they can never have. Then, to encounter someone later in life who was fortunate enough to be born with the ability to make use of it is all the more distressing – if they accept magick as real their entire worldview is shown to be incorrect, and not only that, knowing that they lack it reinforces their own sense of inferiority. It is only natural for humans to hate anything that creates that sort of dissonance."

"Jonas is really good at figuring people out," sighed Michael. "Someday I hope to be half as insightful."

"All it takes is practice," said Jonas with a shrug. "And, of

103

course, a bit of enhanced awareness here and there. As I was saying, anyone raised with the cultural expectations of the modern world will have problems using magick, let alone working with a practical system like ours. Even if they have the aptitude, it is so difficult getting them past their own prejudices and blockages that it usually is not worth it, whereas we raise our own children with the idea that magick works just like electricity or sunlight. That is really the only way to prevent biases from creeping in from the surrounding culture. The few exceptions to this principle are the very powerful, like you. In your case, your aptitude was extreme enough that it shaped other areas of your life in such a way that allowed and perhaps even required your power to express itself. Even though we never contacted you, you clearly have still developed your magical abilities."

"I didn't really have a choice about that," she said slowly. "I mean, it didn't feel that way. It's like there's this force inside you that won't leave you alone. It wants to live."

"Yes," agreed Jonas. "Strength is its own burden. As a teenager, Michael pursued his studies at the expense of his family and friends. I was born into the Guild, but I never thought for a moment that I would be able to walk away from it. We cultivate the Great Families because they make it easier for the next generation to continue our traditions. But sometimes outsiders are required, to keep the bloodlines from becoming concentrated to the point that magical gifts are not enough to offset various genetic problems that inevitably arise. Because of this, around the time Michael was admitted, we also considered admitting you. There was some disagreement on the council as to how many outsiders we should bring in, and the vote settled on one. The politics were such that Michael was chosen over you, so it was less a statement about your ability than a statement about the conservative nature of the Council at that time. I understand from Michael you are a member of another order working in the local area, the A∴A∴."

"I joined when I was nineteen, and I've been working with their system ever since," explained Samantha. "My instructor is an older magician named Daria Edwards. She's a good teacher, but sometimes I think she's scared to death of practical magick. I've learned a lot over the years, but it seems like it's not as useful as it should be. That's why I'm interested in studying with you in the first place."

"What initially caused you to seek us out, if I may ask?" Jonas continued.

"My order," she replied. "Daria detected the Morpheus explosion, just like every other passable magician on the planet – or so it seems meeting all of you. She identified Michael on the scene and looked up some information on him. My order's Council wanted me to do it because I'm a perpetual gadfly," she added with a chuckle.

"What do you mean?" asked Jonas, bemused.

"I'm the one who's always telling them that we have all these magical techniques and we should actually do something with them," she explained. "Daria is one of those learned intellectuals who thinks that using magick for practical purposes somehow debases it. I know that spiritual development is important, but I've always felt that all these things that we can do should be useful too. It's like saying developing a piece of technology is high-minded and noble as long as you never actually try to build a working machine. The A∴A∴ motto is 'the method of science, the aim of religion.' If nothing else, a big part of the scientific method is experimenting and testing. If you never do anything practical, how can you possibly measure your results? I understand that many of the others in my order don't see it that way, but I sometimes wonder if that's because they've tried it and it doesn't work for them. You say I've got such high aptitude, but it still doesn't really work for me – not all that reliably, anyway. And at the same time, I've always felt like it somehow *should*. I don't know if any of them ever have felt that way."

"I think you will find working with practical magick to be much easier than you expect. Have you ever used a pendulum?"

Samantha shook her head.

105

Jonas produced a small amethyst crystal suspended on a silver chain. "Hold it like this," he demonstrated, taking the chain between his thumb and forefinger so that the crystal could swing freely. "This is a simple means of divination. You ask a question and hold your hand as still as possible. Depending on which way the pendulum swings, the answer to your question is either yes or no. For most people it swings either side to side or front to back, though every so often I come across someone for whom it rotates either clockwise or counter-clockwise."

Taking the pendulum, she let it dangle from her fingers. "What question should I ask?"

"No question," he replied. "Focus your mind on the word 'yes' and the associations it brings to mind. The pendulum will move, even if you try to keep your hand still."

Samantha's training allowed her to hold a single thought in her mind easily. She did so, and sure enough, the pendulum swung back and forth right away.

"Now try the word 'no.'"

This time the pendulum swung from side to side.

"Good," said Jonas with a smile. "Most people, aptitude or no, can do that. When the mind is focused on an idea the body follows suit. In that situation the pendulum does not move of its own accord, even though it may seem that way. Unconscious tremors from your nervous system are transmitted to the chain, which picks up the movement. Without the necessary magical aptitude, it is an interesting exercise, but not a particularly useful one." He took the pendulum from her and walked across the room to a low wooden table. On the table was a device consisting of a metal frame from which the pendulum could be suspended. "This is somewhat more enlightening," he remarked. "Come over here and sit on the floor facing the pendulum."

She followed his instructions, and sat on the floor staring at the stone hanging from its frame.

"Now think yes, just as though you were holding the chain. Hold the thought in your mind as long as possible, and concentrate all of your attention on the stone."

Sinking into a meditative trance, she focused her mind on the single thought of the word yes – affirmation, positivity, agreement. A minute crept by, then two, then five, and suddenly the pendulum moved slightly, as though brushed by a breeze. Another minute and it was clearly swinging back and forth. The movement was not nearly as dramatic as when the chain was held, but it was movement nonetheless. Surprised, she snapped back into waking consciousness and the movement of the pendulum began to slow and become more random. "Did I do that?" she asked, already sensing the answer.

Jonas nodded. "Energy follows attention," he explained. "Because you are capable of this sort of magick, your attention is able to convert a small amount of the heat in this room into energy that makes the pendulum swing a little. It is now about a degree colder in here than it was when you started, though I doubt you've noticed."

"Is that why ghosts make cold spots, then?" she asked.

"Precisely. So have you then figured out what operant magick is?"

"No," she replied. "I don't know. Does anyone?"

"But you have a suspicion," he pressed. "Explain it."

She did have suspicion, but it seemed only a glimmer of understanding welling up from the depths of her mind. She tried to explain, even though she wasn't sure the right words existed. "Well, it seems like what you're doing is on the quantum level. You can shift particles and photons around... but that doesn't explain how you could make something much larger happen unless it was linked to a quantum particle, like in the Schroedinger's cat thought-experiment."

"You are right, that does not explain the effect in any meaningful way. Think deeper. What is the commonality between a curse that makes a person unlucky and making kinetic and thermal energy move as you direct?"

"Well..." She thought hard and long about the two

107

concepts, comparing them as best she could. Suddenly, it came to her. She knew it was right; it had to be. She had sensed it when she divined the future, when she tried to make sense of the timelines that spread out from any point in the present. "It's probability, isn't it? You make a certain condition more or less likely by directing your will in a particular way!"

Jonas nodded. "Correct. What we are doing in scientific terms, as far as we can tell, is shifting the level of reality below quantum space. If you change the way space is shaped on a very small scale, you make the particles moving across that space behave differently. I have often wondered myself why cosmologists have not hit upon such a simple truth in their quest for a unified theory of physics – large ripples in space and time produce gravity and other relativistic effects, and small vibrations of the same sort produce quantum effects. Maybe one just has to be a mage and know what the flow of energy feels like to see it. Few scientists, after all, practice magick."

"I did read something kind of like that in physics though, years back," she replied, remembering a book she had read in college. "There was a scientist named David Bohm who proposed that quantum effects were caused by solid, physical particles moving through a kind of space in which they created something like a ripple. He called the ripple a 'pilot wave,' and according to his model, quantum particles behave strangely and unpredictably because they're moving through space like boats passing through their own wakes. There's no real way to test it because the math involved corresponds exactly to the standard model, but it's an interesting idea. It's not a big step from Bohm's model to some sort of unified theory, where a lot of particles concentrated in one place bend space and time dramatically enough to create gravity."

"Interesting," said Jonas. "Perhaps someday we will then see a scientific model that explains magick. But I hope not."

"What do you mean?" she demanded. "Scientific understanding is important. People might finally think of us as something other than flaky head-cases."

"The most attractive thing about being thought of as a flaky head-case is that in most peoples' eyes you are harmless," countered Jonas. "In every country in the world where the majority still believes magick is real people are executed as 'witches' from time to time, whether or not they have done anything besides irritating their neighbors. Fundamentalists may believe that we are damned and rail against us, but they are not going to convince the materialist majority that it is even possible to, say, destroy a building by means of a curse. In this we have allies: the skeptic movement."

"How are the skeptics our allies?" she asked, confused. "As far as I can tell, they're a bunch of intolerant naysayers."

"Yes, they are," agreed Jonas. "But they perform a legitimate service by debunking phony psychics. There are many people who advertise powers they do not have in order to cheat others out of money. Since magick is probability it doesn't work all the time. As a result, most people who appear to be able to use it reliably enough to make a living are fakes."

"You know how hard it is to read most people," pointed out Michael. "Their minds are a disorganized jumble. Could you pick just one thought out of that kind of mess? I sure have trouble doing it. But these 'psychics' say that they can do it easily, all the time."

"Or foretell the future, when there are so many timelines to follow when I try to look," she added. "I always found that suspicious."

"You also cannot usually communicate with the spirits of the dead because they either reincarnate or pass on to higher spiritual realms within about three days," continued Jonas. "But look at how many mediums are out there who claim otherwise. There are many spirits with whom one may communicate floating around this plane, but few of them were ever human. Aside from the occasional ghost, few human spirits ever hang around. A genuine medium might be talking to something, but odds are it is not a deceased relative."

109

She chuckled. "Crowley wrote about that. He called spiritualism 'low-grade necromancy.' From his writings, it sounds like he ran into his share of fakes back in the twenties and thirties. That was kind of the heyday of mediums. I used to play around with Ouija boards when I was a kid, too, and it really seemed like whatever I was talking to just told me whatever I wanted to hear."

"That could either have been your own unconscious mind or a spirit looking to befriend you," said Jonas. "Either way, like the pendulum, your own unconscious impulses are transmitted to the planchette, unless of course it moved on its own?"

She shook her head. "It was plastic. That would never work, would it?"

"No," said Jonas. "Plastic will not usually hold a magical field of any sort. You would not have been able to move a plastic pendulum, for example."

"I had some friends who used a crystal wine glass, though."

The older mage shook his head. "Too heavy. The friction is hard to overcome. The pendulum only works this way because it is very small and very light. Even the most powerful mage can only transform a tiny amount of heat into kinetic energy."

Samantha turned to Michael. "Can you do this?" she asked, pointing to the pendulum.

He nodded. "Watch." He deepened his concentration, letting the amethyst fill his mind. His magical sight showed him the bright streamers of light that extended along his line of attention to encompass the stone, and as they surrounded it, it began to swing almost immediately.

"That was fast," she commented, clearly impressed. "Less than a minute. How long did I take?"

"A little over five," he answered. "But I wasn't nearly as good as you when I started out. I couldn't make it move at all. As I said at the Loring, you've obviously been doing enough practice to develop your abilities, at least somewhat. "

"What sort of ritual practices do you currently perform?"

asked Jonas. "From what I know of your order, I assume they are fairly extensive."

"Liber Resh – Crowley's solar adorations – at sunrise, noon, sunset, and midnight, preceded by a banishing Star Ruby and Star Sapphire – those are Crowley's pentagram and hexagram rituals," she replied. "I follow the adorations with the Animadversion to the Aeon from Crowley's Liber Reguli, which is an invocation of the Thelemic gods and magical formulas. I also perform Liber Reguli itself daily. I say Will before every meal, and I usually meditate at least an hour a day. That's aside from studying and research."

"Wow," commented Michael. "That's a lot."

"Really? What do you do?"

"I try to do the Lesser Rituals of the Pentagram and Hexagram at least twice a day, more if I need it, our Enochian pentagram and heptagram rituals once a day, and I meditate an hour a day or so if my mind is feeling clouded or confused," replied Michael. "I sometimes skip it, though, if it just doesn't feel right. Given your set of practices and our earlier discussion, I take it your order is more regular about practice than we are."

"I guess so. You find that your magick still works, even with less practice?" she asked. "I suppose it would have to," she continued, answering her own question, "if you can just move the pendulum like that."

"That is what our schedule of practices is based on," said Jonas. "What works. If you are doing practical magick, you can usually tell when you are doing something wrong, or not practicing enough. I notice you mentioned the banishing pentagram and hexagram rituals, which you perform four times daily. Is that correct?"

She nodded.

"Why do you perform them that way? As banishings, I mean."

"In Crowley's writings he says that the banishing rituals should precede any ceremony whatsoever. The solar adorations count."

"That is true," agreed Jonas. "We precede our practical ceremonial rituals with the pentagram and hexagram or heptagram rituals as well, with this difference: the pentagram ritual is performed as a banishing, but the hexagram or heptagram ritual is performed as an invocation."

"But that's wrong," she protested. "The forms need to correspond. Otherwise the energy gets distorted."

"Have you tried it?"

"Well, no," she said slowly. "But it's just basic logic. A banishing is the opposite of an invocation, so you can't put the two together."

"No," disagreed Jonas. "You need to unify yourself and the universe to get a practical effect to work in the physical world. You know that the pentagram is microcosmic, focused on you, and the hexagram is macrocosmic, focused on the universe, correct?"

She nodded again.

"Visualize what happens if you clear out space within yourself and call upon the outside universe to fill that space. The macrocosm is now within the microcosm, the exact opposite of the usual arrangement. This artificial condition creates a union between the two realms. In a sense, they interlock. I can assure you from our research, it is the only way to make operant magick work effectively. Practice it and you will see."

"That might actually be in Crowley!" she exclaimed as a sudden insight crossed her mind. "If so, though, it's subtle. In The Book of Lies, Chapter 69. He talks about the Holy Hexagram, which is the reverse of the hexagram of nature. That could be what he's talking about, couldn't it? The text can be read on more than one level, but maybe it also means that you reverse the form of the hexagram ritual from what you would expect along with the hexagram itself."

Jonas considered for a moment. "That seems to be a reasonably correct description. I am not familiar with that particular text, though."

"It's where Crowley talks about reversing the Golden

Dawn hexagram in the Star Sapphire ritual," she explained. "But he's also saying that the hexagram ritual needs to be performed as an invocation, isn't he? Two banishings would separate, whereas he's talking about achieving union. That makes sense now. The one thing that I still don't understand, though, is that we have notes from some of his rituals, and he always starts with a banishing pentagram and a banishing hexagram."

"What was the object of those rituals?" asked Jonas.

"Evoking or invoking spirits, usually to communicate with them."

"That would be why."

"I though you just said that…"

"I said that the hexagram is performed in the invoking form for practical magick," corrected Jonas. "There are cases in which you would not want to do this, though. If you were summoning a potentially hostile spirit, it would be able to use a magical field just like you could. Would you want to give it that option? If all you are seeking is information, again, you have no need to build such a field and might not want to. Holding the two worlds together takes energy that you do not need to expend in order to communicate."

"And Crowley was at least somewhat wary about practical magick, wasn't he?" added Michael. "You said before that's why your order has the attitude it does. He might have just been being cautious, which is not a bad idea in a lot of cases."

"True," she admitted. "So you use the invoking hexagram for daily practice?"

"Yes," said Jonas. "The banishing form is only used for specific cases. You will find that by making that one change, your ability to perform practical spells will increase."

"Okay. I'll do that."

"I also have something of an assignment for you," continued Jonas. "In the wake of the whole Morpheus situation, there is another matter that has been somewhat overlooked by the Guild, but it is important. Michael already knows about it, but I will explain for your benefit. Two nights before the explosion at Morpheus, I sensed something enter this world, a dark power of great strength. I believe that the magick used was a form of demonology, which is dangerous in the extreme, but I have had no luck divining anything about the magician responsible. I do know where it happened, though – outside Rochester. Have you ever been there, or know anyone there? Maybe someone in your order?"

"I don't know anyone in my order besides Daria on a personal level, and she lives out in Minnetonka. I've been to Rochester once or twice, but not since I was a kid."

"I would like you and Michael to travel there and see if you can find out anything about the occult activity going on in the city. Any information you can obtain will be very helpful in assessing the nature of the threat, if there indeed is one. Are you willing to do this?"

"Sure," she replied. "When do we leave?"

"As soon as possible."

"How's tomorrow? I took tomorrow and Friday off of work, because I wanted to focus on whatever you were going to teach me. But we can make a long weekend of it. Does that work for you, Michael?"

"Sounds fine. I'll pick you up tomorrow morning, then."

"Not too early, if that's okay," she said. "I like to sleep in when I'm off work."

"Give me a call, then, when you're up, and we can go from there."

"I'll do that."

"So is that enough to work on for one evening?" asked Jonas.

"I think so. I need to work with it before I can really come back to you with any questions, but I'm sure that I'll have some for next time – if there's going to be a next time, that is," she added hastily.

"Of course," said Jonas with a nod and a smile. "Welcome to the Guild."

VI. The Lovers

The Children of the Voice: the Oracles of the Mighty Gods
The Sign Gemini

Samantha called Michael at ten-thirty the following morning. Since he had already completed his morning routine and ritual practices, he set out right away for her apartment in Minneapolis. He hoped that they could make it to Rochester by noon so that they could get some lunch before their meeting with police forensic investigators at one o'clock. Jonas had emailed him the details and contact information the night before, and it sounded like the police were looking forward to the help. Michael wasn't sure, but he suspected that the Rochester police had little experience with the occult. He thought about what the whole situation could mean.

Jonas had mentioned demonology the night before, a specialized field of magick that developed during the medieval period. It was based on the strict dualism of good and evil put forth by the monolithic Catholic Church of that time, and relied on summoning demons in the name of the Christian God to perform various tasks. If you could actually manage to attract a demon, which was actually pretty difficult despite the insistence of both the Catholic Church and fundamentalist Christians to the contrary, demonology could provide a way of working operant magick without a great deal of aptitude. As a result, if a mage of some sort was involved in the murders, it could be almost anyone. Demons could also possess humans, though that generally only worked on the exceptionally weak-minded or the mentally ill, so it was more than likely that the murders were committed for a purpose. Twelve people made for a powerful sacrifice, and apparently one of the techniques for summoning powerful demons from the Abyss involved the sacrifice of living souls.

He still found it odd that Jonas seemed afraid, given his usual calm. He thought this was maybe because demon magick played by different rules than that of humans. In some ways it

115

was much more powerful, but it also had some curious limitations. Since the Guild worked mostly with humans of very high magical aptitude, the allure of demonology wasn't very strong – in fact, it really was not studied except in passing even at the level of the Inner Order. He saw why it was practiced, though. If he had been born with the drive to be a mage but without the talent, would he have gone that route? Would Samantha, if she hadn't found the A∴A∴?

As Michael turned onto the freeway, lost in his own thoughts, he was not aware of the hulking vehicle lumbering awkwardly down the narrow alley that ran behind his house and into his driveway.

"So when did you say he left?" asked Jim, as he parked his bulky black sport-utility behind the house. He had managed to maneuver it down the narrow alley and into the driveway without hitting anything, which given the sheer size of the vehicle was a real accomplishment.

"About five minutes ago," replied Elspeth, looking up from the scrying crystal cupped in her hands. "We're right on time."

"Isn't this cutting it a little close?"

"Absolutely," she agreed. "But we need to do it while he's distracted – like driving. Otherwise he might sense that I'm here messing with the wards, and the whole point of this is to avoid detection. The trip down to Rochester takes at least an hour, and anyway that new girlfriend of his is likely to be distraction enough. He has to pick her up in Minneapolis, too."

"Are you sure he's not just running out to the store?"

"Of course," she replied dismissively. "I've been watching him in my crystal all day. His girlfriend just called and he's on his way over. We should have time."

"He could drive faster," pointed out Jim. "Isn't his car a racer?"

"Yeah, but there's traffic. My sister tells me that it's practically impossible to get from Minneapolis to Rochester in under an hour during the day and believe me, she's tried," Elspeth replied with a smirk.

"How are we getting into the house?" asked Jim as he got out of the truck. "I have a crowbar in the back. We could make it look like a burglary."

"Don't be ridiculous." she snapped as she carefully lowered herself out of the cab. "I have a key, of course – we dated for four years. If there's evidence that anyone has been here, Michael will know to scry for whoever was here. If he sees nothing in his crystal but the house has been damaged he'll know it was a mage, probably me. So don't touch anything."

"If you can block scrying, you could make a false record or something," suggested Jim. "You know, like gang members trashing the house. Can't you do something like that?"

"Not convincingly," she replied. "It would look contrived and Michael is pretty suspicious. Anyway, since we have a key the physical security doesn't matter. Believe me, it's the least of our worries."

"What do you mean?" he asked, sounding confused. "If you have a key, we should get inside before the neighbors see us."

"I mean that there are magical defenses, pretty good ones. Stand still for a minute."

He did so, impatient to get inside but knowing better than to start a fight.

Elspeth extended her hand and traced a sigil encircled by an invoking hexagram over his body. She then did the same to herself, etching the same pattern of lines and circles in what seemed to her magical sight to be glowing green lines hovering in the air. She traced the sign of Virgo in the center in a pinkish red.

"What's that?" he asked suspiciously.

"A sort of magical invisibility," she explained. "It'll keep Michael's wards and guardians from seeing you. He doesn't have any cameras, so we don't have to worry about that. That's good, because magical invisibility to cameras is just about impossible. With people and guardians you can use concealment spells, since they work by misdirection. I always told him his security was lax," she added with another smirk, "but of course, he never listened to me. Good thing, too."

"Is that it?" he asked, starting toward the house.

"Wait," she ordered, holding him back. He stopped abruptly, rolling his eyes with annoyance but remaining silent. "I need to have a look at this before we go in." She closed her eyes, deepening her magical senses until she saw the house in her mind's eye. A dome of blackish force hung over it, starting at about edge of the porch – the intelligence of Saturn, for protection. As she knew from being in the house many times, Michael's wards didn't extend to the driveway where she was standing, since he just warded his car rather than bothering with the run-down garage or the entire property. Within the dome, various flickering shapes danced back and forth – guardian servitors, artificial souls created to keep the place secure and ward off any hostile magick. She tuned the invisibility field so that it would be optimally effective against the guardians she could make out, and then turned to Jim. "We can go in now. Stay close to me, and as I said, touch nothing. If one thing gets broken, I'll be hearing about it from the Guild."

Obediently, he fell in behind her as she walked slowly up to the back door. The porch creaked, which made him stop abruptly for a moment, but she gestured for him to continue across it to the door, unconcerned about the noise. Carefully, she drew another sigil on the door and inserted the key. She turned the lock over, opened it, and gestured him inside frantically. As soon as he was across the threshold, she closed it quickly behind him. "What was that about?" he whispered.

"State change," she explained at her usual volume. "And you can talk normally. The spell covers the sound. I needed to keep the guardians from sensing that the house had changed its configuration while the door was open – they can still perceive the building, even with us warded. But I think it worked. We'll need to do the same thing on the way out. It's a good thing Michael doesn't like to close his doors – otherwise we'd have to do that every time we walked into a room."

"Yeah, and it's pretty small," he commented, his voice still somewhat restrained. "Searching my parents' house or your place could take forever."

"The temple is over here. I'm betting that's where the book we need is." She led him through the kitchen to the front of the house. Michael's temple had at one time been a parlor; it was in the front of the house adjacent to the foyer and about fifteen feet square. The floor was oak, mostly covered by a circular oriental rug, and the moldings were carved from painstakingly restored mahogany. A fireplace surrounded by am ornate tile mosaic decorated the south end of the room, and on the mantle sat various implements that glowed brightly to her magical sight. Tall bookshelves, also mahogany, lined the room except for in front of the windows and the fireplace. They looked original, except that she knew Michael had cleverly added them in such a way that they matched the building's décor almost perfectly. The ceiling of the room, about twelve feet above the floor, was a painted skyscape in light blue with scattered clouds, and an antique brass chandelier descended from its exact center on a newer, shiny brass chain. Below the chandelier sat the Holy Table, a sort of altar three feet square into which the Enochian angels could be summoned. The table sparkled with an aura of bright yellow.

"Start checking the shelves. Remember to look, but don't touch," she instructed. "We only have about an hour so we have to hurry. Let me know about anything with a blank spine – I'm guessing it won't be labeled."

After a few minutes of checking, Jim spoke up. "Here it is. Liber Iadnamad, right?"

"Stop," she commanded, sensing that he was in the process of reaching for the book even though he was behind her. "Let me look." She walked across the room and examined the book in question. It appeared to be new, leather-bound, and about the right size based on the quantity of the Dee material that she had studied. At first, its aura looked correct as well, but then, looking past that, she realized that an elaborate illusion clung to the book that made it appear to have the right aura for an Enochian text. "It's a decoy," she said finally. "It's not what we came here for. That's interesting – it was made to fool a mage. I wonder if Michael suspected I would try this?"

"I would," commented Jim.

"Oh, thanks a lot!" she exclaimed, glaring at him.

"No, I don't mean that," he amended quickly. "I mean that you're smart and ambitious, and you obviously would want the information the book contains even if you didn't have a deal with what's-his-name. But how do you know it's a decoy without opening it?"

"I just do. Trust me, you don't want to touch it. It probably has some sort of spell on it that'll warn Michael if anyone tampers with it. Since this one is here, the real book probably won't be on the shelves, at least not here. I don't see anything with the kind of aura I'm looking for here anyway."

"So it's in another room, then?"

"It must be. I didn't sense anything in the foyer, so let's try the living room on the other side." She led him through the foyer to another archway, this one opening into the living room. The oak floor and mahogany molding matched the temple, but this room felt much brighter. Instead of the tall, dark bookcases, here there was only a paneled wainscot rising about three feet off the floor. The rest of the walls and the ceiling were painted a bright shade of white. The room was also larger than the temple, a long rectangle about twenty-five by thirteen feet. Scanning the room for auras, she shook her head. "It's not here either. Maybe upstairs?"

As Elspeth and Jim took their search upstairs, Michael parked his GTO on the street next to Samantha's apartment building in downtown Minneapolis. As he turned off the engine, he suddenly felt kind of funny, but searching his mind he could find nothing that explained his apprehension. It wasn't the murders themselves, and it was not anything else he could name. He just felt strange, almost like he was being watched. He quickly scanned the area, but didn't see or sense anything out of the ordinary.

Samantha waved as she walked out the front door of the high-rise carrying a small overnight bag. She opened the passenger door and leaned in. "Do you want this in the trunk, or is the back seat okay?"

"The back seat is fine," he replied.

She tossed the bag over the seat and got into the car. "Nice car," she commented. "1965 GTO?"

He nodded. "I bought it about five years back and restored it as best I could, with a few enhancements and modifications. Elspeth's sister Rochelle is a really amazing mechanic and she did a lot of the work."

"Do you race?"

He laughed. "I used to. I quit a couple years back when I started studying really seriously for the Inner Order – I just didn't have the time for much besides magical work and my job."

"That's too bad. This car looks like a lot of fun to drive."

The odd feeling suddenly intensified for just a second, then faded away. "It is," he replied after a long pause, almost automatically.

"Are you okay?" she asked, noting his detached and distant tone.

"I think so," he said thoughtfully. "There's this old expression about someone walking over your grave. I suddenly felt that way a minute ago, and I can't place it."

"I get that sometimes when I'm stressed. I suppose investigating a murder isn't exactly a stress-free task."

"Maybe that's it," he replied, not really convinced. "I just don't get it."

"It usually goes away, if that's any help."

"I suppose it already has. So did you try out any of Jonas' suggestions?" he asked as he pulled the car away from the curb.

"Yeah, I did," she nodded. "Putting the banishing pentagram ritual with the invoking hexagram ritual seems really

121

weird after so many years of doing the banishing rituals together. It feels powerful, but somehow twisted and not quite right."

"Well, it is a powerful technique," he admitted. "I suppose after doing it one way for years changing it around takes some getting used to."

"I have kind of strange question," she said as they reached the Interstate a few minutes later. "Do you have any idea what this hill looks like where they found the bodies?"

"No," he replied, shaking his head. "But I'm sure we'll be able to check out the crime scene, at least from a distance."

"I suppose so," she replied, remembering the dream. *Was the man she saw the killer?* She had a disturbing feeling that she was about to find out.

Meanwhile, Elspeth and Jim were searching Michael's house from top to bottom, starting with the attic that was remodeled into an open, vaulted master suite. They found various magical implements there, including robes and jewelry of different sorts, sigils of spirits, and dream journals. Part of the room, facing the large stained-glass window in the south, had been turned into a second temple with a circle carved into the hardwood floor and a makeshift altar against the east wall. Elspeth searched that area carefully, looking for hollow panels in the altar and loose floorboards, but found nothing. She checked the master bathroom carefully as well, since she figured a bathroom was a great place to hide something, but to no avail.

Two out of the four bedrooms on the second floor had been remodeled for specific purposes. The first was the computer room, where Michael sometimes worked from home on various programming projects. A large L-shaped desk filled one corner of the room, and on it sat several machines – one of the latest, flashiest Sun workstations, a generic-looking Intel PC, and a sleek new Apple Macintosh. On the wall above the desk the LED's of the hub and router sparkled like Christmas lights. One wall was lined with tall filing cabinets, since the computer room also doubled as an office. Elspeth checked each of the cabinet drawers in turn, feeling the bottom below the hanging files and checking for magical residue. Still finding nothing, she checked each of the cabinets to see if one of them could be slid out from the wall, but found all of them solidly affixed. She also checked the closet, but it was such a mess of cables and old computer hardware that she doubted the book could be kept there and remain accessible. She knew that at this point, Michael most likely studied it daily.

The second bedroom looked more promising at first. Lined with tall shelves like the temple, it served as a second library. Here Michael kept technical manuals, journals, and just about every textbook from his college days. He also had a fair number of newer books on physics, biology, psychology, and paranormal research, which Elspeth knew that he studied in an attempt to stay current with the latest scientific discoveries even though she had always felt such studies were a waste of time. He had a shelf dedicated to Skeptical Inquirer magazine, which she had always found amusing given its anti-paranormal stance, and issues of the hilarious Journal of Irreproducible Results, a publication containing bizarre or meaningless studies that parodied existing scientific research. Going over each shelf for any traces of magical books or secret compartments proved fruitless here too. None of the books had much of an aura to speak of, and magick had probably never been worked in the room.

Both the third and fourth bedrooms were guest rooms, although at one time Michael had slept in the one toward the front of the house before he finished remodeling the attic. Both rooms were completely empty except for a bed, night table, and a dresser. In the closets, Elspeth found boxes containing all sorts of things – computer parts, cables, clothes that looked like they hadn't been worn in years, paperwork of various sorts, several pairs of shoes, and even old window air conditioning units. Judging from the faded aura in the both rooms, he probably hadn't even used them in weeks if not months. When she had stayed at the house, she slept upstairs with him in the attic master suite, and over the last several years she knew he'd had few other guests.

"I guess we head back to the temple," she said finally. "It doesn't seem very intuitive to me that it would be anywhere else, and we've looked all over the place."

"But if it's not on the shelves down there, where is it?" protested Jim as he followed her back down the stairs. "Are you sure that book we found is really a fake?"

Ignoring him, she descended the stairs and returned to the temple. She examined the Holy Table itself, but as it was a tabletop with four spindly legs there was no room to hide anything inside it. She then turned her attention to the mantle of the fireplace, which she examined closely. "Aha!" she exclaimed. "Michael hardly ever dusts."

"What do you mean?" asked Jim, still standing by the archway.

"Look," she ordered, pointing at a spot on the mantle.

He walked over and followed her gesture. "I don't see anything."

"Look really closely, like you were a maid or something. There's a pattern in the dust on the mantle, like the sweep of a door," she elaborated, her hand tracing out the sweep. "There must be a hidden compartment starting about here..." Then, suddenly, there it was – a fine outline in the paneling above the mantle. She couldn't believe she had missed it, until she noticed the concealment spell hanging over the wall. Fortunately for her, the spell didn't extend to the mantle. Otherwise, she might never have found the panel – the spell was a very good one.

"How does that work?" demanded Jim, confused. "I swear that wasn't there until you pointed it out. Now it's obvious!"

"If you know what you're looking for, concealment spells don't work," she explained. "As I said before we walked in, they operate by misdirection – they make your mind skip over whatever they're trying to hide. You can adjust, though, once you know where you should be looking and what you should be seeing."

"So how do you open it?"

"That's what I'm trying to figure out. Let's see here…" she mused, examining the fireplace brick by brick. She then began checking the tile border. "Here," she said, pointing to a tile. "This one isn't dusty, just like the mantle." She carefully warded the scrying crystal that sat on the mantle directly in front of where the door appeared to open and set it off to one side, and then warded the tile and the compartment door. "Here goes," she said, pressing the tile.

Even though the grout around it looked solid, the tile itself could be pressed inward like a ceramic button. With a click, the panel came loose from the wall and slowly swung open. Looking into the secret compartment, her eyes lit up as she spotted the leather-bound volume resting inside. She warded the book itself, removed it from the compartment, and set it on the Holy Table. "This is it," she said as Jim looked on. "<u>Liber Iadnamad</u>. The repository of our Guild's magical knowledge." The binding creaked as she opened it, the smell of the leather still fresh.

From her purse, she produced a digital camera and a high-capacity flash memory card. While Jim looked on, apparently fascinated by either the book itself or its contents, she photographed each of the pages in turn. "Now I'll have a digital copy. I can print one out for Balzador and keep the digital version for myself."

"What script is that?" asked Jim after awhile, pointing to a spot on one of the pages.

"Cursive Angelic," she replied. "It looks like John Dee's own handwriting. I'm guessing the original is pretty valuable, not that the information here isn't by itself."

"So you can read that?"

"Of course. We all can. Most of the incantations I use are in Angelic. It works better than any other language, even Latin or Hebrew, and those are both pretty good. Now if you'll let me finish, we can get out of here. We probably only have about ten more minutes."

Once she was done photographing the book, she put the digital camera and memory card back in her purse and replaced the book in the secret compartment. She swung the panel closed, and as it locked into the wall there was another click as the tile she had pressed popped back into place. She then replaced the scrying crystal on the mantle and unmade her wards. "We're done," said finally. "Now let's go."

On the way out the back, she repeated the process of warding the door, unlocking it, opening it, rushing through, closing the door, locking it, and unmaking the wards. As she clambered back into the truck, she fished her scrying crystal from her pocket and called Michael's image into it. Since he was a mage she could only look so close, but she saw an image of him and his GTO cruising along the highway, just entering the outskirts of the built up commercial area around Rochester. "And he's still on the road," she said with a triumphant smile as Jim hopped into the driver's seat. "Now let's get out of here."

Jim adeptly backed the big vehicle into the alley and headed back toward the side street, again managing to squeeze the truck through without incident.

"I may be a mage, but I have no idea how you do that," remarked Elspeth. "I drive a small car for a reason."

"It's not that hard," said Jim dismissively. "But can I ask you another question?"

"Sure."

"You said that the Angelic language worked better than anything else for incantations. Why is that? Do the words themselves have power?"

"Good question," she replied, surprised. "The use of language is one of those things that mages have argued about for a long time, but from my own experience I think the words do have power of their own – to some extent, anyway. There's a psychological effect that comes from just using a language with which you are unfamiliar, but at least with Angelic, it's more than that. It feels like there's something out there in the universe that certain sounds resonate with. Does that help at all?"

"Not really," he admitted. "See, in all the fantasy novels

126

I've read, the idea is that magick somehow is a collection of words and phrases that make things happen if you just read or pronounce them. The words themselves are powerful. So this Angelic is kind of like that, but kind of not? I don't get it."

"Fantasy novels are just that," she said mockingly. "Fantasy."

"But mythological descriptions are the same way," he added.

"Most mythologies are the fantasy novels of another time. I sometimes wonder if future archaeologists will think that Tolkien's Silmarillion was some kind of a holy text from a real religion," she replied. "Anyway, there's no such thing as a magical ritual that you can just pronounce in such a way that it will work. If that were the case, the world would be crawling with mages. This is the information age, and ritual texts are everywhere. Every sixteen-year-old kid with a copy of one of those fake <u>Necronomicons</u> would be calling up power and summoning 'Elder Gods,' whatever those are. No, magical rituals have to be performed with intention behind them or nothing happens. Magick is will. Since intention has to be trained and cultivated over a lot of years, mages are rare – and that's even assuming that most of them have real aptitude. Does that answer your question?"

"I suppose. I was really just curious. I'd like to learn more about it, if you're willing to teach me."

"Well," said Elspeth, patting her purse and sporting an impish grin, "now I can teach you anything you want to know."

VII. The Chariot

The Child of the Powers of the Waters: the Lord of the Triumph of Light
The Sign Cancer

In 1863 during the Civil War, Dr. William Worral Mayo found himself in the small town of Rochester, Minnesota examining new recruits for the Union Army. After the war, he decided to stay in southern Minnesota and open a medical practice. By the end of the nineteenth century, both of his sons had joined his practice and the clinic they had founded was well on its way to becoming one of the most prestigious in the United States, in addition to being one of the few large medical facilities serving southern Minnesota's rural population. As the twentieth century wore on, the city of Rochester grew up around the now famous Mayo Clinic, and by the turn of the millennium it was the fourth largest city in the state of Minnesota.

"I always liked coming in from the east better," said Michael as he drove his GTO along Highway 52, which connected Rochester and Saint Paul. "You've got cornfields as far as you can see, and all of a sudden it's like you come around a corner and there's a city. It just pops out of nowhere. This highway's been built up over the years, so you know you're getting close from miles out."

"I've never driven that way," replied Samantha, in the passenger seat, "though mind you, I don't get down here very much. I'm a city kid - even Rochester itself is kind of rural for my tastes, and it does have some tall buildings. So what exactly are we looking for, anyway?"

He shook his head. "Jonas didn't know for sure. Apparently, twelve people were found dead on one of the hills around the city the morning after he sensed this 'dark presence' enter the world, though I'm not really sure what he meant by that. I didn't sense anything myself, but I wasn't listening and he was."

"What night was this, again?"

"Two nights before the Morpheus thing. Why?"

"Well, I had a dream the night Morpheus went up, a really weird one," she explained. "It was like I was walking through a forest and I saw this hill, and on top of it there was this *thing* like a tornado of energy. And then all of a sudden, this guy was in front of me and he threw some kind of a magical attack at me and I fell down the hill. And I had this dagger that was somehow really important – but then Daria called and woke me up. It's probably nothing," she added. "It wasn't even the right night. But when I heard about you, I was afraid that you were the man in the dream. Don't worry, you don't look anything like him."

"It's interesting that you would have seen a man the night of the explosion, if it was about Morpheus. You might have sensed Elspeth, but she always looks like herself in other peoples' dreams – and believe me, I know."

"Do we have any specific plans once we're there?" she asked. "You said that we're meeting with the forensics people at one?"

He nodded. "We're supposed to be experts on occultism helping out with the police investigation. According the email I got from Jonas, they're stumped."

"How did we get made experts?"

He smiled. "Well, we are, aren't we? Most of the people who advise the police on occultism these days are inept publicity seekers. We got this particular job because Jonas has connections all over the state and we're doing it because we need all the information on this that the police are willing to share with us as part of the investigation. If this is the work of the magick office, we need to know. They might have summoned up something to destroy the Guild or somehow increase their own power. Or this might have been a failed experiment. Hopefully, we'll be able to tell what was going on from the evidence."

They had lunch at a small downtown café and proceeded on to the forensics lab. A mousy middle-aged man with dark hair and wire-rimmed glasses met them in the lobby of the building. "Are you Jonas' friends?" he asked, walking up to them.

Michael nodded. "I'm Michael Niemand and this is Samantha Davis."

"I'm Dr. Jackson Mitchell," he replied, shaking hands with both of them, "and yes, I have two last names. It's nice to meet both of you. I'm the chief medical examiner, and I'm glad you're here. This case is a real oddity."

"We'll do what we can," said Michael. "I don't know very much about forensics, though."

"I know enough for all three of us," said Mitchell with a wry smile that reminded Michael of Jonas – the two of them were almost certainly friends. The medical examiner then led them further into the building down a long white hallway that smelled of antiseptics. "Jonas tells me that you two are experts on magick and the occult. I have to admit, although I've known him for quite a few years I've always been skeptical of his more esoteric interests. The thing is, this case doesn't make any medical sense and the circumstances under which the bodies were found suggested possible occult involvement. And here we are." He stopped at one of the doors, and then, almost as an afterthought, turned back to them. "Oh, I should probably ask if either of you is particularly squeamish. Jonas said that you might be able to figure something out by examining one of the bodies, so that's where we're headed."

"I'll be all right," said Michael. "I find dead things a little distasteful, but if I have a problem I'll just leave. How about you?"

Samantha shrugged. "Biology major. I never had any trouble with dissection."

"Let's go, then," said Mitchell, opening the door. "This body hasn't been autopsied yet, but I'm sure the cause of death will be the same as the others – indeterminate."

They walked into an examining room. In the center of the room was a metal table of the kind used for autopsies, and on it lay the nude body of a woman. The scene was not disgusting at all, even to Michael's weaker stomach. The woman was pale and clearly dead, but otherwise she simply appeared to be asleep. He did not detect any of the usual septic spiritual energy that often surrounded the recent dead, either. In fact, the body felt more like an inorganic object, as though the life itself had been completely drained from it rather than cut short.

"Now look at this," said Mitchell, lifting one arm. "The body is completely pliable, and it's been in cold storage since we found it. As far as I can tell with the others, there's no rigor mortis to speak of. Sometimes that sort of thing can happen with poisons like cyanide that interrupt the body's energy cycle, but the toxicology is completely clean. There are no wounds, and all the organs look like they could be functional, they just *aren't*. The bodies were found on top of a hill outside town, dressed in robes, and slumped around a circle as though they were suddenly struck dead. At first we thought we might have some kind of cult suicide on our hands, and I still can't rule that out. I don't think that's the case, though – suicide victims usually leave *something* explaining why they did it, like a note or message. And there were thirteen robes found, but only twelve bodies. One of the robes was empty, suggesting another person might have been there."

"Did you find any footprints or tracks?"

Mitchell shook his head. "Nothing distinct. We found the path they made through the woods, but it's all pretty high ground so there wasn't much mud. We didn't find any usable impressions, and as far as we can tell they walked the whole way from the road. Here's another odd thing, by the way. Even after several days, the bodies don't show any signs of decay."

"Well, you said they were in cold storage," said Samantha.

"Oh, I don't mean they show few signs of decay. I mean they show *no* signs of decay. The blood pooled in the usual way, but normally bacteria start breaking down the body almost right away since there's so much of it in places like the digestive tract."

"What if the bacteria inside the body were killed as well?" asked Michael.

Mitchell shook his head. "I don't have any idea how you

would do that, unless you're talking radiation or something else really bizarre. This was weird enough that we scanned for radioactivity too – nothing. No organisms left alive inside the bodies would explain why they haven't started to decay yet, but I don't see how something like that could be done."

"How about the empty robe you mentioned?" asked Michael. "Have you analyzed it for hair or fibers?"

The doctor nodded. "We found a few hairs. Short, brown, really common. They could have come from anybody – probably a man, though, from the length. We could maybe try a hair match if we can come up with a suspect, but so far none are apparent. It looks like there probably was a thirteenth person present, but determining his identity presents us with a real problem. Jonas mentioned that you were psychic or something. Is that correct?"

"Sort of," replied Michael. "Technically, I'm a ritual magician, but we develop some of the same abilities that psychics use. We're just more disciplined about it."

Mitchell smiled. "That's one of the things I always thought was missing from some of the psychics that police have brought in from time to time. They just struck me as so *flaky*. And I can really only think of one case where they came up with useful information. It wasn't anything really profound, either. It could have just been a good guess."

Michael turned to Samantha. "Are you any good at psychometry?"

"Passable at best," she replied. "I've worked on it on my own but my order doesn't really teach it."

"Then I'll try," he said. "If both of you could stand back from the body?" As they did so, he placed his hands over the dead woman's sternum, the *anahata* energy center, and opened his mind.

What he saw was hard to decipher. As was usually the case, the images came fast. He saw a forest, a line of people in robes, a circle, purification and consecration, a man's ordinary face lighting up as power flooded the circle. Then he felt swept up into the air, spinning and rising, only to be met with impenetrable blackness that he slammed into like a brick wall. He heard Samantha gasp as he fell.

Slowly picking himself up off the floor, he turned to Mitchell. "I saw a face," he said, breathless. "The face of their leader, maybe. Do you have photos of the other victims? He might be one of the twelve, or he might be the thirteenth person."

"Sure," replied the doctor. "Give me a minute and I'll get them."

"Are you all right?" Samantha asked as Mitchell left the room.

"I think so. I guess I just got lightheaded. I think Jonas was right – she was sacrificed. At least, the blackness I hit feels like the Abyss, which is where a sacrificed soul would wind up. Her spirit was practically ripped out of her body. That's why it looks like her body's energy cycle just stopped."

"Separation?" Her eyes widened with apprehension. "That's supposed to be one of the dangers of travel in the spirit vision – you know, what they call astral projection these days – but I've never heard of it happening to anyone. Can mages in your Guild just, I don't know, do that? Just separate somebody's spirit from their body?"

"No," he replied, shaking his head. "I've never heard of anyone who could do that. Not even Elspeth – probably, if she could, I wouldn't be alive now. I suppose I can imagine what the technique would have to be - Mars or Saturn, maybe both. Even with regular people, the body of light is pretty resistant to that kind of attack. And this woman was a borderline mage – not fantastically gifted, but with some spiritual awareness and natural power. She didn't see it coming, so it wasn't like she was starting to leave her body and then got hit. Whoever did this just *did it*, no buildup, no preparation, no ritual, nothing. I'll tell you something else – it was probably a general spell if it killed all the bacteria inside her body as well."

"So it affects an area?" she asked, incredulous.

134

He nodded. "Maybe the whole circle."

"How could you possibly block something like that?"

"I don't know," he replied thoughtfully. "It would be difficult, I can tell you that much. I'm starting to think that Jonas has good reason to be scared."

Mitchell walked back into the room carrying a large manila envelope. "Here are the other victims," he said, taking out a sheaf of photos and handing them to Michael, who paged through them quickly. He saw no one who even resembled the excruciatingly ordinary man with the maniacal grin.

"He's not in here. I think I saw the thirteenth person's face. Even if he's not the killer, he's probably someone you would want to interview. I think his hair was brown, too, though it's kind of hard to tell in a hooded robe."

"Could you talk with one our forensic artists?" suggested the doctor. "We can at least circulate a sketch. It's more than we have to go on at the moment."

"Okay," agreed Michael. "Is there one in the building?"

Mitchell nodded. "It's in the other wing. I'll show you." He led them back down the long hallway and took another branching corridor from the lobby into the other wing of the building.

The sketch artist proved to be a young woman in her early twenties with short blond hair who introduced herself as Jessica. She went through the standard set of questions, and after awhile came up with a drawing that looked like the man Michael had seen. She drew the hair short and brown based on the hair taken off the robe, which Mitchell had assumed belonged to the killer.

"Is that really him?" asked the artist when she was done.

"It looks close. Why do you ask?"

"Because this doesn't even look like a real person," she explained. "It's more like a textbook example – average face, average hair, average eyes. I don't think I've ever seen anyone who looks this, well, *normal*. You aren't making this up, are you? Sometimes people do, and you'll be in less trouble now than if we find out later."

"No," he insisted. "That's really the man I saw."

"Where did you see him?" she asked. "Were you there?"

"No," he replied, shaking his head. "I saw him in a kind of a vision, I guess. I suppose you could call me a psychic, though that's not exactly what I am."

Her brow furrowed. "Is that so," she said skeptically.

"Well, I'm not a con artist, if that's what you're thinking," said Michael. "I'm not getting paid for this or anything, and I certainly couldn't care less about notoriety. I'm only doing this as a favor to a friend."

"So is this that weird occult case you're working on?" she asked. "The bodies they found up on the hill?"

He nodded.

"Do they have any idea what happened?"

"Not yet, or at least nothing that I've been told. Do you know something about it?"

"Well, sort of. Not about the case itself, but I used to see one of the women they found up there all the time. It's strange seeing somebody who's a fixture around town just taken out. Especially like that." As she spoke, she shuddered involuntarily, clearly bothered by the whole situation.

"So you knew one of the victims?" asked Michael.

"Not that well," replied the artist. "As I said, I saw her around. She was one of those spooky types who went around claiming to be some kind of witch or something, you know? I already told the investigators everything I know, but it isn't much."

"I take it you're not into that sort of thing, then?"

"Well, I went to a couple of circles a few years back, but I thought it was kind of silly. I'm not really even all that spiritual. She was there, though. I think it was the same woman Dr. Mitchell had you examine."

"Was there anywhere she spent a lot of time?"

"Sure," she answered immediately. "The Barnes and Noble bookstore. It's the biggest bookstore in town, and it's a really cool space. They remodeled an old theater into the store, so it's got a stage and everything – the whole place is one big open room. They've also got a café there, and she and her friends hung out there a lot. It's one of the only places in town where you can get books on Wicca and the occult."

"I take it you don't recognize the sketch as anyone who spent time with them."

"No," she replied, shaking her head. "Although as I said, this is one of the most ordinary-looking people I've ever seen. If I saw him in person, I'd probably have forgotten already."

"Good point," agreed Michael. "Can I get directions to this bookstore, and a copy of that sketch?"

"Sure," agreed the artist. She quickly made a photocopy of the sketch, and wrote the directions on the back. "I wish you the best of luck in finding the killer. The whole city's pretty spooked."

He met Samantha in the lobby and showed her the sketch. "That's really all you saw?" she asked dubiously. "That can't be a real person."

"It does look like a projection," he agreed.

"A what?" she asked blankly.

"A projection," he repeated. "If you're worried about another mage scrying you, you can create a kind of artificial image that anyone scrying you will see instead of your real appearance. Usually, they're pretty generic because that's the best a lot of mages can come up with."

"That has to be it."

"I'm not so sure," he said thoughtfully. "The thing is, it didn't *feel* like a projection, and somebody would have to be fairly powerful to put one up that I would miss. Elspeth is only able to do it about half the time. If we're talking about somebody on her level who can kill at a distance, then we all should be scared. Where did Dr. Mitchell go?"

"He's over there," she said, pointing to the reception desk. Mitchell was standing there, talking with two men who Michael guessed were the detectives working on the case.

"Are you ready to check out the crime scene?" he asked Samantha in a low voice. "You seemed nervous about it in the car."

"I think so," she said, a touch uncertain but determined. "It was just a dream, after all, and I'm sure there's nothing there now, unless our killer is pretty stupid and has hung around all this time." Even though the statement was almost certainly true, it did little to comfort her.

"We could wait another day if you would rather."

"No," she insisted. "I'm fine. Let's just get it over with."

They walked across the lobby to where Mitchell stood talking with the two other men. "Are you done with the artist?" asked the medical examiner.

Michael nodded.

"Well, let's see, then." Mitchell took one look at the sketch and his face fell. "You're kidding, right? This can't be a real person. If this is all you saw, I don't see how it can be of any use to us." He showed it to the two men, one of whom just shook his head. "Oh, I should introduce you. Michael and Samantha, these two gentlemen are Philip Roth and Robert Walker, the two lead detectives on this case."

"Call me Bob," said Robert, a young man with sandy hair and an amiable smile.

"Are you ready to view the crime scene?" asked Philip, the older of the two.

"I think so," replied Michael.

"Well, let's go, then, while it's still light out. It's a bit of a walk through the woods."

Samantha and Michael followed the two detectives to an unmarked squad car outside. They sat together in the back seat.

"So do you know anything about that medium guy on TV?" asked Bob as the car pulled away from the curb. "You know, he talks to dead relatives and stuff."

"No, I can't say that I do," replied Michael. "I can tell you

138

that most mediums are fakes, though."

"Really?" The detective looked genuinely surprised, though Michael wasn't sure if that was because he thought the medium was for real of because he expected psychics of whatever sort to stick up for each other. "The other psychics we work with swear he's genuine. He comes up with things he couldn't possibly know any other way."

"Well, that could be, but then you never know if he's a psychic but not a medium," said Samantha.

"What do you mean?" asked the detective.

"He might be reading the information out of the minds of whoever they are trying to help contact the dead," she explained. "To really be sure it was coming from somewhere else, your medium would have to come up with a piece of information that the dead relative knew but the person he is speaking to doesn't. That doesn't make for very good television, and I've never seen it on one of those shows."

"I don't know from personal experience how accurate the information necessarily is," added Michael, "but I was always taught that spirits of the dead only hang around the Earth for about three days or so except in really unusual situations where you wind up with a ghost. If that's true, anybody who can talk to the dead relatives of half the people in the room has to be a fake, or at best a psychic reader. You don't need to be psychic to read people, either – I'm sure you know from experience that con artists can do it just by looking at body language and picking up on details here and there."

"You're right about that," said Philip, finally speaking up. "I have to admit, that's what I think of most of you fortune-teller types. I'm only doing this because we're really stuck. Even if you two don't help us, I figure listening to what you have to say can't hurt. After all, we're not paying you."

"Fair enough," replied Michael. "I just hope that we can prove you wrong."

They left the city and headed east, deeper into the bluff

139

country of southern Minnesota. To the south and east, Rochester was not nearly as built up as it was to the north and soon they were cruising along a highway lined with nothing but cleared agricultural fields on both sides. Most of the snow had melted, but here and there patches were still visible, usually around trees or other natural features that shielded them from the sun. Another ten minutes or so down the road, the fields gave way to a section of oak forest that was just beginning to bud. Philip turned off the highway onto a disused dirt road that took them deeper into the woods. "There's a walking trail that goes further back at the end of the road," he explained.

"Did the killer drive this way?" asked Michael.

"We don't think so," replied the detective. "We found four cars parked in the field at the end of the road, and each of them belonged to one of the victims. The killer probably carpooled out here with the others, though how he went anywhere after that isn't really clear. It was cold that night, and this is a ways out of town. It would take a long time to walk it, unless he hitchhiked or something."

"Do you think the killer is a man?" asked Samantha. "I mean, you just said he, or is that a figure of speech?"

Philip shrugged. "Mitchell said the hair they found was cut short, your friend says he saw a man in his vision or whatever it was, and yes, I think that's likely. Most mass murderers are male."

"Here's where we found the cars," said Bob, pointing to a field up ahead. "The road ends, so it's really the only place where you can park. We're pretty sure there wasn't a fifth car since the tracks we found were all from the four that were here."

"Can you stop here?" asked Michael. "I mean, on the road before you drive into the clearing?"

"Sure," replied Philip. "Any particular reason?"

"Yeah. I want to check the area magically."

"Suit yourself," he said with another shrug, and stopped the car.

Michael stepped out onto the road, which was still wet

140

and muddy from the melting snow. Trudging through the mud and slush, he entered the clearing and stood motionless, extending his mind to encompass the immediate area. He then focused his thoughts on the timeline that ran from where he was into the past. He saw the cycles of day and night pass rapidly as his thoughts moved backwards in time, and then he ran into what felt like a wall. It was supple and bright, unlike the hard blackness of the Abyss, but beyond it his perception of the timeline just stopped, cut like piece of string.

"What's he doing?" asked Bob, still in the car.

"He's trying to sense what went on the night of the murder," replied Samantha. "You can sort of project your mind back into the past along the current timeline. It usually works, unless it's blocked."

Michael walked back to the car, shaking his head. "It's cut off," he said as he climbed back into the car. "Somebody knew what they were doing."

Philip pulled the car into the clearing and parked next to where the walking trail meandered into the trees. "We're maybe looking at a ten minute walk up to the hill, but be careful. The ground isn't real good and the trail is pretty overgrown."

"Did this used to be a park or something?" asked Samantha.

"No," replied the older detective. "It's just a place where kids come to party sometimes. I think it's still owned by the guy who runs the last farm we passed, but he's neglected it for years. I hung out here when I was a teenager, to give you some idea how long it's been this way."

They got out of the car and followed Philip into the woods. It was clear that someone had been that way fairly recently, judging by the broken branches and trampled underbrush. With the melting snow the trail was muddy and slippery, so it took more like fifteen or twenty minutes to reach what looked like a natural break in the trees… and there it was. Samantha gasped as she recognized the hill from her dream. It looked identical in every detail except in the dream it had been after nightfall. "That's it," she said softly.

"The hill from your dream?" asked Michael.

She nodded, eyes wide.

"What's with her?" asked Philip, turning around to see what was happening.

"I… I had a dream about this place," explained Samantha. "Only I've never been here. It's strange, that's all."

"What did you see?" asked Bob, immediately interested.

"Nothing about the murders," she replied slowly. "It was just – frightening for some reason." She decided to omit the more unbelievable aspects of the dream, since she was pretty sure the detectives wouldn't find it useful. Anyway, there was little point in undermining her credibility. From the older detective's comments, she and Michael were already on shaky ground.

"Great," said Philip, nonplussed.

They climbed up to the top of the hill along the same path Samantha had taken in her dream, although this time she encountered no adversary. The top of the hill felt stark and empty, devoid of energy and life, though the snow was melted and plants were beginning to peek through the moist ground. Michael knelt down and checked the area of the hill, but the result was the same as on the dirt road leading to the site. He deepened his concentration, trying to push through the overbearing energy field that blocked his senses, but it was no use. He emerged from his sensing trance with nothing but a dull headache.

"There's nothing here," said Michael finally, shaking his head. "I can't see anything."

"Okay," replied Philip, sounding a little exasperated. "At least we can tell Mitchell and the Captain we tried. Let's head back."

"So you couldn't see anything at all?" asked Samantha as they headed back to the car.

"Nothing. But it was worth coming here."

"How so?"

"I know that the situation is much worse than I thought,"

said Michael in a low voice. "This is no fringe cult or group delusion – we're up against someone who can not only use magick to kill, but who knows how to cover his tracks the likes of which I've never come across. I think we'll need to do some real police work on this one."

"The bookstore?" she asked, already knowing the answer. He nodded.

The ride back into town was a quiet one. Philip seemed more annoyed than anything else at wasting his time and Bob seemed disappointed that Michael and Samantha could offer them no additional information on the murders. Still, they were both cordial and polite as they dropped off the two mages outside the Medical Examiner's office. They walked into the building only to practically run into Mitchell on his way back to the wing of the building that housed his laboratory.

"Ah, Samantha and Michael," he said with his usual smile. "Did you find out anything at the site?"

"Nothing," replied Michael. "I'm sorry I couldn't be more helpful. I think Philip is a little irritated with us."

"Maybe so," admitted Mitchell, "but he knows that investigation is hit or miss. For what it's worth, I wrote up a report including your observations on the body, though it will probably be controversial and I might have to redo it before submitting it. I appreciate you taking the time to come down here and check it out. Do you have any other business in town?"

"No," replied Michael, "though you should have the investigators talk to Jessica, the sketch artist, if they haven't already. She told me that she knew one of the victims, though not well. She says that the woman she knew used to spend time at the Barnes and Noble bookstore, so we're going to check that out before we leave. I'll let you know if we find out anything else, but after trying to check the site I doubt that will be the case. I do think this done by magick, but it was done by someone who really knows how to cover their tracks."

"I'll be sure to pass along my thanks to Jonas," said Mitchell.

"You may not have seen much, but you've given us more than we had yesterday. I have a feeling it may prove useful."

From the forensics lab, it was only a walk of a few blocks to the Barnes and Noble, which was housed in a remodeled theater of a design popular about fifty years ago. The seats had been taken out and replaced with bookshelves, and what was once the concession area was now an open space that served as a café. The ceiling was brightly painted to look like a sky with clouds across which colorful shapes danced playfully, lending a truly unique ambiance to the store.

"So much for spending the long weekend here," said Samantha as she and Michael walked into the store.

"Yeah," he agreed. "It doesn't look like there's much here to pursue. This is probably a waste of time, too, but I need to be sure. If the killer spent time with the victims here, I may be able to find something out by scanning the store. The more time that was spent here, the more difficult it would be to wipe it all out."

"How exactly do you scan places?" asked Samantha. "I didn't ask earlier because I figured you wouldn't want to answer any pointless questions about it that the detectives might ask, but I am curious."

"Well, it's kind of like looking into the future, only you look backwards into the past. Unlike psychometry, it doesn't require an object, just an area. You kind of stretch out your mind, then visualize a curtain with the symbol of Saturn on it."

"That makes sense, with Saturn as the ruler of time," she agreed.

"Then you visualize yourself parting the curtain and stepping through it, into the past. You should see the past of the area you're in. It's going to be tricky here, since I don't know the exact time and with all the people coming and going I essentially have to scan through everything and hope that I see the face of the killer. Let's sit down."

They sat at one of the tables adjacent to the coffee bar. Samantha stepped up to the counter and ordered two Cafe Mochas

144

while Michael began to put himself into the trance that would enable him to scan the store. Beyond the curtain, he found himself in the store just as it was, and then he began to move backwards in time, concentrating his will so that the images would come in a slow and ordered fashion. He saw Samantha walking up to the counter, the two of them entering the store, and then the flow of patrons in and out as it had happened earlier in the day, followed by the store closed and empty for the night. He allowed the images to speed up a little, moving back through the preceding days to before the night on which the murders had taken place. He then slowed the images down again. *So far so good*, he said to himself. *No blocks.* Could the killer have been clever enough to block everything at the scene, but careless enough to ignore any magical traces in the store thinking that no mage would ever try to scan it?

He realized suddenly that this was indeed the case, as the image that flashed before him was that of the killer and the woman whose body he had examined, two tables over from where he sat in meditation. He wasn't quite sure of the exact time, but from the flow of images it felt like about two days before the murders.

The excruciatingly ordinary-looking man – and that appeared to be what he really looked like – sat across the table from the woman, his face a bemused grin. "Is your coven ready to help me now?" he was asking. "You understand, of course, that most would consider the summoning of the Dark Lord to be black magick."

"Yes," replied the woman with a nod. "We are ready, provided that the Dark One will reward us as you have promised in return for our pledge of service."

"Naturally," replied the man. "It has always been thus, since the Middle Ages and beyond. When the Dark Lord appears, he will reward those with the courage to call him into the world by fulfilling their deepest desires, so long as they remain in his service. The power that he will grant us will shake the foundations of the world."

"When are the stars right?" she asked, her eyes wide and

expectant.

"Two nights from now," replied the man. "Inform your followers that we will be meeting at the usual place. The ritual must be performed in the light of the full moon, so we will begin three hours after sunset."

The woman nodded again. "Very well. We'll be there." She stood up and left the table, then walked out of the store. The man simply sat for what felt like a long time before following suit.

Michael opened his eyes to see Samantha finishing her mocha. "You were under for a long time," she commented. "Your coffee is probably cold by now. Did you see him?"

"I did," he replied, "though I'm not sure if what I saw was particularly useful. The group was a coven of some kind, and the killer promised them that they would be granted power if they helped him summon a being that he called the Dark Lord. I'm guessing it's Coronzon, but I hope I'm wrong."

"Me too," she agreed. "He's just about the last demon I would want to tangle with."

"I'd better call Jonas." He took the cell phone from his pocket and dialed the number that was becoming all too familiar.

"Hello, Michael," said Jonas, sounding like he was expecting the call. "Are you in Rochester?"

"Yes. There's not a lot of information here, though. I think we're heading back tonight."

"Good. I was going to call you and let you know that you needed to be back tomorrow, regardless of what you had found. The council members are arriving today, not next week, and they want to step up the meeting. It's scheduled for tomorrow evening, and you will need to be there."

"Understood," said Michael. "I'll see you then."

"What's up?" asked Samantha as he hung up the phone.

"The council meeting is tomorrow, not next week. The Supreme Council must really want this situation with Elspeth resolved right away."

"I would if I were them," she admitted. "Especially if they

think they may be confronting another threat soon."

"I'm just worried," he said slowly. "It's not every day that someone I care about might be executed by the same people who have trained me and practically been my family for half of my life. I do understand the reasons for the rules, but I still feel conflicted. Elspeth may have tried to kill me, though I'm sure she felt that I was up to countering whatever she could throw at me, but I can't help but feel for her. She needs help, not condemnation."

"You're remarkably forgiving, then," observed Samantha. "Not very many people would feel that way. But the members of your council are wise, aren't they? Jonas seems to be. You'll just have to trust them to make the right decision."

"I know," he replied. "But somehow I feel that in the end, it will come down to me. What I say, how I phrase things, how I describe the events... it's all about how my statements are perceived. I don't want her to die, but I'm not sure I can prevent the inevitable."

"You'll find a way," said Samantha calmly.

Looking into her eyes, he knew that she really believed he could do it, even in the face of the council itself. It surprised him – he had only known her a few days, and yet in that time she seemed to trust him completely. He wondered what that meant, and he hoped that her trust was not misplaced.

VIII. Adjustment, or Justice

The Daughter of the Lords of Truth: The Ruler of the Balance
The Sign Libra

"This meeting of the Supreme Council will now come to order," proclaimed Aleric Sprengel as he struck the marble top of his ornate dining room table with the ceremonial wooden gavel that had began every meeting of the Council for over a hundred years. The seven members of the Supreme Council were seated around the table, gathered from all over the world, while Michael and Elspeth sat in two carved antique chairs placed against the north wall.

Elspeth was quiet and resigned. Even though she and Michael had both arrived early, she had said nothing to him but the standard formal greeting, acknowledging his higher rank in the Guild hierarchy. She was dressed well, as usual, in a semi-formal gray dress that nearly matched the steely hue of her eyes, and she had bound back her long hair so that it fell to the small of her back like a thick rope.

Michael sensed her fear and profound uncertainty about her position, and felt for her. Even after everything she had done, he wanted to tell her what he was fairly sure the Supreme Council's decision would be, that she was in fact not about to be condemned to death, but he knew that the rules of procedure prohibited it. In point of fact, telling her would be premature anyway. From his meeting with Aleric and Jonas, he only knew the status of two votes. The Council would hear the facts, and then they would announce their ruling.

Aleric and Jonas were the only members of the Council in the Twin Cities area, and were also the only members that Michael knew. The other five had arrived quietly and filed into Aleric's formal dining room, waiting patiently for the full council to assemble. Once the entire council was present, Aleric invited Michael and Elspeth into the makeshift council chamber and closed the heavy double doors that led into the room.

"Before we begin, introductions are in order," said Aleric formally. "The two individuals who stand before us are Adept Michael Niemand and Portal Elspeth Sprengel, my granddaughter." Turning to Michael and Elspeth, he continued. "You already know Jonas Votan, Master of the United States. Going around the table, we have Roslyn Sherrington, Master of Great Britain and Ireland; Stefan Adler, Master of Germany and Austria; Robert McCloud, Master of Canada; William Kendall, Master of Australia; and Sofia Borgia, Master of Italy."

Michael felt a sense of awe scanning the faces at the table. Most were old but healthy, with auras that filled the room with a soft spiritual glow. *Here they are*, he thought to himself. *The most powerful mages in the world.* Before the meeting, Aleric had performed a simple spell that transferred Michael's memories of the destruction of Morpheus into a crystal sphere that he now placed gingerly on the table. The crystal served as an indisputable record, so there would be no contention concerning what took place that night. Given the crystal, Elspeth knew that there was no denying that she had in fact cast the spell that had destroyed the building.

"If there is no objection, I will get started with the issue that has called us here. I direct your attention to this sphere," said Aleric. "It contains the record of what transpired at Morpheus, a club and restaurant that formerly occupied a warehouse in downtown Minneapolis. These memories were taken from Michael, who witnessed the event in question. Elspeth was the other magician involved."

Michael did not see anything at first, but shifting his attention to his magical sight he was suddenly aware of shapes forming in the air above the sphere. Then, there he was, sitting at the table with Elspeth, except that unlike a video recording, it showed the physically invisible rings of magick that encircled each of them. He saw himself stand and fortify his magical defenses while Elspeth focused her intention upon attack. As she pronounced the incantation, he was amazed to see the darkness of the curse strike his defenses and bounce like reflected light,

150

scattering through the club. There was a lot more negative energy than he had thought at the time, which explained why the place had gone up in flames. A detached part of his mind noted that she had not in fact called fire – to do that, she would have needed to use an Angelic word like *ialprg*, burning flames, following *yolcam*, bring forth. Instead, she used the more generic *drilp*, vexation, her usual choice for general bad luck.

As the image faded away, Robert McCloud, a tall white-haired man wearing thick glasses, was the first to speak. "This seems a simple case," he said without inflection. "Our rules prohibit the use of magical power in this fashion. No mage has been sanctioned under them in centuries, but the penalty was and has always been death."

"Those rules were set in the Renaissance," pointed out Sofia. "There was still an active Inquisition in those days and we needed to either keep a low profile or be found and executed." Her English was excellent for a European, with only a slight accent. "In those times, the rules made sense. Today, I think that they do not."

"What about the people who died in the fire?" asked Roslyn. "Do we know that this would have happened without the presence of a curse on the premises? Can you dismiss it as an accident? From the way the magick moved I see that the destruction of the club was a side effect of sorts, but that doesn't excuse it."

"At the very least it reflects profoundly bad judgment," said Stefan. "The vote seems simple to me. We must decide whether or not to apply the ancient penalty of death. If the answer is no, then we can vote on a different penalty. If the answer is yes, then further discussion is pointless." His English was also very good, not surprising, Michael supposed, since most of the founding documents of the Guild were in that language.

The room was silent for a moment. "Do you have anything to add, William?" asked Aleric.

"Not as such," replied the Australian mage. "Does she wish to make any sort of a statement to this council?"

151

"As her instructor, it falls to me to address the council on her behalf," spoke up Jonas. "Elspeth is perhaps the most magically talented student our Guild has ever seen. Yes, her judgment is suspect, but I believe that particular problem can be addressed in her training before she is admitted to the grade of Adept. If this is truly the case, she could become one of our most effective initiates. I will also point out that she represents an enormous investment on the part of the Guild over the last two centuries, in term of the effort we have expended augmenting the Sprengel bloodline. Finally, are we still so barbaric that our only way of dealing with this problem is to kill one of our own?"

"What would you have us do, Jonas?" demanded Robert. "Expel her so that she can join another order and turn its power against us? Her strength is such that she could quickly rise to the top of most magical organizations."

"I would have us keep her in the Guild, at her current rank, until such time as her psychological issues have been addressed and resolved. Many of those issues date back to our own failure to provide adequate security for her family, as this council is well aware."

"You can't lay the blame on us," countered Robert. "There were many possible timelines and we had no way to predict which was the true future. We did what we could. In hindsight, of course, it is clear that we didn't do enough. But that makes the current situation our responsibility? I don't think so."

"That *is* a weak argument," agreed William, "however, if what you say concerning her abilities is true, maybe we would be foolish to destroy such a valuable potential asset."

"Assuming, of course, that her problems can be resolved," reminded Stefan. "Some damage is too extreme to correct, even with magick."

"I have been able to help others in worse condition," commented Sofia. "Some of them are now highly respected members of our order in Italy."

"But that doesn't change the fact that magick was used

152

to take the lives of people who were completely unprepared for it," insisted Roslyn. "We have to do everything we can to keep this from happening again. This isn't about her being an asset to the Guild. This is about murder. Whether spells were used or not shouldn't make a difference."

"Murder is predicated upon intent," reminded Jonas. "I would agree with you if you were to say that this is similar to causing an accidental death, but murder? I think not. As for using magick on people who were unprepared, remember that her intention was to use it against Michael, who she knew to be an initiate. It could even be argued that Michael bears some responsibility because his defenses deflected rather than neutralized the attack, but I do not think that anyone in this room would propose that."

"Do you have an opinion, Aleric?" asked William. "You're remarkably sedate."

"I would think that my opinion could be inferred easily," replied the Guildmaster. "I have raised Elspeth since she was twelve and I love her. Naturally, I don't want to see her killed. This situation is tragic, but I have already spoken at length with Jonas and I believe he is correct."

"I guess I can accept that," said William. "My main concern is whether or not it will happen again. You know, Aleric, that if we decide to spare her life and she winds up killing a bunch of civilians again we're not likely to forgive her a second time."

"Yes," said the Guildmaster softly. "I know that."

"I think that the likelihood of her doing something like this is really what our vote hinges upon," said Jonas. "As her instructor, I believe I can give her the teaching she needs to control her incredible power. I am asking you to believe me. But obviously I cannot force any of you to do so. You must follow your own consciences."

"That does appear to be the issue," agreed Stefan. "Aside from Aleric, Jonas, you are the most respected mage in the Guild. But some things are just too difficult, even for the greatest of us."

The room lay silent for a moment.

"Do I hear a motion?" asked Aleric.

"I'll make it a motion," said Robert. "I move that Elspeth Sprengel be subject to execution in conformance with our ancient customs. Do I hear a second?"

"Second," spoke up Roslyn.

"It has been moved and seconded that Elspeth Sprengel be subject to execution in conformance with our ancient customs," said Aleric. "Is there any further discussion?"

"Get on with it, Aleric," said Robert. "I think all of us have made our positions clear."

"Very well. All in favor?"

Three hands rose – Robert, Roslyn, and Stefan.

"All opposed?"

Four hands rose – Aleric, Jonas, Sofia, and William.

Elspeth breathed a sigh of relief – the vote was four to three against her execution. But then Sofia spoke hesitantly.

"You are the deciding vote, Aleric," she said softly. "I am on your side, but as much as I hate to say it, you know as well as I do that in such a case it represents a conflict of interest to cast a vote affecting the fate your own kin. You must designate another to vote in your place, and I see only one eligible Adept here who could act as a proxy." Her penetrating gaze turned to Michael. "Unless, of course, you wish to postpone the vote for a later date."

Michael's eyes widened. *I am member of the Inner Order now, aren't I?* One of the qualifications to serve on the Council was initiation into the Inner Order, and while he had hoped to serve on the Council one day he had no idea he would be asked so soon and in so personal a capacity. Aleric shot a quick glance at Jonas, who nodded almost imperceptibly.

"No," said the Guildmaster. "This must be decided quickly and as the Council is divided, I think it would be appropriate for Michael, as the object of Elspeth's attack, to decide her fate. All in favor?"

All seven hands shot up around the table. Elspeth's eyes

154

filled with fear.

"Me?" asked Michael, finally speaking up. "I may be an Adept, but I'm not a member of the Council."

"No, but as Guildmaster I can designate as my proxy any mage who has been initiated into the Inner Order, with the approval of the Council," explained Aleric. "So go ahead. Cast your vote."

With the eyes of the seven senior mages on him, he was quiet for what felt like a long time. Elspeth closed her eyes, bracing for the worst. He could feel her magical defenses strengthening as she got ready to run or fight. Although he knew she had no chance of defeating the entire Council, she wasn't planning on going down gently. Jonas and Aleric looked him in the eye expectantly as several of the mages around the table gathered their power to counter anything Elspeth might try. It occurred to him that even if he were in favor of her execution, casting such a vote would set in motion a chain of events that could be catastrophic for him and the rest of the Guild. It was fortunate, then, he mused, that he felt the way he did. "Life," he said finally.

Elspeth's concentration snapped like stretched metal, sending the energy she had summoned careening back into the world around her. She turned her head to stare at Michael, shocked, and he suddenly realized that she had honestly expected him to condemn her to death. She let out another deeper sigh, and her whole body seemed to deflate a little.

"There is still the matter of admission into the Inner Order to consider," said Robert. "I move that in light of this situation, Elspeth Sprengel be barred from admission into the Inner Order until such time as that ruling is reversed by this council."

"Second," said Stefan, raising his hand.

"Very well," said Aleric. "It has been moved and seconded that Elspeth Sprengel be barred from admission into the Inner Order until such time as that decision is reversed by the Supreme Council. Is there any discussion?"

The room was silent.

"There being no discussion," he continued, "I will now call

155

the vote. All in favor?"

Five hands rose – Roslyn, Stefan, Robert, William, and Sofia.

"All opposed?" He raised his hand, as did Jonas. "The motion passes." He struck the table again with the gavel. "Elspeth Sprengel will be barred from entry into the Inner Order until such time as that decision is reversed by the Supreme Council. I believe that concludes the business for which this assembly was called. Are there any other matters that must be brought before this Council?"

Again, the room was silent.

"Then the meeting is concluded." He rapped the gavel on the table once more, and the members of the council rose from their seats.

Aleric opened the heavy double doors and everyone in the room filed out into the foyer. Elspeth said nothing to any of the Council members, not even her grandfather, and headed straight for the front door. Michael quickened his step and followed her out onto the front lawn facing Summit Avenue.

"Hey," he said, catching up to her. "Did you really think I wanted you dead?"

She stopped and stood there on the lawn, her gaze fixed on the downtown Saint Paul skyline off in the distance. "Can I ask you a question?" she said softly, without emotion.

"Of course," he replied. "You can ask me anything you want. You know that."

"Why did you do that? You could have had me killed."

"Why do you think I did it?" he countered. "I love you, of course. I didn't date you for four years because I thought you were an objectionable person who deserved to die. I'd like to see you handle some of your personal issues better, but I'm not going to have you killed just because of that. Are you saying that you would have had me killed if the situation was reversed?"

"I... I don't know," she hedged. "I was really angry when we were at the club – my memories are still cloudy – but I still never meant to cause so much destruction. You have to believe me…"

"I do," he said firmly. "If I really thought you were a homicidal lunatic, you would be dead, no matter how much I liked you as a person. It was an accident – a tragic one, but it probably would have happened another night without your intervention."

"Maybe. But maybe not. Those people would still be alive if I had just stormed out."

"True," he agreed. "But the same disaster could also have happened when I wasn't there to help. I know, it's a small consolation at best, and I can't really imagine how you must be feeling. But even magick can't change the past. Not even your magick, which is…"

"Yes, what about my magick?" she interrupted, anger creeping into her voice. "I've worked to be admitted to the Inner Order for years, and now I'm barred from admission, just like that?"

"The Council could reverse its decision."

"Don't be stupid," she countered viciously. "At five to two? I don't think the same Supreme Council has ever reversed a five to two decision in the entire history of the Guild. My grandfather and Jonas are the oldest members, so they aren't likely to outlive any of the others. If I ever want to advance I'm totally screwed!"

"Don't be angry with me about that," he said evenly. "You know the only decision I had anything to do with was your survival."

"I know, I know," she replied, calming herself somewhat. "It still really upsets me, though. I have problems, I know, but to be told that even if I work through them I'm still out… the Guild needs my power. You know it, my grandfather knows it, and Jonas knows it."

"Yes, Elspeth, we do. We're just trying to figure out the price of that power – to all of us, yourself included." He paused for a moment, wondering if he should say what was really on his mind. Finally, he decided to go ahead and ask the question. "Do you remember how your parents died? I know you don't like to talk about it, but it's important."

"It's hard…" she said softly, the heat of her anger giving way to sadness. Then it was as though a switch turned off in her head, and she was back to her usual mechanical self. "I remember the gun wouldn't shoot at me. My parents got in the way, and they were gone. Their spells didn't do anything to the gun – didn't make it miss, didn't block combustion, nothing. But then for me it wouldn't work. Back then I didn't understand how different my power was. But now I know that's why it happened. The killer was coming for me, not them. My parents died because of me. They died because my power is so different – maybe I'm even a new kind of person. I don't know."

"Maybe," he admitted. "I don't know either. You saved your sister, though, that has to count for something."

"I suppose. Jonas once said… do you know who they were? Can you tell me?"

"I don't know if I should," he said slowly, "but I will. The Inner Order isn't sure who they were, but I think you have a right to know what I've been told. They think that it was the CIA's magick office."

"The what?"

"Apparently the CIA has its own mages," he explained. "They think the assassin was CIA, and they think he was after your entire family – you, Rochelle, and both your parents."

"But because of me," she repeated.

"Probably," he admitted. "But they were also afraid Rochelle was just like you, another prodigy. And they were afraid that your parents would have another child with your abilities."

She sighed, closing her eyes. "I knew it," she said softly.

Michael put his arm around her. She stiffened defensively, but then relaxed and leaned her head on his shoulder, which was a little awkward because she was a few inches taller than him. "People hate and fear what they don't understand," he said carefully. "That's been true for so long that it's a cliché at best. And power like yours is dangerous in the wrong hands. Of course, to anybody else, the Guild is the wrong hands. But you didn't choose to be who you are. They chose for you."

"I wish I had chosen. Even if in the end it was the same."

"Would you really have chosen differently?" he asked. "Do you really hate who you are that much?"

She was quiet for a long time before responding. "Sometimes."

"When I first met Samantha and mentioned some of the things that you could do, do you know what she said?"

Elspeth shook her head.

"She said that she would do anything to be as good as you. Would you really have chosen differently, if it had been up to you? I know you. You wouldn't have. But that doesn't mean that everything what happened was your responsibility. You did the best you could, and you saved Rochelle. You just couldn't save them all, and you need to forgive yourself for that. Guilt can be strong and run deep, but I know you have the power to defeat it."

"I have the power to do anything," she said almost mockingly, her voice still weak. "I know. And sometimes it's such a big responsibility that I feel like whenever the world falls apart whatever happens is my fault. I know it isn't. I know it's silly. But it's been almost twenty years and I'm still not past it. What does that mean? What does that say about me?"

He shook his head. "I don't know, Elspeth. I wish I did."

She suddenly shook herself and stepped away from him. "Thank you, Michael," she said stiffly. "I think you have some idea how hard that is for me to say. Thank you for saving my life. I hope that someday I can return the favor. But right now I just have to get out of here."

Michael let her go, standing there and watching as she began a brisk walk down the lawn to Jim's waiting sport-utility. He hoped that social ineptness aside, his comments would prove helpful. Not being very good with people, though, he was never sure.

"You told her," said Jonas, coming up behind him.

159

"We have too many secrets," he replied curtly. "She deserved to know. Are you about to tell me how comprehensively I just violated the rules or something?"

"No," said Jonas. "I should have told her a long time ago. I was waiting for the right time, but I should have known better. There is no right time for something like that."

"No, there isn't," agreed Michael.

After a long, awkward pause, he spoke again. "On a completely different subject, Samantha and I need to go over what we found in Rochester. Are you going to be available tonight?"

"Certainly," replied the older mage. "Can you stop by after seven or so?"

Michael nodded. "I think so."

They looked on, watching as Elspeth departed. As she reached the truck, she quickly climbed in and slammed the door forcefully.

"Let's go," she said sharply as she dropped into the passenger seat.

"What was going on over there?" demanded Jim. "Are you still sweet on that loser Michael?"

She shot him a look of ice and contempt. "Just drive!"

IX. The Hermit

The Prophet of the Eternal: The Magus of the Voice of Power
The Sign Virgo

"So here is to an eventful journey," said Jonas, lifting a glass of wine that shone crimson in the flickering light of the fire. The sun had set, leaving the fire the room's only source of illumination.

"Indeed," replied Sofia, touching her own glass to his and returning his wry smile. As they drank, their eyes remained locked together. They sat in chairs on either side of the fireplace in Jonas' living room.

"I have not seen such disagreement on the Council in years," he commented, "though I realize that it was for good reason. I was not sure how you would vote, by the way. I thank you for supporting my side, as it were."

"No thanks are necessary," replied the Italian mage. "I voted as I saw fit. I suppose you knew how Michael was going to vote?"

Jonas nodded. "Believe me, if I had not, I would have moved to postpone the vote following your objection."

She laughed. "Ever the schemer."

"Coming from a Borgia," he noted, "that seems a trifle ironic."

"Well, that was a long time ago," she replied with a shrug. "There haven't been Popes in our bloodline for centuries. If there were, I suspect the Roman Catholic magical system would not be in such disarray today. After Vatican II, there was almost nothing left."

"I do not mean to pry," he said slowly, "but why did you vote as you did? You have always been a proponent of applying our rules by the letter."

"You know why," she replied forcefully. "Since my elevation to the Supreme Order, I have seen things differently than I once did. All true Masters do. The others are high-ranking

161

Adepts, but the Supreme Order is now down to you, Aleric, and myself. We weathered the twentieth century, but barely."

"I know," he said with a sigh. "And it is the current generation that must save us. All of them are precious, not to be squandered. We cannot fail for heirs."

"Especially one who will follow you as Guildmaster, as you will follow Aleric. You have foreseen that too, have you not?"

Jonas' face softened with recognition, and he nodded again. "But I fear for that future. I see two principle timelines. In one, Elspeth goes on as she has, seizes the reins of the Guild by force, and becomes a holy terror with the potential to consume the entire world. In the other, she changes course and becomes a powerful force for positive change. In both lines, she is Guildmaster, a true Master, one who and has attained all of the things we hope she will achieve. The difference is one of perspective."

"If she sees the world as sorrow, she will destroy it, and if she sees the world as joy, she will preserve it. In both cases, she will believe herself to be doing what is right."

"Yes," he agreed. "But what she needs to understand is that both of those perspectives are really one in the same. Then, and only then, will it be possible for her to move beyond them. Elspeth will not preserve the world. She has seen too much of it to believe it worth preserving in its current form. She will either destroy it completely or take humanity in a new and prosperous direction. And I hope that I am right in my belief that her first step down the right road happened at that Council meeting."

Sofia smiled ruefully. "She was shocked. She really expected that Michael would condemn her and you and Aleric would let him do it. That field she had going was impressive. She was getting ready to fight, wasn't she?"

Jonas took another sip of wine from his glass. "Had we attempted to destroy her," he said finally, "we might have lost two or three of the Council, and maybe Michael as well. It was a mistake for me to keep the information we have about the death of her parents from her. I had hoped to keep her saner by sparing her the pain, but I was foolish. I have seen her two possible futures from the time she was born, and I acted from fear. I feared what she might become, so I tried to insulate her from trauma. And, of course, in doing so, I made her what she is."

"You didn't know, though," countered Sofia. "Even mages like us are not omniscient."

"But I should have guessed," he insisted, shaking his head. "We knew about the government's magick program, we just did not think they had any mages of great power. Someone in their organization saw the same future that we did, and they acted. If you somehow knew that a child would become the next Mussolini, or even that there was a fifty-fifty chance of that happening, what would you do? You would kill the child, of course. And that's what they tried."

The Italian mage nodded. "And thus we lost two members of a generation that for the most part ignored our order. But it is not your fault. We can't foresee everything."

"That is a true thing," he agreed, his voice relaxing momentarily. "I need to keep it in mind."

"It's not that your perfectionism isn't appreciated," added Sofia, "but I sometimes worry that you take on too much responsibility for things that are genuinely out of your hands. Sometimes the future is poorly defined, like it is at this moment. Too many strands are coming together, and too many outcomes are possible."

The room seemed quiet for a long time before Jonas spoke again. "Have you performed any divinations regarding the situation in Rochester? As you say, the timelines are incredibly jumbled and confused there, and unlike the case of Elspeth's future, I can see nothing of consequence. That unnerves me."

"All I have seen are fragments there, nothing more. I have a sense that the one who opened the Abyss was not fully human, but still not fully an Archon or Demon. I don't know what that means."

"I have seen the same, and I fear that I do," he replied

reluctantly, "but I was hoping that I was wrong."

"What is it?" she pressed.

"Not what, who," he said softly. "Balzador. The former deputy of Coronzon, Lord of the Abyss. I found a brief mention of him in the notes of Robert Fludd. Apparently, the members of Fludd's circle were told by one of the Enochian spirits that when Balzador rebelled against Coronzon, he was not destroyed because the spirit of so powerful a demon is immortal and incorruptible. Instead, he was banished to the earth and forced by the power of Coronzon to inhabit a human body. Every time the body he inhabits dies, he reincarnates as human rather than returning to the Abyss. That would explain what both of us have seen, would it not? A being that is both human and demonic."

"It would, if the story is indeed true," she agreed with a sigh.

"Anna Sprengel's magical diaries actually mention encountering a being who claimed to be Balzador in the early part of the nineteenth century. He was trying to gather a circle of followers and came up against the Guild. She defeated him by calling down the magick of the Archons, and his body was destroyed. Of course, if Fludd's account is accurate, Balzador simply would have been reborn elsewhere in the world to cause more chaos once he grew to maturity. At the time, Anna did not have access to Fludd's notes, so she would not have known. She probably just assumed the poor man was possessed in the usual way. But from that interaction Balzador would have learned of the Guild."

"And he would understand that if he ever wanted to build a circle of followers he would have to destroy us," added Sofia. "Do you think that is what he is planning?"

"That is a possible motive, but a few pieces still don't fit. Why would he open the Abyss and summon Coronzon, who cursed him in the first place? Why would he sacrifice his only followers to do it if he planned on building his own circle? Mages are hard to come by, and are not expendable."

164

"Indeed," she said thoughtfully. "What if he had found a way to bind Coronzon? We both know that it is possible, in theory anyway, and it would be a perfect form of revenge. But then, if he had bound the Lord of the Abyss, why would he remain here? With access to the Dark Lord's powers, he could release himself from the curse that binds him to Earth. And he must still be here – otherwise, we would have found his body up on that hill as well. Could he have made an attempt to bind Coronzon that failed?"

"It remains a mystery. Michael and Samantha will be arriving soon to discuss what they found in Rochester, though judging from the phone call I received yesterday and my own sense of the situation, I doubt that they found much."

"Ah, yes," said Sofia with a glint in her eye. "Samantha. So you finally managed to bring her in."

"Of course," Jonas replied with a satisfied smile. "I have always managed to get my way in the Guild, even though it sometimes takes a while. Fortunately, I am patient. It tempers my innate stubbornness."

She returned his smile. "Do you think she and Michael will start a new great family, then?"

He shook his head. "It is too early to tell, but perhaps. They certainly seem to enjoy spending time together. I must admit, a new great family would be an intriguing development, especially considering that both of them are essentially natural talents. Their genetic mix is likely quite different from that of any of the other families, who are all somewhat intertwined, and that could help us immeasurably in the years to come."

"Michael is certainly more stable than most in the great families," she continued, "and from the scrying I've done I would have to say Samantha is as well. I sometimes wonder if we could be running into the same problem that European nobility encountered during the Renaissance. We have managed to heighten the magical aptitude trait we value, but every generation seems less psychologically grounded than the one before it. We may need an infusion of new blood into the lines even more than we think.

165

Imagining all of Elspeth's traits heightened further is not a pretty thought."

"No," agreed Jonas. "It is not. Elspeth has been difficult enough to teach, even though she has more talent than any mage I have ever encountered. She is too stubborn and too sure of herself to learn many of our techniques, particularly those related to balancing the psyche."

"I can imagine," she replied with a nod. "She's not a pupil I would relish having to train. I am amazed that you have done as well as you have, even given what has happened. I would have expected something similar sooner with any other instructor."

"Well, I am glad that you think so well of me, my dear. Naturally, I wish my teaching had been good enough to keep it from happening at all, but maybe you are right in your assessment. I suspect I will have to meditate on the incident for some time."

The silence in the room lingered before Sophia spoke again. "When are Michael and Samantha arriving?"

"Any time now. I should get us some more wine." Jonas slowly rose to his feet and left the room through the swinging wooden door leading into the kitchen.

Just then, the doorbell rang.

Sofia, who Michael had not expected to see, answered the door. "It's good to see you again, Michael," she said with her usual winning smile as she ushered them into the living room.

"It's good to see you too," he replied. "This is Samantha Davis. Samantha, this is Sofia Borgia, Master of Italy."

"Pleased to meet you," said Samantha, shaking hands with the older mage.

"I remember you, you know," said Sofia as the three of them sat down in the living room to wait for Jonas. "We have never met, but fifteen years ago I spent a lot of time watching both you and Michael via scrying. So Jonas finally managed to bring you in, did he?"

"I suppose so."

"It is not surprising, really. Once he sets his mind on

something he rarely fails."

"Singing my praises, Sofia?" asked Jonas playfully as he entered the room with a freshly opened bottle of Merlot.

"No," she replied, "I am telling them just how stubborn you are when you set your mind on something."

"That is true," he agreed, sitting back down in his favorite chair and handing the bottle to Sofia. "Persistence and determination alone are omnipotent. Would either of you care for some wine?"

Michael and Samantha both nodded, and the Italian mage filled two more glasses.

"So what can you tell us about what you found in Rochester?" asked Jonas.

"Several things," began Michael, taking a sip of the red wine that glinted like garnet in the soft light. "First of all, the victims were killed by magick. By that, I mean directly killed, using what must be some kind of attack spell. It looks like it works by separating the body and spirit, though how that would work I have no idea. The spell is general enough to kill off the bacteria within the body, so it's pretty thorough. I was able to see an image of the caster, but it didn't look very convincing to the sketch artist – too generic, really, like it wasn't a real person."

"A projection?" asked Sofia.

"Maybe by somebody really good. It didn't feel like one, though."

"I suppose someone who could cast a death spell reliably would have to be in the 'really good' category," said Jonas thoughtfully. "But continue."

"The victims were definitely sacrificed as far as I can tell, and what you sensed was almost certainly the opening of the Abyss. We went out to the area, but it was blocked so I couldn't use psychometry there – another really good magick trick. That means whoever did it expected mages to sense the energy surge and come looking there, and I can only think of one being that would require twelve victims."

"Coronzon," said Jonas.

167

"Yes," replied Michael with a nod. "What we have is a powerful mage who gathered a group of followers only to sacrifice them in order to summon the Lord of the Abyss."

"Did you find out anything about the victims?" asked Sofia.

"Not much," said Samantha. "It seems like they were a group of low-power mages who were looking for training or guidance. They just ran into the wrong teacher."

"I have a theory concerning the identity of our killer," said Jonas. "It is consistent with my own divinations and with Sofia's, and while I'm not sure that I understand the motive just yet, I believe that we are dealing with a very dangerous adversary – the demon Balzador."

"Balzador?" asked Samantha blankly.

"Balzador," said Michael. "A renegade demon. The legend goes that he challenged Coronzon for rulership of the Abyss and was defeated over a thousand years ago. But how is that possible? The person I saw in the vision was a human being, I'm sure of it. Demons don't have physical forms."

"He clearly has managed to obtain a body," replied Jonas.

"So this guy is possessed?" asked Michael.

"That is possible, though my researches have uncovered another possibility, and it is much worse. Based on accounts going back several centuries, I believe that Balzador was not destroyed when he challenged Coronzon's throne. Instead, he was banished to earth and forced into human form. Because demons are discarnate and thus without physical bodies, he was held here by what is essentially a curse that forces him to occupy a human body. He is thus reincarnated through the centuries as his host bodies age and die, like some sort of spiritual parasite. Apparently Anna Sprengel defeated him once back in the early nineteenth century, and according to her he had access to demon magick at a much higher level than any human."

"You're sure of this?" asked Michael. "I have to admit, it sounds a little far-fetched to me."

"I don't know about that," said Samantha. "Let's say you're the Dark Lord and you've just defeated a rival who tried to claim your throne. What would you do to your enemy?"

"Destroy him," said Michael immediately.

"That is impossible," countered Jonas. "Demons are immortal. They cannot truly be destroyed. Even when a demon's form is disrupted its spirit returns to the Abyss. Its power is greatly depleted for centuries, but it still exists."

"Well, I'd get rid of him somehow, then," amended Michael. "I wouldn't want him to give others ideas. Demons are only ruled by fear."

"And where would you put him?" pressed Samantha. "Why not here, on Earth? If Balzador were forced to inhabit a human body, it would essentially trap him. That would get him out of the way once and for all. In that light, it makes perfect sense."

"I suppose so," agreed Michael. "But if that's the case, what does he want?"

"Probably to destroy the Guild so that he can gather mages around him without interference," replied Jonas. "Given his history, I suspect he seeks power, and certainly establishing himself as some kind of spiritual leader would allow him to acquire a great deal of it. He certainly has the magick to do it."

"So we have to stop him before he can kill us all. Great. Any ideas how to do that?" asked Michael.

"No good ones," answered Jonas. "There are various ways to bind a demon, and one of them might work. The problem is that I do not know enough about how human and demonic magick interact. I also do not know if disrupting his form is likely to work. Normally that would send him back to the Abyss, except if he really is banished I have no idea what the result of that would be. He might just jump to a new body."

"Mind you," added Sofia, "if I were confronted with him I would still try it."

"I wonder if he can take over an adult body, or if he's forced to start over – you know, reincarnate as a baby," mused

Samantha. "If he has to grow up again that would give us some time."

"If Anna was able to apparently destroy him, that probably is the case," said Michael, "but then again, maybe he decided that attacking the Guild after being 'destroyed' would give him away or something like that."

"That could be," agreed Jonas, "demons are clever creatures, and Balzador is one of the most cunning of his kind if the old grimoires are to be believed. Perhaps he thought he had the strength then but was wrong, and has been biding his time ever since. If that is the case, something must have given him greater power or greater knowledge – some kind of edge that he thinks he can exploit."

"Unless, of course, that edge is our order's own weakness," said Sofia thoughtfully.

"What do you mean?" asked Samantha, surprised.

"She means that the Guild was once much larger than it is today," replied Michael. "Our golden age was over a century ago. Today our members are stronger individually, like Elspeth, but there are far fewer of us."

"Our order flourished along with other fraternal organizations in Victorian America," explained Jonas. "The sheer popularity of lodge work and fraternal ties was one of the factors that prompted our expansion into the United States around the turn of the last century. The Twin Cities has the highest concentration of Guild mages that you will find in any American city, and there are only seven of us here – counting you, Samantha. In Europe, the order is even smaller. We have only a hundred or so members worldwide, only a handful of whom have never reached the Inner Order, in fact – and before the Second World War that membership was in the thousands. The holocaust practically wiped out everyone in Europe, since the fascist governments of the axis powers had no interest in spiritual power that they did not control. Sofia nearly wound up in an internment camp herself."

"Fortunately, I managed to get out of the country before

170

that order could be carried out," added Sofia. "I spent most of the war here in the United States, where I got to know Jonas, and only went back to Italy after the allied victory. That's also why my English is so good, by the way. Most of the others in Italy felt that their powers could protect them, that somehow they would be able to hide or even use their magical abilities to bring down the fascists. They stayed and they died. Magick might stop a single gun some of the time, but it won't stop a firing squad."

"At any rate," said Jonas softly, "in Anna's time the order was strong and today it is weak. That may be just the situation our demon friend has been waiting for all these years. He may believe that we lack the strength to stop him, and this time he might be right."

"I didn't realize..." said Samantha, her voice trailing off.

"You are surprised that we lack numbers?" asked Jonas, his smile returning to warm his features. "Only fifteen years ago the council was still dominated by those who believed that new blood was the last thing our order needed. *That* is what I find so surprising, and to some extent humorous, despite the seriousness of the situation with which we are now faced. The fact is that you should have been recruited as a member yourself, Samantha, and you would have been had the Council seen things my way. We should have found others at that time too, even if they lacked your level of innate power."

"It just seems so staggeringly shortsighted," replied Samantha. "Clearly your 'great families' aren't viable, no matter how much wealth and genetic aptitude they can build up. If individual ability can't make up for the combined power of numbers, it seems obvious that you would *need* new members all the time to avoid being stuck in the current situation. I mean, with so few mages, is there anything you – I should really say we – can do?"

"Of course," said Jonas calmly. "Bear in mind that Sofia, Aleric, and myself should all be capable of dispelling a demon, even if all that means is that he jumps to the body of an unborn child. As you say, Samantha, that will give us time, so the situation

171

is not entirely grim. Another twenty years or so and we should be able to find those we need to rebuild our membership. At least, that would be my hope."

"But won't we need to find Balzador in order to stop him?" asked Michael.

"I doubt it," replied Jonas gravely. "In order to destroy the Guild, he will have to come to us. So be ready."

X. Fortune

The Lord of the Forces of Life
The Planet Jupiter

"So he's on his way?" asked Jim, seated in his usual spot on the antique sofa in Elspeth's parlor.

"That's what he said," she replied. She had called the number on the card over an hour ago, and Balzador had called back twenty minutes later. He claimed that he was on his way, though he did not say from where. The printouts of <u>Liber Iadnamad</u> and a copy of the disk on which the files were stored sat in a manila folder on the mahogany coffee table. "You know, I feel weird about this."

"What do you mean, weird?" he demanded. "It makes perfect sense to me. Why not make a deal that will secure your advancement as a magician?"

"It's just that I thought they were going to kill me, you know? And now they aren't. It makes the situation different."

"The hell it does," he replied. "They've barred you from their Inner Order. I know that you want in. You said yourself that the Supreme Council has never reversed a 5-2 decision. After the Morpheus thing, they're never going to trust you."

"I know, I know," she said with a sigh. "I just feel bad about turning on them."

"They turned on you, as I recall," he corrected. "Or is this about turning on Michael? I saw the two of you the other day, remember?"

"What about it?" she snapped, her eyes like flames. "You know, Michael is not the loser you seem to think he is, whatever happened between us. Are you so insecure and jealous you can't tolerate us getting along? I'm with you now, remember?"

"All I'm saying is that you've come this far," he said, softening his tone. "You can't change your mind now. Don't sell yourself short because you're feeling guilty. That's a big waste of time. Soon this'll all be over and you'll be a master or whatever you call it. And then you won't have to worry about what any of your would-be peers think. You'll be above them all, which is as it should be."

"I suppose you're right," she admitted, "but it's still hard for me. The Guild is like my family. I've barely known anyone else my whole life. I suppose it doesn't really matter, though. I mean, why would they care whether Balzador or Coronzon is lord of the Abyss? The only one it really affects is me, once I can cross over."

"Exactly," he agreed. "So it makes sense and you shouldn't feel bad. End of story."

She shook her head. "I just can't shake the feeling that doing this is really *wrong*. You know me. I didn't feel that way about blasting Michael at the club, or anything else I've done, really. I'm so tempted to just draw this thing and take him out when he walks in the door." Her hand clutched the enchanted dagger that she still wore at her belt.

"Do that and you'll never advance," Jim said bluntly. "Balzador's your only chance, unless you want to find another order. Maybe you could bargain with another group for the book or something, but you would still lose access to the knowledge of the older Guild mages and you would still have to try the crossing on your own, right? At least, that's what it sounds like from what you've told me."

"That's true," she agreed. "And you're right. I think I'm just nervous."

The chimes of the doorbell rang a few minutes later. Elspeth got up from the sofa, walked across the entry hall to the front door, and was greeted by Balzador's smiling face as she opened it. "So you have the book," he said without inflection. "Excellent."

"There are still a few matters I want to discuss concerning our arrangement," she said quickly. "Can you accompany me to the study?"

"As you wish," he replied agreeably. He followed her down the hall that led to the study, the room in which they had struck their original bargain. Elspeth again seated herself behind the antique desk and Balzador planted himself in one of the opposing chairs. "What is it you wish to discuss?" he asked politely.

"My crossing of the Abyss," she replied. "How do I know that you'll keep your word? I know demons are not usually that trustworthy, and I want some assurances that once you've conquered the Abyss that I will indeed be allowed to cross safely."

"Obviously, some of that depends on my success against Coronzon," he said matter-of-factly, "since if I fail in my bid for conquest all of this will be in vain. However, I think I may be able to offer you some assurance if we accept my victory as a foregone conclusion. This is not far from the truth, for once I have the spells contained in <u>Liber Iadnamad</u> I will have access to magick far greater than that of the Dark Lord."

"What sort of assurance?" she pressed.

"This," he replied, holding up a small crystal talisman. "It is tuned to the energy of my aura. Feel free to verify this for yourself." He set the crystal in her waiting hand.

Clearing her mind, she projected it into the crystal. Its energy certainly felt like the aura that surrounded the demon, and projecting further, she felt the magical link to his field. Satisfied that he spoke the truth, she opened her eyes. "So this gets me exactly what?" she asked.

"That is your ticket across the Abyss. Once I am the Dark Lord and Coronzon is vanquished, hold it in your hand when you attempt your crossing. The field it sends forth will convince the guardians there that you and I are the same being. If they attempt to oppose you, command them to let you pass, and they will obey. Is that enough assurance for you?"

"I suppose so," she agreed. Magically, it made sense. Even if he was being untruthful about the guardians obeying the bearer of the crystal, it would not be difficult for her to synchronize her aura with that of the crystal and complete the crossing that way. According to everything she had been taught he was correct – the denizens of the Abyss obeyed whoever was the reigning Dark Lord, and she now had a way to assume the appearance of such temporarily. "How long will it take you to perform the ritual that will allow you to conquer the Abyss?"

"Probably no more than a few days. The ley lines are beginning to align themselves as we speak."

"I thought ley lines were part of the earth," she said skeptically. "How can they move?"

"Your order has taught you poorly if that's what you've learned," replied the demon. "As above, so below. As matter moves, so does spiritual energy. The Twin Cities are in many ways an ideal site in terms of available energy. They are positioned at the confluence of the major water ley on this continent, the Mississippi River, and the major air ley, the jet stream. On the banks of the Mississippi, with the jet stream overhead, the energy is as strong as I am likely to find anywhere in North America. That will make the ritual possible here, which is one of the reasons I am still in this city. Now, may I have the book?"

"Yes," she answered after a long, awkward pause, pocketing the crystal. She rose from the desk and led him back down the hallway to the parlor, where Jim waited on the sofa. She picked up the manila folder and handed it to the demon, who smiled and nodded politely.

"Thank you very much," he said as he tucked the folder under his arm and stepped into the entry hall. "I will see you again soon, Elspeth Sprengel, on the other side."

She closed and locked the door, and then returned to the parlor. "So it's done," she said with a sigh as she sat down on the sofa.

"Do you feel better?" asked Jim.

"Not really," she admitted. "It still feels weird. But there's nothing I can do about it now."

"So he convinced you he was being truthful?"

"Not exactly," she replied, "but he gave me a crystal enchanted with his aura. When he becomes the Dark Lord, I'll be able to use it to get across unless for some reason he can unlink from it. There's no reason for him to do that, since it's nothing to him whether I cross or not. So I've done it – I'll be able to keep developing my power with or without the Guild's approval. I just thought it would feel better, that's all."

He put his arm around her. "You just never know," he said reassuringly. "See how you feel once you've crossed the Abyss and this whole thing is behind you. I'll bet you'll feel a whole lot better."

She leaned her head on his shoulder. "I sure hope so."

Balzador stepped into his waiting Audi sedan and backed out of the driveway. Cars were simply annoying; although they were an immense improvement over the horse, he had never stopped wishing that teleportation worked on this side of the veil. If his calculations were right, the moment at which he could begin the rite that would summon all the magick of the world and bind it to his command was only two nights away. As he pulled out onto the street, he possessively patted the folder he had tossed onto the passenger seat. Before he could proceed, he would need to familiarize himself with its contents quickly.

It was ironic, really, he mused as he drove off into the night, that after being trapped for thousands of years on earth moving through lifetime after lifetime, his liberation still seemed far off. His anticipation of the moment slowed time to a crawl, which he found incredibly irritating. He suspected that his demonic consciousness, accustomed to the easy ebb and flow of time in the Abyss, was more bothered by this phenomenon than were humans, though never having truly been one of them, he doubted he would ever know.

Now the Guild was weak.

He had not even know of their order a century and a half ago, when the late Anna Sprengel and her circle had appeared out of nowhere to stop his bid to make himself the living god of this miserable world. At the time, he knew too little of the nature of magick to have any greater aspirations, and had resigned himself to a life on earth that would last until Coronzon needed him again, perhaps in a new offensive against the Archons that required his power. It was true that becoming god of the earth was not that impressive all things considered, but like most demons he enjoyed luxuries in addition to power and figured that a living god would be invited to all the best parties. Everything had been prepared – a new theology, a new political structure, a new social order, all backed up by the 'miracles' that his demonic powers made possible – and then, on the last day before his apocalypse, he had come face to face with Anna and the Supreme Council of the Guild, who destroyed his physical body and ended his incarnation.

It gave him great joy to know that it was Anna's own great-granddaughter who had provided him with the means to tame the force that the Guild had labored for centuries to master, and would thus be the order's undoing. He had thought it through this time, studied the Guild, and had waited patiently as its members had died off through the twentieth century. Still, there was always the possibility that something could go wrong, and after planning for almost a hundred years, he knew that he needed to be cautious. The weapon that never left his side was his insurance – a nonmetallic Glock pistol with a polycarbonate barrel. Not only had the twentieth century depleted most of the Guild's strength, it also had provided him with plastic, a material completely resistant to magick. Demon-killing spells only worked on line of sight, and then at short distances. As long as he had time to draw the gun, no magician in the world without body armor could stop him.

As he crossed the Mississippi River on Interstate 94, he reached out with his mind to feel the water energy pulsing through the ley. The melting snow had pushed the river close to flood stage and power raced along its banks. He could not feel the energy of the jet stream just yet, but he knew from the weather charts it was about a hundred miles north, between the Twin Cities and Duluth, and slowly shifting southward. As it moved within range, the field would intensify like an electric current, amplifying his magick to the point where he could bind the energies of the world. He had to begin studying the rites of Liber Iadnamad immediately, though this was easier for him because being a demon, he could

178

go without sleep for days if necessary. Once he regained his true form, he would not need to make it up, either – the need for sleep was merely a consequence of being bound into a human body.

He left the freeway at the Huron Avenue exit, headed north, and then turned right and merged onto University Avenue, the street on which he currently lived. Passing businesses and restaurants, he finally turned into the driveway of the house he had been renting for the past five years. He had come to Minneapolis in search of the Guild's seat of power – the Twin Cities were one of the last metropolitan areas in the United States that had more than two or three members, and of course were home to the reigning Guildmaster and his likely successor, Jonas Votan. Turning off the car, he gingerly scooped up the manila folder and headed into the house.

The place was practically devoid of furniture and seemed barely inhabited. A brand new computer sat on a cheap desk against one wall of the living room next to a reclining chair facing a huge plasma television set. Like most demons, Balzador found human beings fascinating, and as such he spent many hours in front of the best television he could afford watching their antics. It was not so much that he couldn't afford luxuries if he wanted them – his money had been compounded for centuries and had grown to an unbelievable sum – but it was just that he did not care. As otherworldly creatures furnished their abodes by molding the stuff of the astral plane into the things they desired, and only the things they desired, everything in the house served his will. Anything that did not was dispensed with quickly and without regret.

The dining room did have a table, but only one chair. Like most demons, he never entertained. Stopping to take the floppy disk from the folder and set it next to the computer, he then seated himself at the table and spread out the copied pages of Liber Iadnamad before him and began to take in the information as quickly as he could. The modality of the magick was unfamiliar and would require some adaptation – Dee and Kelly had contacted agents of the Archons, and the magick of light would need to

179

be attuned to his nature for his demonic powers to work with it. Fortunately, the modular construction of the rituals made this a relatively simple prospect. He could do this in two days without difficulty. He had hoped it would be such, but had not been sure without seeing the text. Sure enough, one more potential obstacle that he didn't need to worry about.

He rose to his feet and walked into the kitchen, where he poured himself a cup of cold coffee and put it in the microwave. Coffee was one of things he would miss when he was back in the Abyss, though he supposed once he held Coronzon's throne he could conjure some up whenever he wanted. Once the microwave beeped, he took out the hot cup and sipped at his beloved nectar of the gods. He then returned to his studies, setting the cup down next to him as he worked through the next section of the Guild's grimoire. In another day, he would be ready. The day after that, he would bind the magick of the world to his will, rendering the Guild powerless. Finally, at the next new moon, he would summon Coronzon, make good on his deal, and once he was returned to the Abyss he would wait for the right moment to strike down the Dark Lord and ascend to his throne. Finally, wielding the combined power of magick and darkness like a nuclear weapon, he would move against the minions of the Most High, the hated Archons, and with their defeat plunge the multiverse into greater chaos than anything it had ever witnessed.

As he sipped and pondered, he looked upon his vision of the future, and beheld its beauty. Soon the world, and eventually all worlds everywhere, would be his.

00. Interlude
Ain Soph – No Limit

At night, the public telephone adjacent to the park services building on Lake Calhoun was shrouded in shadows cast by the looming structure itself and the ancient trees that lined Lake Street and the parkway. Off on its own and outside the warm glow of the circle of lights that lined the lake, the phone was rarely used after sunset. This night, though, an unusually indistinct figure stepped from the lit path along the parkway and gingerly picked up the receiver. It was not only the low light that hid the man's features, but a murky cloud of what could only be some sort of magical concealment that made observing eyes simply slide past him without taking notice of any details. The man dialed a long series of numbers, a telephone number along with some sort of code, and waited while the phone on the other end rang.

"Johnston Institute," said a woman's sunny lilt on the other end.

The man rolled his eyes involuntarily. "Dr. Johnston, please," he said in a low, indistinct voice.

"Just a moment," replied the receptionist with practiced inflection. The man waited impatiently as she transferred the call, irritated by the bouncy, upbeat elevator music that for some reason was considered soothing by the psychiatric community. In his experience, after listening to the stuff for hours many otherwise normal people found themselves ready to take a hatchet to innocent bystanders.

"Hello?" said a deep voice as the call was picked up. "This is Johnston."

"This is Stargazer reporting in," said the man softly. "The code is bravo alpha nebula twenty-seven nexus."

"The sky is clear tonight," began the voice warily.

"The northern lights are blazing," said Stargazer. "Good evening, Dr. Johnston."

"Good evening. Is there a reason you're using a public

181

phone? Even with the codes and so forth that always makes me suspicious."

"I'm just being extra careful on my end. It's always possible that my cell phone records could be compromised. As you know, the group you assigned me to infiltrate has impressive financial resources, not to mention contacts in law enforcement."

Johnston's tone became more relaxed. "What do you have to report?" he asked with bureaucratic precision. Clearly, he was getting ready to take notes.

"A great deal," replied Stargazer with a hint of arrogant pride. "As you instructed, I have infiltrated the Guild and become close to one of its members. As we suspected, their knowledge of practical magick is extensive. Apparently, much of that knowledge comes from a grimoire called <u>Liber Iadnamad</u>, which is attributed to John Dee, the English Renaissance magician. It contains a sort of key to the working of Enochian magick that the Guild uses to construct and execute its rituals. "

"Our scholars have suspected for several years that something of the sort must exist, since Dee lived for such a long time and his diaries are so fragmentary," commented the psychiatrist. "This is excellent – if we can learn the secrets of this grimoire we will have something more to offer our country in warfare besides remote viewing and good-luck spells. It couldn't have come at a better time."

Stargazer sounded confused. "How so?"

"The CIA is reviewing funding of the magick office within the next few weeks," explained Johnston. "While some of our superiors recognize the value of our work, others feel it is a waste of time and resources. The same people who closed the remote viewing project are doing everything they can to shut us down, but if we can show them concrete proof of the effectiveness of magick, I believe that they can be convinced to support our funding. Most of them oppose us simply because they do not believe that magick exists."

"That's not surprising given the skeptic groups out there

and their exposure to the media. You would think that after the documented success of the remote viewing program there would be enough data to support our budget," remarked Stargazer. "Then again, it is the government. Data doesn't mean much to them if they have a political agenda."

"It would help if the real success rate could be released," added Johnston. "It also would help if the budget analysts were cleared for that level of security. But a demonstration of a successful magical effect could go a long way toward convincing them of its usefulness. Do you know where copies of these grimoires are kept?"

"Every member of the Guild above a certain rank has a copy. I have their addresses."

"Wonderful!" The psychiatrist's voice sounded positively enthused. "We can send out a team to pick one of them up. What about new recruits? Have you identified any potential agents?"

The man's voice darkened. "No, unfortunately. Elspeth Sprengel was a possibility, but the Guild has decided to let her live. That limits my bargaining power."

"They kill their own members?" Johnston sounded positively shocked. "What on earth for?"

"The nightclub explosion in Minneapolis last week. She caused it by magick. They have strict rules about using magick against people they consider innocent and using it in ways that will reveal their level of ability to the public at large."

Now he just sounded nervous. "She used magick to destroy a building?"

"She's very powerful, way beyond anyone we have. She's also overly emotional and easy to manipulate, so she would be perfect for the program. However, if she's not afraid of the Guild's justice, I doubt I can manipulate her into betraying her order."

"A pity. Is she the only one you are tracking?"

"No, but she was the best prospect. Members of the Guild are surprisingly loyal, though much of that is because its membership tends to run in families."

Johnston sighed. "I suspected it would be that way. All of our research on magical aptitude and heredity indicates that the only way to create really powerful mages is by selective breeding. There are just too many different genes and characteristics involved for such ability to manifest itself by chance very often. By creating an insular social group made up of interlocking bloodlines, though, you can magnify the appropriate traits as long as you're willing to risk a few throwbacks."

"Throwbacks?"

"Genetics can be pretty can be unpredictable," replied the psychiatrist. "For example, I take it Elspeth's sister is the same as ever – no sudden flashes of superior ability?"

"She has a fair amount of talent, but I would rate her at about medium strength for the Guild. That, of course, means that she is far beyond anyone in the general population, but she is nothing like Elspeth."

The line was silent for a moment before Johnston continued. "I suppose the point could be made that their third child might have been another prodigy, but I suspect now that Elspeth is an aberration, more an accident than a carefully planned superhuman." Finally, he asked, "Well, do you have anything else to report?"

"Unfortunately, yes," replied Stargazer. "There's a new complication that we have to deal with. Balzador is here."

"*The* Balzador?" demanded Johnston, incredulous. "The demon that lost the battle for the Abyss to Coronzon?"

"Yes – at least someone who thinks he's *the* Balzador. I believe he may have been responsible for those murders outside Rochester. I don't have proof yet, but it wouldn't surprise me. It's the sort of thing someone who identified themselves with a demon would do."

"And here I thought we might finally have a real Satanic Cult on our hands. I mean, you would think that after looking for over twenty years we'd be able to find *one* besides that silly Church of Satan. Have you witnessed his presence yourself?"

184

"Well, yes and no. I have seen his human form. He felt like a normal person to me, but he seems to have convinced Elspeth and that's difficult to do. Conveniently, the legends don't really mention what happened to him after his defeat. He told Elspeth he had been banished to this world, which is a pretty common explanation given by the delusional people I've interviewed. "

"Interesting," mused the psychiatrist. "I would surmise that to be convincing he would have to be extremely powerful, like one would expect a mythological creature in human form to be. Did you see any evidence of this?"

"No, but Elspeth believes it. She's pretty hard to convince that anything is more powerful than she is, and she pretty much indicated that to me. If that's true, he would make a valuable subject for research."

"So what is he supposedly doing here, now? And why deal with Elspeth?"

"I suspect it's for the same reason we wanted to. She's powerful and easily manipulated. He convinced her to make a copy of Liber Iadnamad for him, and she delivered it to him tonight. Of course, a real demon wouldn't need her to steal a book for him given his enhanced powers, unless there must have been some reason he couldn't do it himself, so that makes me doubt he's for real right there."

"A demon might have some additional weaknesses that offset his powers. Vulnerability to wards, perhaps, or something of the sort. Humans don't have that kind of susceptibility."

"I suppose that could be," agreed the figure. "Anyway, it occurs to me that in the confusion we might be able to obtain a copy of the book, either the one that our would-be Balzador has or yet another copy that we could steal off of Elspeth's computer – she made digital photos of each page. As for our demon, we can deal with him once we've secured the grimoire."

"I like the way you think," replied Johnston. "Very well, do it. Get a copy of the book, and once you have it bring it back here. Then we can examine it in greater detail."

"I would rather have a strike team here in the Twin Cities, if we can manage it. Clearly Balzador is dangerous if he is indeed behind the murders in Rochester, and if he truly identifies with a Minion of Evil he's likely to be extremely unpredictable."

"Make sure there's no bloodshed. I want him contained, not killed," said Johnston firmly. "I can get you a good strike team and anyone who can successfully impersonate a demon has the potential to be a powerful tool," he added quickly. "A real demon would be even better, and though I doubt that we have the capability to trap or use it in the long term, we might be able to do so for a short period of time, long enough to do some serious research into its nature."

"Considering that we've never encountered an actual demon, I think that possibility is pretty remote," countered Stargazer. "We're almost certainly dealing with a powerful but insane individual – but that also makes him a worthwhile target. If his powers are indeed enough to impress Elspeth, I think a demonstration should be possible and I know we've wanted something really impressive to show Congress for some time to justify our budget. I'll see what I can do. Can you have the strike team standing ready? I'll probably need them, especially if you want this 'Balzador' captured."

"Of course. They can be in the Twin Cities in three days. Will that suffice?"

"It should. Meanwhile, I'll see what I can do about getting a copy of the book off Elspeth's computer. I'll talk to you again soon."

Stargazer hung up the phone and walked back toward the path. As he approached the lights, he made a subdued gesture with his right hand and the magical concealment lifted and changed, shifting the air and then fading away into nothingness like a silk veil cast aside. Dressed impeccably in his preppy best, it was Jim who stepped out onto the path and continued on his walk around the lake.

Later, back in Elspeth's parlor, Jim opened the leather briefcase he had carried in from his SUV when he arrived. From the case, he took a compact notebook computer, which he set up on the coffee table and booted. Taking the disk from the manila folder, he placed it in the floppy drive and began making a copy onto the hard disk. Once the copy was complete, he replaced the disk in the folder, shut down the computer, and returned it to the briefcase. Focusing his will, he traced a sigil over the folder and the briefcase to hide any trace of what he had done from future scrying.

"I didn't hear you get up," said a voice from the stairs.

Jim turned with a start. Elspeth stood on the stairs dressed in her long blue nightgown. Her voice was still sleepy and her hair was messy and tangled. "I went for a walk," Jim said quickly, his voice not missing a beat. "I couldn't sleep."

"I know the feeling," she replied as she slowly walked down the stairs. "Do you really think we did the right thing? My dreams are chaotic and confused. You sounded so sure before, but are you having second thoughts now, too?"

He rose to his feet and crossed the room, his face sinking into its usual reassuring smile. "Of course not, darling," he said, taking her in his arms. "As I said, it's like anything – if you want to accomplish something you have to do it yourself, and you have to make it happen."

"I just... I know that sometimes I seem like I really know what I want and what I have to do to get it, but there's always this part of me that wonders if I'm really good enough, or if what seems like the smartest thing in the world to me really is. I try not to think too hard, to go with what the universe seems to be telling me... I don't know that Michael ever really understood that, and I think that's why I'm with you. Does that make any sense?"

"Of course it does," he replied, his voice measured and soothing. "I can't imagine the responsibility of being the most powerful mage in the world. Don't get me wrong, being as powerful as you are sounds great until you think it through. But then you wonder – if you see a situation and decide not to take action when you have the ability, is the outcome your fault? What if you try to fix something and you do it wrong? I can see where you would be worried all the time and be scared that you might not live up to everyone's expectations."

"And this whole situation just makes everything worse. It's gone way beyond anything I could predict. The club, Balzador, Liber Iadnamad... I sure hope I made the right decision, because there are a lot of ways this could go very wrong." She fingered Balzador's crystal nervously.

"But it won't," he said, his voice ringing with absolute assurance. "When you're on top of the world you'll look back at tonight and it will seem like the smartest thing you ever did. Trust me."

Elspeth held him tighter. "Then let's go to bed," she said softly. She turned and led him by the hand back up the long stairway.

XI. Lust, or Strength

The Daughter of the Flaming Sword
The Sign Leo

The next morning, Samantha was surprised to find Daria knocking on her door at a half hour past sunrise. While she and her teacher communicated often by phone and e-mail they only rarely met in person, at most every few months. Daria always seemed to give off an aura of what could only described as neatness, facilitated by both her conservative but excellent fashion sense and some sort of spell that never failed to put regular people at ease. She was dressed simply in black slacks, a medium blue sweater, and a light jacket well suited to the weather, all of which matched perfectly and complement her short dark hair and light blue eyes. Her timing was also perfect, arriving just as Samantha was getting up from her regular morning meditation.

"Good morning," Samantha said brightly as she showed her teacher into her living room. "What brings you here, Daria? Trying to make sure I don't go back to bed?" She sat down on the large black leather sofa lining the south wall opposite the door, and gestured for her instructor to do the same.

Daria smiled as she sat down. "Just checking up on you. The magical field over the Twin Cities shifted again last night. It's like watching a game of chess when you can only see a few of the pieces, but I can feel movement toward some sort of conclusion. Since I don't know what that conclusion might be, I am naturally worried. What have you found out?"

"Well, I would have called you last night if I had gotten back earlier, but I think I know at least part of it. Do any of our order's teachings concern the demon Balzador?"

Daria looked thoughtful. "I can't say that I've ever heard the name," she replied slowly, "but then, I'm not really an expert demonologist and I'm not sure if I know of anyone who might qualify in that area. As you know, aside from Goetic and Abramelin demons, it really is a subject beyond our studies. I can tell you that

189

the name Balzador is not found in either grimoire but not much beyond that. Why do you ask?"

"I told you about my dream, right? The one I think had to do with the murders in Rochester? It was in the most recent chapter I sent you of my magical journal."

"The one with the forest and the hill and the rival magician?"

"Yes. Only I don't think it was a rival magician. I think it was a demon named Balzador who has taken human form and is trying to destroy the Guild. Apparently he's been on Earth a long time and tried the same thing a hundred years ago. Every time his body dies he reincarnates as his full demonic self, and now that the Guild is a lot smaller than it was during the last century, he's making a move now."

She considered thoughtfully. "Why the Guild, I wonder?" she said finally. "There are certainly other magical orders of some power in the world, including our own."

"I don't know," Samantha replied. "I've been studying with them for about a week now, and while they do have some techniques that seem to work better, the difference between our system and theirs is more incremental than revolutionary. Their Enochian system is probably the most divergent – they switch some of the quadrants on the Great Table and they attribute the directions differently, based on the final version of John Dee's Enochian grimoire. You can actually find some of the revised attributions in the True and Faithful Relation, by the way, but it does require a close reading of the text. I just picked it up and I've been spending a lot of time studying it lately." She directed her teacher's attention to the large book that lay open on her desk next to pad covered with notes.

"I was going to comment on that but you beat me to it," said Daria, gesturing to the Enochian tablets that hung on the four walls of the room. "I see that you've moved your tablets. I don't think I've ever seen this arrangement."

"Going clockwise from the east the elements follow the

190

old alchemical density arrangement – Fire, Air, Water, Earth. That's actually not all that surprising considering how Dee's interest in alchemy."

"There were a few other Renaissance magicians who used that arrangement. The directions weren't really codified until the early nineteenth century. Does it work better?"

"Well, I haven't worked with the new arrangement enough to really evaluate how well it works, but if Balzador has decided that the Guild is his only threat it either works a lot better or he's simply targeting the group because of their emphasis on practical magick."

"Do think their emphasis is that significant?"

"Well, if Balzador walked in the door right now, what could you do without any references in front of you?"

"Banishings, of course. Then I could follow them with a Solar or Martial invocation. That usually works against hostile enemies of whatever sort."

"And maybe that's not enough," Samantha mused. "Since Balzador is in human form, his body is going to protect him to some degree from basic magical effects. You've never tried that against a corporeal entity, have you?"

"Well, no," admitted Daria. "I suppose it makes sense that you might need a more material sort of magick to deal with that kind of an enemy."

"Or maybe the difference isn't technical at all, and the whole matter is personal," continued Samantha with a shrug. "According to Guild history, Balzador was defeated by a group of their members in Europe a little over a hundred and twenty years ago. He could just be out for revenge, in which case our order wouldn't be a target."

"But if the Guild loses, we'll have to face him, won't we?" asked Daria, more a statement of fact than a question.

"That would be my assessment, yes," Samantha said with a nod. "I doubt that a demon would stop once he had one victory under his belt. So it's a very good thing that I'm learning everything

191

I can of the Guild system. There may come a day when our order will need their teachings. The trouble is that I'm not sure how many of our order could really make use of them."

"How do you mean?" her instructor asked, surprised.

"Remember when we talked, years ago, about the idea of trying to concentrate the genes that increase magical aptitude? As I recall, you thought I was being ridiculous, because enlightenment doesn't depend on any particular genetic trait."

"Of course I remember," replied Daria with wry grin. "It was a rather heated discussion."

"Well, the Guild has done it."

"What do you mean?" Daria asked, her eyebrows furrowed.

"It goes something like this. The Guild is made up of what they call the 'Great Families.' They've been encouraging people with high magical aptitude to marry for centuries. The end of the line, as it currently sits, is Michael Niemand's ex-girlfriend, Elspeth Sprengel – a direct descendant of the supposedly mythical Anna, I might add. She's the one who blasted the club. They were both there that night. She was upset with him and threw a general curse in an old building that was probably below code, and the result was that the furnace exploded."

Daria looked very pale. "But... that shouldn't be possible. Maybe if you gave the spell a week something would happen..."

"Three minutes, tops," countered Samantha. "According to Michael it was just about an instantaneous effect."

"Are you sure?"

"Well, I only know what he told me, of course, but I'm inclined to believe him. What it shows is that there really is a connection between genetics and magical ability, at least on the physical plane. You shouldn't be so surprised - it's just like any other human ability. I could have trained from the time I was two years old and I still wouldn't be able to run a forty-yard dash in four seconds. My genes just aren't that athletic. Maybe influencing the physical world directly is just hard enough that only people

192

with the highest level of aptitude can even learn to do it reliably."

"If that's true, then, can we do anything with their techniques?" asked her teacher slowly.

"That's what I'm wondering," replied Samantha. "It may be that the Guild's ritual style is so heavily based on aptitude that it might not work for anyone else."

"But it works for you, right?"

Samantha sighed. "That's another story."

"How so?"

"According to what Jonas, Michael's teacher, told me, sometimes people are born with high aptitude outside the Great Families and the Guild recruits them. That's what happened to Michael, whose parents aren't mages, and it's what almost happened to me. I'd be tempted to think they were just flattering me like a lot of cults do, but it makes sense with how I've felt the last few years – like something in my training is missing. I've always wanted to work practical magick – you know that."

"Yes, I do," Daria replied with a soft laugh. "From the first day we spoke. I never told you, because I didn't want to encourage you in that direction, but you have always been very good, even when you were just starting out. There's a reason you're one of our order's youngest full Adepts. When you would do rituals with me all sorts of weird synchronicities would happen around me and around the ritual space. It took me years to get to that point, but you could just do it. I don't think they're making it up, Samantha. In fact, knowing you have unusual natural ability answers a lot of questions that have been on my mind for a long time. But if your ability is so high, why didn't they recruit you?"

"Because they wanted Michael for their breeding program."

"What?" asked Daria, looking confused and a little shocked.

"Seriously. The Council that runs the Guild didn't want to bring in two new members at the time, and they most needed new blood for the Sprengel family line. Since both of the Sprengel

193

children were daughters, it made sense to bring in a male initiate and not a female one. So that was why Michael got in, but not me."

"Wait a minute. They have a breeding program?"

"I'm exaggerating a little for effect," Samantha admitted. "It's not like something out of Nazi Germany, more like subtle persuasion. They did hope, though, that Michael would get involved with Elspeth or her sister, and apparently he and Elspeth dated for a number of years."

"But they're willing to let you study with them now?"

"Yes, because the composition of their Supreme Council has changed, and because their numbers are pretty low at this point."

"Just like ours," commented Daria, a touch of sadness in her voice. "Magical orders don't hold the appeal that they once did for a lot of people. Everyone thinks they can just download some spells off the Internet, and then they get upset when the spells don't work and give up on occultism. Either that, or their spells work and they decide they can do it on their own. It's not just occult groups, either – you see the same thing in most initiatory groups. The Masons used to be enormous and influential to the point where you practically had to be one to be a businessman, but they're also shrinking fast."

"I had no idea," replied Samantha, surprised. "The structure of our order makes it hard to *have* any idea, of course."

"That's the whole point. It's a needless distraction to doing the work." Her teacher paused for a moment, considering her next words. "So are you planning on being a part of the Guild's 'breeding program,' as you say?" he asked finally.

Now it was Samantha's turn to look shocked. "Well... I haven't given it much thought, honestly. According to Jonas, Michael's teacher and now mine, mages just tend to be attracted to each other."

"And are you?"

"To who? Michael?"

194

Daria smiled and nodded. "I've just been noticing a brightness in your voice and your aura when you mention him. Or am I imagining things?"

"Probably not," admitted Samantha. "I do like him – he's friendly, intelligent, and reasonably attractive – but I couldn't really tell you if I see him as a romantic prospect. Everybody tells me that rebound relationships are a bad idea, and his last girlfriend didn't just dump him, she almost blew him up. I'd think that would make it an even worse idea. Anyway, we really barely know each other."

"But you do like him," said Daria.

"That is what I said, isn't it? I just think if we were going to pursue anything, we would need more time, maybe a lot more. Right now, there's the whole situation with Balzador that needs to be dealt with and I really don't feel like either of us can afford the distraction. Once we've taken care of that, I guess we'll see where life takes us."

Her instructor smiled. "Fair enough."

"So what *do* you know about demonology?" asked Samantha. "The Guild seems to be... well, not exactly lost, but not all that knowledgeable. They don't teach it at all."

Daria looked thoughtful. "As I said, for the most part we don't either."

"How about the Goetic and Abramelin demons, then, like you mentioned? The Guild doesn't even study *them*. Right now just about anything would help."

"Well, I'll tell you what I know. There are a lot of proponents of Goetia who think that the entities summoned are aspects of the magician's personality. Even some of Crowley reads like that, though he adds in <u>Magick in Theory and Practice</u> that the magician must treat the entities as though they are independent beings to get results," Daria explained carefully. "Obviously, if the system is talking about psychological baggage, it won't be of much use against a flesh-and-blood demon. How it works is that you set up a circle with a triangle outside it, and then place the sigil of the

195

demon you want to summon into the circle. There are all sorts of ways to set it up – some magicians use a dark mirror and draw the sigil on the mirror, some use thick incense smoke and place the sigil underneath the burner, and so forth. Then you read the conjurations and call the demon into the triangle by the name of the Judeo-Christian god. You can, of course, use the Thelemic pantheon and it works just fine, but if you're talking about the original system, it's Medieval European and thus essentially Christian with some Qabalistic influences."

"So maybe there would be a way to trap Balzador," Samantha mused. "That might get around the problem of trying to keep him from reincarnating, since it sounds like that's what happens when his body dies."

"Possibly," said Daria thoughtfully. "You would have to find a way to keep the conjurations up indefinitely, though, and I can't think of any way to do that. You eventually would have to sleep, and even if you had a group working on it, the strain would be very difficult to handle for weeks or months."

"So we would really get a lot more utility out of just killing his body. I mean, he would return, but assuming he reincarnates as a baby it should take eighteen years or so for him to reach adulthood again. We could never keep spells like that up for eighteen years – he would escape sooner than that."

"Most likely, yes," agreed Daria. "I will ask around, though, if anyone else in the order with more experience than I might have another suggestion. There might be a way to power a containment spell automatically, but of course then the problem arises of where we could put the triangle so that it wouldn't be discovered. I would think that it would have to contain his physical body, so we couldn't make it all that small."

"That's good to hear. Let me know if you find out anything as soon as possible."

"I'll be sure to do that," said her instructor as the two of them rose to their feet. "Thank you for updating me on the situation. I'll start my inquiries at once, and I'll be in touch."

"Thank you," said Samantha as she walked Daria to the door. "I'm sure anything you can come up with will be helpful. We'll talk soon."

She returned to the sofa to meditate on powering a containment spell indefinitely, but was interrupted by the phone a few minutes later.

"Good morning," said Michael.

"Good morning to you. What are you doing up so early? You haven't started morning practices, have you?"

He laughed. "Not at this point, though you never know what the future might hold. I was just thinking about you and wondering if you wanted to do something tonight that didn't involve chasing down murder suspects or magical training."

"Sure," she replied. "We've certainly done enough work lately. Can I ask you a question, though?"

"Of course."

"Well, this is probably going to sound really forward, but I try to communicate as directly as I can, and as far as I can tell, so do you. So I'm just going to ask what's on my mind – does the Guild have plans for me?"

"What do you mean?"

"I mean as far as your 'Great Families' go."

"Well, I really don't know," he replied. "I haven't heard anything like that, if that's what you're wondering about. As far as I know the only 'plan' Jonas has is to train you in our magical system. Why do you ask?"

"I just got to thinking about it."

"To tell you the truth, I'm still wondering whether Elspeth might be the end of the whole thing, with how she turned out," he mused. "See, if we can make people powerful without making them any wiser, is that really such a good thing? We're the ones who are stuck doing damage control when one of them throws a stupid curse somewhere. I don't know how Elspeth's parents did it. I suppose like the rest of us her magical power didn't really turn on until she was a teenager, and at that point she was being raised by

Aleric who was more than powerful enough to deal with her, but can you imagine? A kid who throws a temper tantrum and part of the house burns down?"

"I suppose if that's the case you could be right, but I have a hard time thinking that they would just abandon it after so many years, especially since Elspeth is just one example. She could be a fluke."

"That's true," he admitted. "I'm well aware that I could be wrong."

"If you're not, this maybe doesn't matter, but I'm going to ask anyway. Would you and I be discouraged from getting involved with each other? I mean, hypothetically," she added quickly. "My degree is in biology and I know that if you have a limited animal population that's fairly inbred and you have two new individuals that are more genetically diverse, it makes the most sense to mate each of them with a different animal from the original population. Then you wind up with three lines that are diverse from each other instead of two, which is better for the long-term viability of the population."

"That's true, but as I've tried to explain, it's not like we're breeding goats and we don't force anyone to do anything. Are you asking because you're interested? Or because you think you might be?"

"Well, are you?" she asked.

His voice brightened. "At some point in the future, and maybe not that far in the future, absolutely. Right now I'm still sorting out my feelings for Elspeth, and I wouldn't want to start a new relationship and have that get in the way. I've felt drawn to you from that first night we met, though, and I don't want to give the impression that I'm trying to make some kind of an excuse. I wouldn't be inviting you out if I didn't want to see you. It's just that so much has happened."

"I know. There's the whole matter of Balzador, too."

"I'll tell you one thing, though. Once this is all behind us, I really do want to get to know you a whole lot better. And that's the truth."

"I suppose I'll leave it that for now," she said playfully. "So what would you like to do tonight?"

"Why don't I pick you up around seven and we can make up our minds then. I can think of a lot of good restaurants around downtown, but I'm not quite sure what I'll be in the mood for tonight."

"Sounds good. Let's hope Balzador keeps lying low for at least another day or two – I could really use a relaxing night out."

"Any thoughts on where you might like to go?"

"How about back to the Loring?" she suggested. "I need to stop by Magus and pick up a couple of things this evening anyway and we could meet up there afterwards, if you're game."

"Sure," he replied. "It's one of my favorite restaurants. How does around seven sound?"

"Great. I'll see you then."

Michael made it to the restaurant a little before seven that evening. He had spent years overcoming his natural tendency to always think that he could get one more thing done before heading out the door and as a result usually showed up to appointments a few minutes early. It was a good thing, too, as this particular evening the place was nearly full and from the number people sitting around the lobby it looked like there was a wait of a least a half hour for anyone walking in off the street.

"Niemand, reservation for two at seven," he said as he stepped up to the young woman working the front. He smiled as he recognized the waitress from his first evening here with Samantha.

She returned his smile despite looking a bit harried. "Give us about five minutes. Is that okay?"

"Sure," he replied. "My date's not here yet anyway." With no empty seats left in the lobby he found a spot near the door to stand and wait. He wondered if Samantha would arrive on time seeing as Roger usually couldn't help chatting up any real magician

199

who walked in the door about some new limited edition grimoire. Maybe that was why there was no visible clock in the store.

Nonetheless, she walked in the door right at seven. She wore a light coat over a simple but formal black dress. Michael was surprised to see what looked like a cross hanging around her neck, but as she came closer he realized that the design was far more intricate than that of a usual Christian cross. On the other hand, he was unsurprised to see her carrying a medium-sized bag emblazoned with the Magus Books logo.

"Is there a wait?" she asked as she looked around the room.

"Only a few more minutes. I made reservations for once, and it's a good thing I did. The place is packed. You look really beautiful," he found himself saying. It was true, but he usually wasn't nearly so forward.

She smiled warmly. "Thanks. I don't dress up much so it's fun once in awhile. Do you like the cross?"

She held up the necklace and he examined the design. It was the Golden Dawn rose cross, a design that included the Hebrew letters in the center that were normally used to trace sigils and pentagrams at the cross-quarter points. "Cool," he said, looking it over. "Another new toy from Roger?"

"Of course. I'm looking forward to wearing it around and seeing if anybody treats me differently because they assume I'm Christian. I mean, you're a Hermetic and you wear a unicursal hexagram, so I figure that even though I'm a Thelemite I can wear a Hermetic rose cross. It makes us even, sort of."

He chuckled. "I suppose so. What else do you have in the bag?"

"A few more Enochian books, naturally."

"Another happy customer."

"Of course," she said with a laugh.

"Niemand, party of two," said a voice from across the room. Michael looked over to see the waitress ready for him and Samantha. "Right this way."

The waitress showed the two of them to a small table on the main floor of the restaurant. It was not as isolated as the upstairs table they had found the previous night, but with the restaurant so full there was little choice. "This will be fine," said Michael as he and Samantha sat down.

"I'm really glad I invited you," he said warmly.

"I was wondering if you would. I probably would have asked myself in another day or so, but it's nice to not have to. Sometimes regular folks find me a little pushy."

"I suppose being able to control events with your mind doesn't help what they think."

"Nope," she replied, shaking her head. "Not unless I hit them with an old-fashioned mind control spell, and doing that has its own difficulties. But you sound almost surprised that you asked. Are you usually shy?"

"Believe it or not, I can be. One of the things about being a magician for a long time is that it makes you kind of a control freak. Not in the sense that you want to meddle in other peoples' business, but in the sense that any situation in which you can't use your powers gets kind of scary. Most of the time when I interact with people I spend enough time shaping their reality that I always know what they're going to do, but when you want to ask somebody out on a date doing that defeats the whole purpose. Not only that, but when you pretty much only date magicians those kinds of manipulations don't work."

"You don't need your powers to be who you are, though."

"I wonder sometimes. I mean, without our abilities what are we? Smart people with esoteric interests?"

"Well, yeah, but you say that like there's something wrong with it. Most people couldn't care less how the nuts and bolts of the universe are put together. Even without the powers there's value in knowing and in having a coherent understanding of how it all works."

"But the powers are nice," he commented.

She smiled again. "That they are."

201

As the evening wore on they talked and laughed and told each other their best stories and for a while managed to forget about the murders in Rochester and the renegade demon who was still on the loose and nowhere to be found. Simply enjoying each other's company, they managed to lose themselves in the moment. Perhaps the crisis could wait, at least for one perfect night.

Unfortunately for Michael, Samantha, and the Guild, Balzador had other plans.

XII. The Hanged Man

The Spirit of the Mighty Waters
The Element of Water

The banks of the upper Mississippi river are home to one of the most unique ecosystems in the world. From Lake Itasca to the plains of southern Minnesota, the river cuts its way through limestone bluffs and hills, leaving a deep valley with steep slopes. After the extensive flooding of the 1990's, the Army Corps of Engineers called on the state to authorize converting the slopes that lined the river into enormous concrete channels with bigger and more effective locks to protect the cities of the southern plains, but the Minnesota Department of Natural Resources would not hear of it. Years ago, the cities of Minneapolis and Saint Paul had turned much of the land along the river into parks in order to preserve the extensive collection of wildlife that called the river valley home. Since they added some much-needed greenery to the two otherwise stark and industrial downtown areas, city dwellers extensively used and enjoyed the parks, and were not about to part with them.

One of these areas was Hidden Falls Park, located near the western end of St. Paul's exclusive Summit Avenue where East River Road ran along the edge of the river valley. A creek ran through the park, draining much of the hillside into the Mississippi, and a flight of stone steps led down the bank to a place where the creek fell about thirty feet. The falls themselves were located in a natural ravine, hidden from boats patrolling the river and onlookers driving along the road above, and as such the area around them was a perfect place to work unseen.

Although the park was closed after dark, that night a stealthy figure descended the stairway leading to below the falls. Dressed in a black dress shirt and slacks and clutching a sheaf of printouts in one hand, Balzador reached the bottom of the stairs and flipped through the reproduced pages of Liber Iadnamad. He held his left hand up to the heavens, sensing the state of both the

203

weather and the flow of magical energy around him. Satisfied, he then consulted the pages and began reading the First Angelic Call, weaving his demonic magick into the odd-sounding intonations. The Call took on a somber, dark tone, like a piece of triumphant music dropped into a minor key, and along the edges of the ravine shadows began to move and consolidate. The spiritual energy of the world welled up around him and began to swirl as he completed the First Call and moved on to the Second, then the Third and Fourth. A pillar of magical light constrained within a web of dark threads began to spin before him as the energy gained structure and form, bound by the spell.

Entranced by the concentration necessary to keep the spell going, he did not hear the sound of a car swerving rapidly into the parking lot at the top of the ravine, or the sound of one of its doors opening and then slamming sharply closed, followed by footsteps on the stone stairway. "That will be enough, demon," said a voice from above. "*Adrpan lonshi.*"

Balzador looked up, jerked out of his reverie as the carefully constructed magical field disintegrated around him, throwing splinters of brightness everywhere. "Who are you?" he demanded violently, fixing his gaze on the intruder. "How dare you disturb my ritual?" He spread his fingers wide and intoned the same incantation he had used to make his sacrifice to Coronzon. "*Yolcam teloch!*" The death spell raced toward the stranger, but met resistance and shattered like breaking glass. "So," said the demon. "You are not just a mage, but a skilled one."

Aleric stepped from the bottom of the stairway into the moonlight. "I am Aleric Sprengel, Guildmaster," he said softly. In the midst of a ritual at his home, just up Summit Avenue, he had felt the draw of Balzador's spell. Knowing it for what it was, he had raced to the park without delay. "The pages you are holding belong to my order. Did you think you could perform such a ritual practically on my doorstep without being detected? Give me the pages, and I will let you leave here."

The demon glared at the Guildmaster contemptuously, a

touch of amusement crossing his features. "Sprengel," he muttered to himself. *Could his vengeance already be at hand?* "I am an immortal," he replied dismissively. "I do not acknowledge the orders of a mere human."

"Really?" asked Aleric facetiously. "Do you think I don't recognize you for what you are, Balzador? You are an outcast, an exile, and while you may be an immortal I also know that the magick of Coronzon binds you here. That means you cannot escape, and you will obey my commands or suffer forever. Return the pages now. *Adrpan lonshi vovina!*"

Balzador effortlessly raised his hand to counter the spell, but suddenly he began to shake and a wave of weakness washed over him. He struggled to hold onto the pages, but a few sheets still managed to fall from his grip and float away in the night breeze.

"How about now?" asked the Guildmaster, his voice conversational but firm. "You know as well as I do how vulnerable you are to the magick of light. I'll ask again – hand over the pages, and I will let you leave. Otherwise, I can torture you for a very long time."

Balzador stretched forth his hand to throw another counterspell, but now the power was wrenched from his grasp and nothing happened. "You will die for this, human!" he exclaimed between clenched teeth. His features shifted as he struggled, his demonic nature now apparent.

"I don't think so," replied Aleric. "Others will be here soon, and now you will not escape." Raising his voice, he spoke a longer and more powerful incantation. "*Yolcam olpirt Iaida! Mad, zacare od adrpan Balzador, hoath drilp!*"

Pain shot through the demon's body like lances of flame as blazing magical light began to consume the demonic soul that animated his human form. The printouts fell from his grasp as he doubled over and then was forced to his knees. Still, he groped for the papers, trying to keep the wind from scattering them around the park. Aleric stood calmly at the foot of the stairs, calling down the magick of the Archons, toxic to all demonic beings. Finally, nearly incapacitated, Balzador pulled the Glock from his belt and tried with all the volition he had left to target the Guildmaster, who almost effortlessly increased the flow of magick and threw a field of stasis at the gun.

It fired anyway.

Aleric's eyes widened with surprise as he felt the bullet hit. Years of magical discipline enabled him to maintain his concentration, but the disruption of his aura from the injury was severe. The power continued to flow, but its intensity was vastly reduced. He tried to direct healing energy to the wound, but as he did so he suddenly became dizzy and fell to the ground. It was only then that he became aware of the pain.

Balzador rose to his feet, almost immediately recovering his strength as the spell broke. He walked slowly across the bottom of the ravine to where the Guildmaster lay. "Polycarbonate," said the demon softly, a victorious grin playing across his face as he leaned over and showed Aleric the gun. "Plastic."

He sighed, shaking his head weakly. He should have thought of that.

"My dear Guildmaster," gloated the demon, "you may have disrupted my ritual for this evening, but you know as well as I do that you will not survive. I can see the power leaking out of you like water from a broken vessel, and soon your spirit will follow. I would have liked nothing better than to torture you for centuries once I became the lord of all magick upon this plane, so you can take some comfort from the fact that your death here and now will deprive me of the opportunity. But you should never have opposed me." He then stood up without a backward glance and meticulously gathered up the pages that had scattered around the ravine. Once he had them all, he strode off nonchalantly into the park.

A few minutes later, lights shone up above and the growl of an overpowered engine echoed across the ravine. The engine stopped, and two car doors opened and closed. Jonas and Rochelle raced down the stairway to find Aleric at the bottom, weak and barely conscious.

"He's hurt," said Jonas, checking him for injury. "It looks like a gunshot to the chest. It missed his heart, but he's already lost a lot of blood."

"Oh, no!" exclaimed Rochelle under her breath, momentarily stunned. She realized that it had never before occurred to her that anything could harm her grandfather, who she knew to be the most powerful mage in the world. But then, even with the greatest magick, it was still hard to stop a bullet. "Is there anything we can do?"

Jonas was already holding his hands over the wound, directing as much healing energy into it as he could manage. "Nothing beyond this. We need an ambulance."

Rochelle began to dial on her cell phone, but Jonas held up a hand.

"No," he said quickly. "I need to call. I want you to leave before they get here, and they record most 911 calls. If your voice is on the recording, they will know you were here. There will be some awkward questions, and I do not want you involved." He took his own cell phone from the sheath on his belt and dialed.

"911 emergency," said the voice on the other end.

"I need an ambulance. My friend has been shot," said Jonas. "He is at Hidden Falls Park in Saint Paul, right by the falls. Do they know how to get here?"

"Yes, sir," said the operator. "I'll dispatch an ambulance right away."

"Jonas," rasped Aleric, coming to. "The signature. You were right. It was him. It was Balzador! The murders in Rochester. The dark power!"

"Just rest. The ambulance is coming," he replied in soothing tones.

"No," insisted the Guildmaster. "He has <u>Liber Iadnamad</u>. I don't know how. He was summoning magick. All of it. All of it in the entire world. You have to stop him."

Jonas' eyes widened as another piece of the puzzle fell into

207

place. "Please. Lie still," he directed as he opened the Guildmaster's shirt and examined the wound. He then turned to Rochelle. "Go. I'll call you from the hospital. Try not to get any blood on you – you're one of his heirs, so you might become a suspect if he doesn't survive. And he may not."

"What is it?" demanded Rochelle, noting his expression. "You're afraid. But not of losing him. It's something else."

"We can discuss it later," he said, shaking his head. "Just go. They'll be here any minute." Maintaining the flow of healing energy with his mind, he washed off the blood that had transferred onto his hands in the freezing water of the creek. He then returned to holding them over the wound, the energy flow warming them back up quickly. As he did so, Rochelle hurried up the stairs without a word. He heard the door slam, the engine start, and the car race off along East River Road.

The paramedics and police arrived a few minutes after that. The gate into the park was locked, so they parked at the top of the hill and came down the stone stairway with a stretcher. They loaded the Guildmaster onto it and quickly began carrying him up the steps to the waiting ambulance. Jonas shaped a sigil in his mind that would hold the magical energy of healing around Aleric as long as possible, but he suspected it was futile. The Guildmaster was an old man, long past his physical prime. The gunshot wound hadn't been immediately fatal, but it was bad.

The two detectives who had arrived with the paramedics stayed below to examine the crime scene along with several forensic technicians who got to work right away gathering evidence. "Is that you, Jonas?" asked one of the detectives, a middle-aged man with a thick, dark mustache.

The mage recognized the detective right away as Thomas Anderson, who he had known for more than ten years. "Hello, Tom," he said softly. "Yes, it's me."

"You know him?" asked the other detective, a younger blond-haired man with suspicious eyes.

"Jonas Votan," replied Tom. "He's an old friend. Jonas, this

208

is Dan Watson, my partner."

"Pleased to meet you," replied Jonas. "I would shake your hand but I assume you'll want to test mine for traces of powder to exclude me from your list of suspects."

Tom nodded, and gestured one of the forensic technicians over.

"What were you doing in the park after hours?" asked Watson immediately. "Did you know the victim?"

"Yes. Aleric Sprengel, another old friend. I think I introduced you to him eight or nine years ago. He lives up on Summit Avenue and we sometimes meet down here after the park is closed to go walking along the river - it's very beautiful at night. I know it's illegal and potentially dangerous, and I suppose this is why. We were going to meet tonight, but when I got here I found him lying at the bottom of the stairs, shot. That's when I called the ambulance."

"Is that your Jaguar in the parking lot up above?" asked Tom.

"No," replied Jonas, "it's Aleric's."

"I take it your friend is pretty well off, then," commented the detective. "Cars like that aren't cheap."

"Not to mention they break down every five minutes," interjected Watson. "Nobody's only car is an XJS."

"Well, yes, he is quite well off, as you say," replied Jonas. "By the way, Detective Watson, you're absolutely correct about the car's reliability. The only reason it runs at all is that Aleric's granddaughter is a rather inspired mechanic."

"Did you see or hear anyone else here?" asked Tom.

"No," replied Jonas. "I didn't hear the gun, either."

"911 did get a call a few minutes before yours from someone in the neighborhood claiming they heard a sound like a single gunshot. You must have just missed the assailant. We have the park cordoned off on both sides, but there aren't any cars in either lot besides your friend's Jaguar. How did you arrive? Did you walk?"

"Aleric's granddaughter Rochelle dropped me off. She was at my house this evening taking a look at my car, which has also had some problems lately. It's a Mercedes, but it's getting up in years. I was planning on getting a ride home with Aleric, though of course that doesn't seem likely now. I'll have to call a cab."

"If you didn't see a car up above, the attacker might be on foot and still in the area," mused Tom. "But he's had a good twenty minutes to make his way into the park. We'll search, but unless this guy is pretty stupid we won't find him."

"Then again, criminals often aren't that bright," pointed out Jonas.

"True enough," agreed the detective. "Maybe we'll get lucky. But I'm guessing the physical evidence here is most of what we'll find."

Tom and Daniel searched the area carefully as a forensics technician tested Jonas' hands for power or residue left over from firing a weapon. "Shell casing," said Daniel suddenly, noting a glint of metal on the ground. "Looks like a nine millimeter. The killer must have been standing here."

"Any footprints?" asked Tom, who was searching the other side of the creek.

"Maybe. It's muddy, but it looks like a lot of people have been through here recently. The weather did just turn a week and a half ago." Daniel gestured to another technician, who began mixing plaster to take molds of the tracks left in the compacted mud.

"I don't mean to be uncooperative," spoke up Jonas, "but is there anything else you need me for? I would like to go to the hospital and attend to Aleric. He's my friend and I think he would want me there. Do you have my address and contact information, Tom?"

"Sure, Jonas. You go on ahead. We can get a statement from you later."

"Are you sure that's wise?" asked Watson. "He's still a suspect."

210

"That's true," replied Tom, "but I've known Jonas for years. He's no killer. And I'm pretty sure that's exactly what our tests will show."

"If you say so," said the young detective, still sounding uncertain.

XIII. Death

*The Child of the Great Transformers: The Lord of the Gate of Death
The Sign Scorpio*

Elspeth arrived at the hospital a few minutes after Rochelle, who had called and updated her on the situation. They met in the lobby, where they were told to wait. They sat down in the brightly painted waiting room.

"What happened?" asked Elspeth quietly.

"He was shot," said Rochelle slowly, her eyes welling up with tears.

"How?"

"He interrupted something. Some kind of a ritual. Jonas called just before you and is on his way. Aleric told him it was Balzador, you know, the demon."

"What?!"

Rochelle, her eyes bleary, completely missed the look of fear and recognition that crossed her sister's face. "Grandfather also said something about summoning all of the magick in the world, and that Balzador had <u>Liber Iadnamad</u>. Where the hell would he get a copy of that?"

"I... I don't know," said Elspeth softly. "Why would he be summoning all the magick in the world? To use against Coronzon, or the Archons?"

Rochelle shook her head. "I'm not sure. He was having a hard time talking. But Jonas seemed like he knew."

"He's not going to be all right, is he?"

"I don't think so," replied Rochelle haltingly through another wave of tears. "He's too old. The spells aren't holding properly."

"I have to see him," said Elspeth, rising to her feet.

"They won't let you in," replied Rochelle. "I already tried."

Elspeth's eyes were cold and angry. "They won't have to. Do you know where they took him?"

213

"No, they wouldn't tell me. Please don't," she begged, her face infinitely weary. "The last thing I want to be around now is you blasting the staff."

Elspeth laid her hand reassuringly on her sister's shoulder. "There's no need for anything like that. I'm just going to slip by them. I need to see him, Rochelle."

She sighed and shook her head. "Be careful, then."

Elspeth focused her will and began to shape the space around her. To the four directions, and above and below her, she traced the sign of the Rose Cross, a cross and circle superimposed. She then clasped her hands over her heart and whispered, so the nursing staff would not hear, "*Yolcam ehnub ror.*" The cube that the rose crosses formed around her shimmered and solidified, and even to Rochelle's trained magical sight her sister simply disappeared.

Elspeth slid through the door of the waiting room into the hospital. She still had to be careful, she reminded herself. Magical invisibility was much more like a concealment spell than physical transparency – it worked on the principle of diverting the attention of others in such a way that she would not be noticed, even by someone looking directly at her, unless she did something obvious like opening a door in plain sight or knocking something over. Since it depended upon the nature of conscious attention it wouldn't affect the hospital's security tapes, but by the time they were reviewed it wasn't likely to make any difference.

She stood in the corridor beyond the door for a moment holding the image of her grandfather in her mind. Shortly a sense of his location drifted into her thoughts, and she started down the maze of corridors to find him. Navigating past stretchers, carts, and teams of nurses, she managed to find the room after doubling back on her tracks several times. Her spell held beautifully – none of the doctors or nurses she passed gave any sign of noticing her.

Aleric lay in a room in the intensive care ward, wired up to more machines than Elspeth had ever seen. His weak and fading aura confirmed the worst - he was clearly dying, though Jonas' spells had slowed the process considerably. She concentrated and added her own healing spells to the invisible spiritual tracings that lined his immobile form, and was gratified to see his aura brighten. It probably wasn't enough to save him, but it would at least spare him a lot of pain.

Once the healing spell was in place, she leaned down by his side and spoke, negating the effect of the invisibility spell on him. "It's Elspeth, grandfather," she said softly so as not to draw the attention of the nurses outside the door.

His eyes flickered open. "Elspeth," he said weakly. "You came. That's good. I wanted to see you before the end."

"Don't talk like that," she said tentatively, knowing it would do no good.

He did his best to shake his head. "I know the end."

"Grandfather, what happened?"

"You are strong, child, and they will need you."

"What?" she asked, not sure what he meant.

"Balzador – a demon," said Aleric haltingly. "I told Jonas. He's in human form. He has Liber Iadnamad. There is a way – demon magick combined with our own techniques – to bind the magick of the world. I used Archon magick to stop him. It might have worked, but he shot me. The gun was some kind of plastic so the stasis field didn't work. He has to be stopped, or all the magick in the world will be his. He'll kill us all before any of us can stop him." Elspeth's eyes widened with horror as her grandfather continued. "The others will need your power. Promise me you will help them. Promise me you will destroy Balzador. The ruling of the Council against you can be reversed."

Anger shot through her veins like molten ice. The demon had betrayed her, and not only that, he had mortally wounded the man who had raised her from childhood. *I'll kill him, all right*, she said to herself. *I'll annihilate his soul.* Her eyes hardened like cold metal as she gently took her grandfather's hand. "I promise," she said her voice shaking. "I will stop him."

"Good," said Aleric, relaxing a little. "Good. I needed to know. Now wish me a pleasant journey, my dear. You've been like

215

a daughter to me all these years, and I want you to know how much I love you before I go. The end is close now, and I fear I will not see you again. "

She bowed her head. "Travel well, grandfather."

He closed his eyes again, but now his face bore a slight smile as he slipped back into unconsciousness. After watching over him for another hour during which he did not speak again, Elspeth finally rose from his bedside and slipped away unseen, like an image in a dream.

The Guildmaster died at the hospital the next morning. Rochelle, Elspeth, and Jonas had all spent the night meditating and directing spells his way in the waiting room, trying to no avail to use their powers as best they could to keep him alive and free of suffering. In accordance with the custom of the Guild, the remaining members of the Supreme Council held an emergency meeting to choose a new Guildmaster, and since they were already in the Twin Cities the members met at once. There was little argument; only two of the mages on the council, Jonas and Sofia, were members of the Supreme Order, an absolute requirement for the position. More than ten years Sofia's senior, Jonas was selected to succeed Aleric.

All of the mages in the Twin Cities area attended the installation ceremony. Samantha was asked to attend as well, as Jonas' newest student. Michael was uncharacteristically silent, though he did manage a weak smile as she sat down next to him. Their date had gone very well the previous night and both of them had managed to get a break from thinking about having to deal with Balzador, but Aleric's death now darkened the whole situation. *Couldn't the demon have waited one more night?*

The ballroom of the Summit Avenue mansion made a truly impressive temple with its high ceiling and sheer size. Chairs had been placed in the west, leaving most of the room open for the installation ritual. A circle about twenty feet in diameter had been drawn in the center of the room with an Enochian Holy Table placed in its center. The circle was lined with twelve banners made in the four directional colors – red in the eastern quadrant, white in the southern quadrant, green in the western quadrant, and black in the northern quadrant – and bearing the Twelve Holy Names of God from the Enochian Tablets of the four directions.

In the center of the Holy Table, ringed by the seven talismans called the Ensigns of Creation and sitting directly upon the Sigillum Dei Aemeth, the Sigil of God, was a leather-bound book that looked centuries old. *Liber Iadnamad?* she wondered to herself. If it truly was the original of the lost Dee grimoire, it would be priceless. On top of the book, placed in the exact center of its cover, was what looked like a gold ring. Jonas stood to the west of the altar facing east, seemingly lost in thought. She supposed he was as shocked as everyone else by the loss of Aleric.

Looking around the room, she was amazed at how few mages were present. She supposed that she shouldn't be surprised – she had been told the Guild was small, but to actually see how small was still sobering. She assumed that the older mages were the remaining members of the Supreme Council, and one of the two women sitting off to one side of the room could only be Elspeth. She felt a touch of envy as she realized Michael had not been exaggerating – his former girlfriend was indeed one of the most beautiful women she had ever seen, the perfection of her features marred only by her icy expression. Samantha guessed that the shorter, younger woman sitting next to Elspeth was Rochelle, her sister, and the blond young man next to her was Eric Palmer, who Michael had also described. That was it – ten members, eleven counting herself, and five of them from other cities around the world. Based on her earlier conversation with Daria, she wondered if her own order was also as small, but of course she couldn't be sure.

Sofia advanced to the altar from the east of the temple, beginning the rite that had accompanied the installation of Guildmasters for centuries. After opening the strongest magical field Samantha had ever felt with the rituals of the pentagram and hexagram, the Italian mage intoned the haunting Angelic language of the First Enochian Call. She then pronounced the Angelic invocation. Although Samantha often had difficulty seeing auras and other magical effects, there was no mistaking the spiritual brightness that filled the room.

Bataivah, bogpa raas, yolcam lonshi dooaip Oro Ibah Aozodpi!
Raagiosal, bogpa babage, yolcam lonshi dooaip Mehpeh Arsal
Gaiol!
Edalpernaa, bogpa soboln, yolcam lonshi dooaip Oip Tea Pedoce!
Iczodhihal, bogpa lucal, yolcam lonshi dooaip Mor Dial Hectaga!
Dooaip Mad, zacare ca od zamran! odo cicle qaa!
Zorge, lap zirdo hoath Iaida!

Although Samantha didn't catch the full meaning of the Angelic conjuration, she recognized the names of the four Kings of the directions, the three Holy Names of God used to summon them, and the language of the final section – "Move and show yourselves! Open the mysteries of your creation! Be friendly unto me, for I am the true worshipper of the Highest!" She felt the brightness of the room increase further as a distinct presence or presences fell over the temple.

"Place your right hand on the Book of the Spirits," said Sofia. Jonas complied. "Now repeat after me." He did so, repeating the oath line by line.

I, Jonas Votan,
 of my own free will,
In the presence of God
and the powers of the four directions,
do hereby and hereon
most solemnly and sincerely promise and swear
that I will faithfully execute
the office of Guildmaster
according to our ancient laws and customs.

I will protect, nurture, and assist its membership
with every aspect of my being,
that all may eventually apprehend
the clear light of truth.
During my tenure
may the Guild prosper
and send forth its light
to dispel the darkness of the world.

He then sealed the oath by dropping his lips to the book and kissing its heavy leather cover. Everyone else in the room responded with "So mote it be," catching Samantha by surprise.

"Now take the ring," instructed Sofia. Jonas picked up the ring from the center of the book and put it on his finger, and a shudder of energy rippled through the room. "By the True Names of God and the Kings of the Four Winds, I proclaim you Guildmaster. May your tenure be glorious and illuminating unto all."

The Italian Mage then bid the conjured spirits to depart and closed the rite by reversing the opening pentagram and hexagram rituals. The energy that was raised seemed to flow into the ring that Jonas now wore, rather than sinking into the earth.

Amidst the subdued congratulations, the new Guildmaster walked over to Michael and Samantha. "I need to rest now," he said, sounding more tired than she had ever heard him, "but come by my house later today. There are things we need to discuss."

With that, Jonas retired from the room, with Sofia not far behind.

"Shall we go?" said Michael softly, the first words he had spoken to Samantha since she arrived. He rose to his feet.

"We can," said Samantha. "I never met Aleric, but I can see from the reactions of everyone here that he must have been pretty special."

Michael sighed. "That he was. Aleric was the best of all of us. He will be missed."

As they left the mansion and headed out to their cars, he spoke again. "I didn't want to say this in front of everyone, but I'm really scared," he said softly. "I wasn't before this happened, but I am now. If Aleric couldn't stop Balzador, what can we do? He was the most powerful mage in the world."

"I don't know," she replied. "But let's hope Jonas has some answers."

Jim picked Elspeth up after the ceremony. "How are you feeling?" he asked. "I know this is difficult for you…"

"Oh, give it a rest," she snapped. "This is my fault."

"What do you mean?"

"Balzador killed him. My grandfather told me last night, before he died," she said coldly.

"Why would he do that?" asked Jim, confused. He had thought that maybe the magick office had sent an assassin, but he wasn't prepared for such an action on the part of the demon.

"I don't know. It's hard to say, really. But he said something about summoning all the magick in the world. It must have had something to do with his spell to destroy Coronzon. Grandfather stopped the ritual, but Balzador shot him. I never should have helped a demon. I just thought I was going to be killed, you know? It was a way out. But now I don't care."

"What do you mean?"

"I mean I'm going to kill him. To do that I have to find him." She fished the crystal out of her pocket and felt its aura. The link was still there, so it would work to locate him if she was reasonably close.

"How? He could be anywhere."

"No, only one place," she corrected. "He needs to wait until the river and the jet stream align. He told me that the other night. It's cold today, so the jet stream has moved south. He'll probably want to wait until it swings north again. Do you have any idea what the weather is supposed to be like tomorrow?"

"Warmer, according to the forecast."

220

"So I'm guessing it will be tomorrow night. All we need to do is plot out where that will be along the river. Then I can get close enough to find him with the crystal. Then his life ends," she added, her voice like the sweep of a sword.

Jonas met with Michael and Samantha later that day. He looked much better, and appeared to have recovered from the ceremony. "It seems that our suspicions were correct," he said as they seated themselves on the overstuffed sofa in his living room. "Balzador is definitely the mystery man from Rochester."

Samantha sounded confused. "Why would he kill the Guildmaster?"

"At first I thought he simply wanted us out of the way, but Aleric told me that he was trying to summon all of the magical energy of the world using a copy of our own <u>Liber Iadnamad</u>," replied Jonas.

"Is such a thing possible?" asked Michael.

"Yes, I believe it may be," said Jonas thoughtfully. "Aleric certainly did, and stopped whatever ritual the demon was trying to perform at the cost of his own life. It is possible that when combined with the energies of demon magick the Angelic Calls could be used in that fashion – to bind the magick of the world in such a way that it could be directed by a single will."

"What's wrong?" asked Michael, noting that Samantha had turned white.

"The dream," she replied with fear in her voice. "I wasn't sure when I saw the sketch, but now it makes sense. It was a premonition. The man I saw was Balzador, the hill was the place outside Rochester where the bodies were found, and that *thing* on top of the hill was the magical energy of the world brought to a single point. That's why I didn't have any power. All of the magick was going there. I don't know why I had the dream the night I did, though – it happened the night Morpheus burned, but it wasn't about you or Elspeth at all."

"That was probably just a coincidence," agreed Jonas.

"Either that, or you were seeing a timeline that was in some way set in motion by Elspeth's action at the club."

Suddenly a realization crossed Michael's mind. "She copied Liber Iadnamad!" he exclaimed suddenly. "Hell, she probably copied mine – she still has a key to the house and might have been able to get past my magical defenses without being detected. And she did it because she was afraid the Guild would order her death after the Morpheus explosion, or maybe because she felt betrayed after being barred from the Inner Order. Balzador must have promised to protect her from us or something like that. Before the whole Morpheus thing, he would never have been able to talk her into it – Elspeth was too loyal to her grandfather, if nobody else. But her mistake gave him the opportunity."

"And now Aleric is dead," said Jonas. "Do you truly think that it was Elspeth who provided Balzador with Liber Iadnamad?"

"I don't exactly *think* it, but it feels right," he replied, searching his thoughts.

"Well, it does make sense of much of the evidence we have gathered," agreed Jonas reluctantly. "I would have thought better of Elspeth, though."

"So he'll be at the hill," said Samantha.

"What?" asked Michael.

"He'll be at the hill in Rochester when he tries the ritual next," she elaborated. "I must have seen it in the dream because that's where the current timeline leads, right?"

"Probably," admitted Jonas. "I suspect he won't try it in the Twin Cities for fear of alerting us again. Is there anything else you remember? Like how to defeat him, perhaps?"

"I woke up before I could do much," she said slowly. "But wait a minute – I had a weapon of some kind. A dagger, I think. In the dream, it was the only thing that could stop him."

"A dagger with the right enchantment might work," mused Jonas. "You could disrupt his form, perhaps. It is possible that even if he were to jump to a new body, the magical energy of the world would be released. It is maybe even possible that the resulting energy surge might be enough to destroy him, if his body is killed or disrupted at the right moment."

"Can't you do that with a spell, though?" asked Michael.

"Of course."

"Then why didn't Aleric use it? Or did he, and it failed?"

"I don't know," said Jonas thoughtfully. "He did recognize Balzador, and he must have depleted the demon's magick to the point where the ritual couldn't be performed that night. Otherwise, Balzador would have tried to kill me and Rochelle as well when we arrived so he could continue the rite. To shoot Aleric at all he must have either been extremely lucky or used a weapon that is proof against magick."

"Like a polycarbonate Glock," said Samantha immediately. "Do either of you shoot?"

"No," replied Michael. "A Glock is what, a nine millimeter?"

"Yes," said Jonas. "Some of the police officers I know are using them now."

"A Glock has a removable metal barrel," explained Samantha. "The rest of the gun is nonmetallic. The thing is that you can buy a third-party polycarbonate barrel. Once you swap in the new barrel, the whole gun is nonmetallic, and I doubt a spell would work on it."

"You're probably right," admitted Jonas. "And I spoke with one of the doctors at the hospital this morning, when he called to tell me Aleric had passed on. He said the bullet was the right size for a nine millimeter, though the police planned on running a ballistics test to be sure. "

"That does fit," said Michael slowly, "but I think we must still be missing something. Why would a demon bother with this at all? I mean, they *are* obsessed with power, but wouldn't the power of his magick be stronger than anything he could raise here?"

"Possibly not," replied Jonas. "He was, after all defeated. The power of the Dark Lord is almost certainly stronger than the magick of this world, but it may simply be that Balzador would rather rule the Earth than attempt to get back into Coronzon's good graces."

"Or maybe he has bigger plans," said Samantha softly.

"What did you say?" asked Michael.

"Maybe he has bigger plans," she repeated. "With everything we've found, the murders in Rochester still don't make sense. Why would Balzador summon another powerful being from the Abyss, especially if he was banished here?"

"He could have been seeking greater power in order to get the Guild out of the way so he could go forward with his plans," replied Jonas immediately.

"But that doesn't explain why the murders were committed," she countered. "He must be pretty powerful already to be able to kill his followers using magick, all at once, in the middle of a ceremony. Could Elspeth or Aleric have done that?"

"What does she have to do with this?" asked Jonas.

"Nothing. I'm talking about power level here. Those two are the most powerful you've ever seen, right? Could they cast a spell that would instantly kill twelve people by separating their souls from their bodies, even if they were working together?"

"Of course not," replied Jonas. "Perhaps if they directed their power together they could kill one person that quickly, but even then it could still fail. I doubt that I could manage it myself, even now with the might of the order behind me."

"Exactly," she continued. "So it sounds to me like Balzador is already much stronger than any of us, and if that's the case, wouldn't followers be an asset, even if they were fairly weak magicians? More to the point, if he's somehow obtained the ability to summon all the magick of the world and command it, why would he need to summon another high-ranking demon? Wouldn't the magick of the world be power enough?"

"I don't know," said Jonas, shaking his head. "You are right, though – since Balzador is already a demon, he can make use of demonic magick. Combined with the magick of the world that should be more than enough power to accomplish almost anything."

"What if he was making some kind of a bargain?"

"Like a pact?" asked Michael. "He's already a demon."

"Something like that. He could have summoned Coronzon to bargain for his freedom."

"I don't see how he could succeed, though," said Michael. "Why would Coronzon ever release him? If I were the Dark Lord, he would have to offer me something pretty impressive."

"Like all the magick in the world," said Samantha bluntly.

Michael's voice remained skeptical. "Still, what is the magick of one world compared to the power of the Abyss? The Abyss spans the entire universe."

"The entire multiverse," corrected Jonas. "There are, of course, many universes."

Samantha shook her head. "I don't know, then."

"I can think of one possibility," said Jonas slowly. "And unfortunately, to my magical senses it rings true. The forces of order and chaos are closely matched in our universe, and they are very close indeed on this particular world. That is what makes magick possible here. Light and darkness are like the poles of a battery, and when the poles are matched, the magical energy is the most powerful and the most pure. If Balzador can harness all of the magical energy of this world, he could join with Coronzon to repel the minions of order from the Earth. That process could be repeated on other worlds until this universe is completely subjugated to the Abyss. Then the power of this universe could be turned against others that are mostly in balance and so forth. Like a chain reaction, the power of chaos would spread across the multiverse."

"But that would take millennia," objected Samantha. "How many worlds are out there? I'm betting there are a lot of them."

Jonas sighed. "Balzador and Coronzon are both immortal and indestructible. They can wait a long time to accomplish their goals, and are free to think in terms of eons rather than years or

225

even centuries. On that time scale, imbalance is like a virus – it can spread to everything it touches, even if it spreads slowly. So we really do have to stop Balzador, and stop him here and now. The problem is that so far I do not have any reasonable idea of how to go about it. We cannot be vigilant forever, and now that Balzador has <u>Liber Iadnamad</u> he could just go underground and wait. Even if he remains here on Earth, what's a hundred years? What's a thousand? When does it end? Since he's bound to this world, we cannot just kill him. Now that he has seen <u>Liber Iadnamad</u> and knows how to bind the magick of the world, he could simply jump to a new body and perform the ritual once he reaches maturity."

"But I think he'll move soon," said Michael gravely. "It's like in chess. You wait for an opportunity, and then you mobilize your attack. Elspeth was his opportunity. Who knows when he'll get another one? The Guild is weakened now by the death of Aleric, and if Elspeth is any indication our mages are getting stronger over time. In twenty years time we might even manage to rebuild our membership, if the current generation's interest in occultism is any indication. He won't wait a hundred years. I think that now is probably his best chance."

"I fear you're right, Michael," admitted Jonas. "I will meditate on this and let you know if I see any solutions."

"Okay," he replied. "I'm going to head back home. I have an idea of my own, but I want to try it from my own temple space. I'll keep you posted."

Michael and Samantha left the Guildmaster's house and climbed into the waiting GTO parked in the driveway. As Michael started the car and was about to ask where Samantha wanted to be dropped off, she turned to him. "I want to help."

"Are you sure?" he asked, pulling out onto the street. "It could be dangerous. Don't get me wrong, you've already helped a lot and I would like your assistance, but I want to make sure you have some idea what you're getting into. We could wind up dead, too, just like Aleric."

"Well, I have to do *something*," she replied. "I never was very good at sitting around waiting for the end of the world. I want to be involved."

"Okay," he agreed, "you can help. I just needed to make sure it was something you wanted to do of your own free will and accord. This is the Guild's problem, and to some extent my responsibility. It isn't yours, and if you wanted to walk away I wouldn't blame you."

"What do you mean, your responsibility?" she asked. "You're not the one behind this."

"But in a way I am," he insisted. "You know, if I had refused elevation into the Inner Order, none of this would have happened. In a lot of ways, that's where it all started."

"But you would never have refused."

He shook his head. "Of course not," he admitted. "As Jonas said the night you met him, strength is its own burden. It would have pushed me forward regardless of other factors. I would have locked up that blasted grimoire better, but other than that I wouldn't change anything, even knowing what I do now."

"I suppose that's what makes mages dangerous," she said thoughtfully. "We're unwilling to sit still and be content with where we are. We have to push on, regardless of the consequences."

"And I know, had I refused, I'd be no happier," he added. "I'd still be involved with Elspeth, trying to deal with her spoiled-child antics, and I would be deliberately holding myself back. But then, the rest of the universe wouldn't be in danger."

"Nobody can know the outcome of all their actions," she said softly. "Not even us."

"I suppose not. Even when we see the future, most of what we see is that the future is hard to predict. I just hope we can manage to deal with this situation before it's too late for everyone."

XIV. Art, or Temperance

The Daughter of the Reconcilers, the Bringer-forth of Life
The Sign Sagittarius

"So you said you had an idea. What do we do?" asked Samantha, seating herself on the antique sofa in Michael's living room. "We know who the enemy is, but how do we stop him?"

"I'm not sure," replied Michael, sitting down next to her, "but I think I know how we can find out. Are you any good at scrying?"

"Passable. And the new rituals I've been practicing already seem to be helping."

"Good," he replied. "We need to contact one of the higher spiritual beings who knows more about how demons really operate than we do, and I think I know of one who would be perfect."

"Who?"

"Araziel. He's a former archon who went independent. I've worked with him on and off for the last few years, ever since I ran across his palace on the astral plane."

"Archon," she mused. "I've heard that before. From the early Christian Gnostics?"

"The Gnostics knew of them, yes. They're the sworn enemies of demons like Balzador, the embodiments of order rather than chaos. But Araziel, as I said, is an independent. He was originally an archon, but gave up his post a couple thousand years back – at least that's what he's told me, and according to all the magical tests I can devise, he's legitimate. The advantage of working with an independent is that what we're doing is less likely to get back to the archons themselves."

"But why is that bad?" she asked. "If they're the enemies of Balzador, they might help us."

"And they might decide to help themselves to our planet," he countered. "The archons are just as dangerous as the demons. Their obsession with structure is as pathological as the demons' obsession with disorder."

"So what the universe really needs is a balance. I suppose that should be obvious to any magician."

"Yes," he agreed. "A balance between order and chaos creates a world in which life, not to mention magick, can exist and evolve. Balzador is dangerous precisely because if he figures out how to control magick and allies with Coronzon, order could be driven from the world and along with it everything that depends on structure to exist. That everything includes us. But if the situation was reversed, and Balzador happened to be an exiled archon, he might very well attempt the exact same thing and we would still have to stop him. Unbending order is no improvement over rampant chaos."

"So how do we contact this Araziel?" she asked, her thoughts shifting to technique.

"We use my scrying crystal and the Holy Table. I can conjure him into the table using an Enochian evocation, and then we should be able to talk to him and see what he can tell us. Have you worked much Enochian magick?"

"Not a lot outside of the research I've been doing lately," she admitted. "And I don't know your system at all."

"That's okay. I was just checking. In that case, I'll handle the conjurations. I would still like you here, though. You can help me verify the results and you may very well come up with some questions that I won't think of. Are you ready?"

"Right now?" she asked, surprised. "I guess so."

"We don't have very much time, I think, before Balzador gets a chance to complete his ritual. He would have finished it the other night if it wasn't for Aleric. We need to do this right away."

Pulling herself to her feet, she followed him into the temple. From the mantle, he took the scrying crystal and set it in the center of the Holy Table. Pressing the false tile on the fireplace, he opened the secret compartment and removed his copy of Liber Iadnamad. He then set it on the Holy Table and walked back to the coat closet adjacent to the foyer. "You'll want a white linen robe," he explained. "I have a spare here, since I assume you don't have one in your car or something."

"Not linen. Is that important?"

"I find that it helps the energy flow more efficiently. If you'd rather wear your own, it's fine though. I suspect that if your robe is attuned to you and not polyester or something, the aura that it's picked up will more than compensate for the difference in material."

"I'll be right back," she said, opening the front door and walking out to her car.

Michael took off all his clothing in the foyer and pulled the robe over his head. He then carried his clothes upstairs and returned wearing the Enochian lamen carved into a brass plate that hung over his chest. He had also placed the Enochian ring, a piece of gold jewelry bearing a particular combination of Angelic letters, on the index finger of his right hand. He retrieved a lectern-like stand from the living room large enough to hold his copy of <u>Liber Iadnamad</u> and set it in the temple to the west of the Holy Table. Placing the book on the stand, he waited for Samantha.

A moment later she walked back through the front door carrying a black duffel bag. "I carry a few ritual implements with me wherever I go," she explained. "That way, I'm always ready if I need to work some magick on the spot." She dug through the bag, pulling out a white cotton robe. "Is there anything else I need? Wand, chalice, incense…"

"No," he replied, shaking his head. "I have the lamen and the ring, and only one of us needs to be wearing them."

"Okay." She started undressing in the foyer, and then suddenly stopped. "Oh, I should probably ask if you mind me changing here. Some people are more touchy about that than others."

"No, go ahead."

She turned away from him and quickly removed her clothing, throwing the robe over her shoulders and affixing the clasps that ran down the front. Her robe opened in front, so it was easier and faster to put on and take off. It also looked quite a bit more difficult to make, since it fitted her shape better than Michael's loose tunic. He probably would have something similar, he thought to himself, except that using a sewing machine was one of those tasks that had always completely eluded him. Once she was done fastening the clasps, she folded up her clothes and set them on top of the bag in the corner of the foyer.

"Now I'm ready," she said walking into the temple. "Should I close the doors?"

"If you would," he replied.

She shut the two sliding doors that separated the temple from the foyer, and turned to face him. "Now what should I do?" she asked.

"Stand directly opposite the table from me," he instructed. "You want to be east of the table facing west. As I work through the opening calls, I'll be walking clockwise around the table and reading one of the Angelic calls to each of the four directions. You will want to walk around the table the same way I do, so there's always a line of magical energy running between us over the center of the table – in particular, that crystal. One I've returned to the east, I'll perform the final conjuration to call Araziel into the crystal. If everything goes well, we should be able to talk with him and see if there's anything we can do to stop Balzador. Oh, and when I do the banishings, I'll be going around the table the same way, so just stay opposite the table as I do them. Make sense?"

"Sure," she said with a nod.

He smiled. "Then I'll begin."

Michael started with the pentagram ritual, first empowering himself and then calling upon the god-names and archangels of the quarters. He continued with the hexagram ritual, aligning his temple with the exterior world, and the first Enochian call, which filled the Temple with pulsing energy waiting to be tapped. That was the secret of the First Call – it was used for evocation, calling forth a spirit into the Holy Table, and thus it empowered the magician to act along the lines laid out in the Medieval grimoires: *"so that every Spirit of the Firmament and of the Ether: upon the Earth and under the*

232

Earth, on dry land and in the Water, of whirling Air and of rushing Fire, and every spell and Scourge of God may be obedient unto Me."

To each of the four directions in turn Michael then read the four calls that corresponded to the Angels of Transportation, spirits that facilitated the summoning of entities from the astral plane, moving clockwise around the table. Samantha concentrated her will upon the sound of the alien Angelic language and felt her own energy along with his drawn into the magical vortex that was beginning to form over the Holy Table. Arriving back in the west, he then intoned the conjuration of the Angels to the four directions in turn, making one more revolution around the Table. As he completed his second circumambulation the magical field in the room stabilized and solidified. Samantha could feel a tangible presence over the center of the Table now, and wondered if it was invoking spirits like this that led to the near-breakdown of Edward Kelly described in John Dee's diaries. She suspected that if these spirits were indeed moving in her head, her own grip on sanity might rapidly become tenuous.

Michael raised his hands into the air and intoned the final conjuration. "Araziel, I summon thee from the celestial realms! *Araziel, zacare ca od zamran! Odo cicle qaa! Zorge, lap zirdo noco Mad, hoath Iaida!*"

There was silence in the temple. Slowly, Samantha's magical sight began to show her something forming in the crystal, first a kind of sparkling, and then a pattern that looked a little like a face. As the image became clearer, she thought she felt the temperature of the room drop.

"Michael," said a voice, not a physical sound, but words nonetheless flowing into her mind from somewhere. "I don't recognize your friend."

"Her name is Samantha. Present your sigil."

An image formed in the crystal, identical to the one Michael had set on the floor.

"Hello, Araziel," he continued as the sigil faded to be replaced by the face. "I have questions for you concerning Balzador, a demon exiled from the Abyss."

"I knew Balzador," replied the voice. "He is one of the strongest of his kind, strong enough that his exile was met with surprise by the Most High. A demon of his kind, even a rebellious one, makes a powerful ally. Have you encountered him, then, in human form?"

"What do you know about him?"

"When Balzador was exiled onto your world, he was forced to inhabit a human body at all times. Thus, when his current host body dies, he will be forced to take over another, and so forth. He reincarnates much like a human soul, but he retains his personality and, too a degree, memories. Once his new brain is fully developed, he has access to all the memories of his former incarnations and thus his personality remains effectively immortal."

"Just like Anna thought," said Samantha.

"Have you encountered him?" repeated the voice.

"Yes. Not me personally, but members of my order. He has obtained a copy of our Liber Iadnamad, killed our Guildmaster, and is planning a ritual that will allow him to collect the magick of the world to a single point, effectively taking control of it. We need to know how to stop him."

"Aleric is dead?" asked the voice. "A shame. I always liked him."

"Yes," agreed Michael. "We all did. Can you help us?"

"Possibly. But not like this. Come to my palace and I'll see what I can do for you. Before you leave, replace this crystal with a dagger suitable for enchantment. You have one, don't you?"

"Of course. But why can't you just tell me what I need to know?"

"You'll see." There was suddenly a flash from the crystal, and the image was gone.

"Araziel?" asked Michael, surprised. There was no response. "I guess he's gone."

"What do you mean, we have to go there?" asked Samantha. "Astral projection or something?"

"Yes. Do you know how to do that?"

"Sure. I've been doing it on and off for years."

"Good. Then you can accompany me. But first, I need a dagger. It's interesting that he would suggest it without being told about your dream." He headed up the stairs and returned a few minutes later. He had removed the Enochian lamen and ring and carried a long dagger in a black leather sheath. "Check this out," he said, drawing the weapon. The blade was obviously high-quality tempered steel, and the hilt was solid and serviceable. It was not a particularly decorative weapon, but it looked like it would be deadly in a fight.

"Nice," she commented.

"I was saving it for some kind of ritual, and I guess this is it. I saw it at one of the martial arts stores a few weeks back and it just suddenly felt like I needed to buy it." He picked up the crystal, replaced it on the mantle, and set the dagger in the center of the table with the point facing due west. "Since I already have the temple field set up, and you know the technique, this shouldn't be difficult. Meet me on the other side, if you can."

Michael seated himself in a loose cross-legged position, and Samantha followed suit. She had a set of visualizations that she had used to accomplish astral travel for years. She focused her mind on the sigil and mantra she conventionally used, and let her mind still as she directed her attention to her astral body. Before her, her magical sight showed her an image of herself standing before her. Shifting her entire consciousness, she felt it jump to the astral double and suddenly she was looking at herself, dressed in a white robe, sitting on the floor in a meditative trance.

As her meditation deepened, the room seemed to fall away. It was replaced by the amorphous twilight of the lower astral plane, a seemingly endless flat grayness that spread out in all directions. Off in the distance, occasional sparkles of shiny brightness provided the only reference points. No earth lay below her, but since there was no gravity either, this did not constitute a problem. Then again, thought Samantha, she could be falling after all. *In this undifferentiated space, how would I ever know?*

Since she had traveled the astral plane in the course of her own magical studies, the scene was not completely unfamiliar, but it was still as disorienting as ever. She looked around, adapting herself to the sort of motion required to get anywhere without a body. On the astral plane, one did not precisely *move*; as far as she knew, the only way she could get anywhere was to focus her attention where she wanted to go and let her consciousness follow suit. It was like navigating a dream rather a material place.

She saw Michael standing far off to her left – at least, in the direction that felt like her left. She fixed her mind on his location, and suddenly she was standing beside him. Up close, he looked very different than he did in person. His aura was completely visible on the astral, an almost overpowering luminance that clung to him like a cloak of light, and she supposed hers did the same. Beyond that, he looked taller and thinner, with finer and more perfect features. It occurred to her that his astral body had some traits in common with Elspeth's physical appearance, the same sort of elfin beauty. She wondered if that meant magical aptitude of a really extreme order warped and shaped the physical body, or if it simply reflected Michael's own image of perfection.

"You look different," he noted as she materialized beside him.

"Daria tells me that everyone does on the astral," she replied. "We appear as we envision ourselves, not as we look in the material world. Of course, there are no mirrors over here, so I've never seen myself."

He smiled, and gestured to the air or whatever it was beside him and an image formed out of the nothingness.

"How did you do that?" she asked as her own image stood before her. She looked very different as well. She was not wearing glasses, of course, and her own aura surrounded her, as bright as Michael's but different in color and density. His was bright white tinted with just a touch of blue, like electricity, whereas hers was golden like the afternoon sun. She also looked physically different, and noted that her features had undergone a similar shift to his. Apparently, then, the distortion was a general effect, rather than the projection of personal expectations.

"Illusion is really easy over here. You just visualize what you want and it appears, for the most part. It helps to hold in your mind either the energy of the Moon or the sign Pisces, both of which seem to amplify the effect."

"Interesting," she commented. "I'll have to give that a try at some point when we're not as rushed. So where are we going?"

"Here," he said, tracing a figure in the air. It was the sigil that she had seen in the crystal. "Focus on it, and we'll be there."

She concentrated on the figure, turning it over in her mind's eye. Then, suddenly, it seemed as though she was rushing through the image and moving upwards, or what felt like upwards. In front of her a great shining white tower rose out of the dense astral mist, followed by the rest of what looked like a vast castle or fortress. She then found herself and Michael standing before an immense set of double doors cast from what looked like pure gold. There was no knocker or handle of any sort, but as they appeared the doors began to open. Hesitantly, she followed him inside. "So you've been here before?" she asked.

"Twice," he replied. "But you need to be careful. It's an astral structure so it isn't solid. It shifts all the time, and it's looked different each time I've been here."

As they walked into what appeared to be a vast hall, larger than she could easily estimate, a cool breeze wafted through the room. At the end of the hall, atop a high dais, an explosion of flame erupted. Their position shifted, and suddenly they stood before the raised platform, bathed in intense heat. From the flames stepped a creature right out of the Christian mythology Samantha had grown up with, proportioned like the statue of a Greek god and ringed in light. From its back extended an enormous set of white-feathered wings.

"Kneel before Araziel, minion of the Most High!" it commanded, in a booming voice that shook the entire space.

Samantha was nearly overcome by an urge to kneel and prostrate herself before this legendary figure, but her magical training held and she fought off the impulse. She turned to Michael as he simply rolled his eyes.

"Cute," he said flatly.

The flames died, the figure shrunk, and the whole room melted away. They found themselves in a smaller and more intimate room that looked like a study, with a sofa, bookshelves, and a fireplace burning at one end. Araziel had lost the wings, though he was still tall and imposing with features that suggested perfect mythological beauty. He appeared to be dressed in a long white robe, leaning casually against one of the bookshelves.

"We're here on a mission, Araziel," said Michael, who had already seated himself on the sofa. "There's no time for that kind of silliness."

"There's always time, Michael, especially here. Are you forgetting that time, like space, dilates on the astral plane?" he asked playfully. His voice was melodic, like a singer's, rather than the booming violence they had faced in the hall. "As for silliness, that's one of the reasons I quit the service of the Most High, you know – no sense of humor. Anyway, I had to test out your friend. Were she a demon or dark minion, she would have fled, and were she not strong, she would have knelt."

"True," admitted Michael. "But we are in a hurry."

"What are you?" asked Samantha. "An angel?"

Araziel smiled, emoting what could only be described as perfect joy. "Not quite, though there are certainly those who have referred to my kind as such including your Guild's own John Dee as I recall."

"Is this your true form that we're seeing now?"

"That is a complicated question," he replied. "Form is relative. The closest thing I have to what you might call a true form would probably appear to you as something akin to a cloud of energy, had you the ability to perceive it. I appear as an angel to inspire awe and as a human being to facilitate communication with the two of you, but they are both projections of my will."

"So your appearance is whatever you want it to be?"

"In effect. I can appear as a man, a woman, an animal, a cloud of light, an object, or any of a million other shapes and forms. In practice I usually adapt my shape to that of the magician who summons me, in this case that of a human male in response to Michael's conjuration."

"I suppose I should be asking about your true nature, then, rather than what you look like. If you're not an angel, what are you?"

"More properly I am an archon, a creature formed by the Most High to maintain the principle of order in your universe. I quit the service of the Most High about four thousand of your years ago because at that time others of my kind were making a move to subdue your world and drive out all of the demons. I was a terrestrial agent of the Most High, a Watcher, and as such I spent a great deal of time among human beings. Through those interactions I came to realize that perfect order can only lead to oppression and stagnation. I think that my brethren still believe that I was corrupted by concern for your kind, but of course there was really nothing they could do to stop my resignation; I followed the proper procedures when I left, and archons never deviate from procedure under any circumstances. So I became, in effect, a free agent. Since then, I've tried to do what I can to look out for your world, though my resources are not what they once were."

"Araziel is known to the Guild," Michael added. "He's been working with certain of our mages for centuries, and has helped out in a number of situations. As I said earlier, Balzador is close to performing a ritual that will allow him to focus the world's magick. Once he does that, he'll be nearly unstoppable. You said that you could help, but we needed to come here. Now we're here. What gives?"

"Stopping a creature like Balzador is problematic," said the archon thoughtfully. "Both demons and archons like myself are fully immortal. As such, we cannot be killed in any meaningful way.

Were Balzador a usual demon rising from the Abyss to possess a body, this would not be an issue – you could simply perform a ritual to cast him back into the Abyss and he would be gone. However, in Balzador's case it is different. Coronzon's magick prevents him from returning, and it forces him to inhabit a physical body on your world. If you were to kill his human body, he would simply jump to another. In fact, he would be compelled to do so."

"So his form can't be disrupted?" asked Michael. "I was taught that you could disrupt a demon and destroy its form on the spiritual plane."

"That is only correct up to a point. The technique you were taught destroys the spiritual form they have built around themselves, but the essence of the demon itself is cast back into the Abyss. Once it builds a new spiritual form, it can return, though that often takes a long time."

"But since Balzador is barred from returning, he would still jump to another body instead."

"Yes," agreed the archon. "Do you think that if he could be killed he would still exist? He challenged Coronzon's throne, and even the Lord of the Abyss could only banish him. It is possible, mind you, for a demon to unite with the universe and in effect die of its own free will, returning to the infinite, but even this is not possible for Balzador while he is bound by the power of the Dark One."

"What about some kind of energy transfer?" spoke up Samantha. "Maybe you could somehow drain off his power and, oh, I don't know, ground it or something?"

"Or perhaps take on the power yourself?" suggested Azaziel facetiously. "That would also fail. Balzador's consciousness follows his magick. Ground his energy, and he will jump into a new body somewhere to attack you again. Attempt to take on his power yourself, and he would jump from his current body into yours, blotting out your mind and personality with his own. Since your magick is likely greater than that of the body he is currently inhabiting, he would then become even more dangerous."

"How about breaking Coronzon's spell?" she pressed. "Or is that hopeless as well?"

Azaziel nodded. "Coronzon is the most powerful being in your universe next to the Most High, and even that varies from day to day. He's the closest thing to a god you're ever likely to face. Even with many mages, my help, and a legion of other archons, breaking the spell would not be possible. Only the Dark One himself or the Most High could do it. Coronzon won't because he imprisoned Balzador to begin with, and the Most High won't because if Balzador and Coronzon become allies the forces of the Abyss will be strengthened and may be able to overcome the archons in your universe."

"So that's not an option either," mused Michael. "What can we do? I take it you have an idea or you wouldn't have asked us to come here."

"Yes. But if Balzador were to learn of it, he could prepare defenses, and as you can probably guess, he's able to listen to information traveling across the astral just like a mage can. It is possible that he has already figured it out, but I don't think so. He could be imprisoned in an object enchanted to look like a physical body on the spiritual level. If this were, for example, a weapon, you could kill his physical body and in effect catch his spirit when it is forced to jump. Hence the dagger." The archon gestured, and the Holy Table from Michael's temple appeared in front of him with the dagger still in the center. He then walked to a cabinet next to one of the bookshelves and removed a wooden box. Opening it, he took out another dagger. "This is the weapon you need," he explained. "It will trap the demon, assuming that he isn't ready for it. Remember that he can read the minds of people around him. Keep your magical shielding strong, and if possible, think about killing him with the weapon, not imprisoning him. That way, he'll assume that you simply don't understand his nature and dismiss you as insignificant. Pride was always Balzador's weakness, as is often the case with demons. I'll place it into the weapon on your Table, and it will be ready to use."

Walking back to the table, he set the dagger he carried in the center of the table, where its form overlaid that of Michael's weapon. He then held his hands over the table, and muttered something that sounded like Angelic, but which Michael was unable to make out. A flash of magical light suddenly filled the room, and as it faded he saw that the Table and the dagger Araziel had been holding were gone. "Is that it?" asked Michael.

"All I can do, at any rate," replied the archon. "You're the one who has to get close enough to stab him. Given Balzador's magick, that may prove difficult."

"You're telling me," said Michael. "I suppose he'll be able to sense us coming before we're close enough."

"Naturally," replied the Archon. "You'll need to catch him when he's distracted. You mentioned that he means to perform a spell to focus the world's magick. While he's casting the spell, you should have an opportunity to strike."

"Thank you, Araziel," said Michael as he and Samantha bowed their heads respectfully. "I hope this works out well."

"As do I," said Araziel. "Go in peace, and may fortune favor you." The Archon raised his right hand and the room melted away, leaving Michael and Samantha standing in the temple looking down at their inert bodies.

"This is the part I hate," commented Michael. "Going back in is always a bit of shock. You're supposed to get used to it, but I never have."

"Maybe you need to do it more," suggested Samantha.

Michael shook his head. "You sound just like Jonas."

They lowered themselves slowly into the space occupied by their physical bodies, which jolted awake as the astral doubles merged back into their nervous systems. They rose to their feet at once, checking on the dagger in the center of the Holy Table.

"Is it charged?" asked Samantha.

"Very much so," said Michael as he picked up the weapon. "Let's just hope Araziel knows what he's talking about. There's still the problem of figuring out where Balzador will be casting his spell. You're still thinking it'll be the site in Rochester?"

"It has to be, doesn't it? That's what I saw in my dream, I'm sure of it. And let's face it, it's not like we have any other ideas. I've taken the week off work with everything going on, so we could head back down there right away."

Michael looked at her thoughtfully. "I took the week off too – I guess we think alike – so I could go as well. I just wonder why, if he has to be in Rochester to cast his spell, what was he doing at Hidden Falls Park? He must have been trying to perform the binding spell – how else would Aleric know what he was up to?"

"Maybe it isn't necessary, but it would be a good move on his part, wouldn't it?" she asked. "Being that far from the Twin Cities pretty much guarantees that he won't be interrupted. Do you think he would try it again here, with all of us listening for his magick?"

"That's a good point. We should probably head down there and stake out the hill before it gets dark. Shall we?" he asked, offering his arm to her in mock formality.

"I'm game," she replied, taking his arm. "Let's hit it."

"I'll call Jonas and let him know what we're up to. If we're lucky, we may just be able to end this before it gets out of control." He took out his cell phone, dialed, and proceeded to update the Guildmaster concerning their plans.

"So you are sure this weapon of yours will work?" asked Jonas.

"As sure as I can be. I got the design from Araziel, who's usually reliable."

"And you think he'll be at the hill in Rochester?"

"I'm less sure of that," replied Michael, "but Samantha dreamed about him performing the ritual there. It's the only lead we have."

"Best of luck, then," said Jonas. "The hopes of all of us go with you."

XV. The Devil

The Lord of the Gates of Matter, The Child of the Forces of Time
The Sign Capricorn

Gray Cloud Island, in the middle of the Mississippi river just south of the Twin Cities, was held sacred by Native American medicine men long before the arrival of European settlers. Surrounded by the moving water of the river on all sides, it became a battery of incredible magical power when the Jet Stream aligned overhead, and that power could be called upon to assist with any sort of magical rite. The moon overhead was waxing but not quite full, which limited to some extent the energy that could be raised from its silvery rays, though the power traveling along the leys more than made up for it. Aside from the moon, the night was perfect.

Wandering through one of the island's wooded areas along the shoreline Balzador had found a suitable clearing earlier in the day. Now, he set about building a circle and various wards that he had neglected two nights before at Hidden Falls, as this time he was not about to risk detection. He carefully carved the circle into the earth with a ceremonial dagger, and then censed and purified the area as his minions had done on the hill outside Rochester. Tonight there would be no mistakes. Just in case, he threw a field of concealment around the entire area to keep prying eyes at bay. He opened his copy of <u>Liber Iadnamad</u>, which he had placed into a sturdy three-ring binder, and began reading the First Call.

"It has to be here," said Elspeth as she climbed out of Jim's SUV.

"Why here?" he asked.

"I checked the Weather Channel before we left. This is where the Jet Stream is currently running. Feel the wind?"

He nodded.

"According to what Balzador said, he needs to perform the ritual where the Jet Stream and the Mississippi River come together," she explained.

245

"The island isn't that small," observed Jim. "He could be anywhere on it. How can we possibly search it in time?"

"We know he'll be by the water," she replied. "In addition, one of the advantages of having a crystal imprinted with his aura is that it should allow me to find him in an area this size. Aggregate Industries owns most of the island facing the main channel, and their land is way too exposed to be useful. He'll want to be close to the main channel of the river, though, so that's why I had you stop here at the tip of the island. I need to be on foot to track him, and anyway the road ends so we need to walk from here."

"What do we do if he's armed?"

"Oh, he will be," she said gravely. "I'm hoping that he'll be distracted enough by the binding spell that I'll be able to disarm him. As long as I have the crystal, the magick he can use against me is limited — any curse he throws at me will hit him too, so he'll need to attack us indirectly. If he loses the gun we'll have the advantage, and I'll be sure to put my dagger to good use." She ran her hand across the hilt at her belt, reassuring herself of the weapon's presence. She then took the crystal from her pocket and held it between her cupped hands, reaching out with her mind to find the demon's location. Since the crystal was linked to Balzador, it allowed her to sense his presence through his concealment spell. "That way," she said softly, pointing south along the shore. "He's pretty close, so we'll want to be as quiet as possible."

They wandered toward the shore through a stand of trees, picking their way through the branches and underbrush as best they could. From further down the bank she began to hear the Angelic language of the Calls echoing through the woods. They slowed their pace at once and crept forward cautiously to the edge of a clearing that touched the water's edge. Balzador stood at the shoreline facing the river, calling magick from the four quarters of the world and weaving it into an intricate web that he bound with a simple sigil. Elspeth could feel the flow of the energy now, like subtle wind gathering between the palms of his hands as he cast. She silently pointed him out, and suddenly Jim was able to see and

246

hear him as well.

"The gun is on his belt," she whispered to Jim. "Here I go. Be ready to run if you have to." She rose to her feet and visualized the symbol of the Rose Cross to the four directions, above, and below as she had done at the hospital and whispered the incantation. While the magick was flowing into Balzador's spell, it was not yet bound and the field solidified without difficulty. Cloaked in her own magical concealment, she crossed the clearing slowly, careful not to break twigs underfoot or make any unnecessary noise. She made it across without being noticed, and stood within arm's reach of the demon, whose attention remained fixed on calling and binding magick into a unified whole that he could wield like a sword against the archons, Coronzon, and all who opposed him.

For a brief moment she considered just using the dagger. She had him, after all, and if she grabbed the gun she would be noticed immediately. The logical part of her mind dismissed the idea, though — she wasn't completely sure that the dagger would work, and the demon's ability to attack her would be greatly diminished if she could disarm him. If the dagger failed and he was still armed, she would be dead.

As quickly as she could, she reached out and grabbed the gun, pulling it from Balzador's belt. Almost as quickly he whirled around, striking the pistol out of her hand and sending it skidding across the sand of the riverbank. At the same moment, Jim charged from his hiding place at the edge of the clearing and tried to tackle the demon. Balzador was inhumanly fast, though, and sidestepped the attack, sending Jim sprawling into the mud and sand that lined the shore. Almost as a reflex, the demon gestured in the direction of the gun before remembering that, since it was plastic, it was immune to magick and couldn't be called to his hand. He brought his other hand up just in time to meet Elspeth's thrust with the dagger, grabbing her wrist and twisting violently. She cried out as she lost her grip, sending the dagger flying across the clearing as she dropped to her knees. Jim rose to his feet quickly and jumped at the demon again, who gestured and dropped him to the ground, fast asleep, with a quick spell.

"So," said the demon as he tightened his grip on Elspeth's arm like a steel vise, "you betrayed me after all."

"You betrayed me first!" she exclaimed, anger overwhelming the pain as she gestured with her free hand. "You killed my grandfather! *Yolcam drilp!*"

The spell that had completely destroyed the Morpheus nightclub scattered around Balzador in a black miasma that clung only to itself and then sunk into the ground, ignoring the demon's form completely. "Is that the best you can do, mage?" he asked contemptuously. "At least your grandfather knew spells that could actually hurt me. I should kill both of you right now – but were I to use magick do so I would squander my power for yet another night and if I used my bare hands it would take too long for me to complete the spell. So consider yourself lucky." He struck her sharply across the face with his unnatural strength and she collapsed into unconsciousness as the demon released her wrist.

Balzador turned back to the globe of light visible only to magical sight that was beginning to diminish in the air above the riverbank and continued his casting. The magick that had escaped during the short fight was quickly bound back into the sigil, and as he intoned the rest of the Calls it grew in intensity, expanding from a globe into a bright whirling vortex that rose toward the sky. He then closed the binder and began summoning the demonic magick of the abyss to bind the power he had called together. As he raised his hands into the light and concentrated, blackness began to swirl through the tornado, turning the light to darkness. Even to his magical sight, the black whirlwind was now barely visible against the night sky.

Finally, the demon clasped his hands over his heart and intoned the final invocation. "*Yolcam gmicalz vovina lansh!*" Obediently, the vortex shifted its base to the center of his chest, and like water swirling down a drain filled him with its entire contents. The shock of binding his will to the sigil struck him like a bolt of lightning, dropping him to the ground along with Jim and Elspeth.

248

It was some time later that Balzador staggered to his feet. His eyes took in the clearing, the forms of his enemies, the river, and the stars overhead. He reached expectantly into the depths of his consciousness and found what he sought – the magick was there, all of it, bound into a sparkling web of light interspersed with the darkness of his demonic heritage. Experimentally, he called fire to his hand and was rewarded with a bright, continuous hot flame, not the simple explosive flash that constituted the previous limit of his ability. He reached out with his mind and extinguished it, and then concentrated again and found himself levitating into the air. Sinking back to the ground, he smiled. He could kill his enemies after all.

As he pointed at the two prone bodies lying before him and threw the death spell, Elspeth suddenly grabbed Jim's wrist and clutched the crystal in her other hand. Balzador gasped in pain as the spell rebounded on him through his link to the crystal. He staggered on his feet as confusion flooded his awareness. "Move!" she yelled, dragging the still groggy Jim to his feet. She suddenly realized that the gun was only a few feet away and dove for it before the demon could recover from the magical backlash. In a single fluid motion she picked up the gun and transferred the crystal to her other hand, interlocking her fingers with Jim's so that the crystal was held between their palms. Then she aimed as best she could and opened fire.

Years of practice at her exclusive gun club had made Elspeth an excellent shot. Her aim was true, and Balzador was thrown backwards by the bullets as they ripped into his flesh. The pain cleared his head and he began willing the wounds to heal. He then willed the space around him to deflect any further shots, causing the bullets to inexplicably veer off course as she tightened her aim. As she realized what was happening she stopped shooting, but kept the gun trained and ready. The demon contemplated charging and seizing the upstart mage despite being unarmed, as his demonic strength would easily give him the advantage, but as he began to invoke more magical energy to enhance his physical

249

power and strengthen the shield he was surprised to feel the energy weak and distorted. He realized the bullets had hit several major organs, and while the world's magick coursing through him was keeping his body alive, there was little left with which to mount an attack.

"Don't move!" Elspeth commanded Balzador as she backed toward the woods leading Jim along with her. She knew the dagger had landed somewhere in the area and she had to find it before the demon could escape. As she approached the tree line she felt something under her foot. "Take the gun," she said to Jim and handed it to him. "Keep it on him." She then knelt down and picked up the magical weapon, which pulsed with energy. *Even with magick bound it still works*, she thought to herself. Whatever Balzador had done must not have affected magical weapons that were already created when the spell was cast.

"Do you really expect to get close enough to use that?" asked the demon dismissively. "Now I can travel like the wind. I will see you soon, Elspeth Sprengel. Count on it." With that, his body simply faded away into the night air. Jim fired three more shots, but Balzador was already gone.

"Damn!" swore Elspeth. "We were so close!"

"What did he do?" asked Jim, dumbfounded.

"The bastard teleported away!" she exclaimed. "He could be anywhere now."

"Magicians can do that?" demanded Jim incredulously.

"Not usually. Apparently, though, demons who've bound the magick of the world can," she replied, disgusted. "We have to warn the others. I just hope Balzador didn't think to disable your truck."

Fortunately, they found the vehicle in working order and arrived at Jonas' house about a half hour later. The new Guildmaster was surprised to see them but quickly ushered them inside.

"What happened?" he demanded. "Magick no longer appears to work."

"Balzador finished his spell," said Elspeth dejectedly. "Jim and I tried to stop him, but he was too powerful. I shot him with his own plastic gun but he still managed to get away."

"He was here, in the Twin Cities?"

She nodded.

"He should be dead," added Jim. "She shot him a bunch of times."

"How many times?" asked Jonas.

"Five or six, all into the chest and abdomen. I must have hit at least one major organ. It appears, though, that binding magick has made him strong enough to survive serious injury, unless he teleported away to bleed to death somewhere. But he's still alive, isn't he?"

Jonas nodded. "He teleported? Impressive – that is one of those mythical powers that I always wondered about." He considered for a moment, then continued. "I am guessing that magick will only remain bound as long as he lives. If his body dies, it should be released. Though I must admit I cannot be sure."

"So we failed and now magick is his to command. And it's my fault."

"Your fault, my dear?" asked the Guildmaster.

She collapsed onto the sofa. "I gave him a copy of <u>Liber Iadnamad</u>," she said dejectedly. "I made a copy of Michael's. I still had a key to the house and was able to bypass his defenses. Balzador told me that he needed it to defeat Coronzon and in return he would protect me from the Guild. I swear I didn't know what he was really planning. I just thought you were all going to kill me and knew I needed some way to stay alive."

"What kind of magical group kills its own members?" demanded Jim. "That's barbaric. How could you possibly be a part of something like that? She had every right to do what she did."

"Perhaps she did," said Jonas thoughtfully. "Since you were not there, you may not realize that my efforts resulted in the sentence of death being rescinded."

"But they'll reinstate it now," she said quietly, her voice more tired than anything else. "And it's okay. I deserve it. My grandfather is dead because of me and I loved him more than anyone else in the world."

"It's still not right!" insisted Jim. "Nobody deserves to die. You didn't kill your grandfather, Balzador did. He's the one you should kill."

"Oh, I agree!" she spat back at him. "It's just a question of how. Do you have any bright ideas?"

"Michael tells me he has a weapon which may be able to do it," said Jonas. "Also, from what you say, magick-proof guns may work if there are enough of them."

"Maybe," she said, shaking her head. "Did Michael make a dagger or something?"

"As a matter of fact he did," replied Jonas. "It is the best choice for a demon-killer, as you well know."

Jim looked like he was about to say something, but Elspeth glared at him and he remained silent. "It's just that Balzador is fast – I mean, really fast," she said to Jonas, who had missed her frigid glance. "It's like his response time is just about zero. He's strong, too. I don't see any way to get close enough to use a weapon like that."

"There is now only one time left," said Jonas, sitting down in his usual chair. "When he is summoning Coronzon. In the middle of a spell he will be distracted."

"That's what I thought about tonight," countered Elspeth. "I got close enough to take the gun but he reacted before I could do anything."

"It is still our best chance," argued the Guildmaster. "How did you know where to find Balzador? So far, that is the part that has eluded us."

"He told me the ritual needed to be performed at the intersection of the Mississippi River and the Jet Stream," she explained. "All I had to do was check the weather."

"And not at the hill in Rochester," mused Jonas. "Samantha was sure that would be the place. She and Michael went down there this afternoon, thinking he would be there. I suppose he's

252

said nothing to you about where he can summon Coronzon?"

"Of course not," she replied.

"By the way," asked Jonas, "do you still have the gun?"

Elspeth nodded, producing it from her belt.

"Set it over here, if you would," said the Guildmaster. She put the weapon down on the coffee table as he continued. "I have to make a phone call. I have a suspicion that this was most likely the gun used to kill Aleric. Balzador might have purchased it under the name of his human vessel, since a weapon like this is unusual enough that it would be hard to find if he was looking to steal one. It is possible that we can trace him if we can find the place he purchased it. I will return shortly."

Once the Guildmaster had departed, Jim waited a minute or so and then turned to Elspeth. "Why didn't you tell him about the dagger?" he asked in a low voice.

"Because they would take it, of course," she replied softly, "leaving me defenseless against Balzador. It's mine. Why should one of them end up with all of the demon's power? It sounds like I'll have to beat Michael to it, though, if he made one too. You're doing fine," she added reassuringly. "Just let me do the talking."

"If Jonas is calling the police, they'll want to talk to both of us," he countered. "We're sitting here with a murder weapon. Where did we get it? They wouldn't believe the truth, so we should probably get our stories straight. I'm thinking that we were out at Gray Cloud Island, and Balzador approached us and drew the gun. You wrestled it away from him and it went off, but he ran away. Sound good? If they ask why we were out there, we'll say we were on a romantic walk down by the river."

She looked at him quizzically. "That sounds perfect. Have you done this before?"

"No," he replied quickly. "I've just read a lot of crime novels. The police always follow the same procedures."

Jonas returned from making his phone call. "The investigators are in the neighborhood and will be here shortly. They will want to question you about how you acquired the weapon."

"Of course," she replied.

Within fifteen minutes there was a knock at the door. Jonas opened it to admit detectives Tom Anderson and Dan Watson, and introduced them to Jim and Elspeth.

Watson did little to hide his suspicion. "So you say you might have the murder weapon?" he asked. "Where did you get it?"

"We were attacked down on Gray Cloud Island," said Elspeth. "The attacker used it. We got into a struggle and we wrestled it away from him."

"Did it go off?" asked Watson.

"Several times," she replied, "but the attacker ran off. I don't think he was hurt."

"We did hear something over the dispatch about shots fired on the island," said Anderson. "One of the neighbors called it in. When did this happen?"

"Maybe an hour ago," she replied, sticking to the truth as best she could.

"Well, that matches the time of the call," admitted Watson. "Is that the gun?"

"Yes. Unfortunately, it probably has my fingerprints all over it."

Anderson looked at the weapon closely. "There are a few bits of sand in the mechanism," he observed. "Like it was dropped on a beach somewhere and picked up."

"The attacker dropped it in the struggle. We were right by the river and the ground was sandy," explained Elspeth.

"What makes you think that this was the same attacker who killed Aleric Sprengel?" asked Watson.

"Well, I don't know for sure, of course," she replied, "but I'm Aleric's granddaughter. What are the odds of both of us being attacked by someone with the same kind of gun within a week? That's a Glock, isn't it? That's what the doctors said was probably used on my grandfather. I'm starting to think this guy is nuts and has a vendetta against my family. Maybe he followed us out there

254

from my house."

"We'll check it out," said Anderson as he gingerly picked up the gun using a pen through the trigger guard and dropped in into a plastic evidence bag. "Just as a formality, did you have any financial interest in your grandfather's death? I apologize for having to ask - I know it sounds heartless when you've just lost a loved one, but that's the first thing they'll look into down at the station."

"It's okay," she said softly. "My sister and I don't have any interest whatsoever. He set up trust funds for us when we were children, and as a result we're both quite wealthy today, but he didn't leave us any of his assets and he had no life insurance or anything like that."

"Good," said the detective. "That makes this look a lot less suspicious with you having the murder weapon and all, if that's what it turns out to be."

The detectives took separate formal statements from Jim and Elspeth before heading back to the station to look up the registration information on the gun and check it for fingerprints.

Michael and Samantha showed up a few minutes after the police left. "What are you two doing here?" asked Michael, surprised to see Jim and Elspeth as they walked into the house.

"Trying to stop Balzador while you were out goofing around," shot back Jim nastily. "I hear you drove all the way down to Rochester."

Michael rolled his eyes. He had dealt with Jim before. "And that's a problem? We had to look somewhere."

"Maybe if you'd gotten it right we could have stopped him," said Jim. "Four of us would have had a better chance than two."

"Stop it!" ordered Elspeth, glaring at Jim. "Why do you have to be such a jerk? We were guessing too."

"So you saw him?" asked Michael, talking directly to Elspeth and ignoring Jim, who stared at him jealously.

"Shot him, even," she replied, "but he still managed to

finish his ritual. And I owe you an apology."

"For what?"

"For a lot of things, really," she said as Jim continued to glare. "But this situation is my fault. I copied your <u>Liber Iadnamad</u> and gave it to the demon. I didn't know what he was planning, but I know that doesn't excuse it. For what it's worth, I promised Grandfather that I would find Balzador and destroy him, by whatever means necessary. But more than that, I need to fix my mistake. I only did it because I thought the Guild would order me killed, and I wanted to stay alive. He said he could protect me – but I should know better than to listen to a demon."

"Next time talk to me first," he said sternly. "I didn't want you killed either, you know. Or at least you do now. But I accept your apology. Maybe if we work together we can somehow deal with all of this."

Jonas walked back into the room from the kitchen. "I thought I heard you, Michael. As you have almost certainly noticed, we have quite the problem on our hands."

"Indeed," replied Michael as he and Samantha sat down. "I wish one of you would have shared that little point about the Jet Stream and the Mississippi, but what's done is done. You say that you shot him?" he asked, addressing Elspeth.

"Yes. Five times, I think, all of them to the abdomen."

"Wow," he replied, honestly impressed. He knew that she was an excellent shot on the target range, but it was all the more impressive that she was that accurate under stress. "And he still was able to get away?"

"He teleported."

Michael's eyes widened. "You're serious? What am I saying – of course you are."

"It seemed like he was able to heal himself, though the gunshots weakened him considerably and it didn't seem like he could do it instantly. I maybe could have taken him out with a couple more shooters – but he also was able to conjure some kind of a shield. It deflected the bullets off to either side of him. With that up, he would be hard to hit."

"It seems that his physical body is still a potential weakness," spoke up Jonas. "He probably needs to turn the shield spell on, so if we could catch him by surprise we might be able to at least incapacitate him."

"I think that's all we could do," said Elspeth, her voice heavy. "I know I hit several major organs. It slowed him down, but the magick in him wouldn't let him die. He may actually be physically immortal at this point."

"Incapacitation might be good enough," said Michael. "Did Jonas tell you I tried out my idea out for making a weapon to stop him?"

She nodded.

"If we can incapacitate him I can use it. I might be able to stab him in a fight, but I wouldn't count on it."

"Don't," said Elspeth. "He's faster than any human I've ever seen. Jonas thinks we could attack while he's distracted summoning Coronzon, but I'm not so sure. He was distracted tonight and he was still too fast for me."

"Let's hope that he was injured severely and needs a little time to recover," said Jonas. "I'll be speaking to the Council tomorrow morning, and hopefully we can formulate a plan. If we are lucky, perhaps the police will find him before he has healed enough to act against them."

"Since when have we been lucky?" asked Michael ruefully. "We're still alive, but he's out there getting ready to strike. Let's hope the Council figures out some sort of strategy. We have the weapon, but we need to find a way to use it effectively, not to mention figure out where Balzador will be summoning Coronzon."

"We also need to find anything we have that can be used against him," said Jonas. "Michael, have you checked the aura of your dagger tonight, after Balzador's binding spell went up?"

"Damn," he replied, crestfallen. "I never thought of that. If it's bound..."

"Do you have it with you?"

257

"It's in the car," he replied. "I'm almost afraid to check it."

"Go and get it, if you would."

Michael did so, opening the trunk of the GTO and taking the weapon out of the duffel bag he had packed for the Rochester trip. He let out a sigh of relief as he picked it up and felt the warmth of its aura, unchanged from earlier in the evening. He clipped the weapon in its sheath onto his belt, just in case.

"It works," he announced as he walked back into the house.

"That means magical weapons and items constructed before the spell went up will still retain their energy," explained the Guildmaster. "If any of you have magical devices that you built in case of an emergency, this is it. The more such things we can find the better. Balzador will not be expecting us to be able to use magick."

"Would more mages help?" asked Samantha. "Most of us have one or two talismans or devices put away, and I could set up a meeting with the members of my order as early as tomorrow. I know there are a few besides Daria in town."

"Do so," said Jonas. "They may be useful simply because Balzador does not know of them, and he will almost certainly eliminate any other mages he can find once he gains his freedom. In fact, you and Michael should go. As a member of the Inner Order he is empowered to represent the Guild, and I have a meeting set up for tomorrow morning with the Supreme Council that could run much of the day. Any help your friends can give us will be most appreciated."

"Valour and Oppression," Samantha said, at least partially to herself.

"What was that?" asked Michael.

"I did a Tarot reading the day after the Morpheus explosion," she explained. "For querant I drew Valour, the Seven of Wands. For environment, I drew Oppression, the Ten of Wands. I thought that maybe the Seven meant that the future was more dangerous than I expected, but now I see that Crowley's description of the card is strikingly accurate. We have little magick to fall back on, the Guildmaster is dead, and it's up to us to carry the day. I had no idea at the time how Oppression could relate to the environment, but it also fits perfectly. Balzador has bound the magick of nature and turned it to his own ends, destroying everything in his way."

"That's the Celtic Cross layout, right?"

She nodded.

"What was the final resolution?"

Her eyes fell and a heavy sigh escaped her lips. "The Devil," she said finally.

"Don't give up now," he said gently, reaching out and putting his arm around her. "Everything will be fine. It just means that we just have our work cut out for us."

XVI. The Tower

The Lord of the Hosts of the Mighty
The Planet Mars

Chaos reigned in the ballroom of the late Aleric Sprengel's former mansion the following morning. The members of the Supreme Council spoke quickly and nervously to each other, tracing sigils in the air accompanied by the corresponding Angelic incantations. Every spell turned out the same - absolutely nothing happened. Like leaves in an autumn wind, the carefully crafted magical forms were whisked away before the energy could rise to empower them, disappearing without a trace into the ether.

Casting the large double doors open, Jonas strode into the room with Sofia in his wake. He wore one of his finest black suits – dressing for war, as he had been known to explain to his students with all seriousness. All eyes in the room turned to him with looks of fear and anger as he took his place at the head of the Council table. Sofia, dressed in an unobtrusive medium gray dress, quietly took her seat at his right hand. As was her intent, the attention of the Council remained fixated upon Jonas.

"I will have order," he commanded, his voice forceful but without hostility. Obediently, quiet settled over the room.

"What has happened?" demanded Robert, his voice accusatory. "None of our spells work!"

"It happened some time last night," added Stefan matter-of-factly. "All of the personal spells I had running simply stopped, and I can cast nothing new. It's the same for all of us."

"I know," said Jonas softly. "I know. We had hoped to move against Balzador, but we have failed."

"Aleric can't have given his life for nothing," said Roslyn. "He could see the future as we can. He must have known something."

"Do you think so?" demanded Robert bitterly. "When I look ahead, I see nothing but death and destruction. What can we

261

do without magick?"

"My students, Michael and Samantha, have created a weapon that they believe may have the power to stop him," replied the Guildmaster.

"And you're not wielding it right now?" asked Stefan incredulously. "Obviously we are Balzador's most logical targets."

"Using it requires getting very close to him," explained Jonas. "With his heightened senses and powers, that won't be possible in a straight fight. We need to use it while he is summoning Coronzon. The ritual will require his full concentration, so he will not be able to detect anyone approaching him. Otherwise, he needs to be incapacitated in some way."

"I'm not about to wait, and neither should any of you," said the German mage. He took a metal case from under his seat, set it on the table, and opened it. Inside were six handguns, which he began handing around the table. "These are polycarbonate Glock pistols, just like the one Balzador most likely used on Aleric. The mechanisms should be entirely immune to magical effects, so that a spell won't be able to make any of them misfire."

"Destroying his body will only put off dealing with the problem, even if it can be done," countered Jonas. "If he is forced to reincarnate, he will only return in twenty years or so."

"Which gives us twenty years to prepare," replied William. "I know it's not an ideal solution, Jonas, but if this weapon of yours is too touchy to use in a fight, I'll settle for the next best thing." He picked up his pistol, checked the mechanism, and cocked it.

"Elspeth and Jim were there last night trying to stop Balzador from casting his binding spell," said Jonas. "They managed to get his gun away from him and shot him five or six times, but he still managed to complete the spell and escape. We have no way of knowing if these will be enough to kill him."

William offered one of the guns to Roslyn, who waved it away. "I put my faith in the tradition," she explained, her hand resting on the long ritual dagger at her belt. "Enchanted with the power of the Archons, it will do more damage than a bullet."

"Suit yourself," replied the Australian mage. "In theory you're right, of course, but in order to use that you'll need to get awfully close. I prefer some distance myself."

"There is also the matter of finding him," added Sofia, "unless he comes after us."

"I got a call from the police this morning," the Guildmaster continued. "They have identified Balzador's human vessel from his fingerprints and the gun registration. As I suspected, he purchased it on special order from a dealer along with the polycarbonate barrel. They managed to get a fast-track warrant and searched his apartment, but it looks to have been cleaned out, probably last night. They did find some hair and fiber samples that I suggested they send to Rochester to see if he can be linked to the murders there. The results of the ballistic tests will be in later today, but suffice it to say that I have no doubt the tests will prove conclusive. A warrant is being issued for Balzador's arrest, so he will need to avoid the police. That should give us a little breathing room."

"Unless he comes straight here," said Stefan darkly. "That is what I would do. Who else in the world could oppose him? We clearly are the enemies he must destroy in order to be certain of success."

Suddenly they were startled by the sound of an explosion from the front hall. The members of the Supreme Council pointed their guns at the door and ducked beneath the huge table. Even Jonas picked up one of the weapons and trained it on the door. "Speak of the Devil," he said under his breath.

The ancient oak of the door exploded in a ball of flame, sending charred splinters hurtling into the room. Balzador strode into the room dressed in a black magical robe, his aura as blinding as direct sunlight to the assembled mages. "Let me guess," he said glibly. "You've all lost your magick. It seems that I've found it."

"What are you doing here, demon?" demanded Jonas, keeping the gun trained on the demon but slowly stepping out of the other mages' line of fire. Together, the other members of the Council turned the heavy oak table on its side, forming a makeshift

263

barricade.

Balzador smiled and shook his head as he watched the frightened mages cower behind the table. "Killing you, my dear Guildmaster," he replied cheerfully, "and the rest of you as well. With the New Moon tonight and magick bound all of you have become expendable."

From behind the table, the members of the Council opened fire. Jonas began shooting as well. The space around the demon bent and twisted, sending the bullets off to either side of where he stood. He gestured in the direction of his attackers, and another smile crossed his lips when he realized that he was unable to stop the weapons from firing. At least they would be a bit of a challenge. He folded his arms and waited for the firing to subside as the mages realized that the shield rendered shooting pointless.

"Picked up my little plastic gun trick, have you?" he asked condescendingly. "It worked pretty well on Aleric. Mind you, after what Anna did to me, as her descendent he had it coming to him. You see, the trouble with trying to fight someone with thousands of years of memories is that they're always a step ahead of you. More life experience means I notice patterns faster and react ahead of time. If you can't stop a gun, shield yourself from the bullets. Now let me see…" he mused, looking around the room and identifying the exits. He gestured, conjuring magical force to secure the two doors on the opposite side of the room. "There we are," he said with a sinister smile. "Now the only way out is through me. Who wants to try first?"

Stefan suddenly leaped out from behind the table and charged the demon, firing as he closed the distance. As the German mage had suspected, the shield became less effective as he got closer, and at a range of less than ten feet he managed to graze Balzador's shoulder. Surprised, the demon backed quickly toward the door and produced a submachine gun from under his robe. He opened fire on full automatic at point-blank range, throwing Stefan's body backwards and onto the floor where it lay twitching but lifeless.

"I really must work on this shield spell," said the demon, more to himself than anyone else in the room. "You know," he added, turning his attention back to the room, "the best thing about a machine gun is that with all of the magick of the world under my control, none of you can throw spells that will make it jam."

"You cannot bind magick forever," said Jonas, his voice threatening. "Know that we will release it, and return it to its place in the natural world."

"How?" demanded Balzador, laughing almost maniacally at him. "You've already lost! Magick is mine. Now come on, who's next? This is almost as much fun as being back in the Abyss, torturing the souls of the damned."

"Jonas, shoot his gun!" yelled Robert as he and William emerged from either end of the table, charging the demon from opposing directions with guns drawn. Realizing what was happening, Jonas took aim at the machine gun and opened fire as Balzador trained it on William, who was the closest. Much stronger than a normal human and therefore immune to the kick of the weapon, the demon held the gun like a pistol at arm's length which brought it near the edge of the shield. As a result, one of Jonas' shots managed to slam into the body of the weapon gun and throw it out of the demon's hand. Robert and William began firing as they closed in, three more shots grazing Balzador's arms and side. He backed up further, nearly to the door, and for a moment it looked like they might have him.

Then, suddenly, the demon stretched out his hand and a shockwave surged through the room, throwing everyone who lacked the protection of the table away from the door and slamming them into the floor. As they lay there stunned, the demon gestured again, calling his weapon back into his hand. He pulled the trigger, but found that Jonas' shot had lodged in the mechanism, rendering the gun useless. He cast it away, turning his attention to healing his superficial wounds. As he concentrated, the bleeding stopped immediately and the skin began knitting itself back together

"I suppose I'll just have to use spells on the lot of you," he said, feigning disappointment. His confidence was supreme and unshaken by the near-success of the two attacks. "That table is in the way." He pointed, and a bolt of lightning streaked from his fingertip, splintering the ornate tabletop and rendering it useless as cover. "So, anybody else?"

Robert and William had pulled themselves to their feet. They stood up slowly, breathing hard, as though they were going to rest, but then suddenly charged at the demon again, guns firing rapidly. Balzador was startled momentarily, but as soon as he realized what was happening he stretched out his hands toward the charging mages and a burst of fire spurted from each of his palms, engulfing them. They fell to the floor, screaming in pain, still trying to shoot as the fire consumed their bodies. In a few moments, all that remained were two piles of black ash.

The demon laughed viciously. "I'll have to try that again once I make it back home."

"You will never make it home," said Jonas. "The Guild will see to that."

"Well, there aren't very many of you left," replied the demon, matter-of-factly. "From seven down to... wait a minute, where's your friend?"

Jonas looked around the room and realized that Roslyn had disappeared. He glanced over at Sophia, who shrugged.

"I know none of you made it by me, neither of the doors down there opened, and you can't cast spells. Where in this room could someone hide? I wonder." As the demon began looking around the room thoughtfully he suddenly gasped and doubled over in pain. Roslyn flickered into view, gripping the hilt of her dagger that was now embedded in Balzador's abdomen. She slid and twisted the blade, trying to do as much damage as possible. The demon's aura flickered and sputtered like a dying candle as the magick of light and order penetrated the core of his body.

Jonas suddenly recalled that one of the things Roslyn was famous for throughout the Guild was invisibility talismans. She

266

must have been carrying one with her, and since it had been made before the binding spell was cast it still worked. The English mage managed to stab the demon again before he was able to twist the dagger out of her grip. Jonas and Sophia charged forward with their weapons, hoping to get close enough to shoot while Balzador grappled with Roslyn. As the blade left the demon's flesh his aura stabilized, but the Guildmaster could see from its diminished brightness that as Balzador became wounded, his ability to command magick decreased, just like Elspeth had said. Jonas hoped that he could use that fact to his advantage.

Maintaining his grip on her arm, Balzador drew Roslyn close to him and with his other hand gripped her by the throat and turned her around to face her colleagues. She struggled, but the demon was far stronger than she was. "Stop or I kill her," said Balzador. He could feel himself weakening, and knew that the shield would start to fade soon.

Roslyn shook her head as best she could with the demon's hand clutching her throat, but Jonas and Sophia stopped in their tracks. The English mage's eyes fell.

"Now drop the guns," commanded Balzador.

Unable to speak, Roslyn's eyes pleaded with Jonas to press the attack. Blood was beginning to pool on the floor where the demon stood, and his aura was weakening by the minute. He glanced over at Sophia, who nodded. "Let her go now," said Jonas, still pointing his weapon. "You're weakening. If you kill her, we will shoot. I can see that your shield is beginning to fail."

"I still have enough power to take care of you," spat back Balzador. Summoning what reserves of magical strength he had left, he threw a death spell over the entire room. Jonas and Sophia slumped to the floor as he tossed Roslyn's lifeless body away like a rag doll. "So much for the Guild." He closed his eyes and concentrated on his wounds, repairing the two dagger thrusts that had nearly bisected his abdomen. Healing light engulfed his body and the process of repairing the damaged tissue began. As strong as the world's magick was, it was still slow when it came to rebuilding flesh. He needed to be more careful – toying with the mages had almost cost him his victory. Still, he thought to himself with a wry grin, it was more fun that walking in and just killing them all on the spot. Despite his urge to spend more time gloating among the bodies, he realized that if other mages were to arise he was in no shape to defend himself – especially if Elspeth and her crystal were with them. As soon as his strength had recovered enough, he visualized the field outside Rochester where he would return to summon the Dark Lord and faded away.

Jonas came to first. He walked over to Sophia, checked her vital signs, and nudged her awake. She looked up at him, confused. "Why aren't we dead?" she asked drowsily.

"Being a Master of the Temple makes you resistant to most magical effects, remember?" he said softly. "Apparently even high-power death spells just knock us unconscious, and I am guessing that Balzador has no idea we're alive. Otherwise he would have made sure we were dead while we were out."

Sophia let out a painful sigh as she rose to her feet. "The Council," she said softly, her eyes lingering over the remains of her comrades.

"We are all that is left," said Jonas gravely. "We cannot let them all die in vain. First Aleric, now them."

"Jonas!" called a voice from the front hall. Elspeth raced into the room and as she saw the bodies her face turned white. "Oh, no…" she said softly, her voice trailing off. "Balzador?" she asked finally.

"We almost had him – at least, his physical body," said the Guildmaster. "He can shield himself from bullets, but the shield weakens if you are close. If you use plastic weapons, he cannot stop them from firing. Magical items created before the binding spell will still work, even with the spell in effect." He held up his hand, collecting his thoughts, and realized it was shaking. "I feel weak," he said, suddenly sounding out of breath. "Sofia…"

"I feel it too," she said quietly. "That last spell took a lot out of us."

268

"I suspect it was the same death spell he used on those poor victims of his in Rochester. It killed Roslyn instantly," he explained. "Only our greater magical strength saved us."

"What the heck is going on?" demanded Jim, walking into the room. "The front door is blasted. Who are these people? What happened here?"

"Balzador attacked the Supreme Council," said Elspeth. "This is Sofia Borgia, Master of Italy. She and Jonas are the only members still alive."

"And barely at that," commented the Guildmaster. "I'm afraid this is going to fall to you, my dear."

"What is?" asked Elspeth.

"Stopping Balzador. After absorbing that spell, neither of us will last very long against him until we have some time to recover, probably days. He said that he would be in Rochester tonight summoning the Dark Lord. Michael and Samantha are meeting with the members of her order later to secure their support, but if tonight goes well we will not need it. Call Michael. Take him and his weapon with you and make sure Balzador does not succeed. You two are the only mages with the knowledge and training to stop him. Eric or Rochelle would be liabilities, as would Samantha and you, Jim."

"I should go alone," said Elspeth.

"Why?" asked Sofia. "That would be far too dangerous. You will need Michael's weapon to kill the demon."

"I have my own. I built it right after my first encounter with Balzador. I also have a crystal he gave me that's linked to his aura. As long as I carry it, he can't throw death spells or anything else at me. It protects anyone else I touch, but I can't wield a dagger very effectively while holding on to someone else and the crystal."

"You really should bring Michael," insisted Jonas.

"So Balzador could knock him out right away with a death spell, like he did with Roslyn? Don't you trust me?" she asked. "I know, after all I've done, I don't blame you. But this is my mess, and I need to take care of it. I promised Grandfather on his deathbed

269

that I would stop Balzador, and I will. He will not summon the Dark Lord tonight - you have my word on that. Besides, if Samantha is trying to secure the support of her order, someone from ours should be there who has an idea about what's going on. Are either of you in any shape to do that? I know Rochelle and Eric wouldn't be knowledgeable enough to discuss the situation. Where are they, anyway?"

"They went out while we were conducting our meeting," said the Guildmaster. "They should be back soon."

"I'm not leaving until they get here," she said firmly. "Both of you look like you shouldn't be left alone."

"At least update Michael on the situation," insisted Jonas weakly as he lowered himself onto the sofa. "Maybe it will be better to have allies ready in case something goes wrong tonight, and you are right – Balzador could kill Michael if he has no sufficient protection. But you know the crystal works?"

"Yes. He tried to use a death spell on me when we fought on Gray Cloud Island and it rebounded on him."

"Good. Now call. Have Michael and Samantha go through with their meeting and let them know what is happening."

"Okay," agreed Elspeth, taking out her cell phone and dialing.

"Hello?" said Michael's voice as he picked up.

"Hi Michael. It's Elspeth. We've got trouble."

"That sounds bad. What happened?"

"Balzador hit the Supreme Council meeting. Jonas and Sophia are alive, the rest are dead."

There was a long pause on the other end. "Tell me you're joking."

"I wish. We know where he's going to summon Coronzon – the circle in Rochester tonight. I'm going after him, and Jonas wants you to keep your meeting and update Samantha's order on the current situation."

"Why? I should be there! We should have as many members there as possible, so that our strength is at its maximum."

"Balzador can throw a death spell that'll kill you instantly," she explained. "He gave me a crystal imprinted with his aura, which protects me. I have my own weapon, too – it's probably just like yours. We've always thought alike concerning matters of ritual."

"Really? Araziel didn't say anything about…"

"Look, Michael, I will stop the demon," she said quickly. "Please trust me. Just get all the allies you can and have them ready in case Balzador has more tricks up his sleeve. Hopefully I'll see you later tonight and we can all celebrate our victory."

"Okay. Good luck to you – I hope you won't need it, but I'm not enough of an optimist to really believe it. I'll have my phone on. Stay in touch."

"I will," she replied.

Rochelle and Eric walked in as she was concluding the conversation. Rochelle ran to the temple and collapsed to the floor as she surveyed the bodies and the smashed table. Eric went pale, but he stayed standing and helped her to her feet. "Balzador?" she asked softly. Elspeth nodded.

"It'll be okay," said Eric, still holding Rochelle.

"We need to get away from here," she said, her voice soft but almost frantic. "I can outrun any car he's got. Let's just go."

"No," said Jonas. "We cannot run. He will find us. With magick bound into him he can teleport. There is no vehicle on Earth that is faster."

"He'll be in Rochester tonight, and so will I. This is going to end, and I'm going to make sure he can never come after us again."

"Not you, too," she said, shaking her head. "First Grandfather…"

"Stay here and take care of Jonas and Sophia," she said, her voice stern but far calmer than the volcanic hatred that flowed through the core of her being at the mention of her Grandfather's murder. *Balzador would pay dearly for that…*

Rochelle nodded. "Okay," she said. "Just make sure he's dead."

271

"I will," replied Elspeth, never more certain of anything in her life.

XVII. The Star

The Daughter of the Firmament; the Dweller between the Waters
The Sign Aquarius

"So you think you can trust her?" asked Samantha as she and Michael walked up the driveway of Daria's Minnetonka home. It had taken them a little half an hour to drive across the Twin Cities and meander through the sprawling western suburb. Minnetonka surrounded the eastern edge of Lake Minnetonka, a shallow but large body of water with numerous inlets that required the roads to curve along the bays and across the narrow channels in an organic arrangement completely unlike the neat gridded blocks of Minneapolis. A little over a century ago, the lake had been a popular tourist destination lined with opulent hotels, resorts, and steamships carrying passengers from one end of the lake to the other. With the advent of the automobile, the city had slowly become part of the Twin Cities metro area, a playground for wealthy suburbanites who inhabited enormous houses along the waterfront.

"I hope so," replied Michael, "and actually, to tell you the truth, I think so too. Elspeth honors her word, and turning against us now would mean betraying her grandfather. She loved him like a father." In contrast to the mansions of the mansions that lined the lake, Daria's house was an ordinary-looking split-level, probably built in the early seventies. Michael realized that he had expected something larger as he pulled his GTO into the driveway, which was of course silly of him since the A∴A∴ was not made up of Great Families who could call upon centuries of accumulated wealth. On the other hand, ostentation had its own problems and likely contributed to Balzador's ability to find the members of the Guild so easily. The landscaping lining the driveway was conservative but neat, the lawn nicely mowed, and the exterior of the house gave no indication of anything unusual going on inside, such as magical operations.

"You know her better than I do," admitted Samantha. "The whole thing just makes me nervous."

"As well it should," he admitted. "I sure hope Jonas knows what he's doing. If she does have an item that protects against death spells, she's right that nobody else should go with her. She did fight him once before and survive, so she probably has a better idea of what to expect than I do. Still, I have a hard time believing the situation is as it seems."

"So you think she was lying?"

"No, but something isn't right," he replied. "Why would Balzador act so openly? It would be smarter to wait and go through with summoning Coronzon before coming after us, unless he hopes to provoke a counterattack. It might be a trap, and given Elspeth's headstrong nature, I'm worried that she might charge right into it."

"Well, he is a demon," pointed out Samantha. "He may simply be acting out of pride and malice. Now that he has the magick of the world bound, he probably thinks we can't hurt him."

"Well, let's hope your friends can help us prove him wrong."

As she reached the top of the steps she rang the doorbell. Daria answered the door and ushered them inside. He quickly locked the door behind them and led them up a half-flight of stairs to the living room. Only then did he speak.

"Daria Edwards," she said, offering her hand to Michael.

"Michael Niemand," replied Michael, shaking hands with the A.'.A.'. mage. He was somewhat surprised at the appearance of Samantha's teacher, as for the most part she resembled a suburban housewife more than a mage – at least externally. After a moment, though, he could sense the power emanating from her. Maybe Samantha was right that she had some difficulties with practical magick, but her spirit was very strong and she clearly gave off the aura of a devoted and accomplished mystic.

"Here they are," said Daria, gesturing the room. Two men

and one woman had already arrived and were chatting in the living room. They all looked to be about fifty years old, like her.

"Five?" queried Samantha softly, turning to Daria. "That's it?"

"Here in town, yes," she replied. "We have a few more students below the rank of Adept, but none of them would be capable of dealing with the current situation. Let me introduce you." Samantha turned back to the room as her instructor spoke. "Everyone, these are Adepts Samantha Davis of our own order and Michael Niemand of the Guild, with whom who we are here to meet. Understand," she added as an aside to Michael, "that according to our tradition meetings like this are never held. Samantha has never met another member of our order besides me until today."

"It's good to meet you all," said Michael, mustering his most polite smile. It was hard to do under the circumstances, but he managed. *How could only five Adepts, without Guild training, possibly help?*

"These are Adepts David Blake, Robyn Wallace, and Jonathan Morgan. Please, have a seat and let's get started."

"If you don't mind, I think I need to stand for this," said Michael as Samantha sat down in one of the remaining overstuffed chairs. "As of today the situation has worsened considerably."

"Is that why our spells don't seem to be working?" asked Daria, sitting down on the sofa across the room next to David and Robyn.

"Yes. The demon Balzador cast a spell last night that binds all of the magick of the world to him. Until he is defeated, it will remain bound. We believe that tonight he will be attempting to summon Coronzon, the Lord of the Abyss, in Rochester. One of our members has gone there to stop him, but if she fails we will be left with few options. Balzador has killed five of our members in the last week, including four this morning, and has attempted to kill at least three others."

"Are you sure it's really a demon and not some delusional

mass murderer?" asked Robyn, gazing at him critically. "From what I've read, demons don't exist the same way you and I do."

"Well, we've never come up with any way to do a global binding on the world's magick that doesn't involve demonic spells, and you can feel that the binding is working," replied Michael. "Everything we've seen is consistent with the being who calls himself Balzador being who he says he is. In any case, his magical power is now quite strong and we need to stop him if we want to bring unbound magick back into the world. For that matter, if he successfully summons Coronzon into this world, will it really matter?"

"That's true," admitted Robyn, "although Crowley is not very clear on whether Coronzon is a personified being who can take on physical form. Your order teaches that he can?"

"Of course," replied Michael, "at least to the extent that any other spirit can. They're mostly energy rather than matter, but that doesn't mean that they can't influence the physical world. Crowley deliberately invoked Coronzon into himself when he was traversing the Aethyrs – had he not been a Master of the Temple and thus at a higher level of consciousness than the Abyss, that could have turned out rather badly."

"So could your Balzador be someone who did exactly that rather than a demon?" spoke up Jonathan.

"Maybe, but whatever the case he's killed seventeen people so far – the members of our order that I mentioned plus a would-be coven of twelve down in Rochester, who were sacrificed to summon the Lord of the Abyss the first time. He also seems to be mostly immune to bullets and can teleport, which makes it unlikely that the police will be able to do anything to him. Since he seems to be targeting mages I'm pretty sure he'll get to you eventually, whatever he is."

"Samantha has kept me apprised of this situation as it has unfolded, and it seems genuine," added Darius. "It scares me, to tell you the truth, but at the same time part of me feels vindicated. So many people think what we do is nonsense, and yet here's indisputable proof that it's real. I started studying magick to understand the world, but the time has come when our studies may be required to save it. I, for one, don't intend to let the Earth fall into darkness, and I don't think any of you do, either."

"That's not the point, Daria," interjected David. "We're not equipped to take on a mass murderer, demon or not. Magick is bound – what good can we possibly do? With whatever power we might have inaccessible, we're just like everyone else."

"You have two things that others don't," said Michael thoughtfully. "First of all, you have knowledge and therefore some idea of what Balzador can and will do. Second of all, I'm thinking that you have magical talismans and devices that you've constructed over the years. Am I correct?"

The other mages nodded.

"Have you checked them?"

"Well, no," said Darius thoughtfully, his voice trailing off for a moment. "I just assumed that with magick bound they wouldn't work."

"Check them," said Michael. "Our items are still operational, and yours should be as well unless your techniques are really different than ours. The binding spell seems to stop ongoing personal spells and keep anything new from working, but empowered items remain empowered."

"I suppose that's something," said Jonathan, "but what can we do?"

"It seems that would depend on what you have," spoke up Samantha. "How about anything that will disrupt demons?"

"Why would we have built something like that?" asked David. "We don't deal with demons and for the most part they leave us alone. I don't know about anybody else here, but I've never built anything resembling a weapon aside from my Air Dagger."

"Nor have I," added Darius. "Suffice it to say that this situation is unusual. Would something like an Air Dagger or Fire Wand be useful against Balzador?"

"I doubt it," replied Michael. "You would need to get

too close. He's really fast. I have this, which is designed to kill demons and trap their souls," he continued, holding out the dagger enchanted by Araziel, "but it's going to be hard to even touch him with it unless he's distracted somehow."

"What if the weapon were thrown?" asked Daria. "That looks like a nicely balanced dagger, perfect for throwing."

"He'd probably block it," said Michael with a shrug. "As I said, he's fast. If he sees you pull the trigger on a gun he can summon a shield instantly to deflect the bullets, and I can't imagine that a dagger or wand would be more difficult to block."

"They're larger and heavier," countered Robyn.

"But without nearly as much speed. That's what we would need to get something through his shield spell – lots of kinetic energy. We tried polycarbonate Glock pistols, with mechanisms that are immune to magick, but they didn't work for any sort of frontal assault when he attacked our Supreme Council."

"So a direct attack is out of the question," spoke up Jonathan. "Could we help some other way?"

"Perhaps," said Darius suddenly. "What is the worst case scenario if you fail against Balzador? Would he kill you on the spot?"

"Possibly, though he might toy with us first. He certainly has the arrogance of overconfidence of a stereotypical demon."

"Long enough for us to reach you if we were alerted to the attack?"

"I don't see how, unless he starts ranting like a comic book super-villain about how powerful he is, or decides to keep us alive but incapacitated while he summons Coronzon."

"But is it a possibility?" asked Darius.

"At this point anything is," admitted Michael.

"Then I have something for you," said the older mage. "Give me a moment." He rose to his feet and walked across the room to a hallway that presumably led to the home's bedrooms and most likely the temple space. He returned moments later with a medium-sized star opal that shone with an orange glow to

Michael's magical sight.

"What is it?" he asked as Darius placed the stone in his hand.

"A magical locator talisman. If you carry this with you, I can see you in my scrying crystal wherever you are, and with much greater detail than would otherwise be possible. We can wait here, and if anything happens we can back you up."

"How?" demanded Robyn. "We could arrive on the scene and be killed, I suppose."

"You need not help if it is not your will to do so," said Daria sternly. "I will not place any of you in danger without your consent. However, it seems to me that even if we are killed in an attempt to save the world from Coronzon that would be better than sitting around and waiting for the darkness to engulf us along with the rest of the planet. We are mages, and the demons will come for us. However, if we can stop Coronzon's summoning, we at least have a chance."

"I do have a number of talismans," said Jonathan. "Invisibility, good luck, healing, protection, things like that. They would give us more of an advantage than anyone else would have. And you're right, Darius, though I hate to admit it. If we decide not to act in the face of Balzador, we will soon be facing Coronzon as well."

"Elspeth may succeed tonight. If so, we all can relax. She has a magical dagger as well and plans to confront him when he is in the midst of his summoning tonight in Rochester. If we're lucky, we'll wake up tomorrow and our magick will have returned. So don't consider a suicide mission inevitable just yet. I like the idea of the locator, though. Will you watch us, Daria, at least until magick returns, and be ready?"

"We all will," said David. "We can do a better job if we watch in shifts. If anything happens, we'll be there."

"That's the best we can do," said Robyn.

"Know that your assistance is appreciated," said Michael, "and once this is all over I look forward to learning more about your order's techniques. As for Elspeth, let's all send what energy we can to assist her. I have a feeling that she will need it."

XVIII. The Moon

The Ruler of Flux and Reflux, The Child of the Sons of the Mighty
The Sign Pisces

Elspeth stepped into the circle and examined the various implements arrayed upon the altar stone. "This is the place," she said softly. "Balzador has to return here to summon the Dark Lord tonight, unless he wants to come up with more dupes to sacrifice or wait for the next full moon. This is where I have to stop him. You should leave before he gets here."

"Yes, I probably should," agreed Jim emphatically, dialing a number on his cellular phone.

A feeling of wrongness permeated the woods around her, a premonition of confinement and restriction. "What are you doing?" she asked nervously, unable to shake the feeling.

He ignored her question, speaking into the phone. "This is Stargazer. Move in."

Her eyes widened, apprehension sweeping across her body like a cold breeze. "What are you doing?" she demanded, more forcefully. "Who are you talking to?"

He only smiled coolly. "You'll see."

Spotlights from all directions suddenly illuminated the top of the hill. Right out of a Hollywood action movie, several groups of people dressed all in black and carrying what looked like automatic weapons stepped out of the woods and began a slow, careful ascent up the hill.

Elspeth gestured frantically, but nothing happened.

"Your powers are bound, silly," he reminded her, "as are mine, and as are the powers of every other mage upon the earth."

She stared at him, stunned. "Who are you?" she barely managed to ask, her voice weak with fear.

He shrugged. "Well, I spent my senior year at Yale as a member of the Skull and Bones Society, and these are government agents. You're bright – you figure it out."

"You're CIA?"

His smile returned. "Good guess. CIA Magick Office, specifically."

The shock of the statement did not reach her right away, leaving her momentarily dumbfounded. Her mind struggled to make sense of the situation, and as the pieces of the puzzle arranged themselves into place she suddenly understood that the man standing before her might be her lover, but he was also her enemy. "You killed my parents!" she finally exclaimed, clenching her fists as anger struggled to overpower her fear.

"Not me personally, of course," he replied, "but yes, it was our organization that carried out the operation. That was a lot of years ago, long before my time."

"So you're here to finish the job?" she demanded spitefully.

"Not at all," he replied, shaking his head. "There are twenty automatic rifles pointed at you right now and your powers are bound – believe me, from this distance they couldn't *all* miss or jam. If I wanted you dead, you wouldn't still be breathing. I had hoped to recruit you into our organization when the Guild condemned you to death, but of course by refusing to condemn you the Supreme Council thwarted that idea. Still, you've been very useful – more so than you realize, I'm sure."

Her voice was wary. "What do you mean?"

"Well, thanks to you we have a copy of your precious <u>Liber Iadnamad</u>, we know where Balzador will be, and we have a subject for our next round of experiments."

"Do you actually think he'll show up here now? You have enough people running around to set off every magical sense Balzador possesses. He'll just find somewhere else, or do his ritual another night."

Jim chuckled smugly. "Our agents all wear talismans shielding them from magical detection. How do you think we've managed to operate for so long under the proverbial nose of your Guild? Balzador is welcome to scan the area ahead of his arrival – you won't register because you still have that crystal of his and the rest of us are shielded. He may not even bother, though – if he were truly being cautious, he would have thrown a death spell at the members of the Council right away rather than toying with them like he did before using his full powers. He certainly seems to be as arrogant and careless as the folklore regarding demons would suggest."

"And what about your vehicles?" she pressed. "Or did you find somewhere less obvious to park them than along the road leading in here?" It also occurred to her that she had not considered how obvious Jim's enormous SUV would be parked on the road when they first arrived, but he had said nothing at the time and clearly did not consider it a problem.

"No, they're parked next to my truck," he replied. "They were following us and pulled in a few minutes after we did. But Balzador teleports, remember? We both saw it. Why would he teleport to the road when he can just materialize at the base of the hill and be that much closer to this makeshift circle of his? He won't be able to see the cars parked on the road from here."

"I could drop the crystal."

"And trust me, my friends will not hesitate to shoot the moment you try it. Why would you want to scare Balzador off, anyway? When I mentioned a subject for our next round of experiments, I was talking about you – we certainly don't intend to capture someone as dangerous as our would-be demon. He won't leave the circle alive, and didn't you promise your grandfather you would kill him? My team is doing you a favor – even if we fail to gain the advantage of surprise, or if Balzador really is too fast to attack, there are too many of us and too many weapons here for him to escape. If we'd had this many shooters on Gray Cloud Island we would have won."

"So I'm an experimental subject?" she demanded, her voice rising.

"Yes!" shot back Jim. "And keep your voice down. Sequencing your DNA will show us where your amazing abilities come from, and how we can engineer more powerful magicians.

Normally that would take decades, but with the magick of the world to assist us we should be able to accelerate the process."

"What are you talking about?" Her voice was lower but still smoldering with rage. Before Jim could respond, though, a sense of foreboding and loss replaced her anger as she realized what his answer would be.

"What I'm talking about is that we also will have the power to bind all the magick upon the earth once Balzador shows up, thanks to your little creation." He gestured to the dagger, still sheathed at her belt.

"You're not taking it," she insisted desperately.

"Oh, I believe I am. You will give it to me, or I assure you my associates won't hesitate to shoot you. I would miss you, as would our program, but we would still have the dagger and even dead your genetic material will prove useful. Now hand it over."

Her eyes darted around the circle, looking for an opening or a way to escape, but nothing came to mind. She was ringed by armed men and women who obviously were well trained, and without her powers, she didn't know what to do. She wondered how regular people managed to survive without the ability to shape the physical world - she was out of options, and there was really only one way out of the situation alive. Though the totality of her being resisted the inevitable conclusion, there was nothing else to be done. She had to give up.

"Do it!" ordered Jim. "Your powers are gone and you're out of options. Please..." he added softly. Elspeth was not sure, but it seemed as though she could hear genuine concern in his voice. Maybe he really did care for her underneath it all.

With a defeated sigh, she unclipped the dagger from her belt and handed it to him. "I guess you win," she said slowly, sounding infinitely weary.

He smiled triumphantly as he took the weapon. "Now we wait. We'll be out of Balzador's line of sight over here."

"Tell me something," she said, seating herself on the cold earth. "Why did your people kill my parents?"

His eyes softened. "I'll tell you what I know. According to Johnston, it was fear," he replied. "In the early days, remote viewing was the cover for the magick office, and Johnston has been the head of the program for almost thirty-five years. He's a good scientist, but he's not a mage – he doesn't know what it's like to be born with power. There were only a few mages in the program back then, and one day one of them came to him with a dream about a child adept born with unspeakable strength and aptitude – you. The CIA knew that your parents were part of some secret magical order, but they knew almost nothing about it except that it was international, and this was in the days of the cold war. They sent an assassin because they knew they wouldn't be able to turn you away from your parents, and because they thought you had potential as a weapon. Once you were dead, the agent was supposed to collect blood samples and other biological information to see if there was any physiological difference that we could measure between mages and normal people. Of course, that effort failed. By the way, I find the whole situation tragic, not that it makes much difference now."

"Tragic? You mean you wouldn't have ordered it if you had been running the show?"

"No!" he replied immediately, sounding amazed at the question. "I'm a mage. I do what I can to avoid harming my own kind, whether you believe that or not. We're the chosen, gifted with the power to channel what the ancients called the divine light. One of us is worth a thousand regular people, maybe a million. I would rather destroy a priceless work of art than kill one of my own."

"You talk like we're a separate species."

"Well, aren't we? Think about it. In the book of Genesis, which is thousands of years old, we read the story of the Nephilim, the offspring of humans and angels who became the 'ancient men of renown.' That sounds like a story about mages to me."

"You think we're descended from angels?" she asked dubiously.

"Not at all," he replied, shaking his head dismissively.

"Those are mythological stories. But they were created to explain a real truth - mages have existed since the beginning of time. To a primitive Bedouin hiking around the wilderness of the Middle East, what better explanation could there be for someone like you? A person who wields the power of a god must be divine in some way. Look at Jesus himself - how many of his miracles could you perform? Taking into account a century or so of exaggeration on the part of his followers, it seems to me that the most reasonable explanation there is that he was also a powerful mage, not some mythological child of a god humans created in their own image."

"But... how can you not believe any of that and then stand here waiting for a demon to show up? That doesn't make any sense."

"Of course it does. Balzador isn't a demon. I was apprehensive at first, but all of our research says that demons lack material forms, and he looks pretty material to me. He's a mage like us, but delusional and with powers beyond our understanding. Don't look so surprised," he added. "There's always someone bigger and tougher, no matter how good you think you are. Somehow, this particular mage has managed to bind the magick of the world into himself, and when I use this dagger against him that power will be mine. Johnston will make me head of the magick office, and we'll use what we can learn from your DNA and our would-be Balzador's to create a new race of mages who may one day rule over the earth as gods. After all, why not replace the current worship of mages long dead with the worship of mages who are still living? You could help me, you know. It's not too late for you to join us. Your power would be a great asset to our organization."

"No deals," she said firmly. "I've learned my lesson on that one."

"That's a shame," he replied, sounding genuinely disappointed. "We'll just have to keep you under lock and key for study, then."

"You know," she said after what felt like a long time, "I didn't understand before why the Guild is so opposed to using

286

magick to shape the course of the world. We all use it as a matter of course in our personal lives. What harm could there be in using our power overtly? But listening to you I get it. We're not some sort of separate race of humanity. We're just people with a particular heightened ability, like scientific geniuses or professional athletes. Maybe we should be allotted some kind of status within society, like the shamans and medicine men of ancient times, but we're not gods. We don't deserve worship."

"That all depends on your definition of a god," he countered. "Spirituality is just another term for psychic awareness. Psychic power is the ability to manipulate that awareness. Some people have it, and some people don't. It seems to me obvious and logical that our kind should rule, as we represent the next phase of human evolution, and it surprises me that you would disagree with that assertion. But in the immortal words of Aleister Crowley, do what thou wilt. In a little while it won't make any difference anyway." He turned to one of the gunmen. "Put her below in the truck."

As Elspeth was taken down the side of the hill opposite the road, one of the agents stepped up to Jim and gestured to the readout on some sort of handheld electronic device. Remaining silent, he gestured for the other agents to hide as he unsheathed the dagger. Sure enough, it still held its power, having been enchanted before Balzador's spell bound the magick of the world. He ducked down behind some of the underbrush as the agents did the same. With the New Moon the night was very dark, and the agents seemed to sink into the shadows and vanish completely.

Rather than hiding, the agents leading Elspeth brought her to a large black truck parked at the base of the hill facing away from the road, where the demon would not see it on his approach. She mused that it must have been pretty difficult to get it so far into the wooded area, even with military-grade all-wheel drive. One of the agents opened the heavy metal doors in the back of the vehicle, which swung open almost silently, and the other pushed her inside.

At that moment Balzador stepped out of the woods. He ascended the hill and walked to the makeshift altar, where he set his binder bearing the pages of Liber Iadnamad. As he opened the binder, the pages fluttered in the wind, but with a wave of his hand the demon calmed the air. An oppressive stillness settled over the hill as the moon reached its apex. *"Adrpan comselah madriax."* He gestured to the altar stone and the whirlwind of darkness and stolen souls suddenly reappeared, shadows revolving in the center of the circle. "Coronzon!" he cried, his voice echoing through the forest. "Lord of the Darkness, Master of the Abyss, I conjure you to this place! Come forth, o mighty one, and…"

The demon gasped with shock in mid-sentence as Jim, stepping silently from the underbrush, expertly buried the dagger between Balzador's shoulder blades.

"No…" whispered Elspeth to herself, feeling the energy of the universe shift. The power that should have been hers was about to become Jim's to command.

The chaotic energy field granted her the use of her powers momentarily, and she made the most of it, throwing spells of distraction on the two agents who were about to lock her in. Carefully sliding the door of the truck open, she ran for it into the woods sowing as much concealment behind her as she could manage. She had to get word to the other mages, if she could find them.

Atop the hill Jim clutched the dagger as the power flow nearly overwhelmed him. Marshalling his magical training, he shaped his thoughts into a vessel that would hold the combined energies of nature. Flooding into him, he felt the ancient elements, the planets, and the wheel of the zodiac. Angels and demons alike filled the air, bound and subservient to his will. Now he was indeed a god, the lord of all magick, the master of the world. He would take the magick office first, then the United States, then the whole earth. His newfound powers would smite his enemies so that none could stand against him.

None, that is, but the alien intelligence rapidly filling his mind.

In his last few seconds he realized what was happening, why Elspeth's theory concerning the dagger was flawed, and what exactly happened to mages who attempted to lay claim to the powers of a demon. But then it was too late.

Balzador stood on summit of the hill, clothed in Jim's flesh. The fog of momentary disorientation lifted, and he looked out upon the hill from his new set of eyes. His old body crumpled to the ground before him, and he looked down at the dagger, coated with blood. "Fascinating," he muttered to himself. "Such an interesting toy…"

"Agent Warwick?" asked one of the men gathered around the hill.

Jim's memories filled through the demon's mind, merging with his own. "Yes, Agent… Robinson," he replied slowly. In addition to the names of his fellow agents, he suddenly realized that as long as he could capture the members of the Guild to sacrifice at a new location, the magick office had a way to defeat Coronzon. As that had been the most questionable part of his plan to conquer the Abyss he could not believe his luck. He already had one Guild mage, and capturing the others would be easy.

"Are you all right?"

"Just fine," he replied smoothly. "We'll need to bring the body to the new command post in Rochester. Dr. Johnston will be arriving in the Twin Cities in the morning." The interruption of the ritual had wasted the power of the moon, which he needed to call the Dark One without sacrifices. Still, it was only a momentary inconvenience after over a thousand years of waiting. He reviewed Jim's carefully articulated plans for world domination, and was forced to admit that they were clever. He would have to consider such a thing himself should Coronzon break his word, now that he found himself a high-ranking magick office operative.

"Agent Warwick!" echoed a voice from the bottom of the hill. "The woman's escaped!"

Balzador's eyes smoldered. "She's resourceful. Still, she

289

can't have gone far. Fan out and hunt her down." As his heightened senses picked up the sound of a car from the clearing where Jim and Elspeth had parked, his lips formed a snarl. Reaching out with his mind, he threw fire into the tank of the black SUV, which exploded in a plume of flame that rose from the clearing.

The sound of the car continued, fading into the distance. He gestured again, trying to target the sound, but nothing happened.

"She's on the road into Rochester," he said angrily. "Radio the police."

"Yes, sir," said Robinson. "What should we do with the body?"

"Call the medical examiner. Once he's here, I want to see if there are any physiological or neurological differences that might explain this man's magical abilities. Assuming that the police can catch the woman on her way back into town, we should be able to make some comparisons between the two of them and come up with something useful."

Robinson nodded, taking the two-way radio off his belt and talking briskly into it. He contacted the police dispatcher almost at once, who assured him that a car was in the vicinity and on its way. There was only one major road back to Highway 52, and the police were sure to catch Elspeth on their way out of Rochester. Ten minutes later, however, Balzador was not amused. The police cruiser had arrived, but Detectives Roth and Walker swore that they hadn't passed anyone on the road. Deciding not to press the issue, the demon hid his frustration and led them up the path to where his old body lay before the altar in the center of the stone circle.

"I'll be damned," said Walker, gazing at the body's too-average features. "Do you think those psychics could have been right?"

"What are you talking about?" asked Balzador as pleasantly as he could manage.

"There were a couple of occult experts that came down here last week," explained Roth. "One of them saw an image of the killer and described it to one of our sketch artists, but the features looked too stereotypical to be those of a real person. Still, I swear this is the man."

Walker nodded in agreement.

"Do you think so?" asked the demon. "He was performing some kind of ritual. There was also a young woman here, maybe a follower of his, but she stabbed him in the back with this ritual dagger as he was completing whatever it was he was doing." Robinson started to speak up, but the demon gestured him to stay silent. "Mind you, I've read up on the case and if she was about to be sacrificed, it probably was self-defense."

"With him, it almost certainly was," said Walker. "We've got five more counts of murder and two of attempted murder up in St. Paul that might be linked to this guy. He was bad news, that's for sure. We'll check the prints and DNA against the evidence from the Cities, and the hairs against the ones we found after the murders here, but I'm guessing this is our man."

"I'm glad my organization could help, then," replied the demon.

"I know I'll sleep better with this nut off the street," said Walker. He turned to Roth. "Get on the radio and get Dr. Mitchell out here. We'll want to take the body back for autopsy and run some DNA tests."

Balzador walked across the top of the hill to one of the agents, a woman in her mid-thirties who was in the process of conducting tests on the area. "The medical examiner will be arriving soon. Work with him and make sure you get all the samples we'll need back in Washington." She nodded, and returned to her testing. He then took out his cell phone and dialed the Minneapolis office.

"Johnston Institute Minneapolis," said the voice on the other end of the line.

"This is Stargazer," he said quickly. "Verify the phone number."

"You're clear, Stargazer," said the voice. "What are your

291

instructions?"

"Access the contact database for a group called the Guild. Look up the addresses under that listing and send a team to each house. Start with the address on Summit Avenue, then the one in Kenwood, and then the others. We're looking for Elspeth Sprengel. Her information should be in the database as well."

"Affirmative, Stargazer. We'll be on it within the hour."

"Do as quickly as you can. She has a head start. Contact me once you've found her, but don't move in right away."

"Yes, sir."

Balzador disconnected the call and returned to where the detectives were examining the body. "I need to return to the Twin Cities at once," he explained. "I'll be leaving Agent Robinson in charge until the medical examiner arrives and we can conduct our own tests on the body."

"For what?" asked Walker.

"It's a matter of national security, detective, and unfortunately that's all I can tell you. Suffice it to say that this individual may be part of a terrorist organization in addition to being a murderer. We need to know for sure."

"Understood," replied the detective with a nod.

"I'll be taking another of the cruisers since my vehicle is no longer operational," announced the demon. "Since the woman is no longer in custody there will be room in the truck for additional passengers. Agent Robinson is in charge in my absence, and I'll be seeing you all tomorrow in the Twin Cities. Make sure your investigation is thorough."

With that, he headed back down the hill, and as soon as he was out of sight he visualized Aleric's mansion and summoned the necessary energy to teleport there ahead of Elspeth. He was met with resistance like an impenetrable wall that slammed into his consciousness, disorienting him much like the rebounding death spell he had cast on Gray Cloud Island. As he came to his senses, he swore under his breath as he realized what had happened. Even with all the magick of the world bound to him, Jim's body was simply an inferior vessel and lacked the magical aptitude of the demon's previous form, and as a result it was not capable of teleportation. Perhaps in time he could figure out what he needed to do to make it work, but his time was short if he wanted to catch Elspeth before she could warn the other mages of him.

A scowl on his face, he climbed into one of the unmarked CIA sedans. Minutes later, he was on his way back to the mansion in St. Paul. He hoped that his agents would get there first.

XIX. The Sun

The Lord of the Fire of the World
The Sun

On the road leading back to Highway 52, Elspeth felt her powers drop off as the energy transfer from Balzador to Jim completed. As she watched the SUV explode behind her, she sighed with relief that she had taken one of the gray unmarked police cruisers used by the CIA instead. Rochelle had taught her how to hotwire a car when they were teenagers, and she had honestly expected never to need the skill. She hoped that the spells she had thrown on the car would hold, a mixture of concealment and separation that should prevent any mage, even Jim at the helm of the world's magick, from sending fire to destroy the vehicle or a curse that would disable it. *So much for being more willing to destroy a priceless work of art than kill his own kind,* she mused to herself. *He'd said it what, fifteen minutes before trying to incinerate her?*

Far off in the distance she heard an approaching siren.

Having never been in trouble with the law before, she wasn't sure what to do if the spells didn't work. The police would spot her, and without any more magick she wouldn't be able to hide. She had seen enough chases on television to know that even the best drivers rarely escaped, and although she could tell the cruiser was fast by the way it accelerated there was no way she could outrun a radio. As a government agent, Jim would probably be able to call in the FBI or any other Federal agency. He could probably also frame her for the murder of Balzador's human vessel if his team was loyal enough to testify against her, and she suspected that even if they weren't, his newfound powers would allow him to arrange for them to see whatever he wanted them to at the scene.

The unmarked police cruiser sped by her, nearly blinding her momentarily with its flashing strobes. She looked into the rear-view mirror expectantly, but the car kept on its way down the highway without any sign of turning around. She breathed a sigh of relief. For now, at least, she was invisible. Up ahead she saw the overpass that marked Highway 52, turned the car onto the northbound ramp, and sped back toward the Twin Cities. She knew that her time was running out, and she had to warn the other mages of this new threat. She took out her cell phone and dialed Michael.

"What just happened?" he asked, without even saying hello. "It felt like the binding spell broke for a minute or two, but now it's back up."

"Balzador's dead," she replied, "but we can't celebrate just yet. It wasn't me who killed him – it was Jim. He's CIA, and he's probably got agents on my tail right now. I'm on my way back to St. Paul."

"Wait a minute. Jim is CIA? I don't mean to be snide, but he always struck me as way too ineffectual to be dangerous. That's some cover."

"Well, as I said, he killed Balzador, so that just makes it worse."

"Why?" asked Michael. "I don't get it. Magick should be unbound with Balzador dead. Or did it somehow die off with him?"

"What do you mean, you don't get it?" she snapped. "When the energy transfer spell went off Jim was holding the dagger instead of me. So now the magical energy of the world is bound to him."

The other end of the line was silent.

"What?" demanded Elspeth after a moment. "Are you telling that me yours works differently?"

"Well, yes," he said slowly. "I consulted with Araziel to help in making mine. It works like a container to trap Balzador's spirit if the dagger is used to kill his physical body. I originally thought about building some kind of transfer device, but according to Araziel, something like that won't work."

"What do you mean?" she asked, confused. "It did work. Jim now controls the world's magick."

"Maybe it looks that way," he said slowly, "but I don't think

296

Balzador is dead. Araziel told me his consciousness follows his power. That means we now have a demon to deal with who's in the body of a CIA operative, and I'm guessing Jim no longer exists. I'm sorry," he added quickly, "but you should be thankful that it wasn't you."

"I was so sure it would work…" she said softly. "Are you positive?"

"I know that according to Jonas, some portions of the binding spell can only be sustained by demonic magick. For the minute or so that Jim was still Jim, the spell was partially broken because human magick can't completely bind the energy of the world. Once Balzador's soul transferred into Jim's body, the spell came back in force."

"Can it be undone?"

"I don't know," said Michael thoughtfully. "I can ask Jonas, but if what he told me about Anna Sprengel's encounter with Balzador is true, I don't think they found a way. All they could do was to kill his physical body, and usually that's a tactic of last resort when dealing with possession."

"Where are you?" she asked finally.

"At Aleric's, with everybody who's left."

"Get out of there," she said firmly. "We need to meet somewhere that both Jim and Balzador don't know about. He might have agents in the Twin Cities, and if I were him I would have put in a call already to stake out everywhere we might meet."

"My place?" suggested Michael.

"No good. Jim was with me when I copied your <u>Liber Iadnamad</u>."

"Well… he's also been to Jonas' house, your place, Aleric's mansion… We could try Daria's place – she's Samantha's senior in the A∴A∴- but they're our backup if something goes wrong and we shouldn't all be in one place. How about Samantha's apartment? I'll check, but I'm sure she'll let us hide out there under the circumstances."

"Sounds like a plan. Where is it?"

"Downtown Minneapolis," he replied, and gave her the street address. "Do you know where that is?"

"Well enough to find it. I'll be there in an hour."

She encountered no more police cars on the road back to Minneapolis, which was either a good sign or a very bad one. With the luck she had been having lately, she feared that it might be the latter. No police likely meant that Jim had decided to find her himself using his own resources in the magick office. For that matter, he also had the power of the world's magick to call upon and her concealment spell would not last forever. She was lucky nonetheless that the traffic was light. Driving the vehicle in rush hour traffic would have been incredibly dangerous, since concealing the car hid it from everyone including other motorists. With only a few cars on the road she could maintain enough distance that she could evade any driver who failed to notice her stolen sedan.

While watching out for other cars in theory took concentrated attention, she still found herself lost in her own thoughts as the freeway stretched out ahead of her, cutting through the rural farmland of southern Minnesota. *Could Michael really be right?* She had not considered the possibility that Balzador's power and consciousness might be connected, and had made not provision in the design of her dagger to separate the energy channeled by the weapon from its structure – doing so would have in fact defeated the original purpose of transferring some of the demon's specialized abilities to the wielder. Maybe Jim was not on her tail because he had simply teleported ahead and was waiting, either at her house or the Guild headquarters previously owned by her grandfather. At least she was not headed there.

As she finally approached the metro area, she suddenly cursed to herself when she remembered that magick was bound. The fastest way to get to downtown Minneapolis was to take Highway 55 where it veered off from Highway 52 – that is, for anyone who happened to be able to cast effective spells. Highway 52 ran into downtown St. Paul, and while it was possible to take Interstate 94 from there to Minneapolis the distance was further. Highway 55,

298

which became Hiawatha Avenue as it traversed South Minneapolis, looked perfect on a map, since it was a straight road that ran all the way to the main downtown exits. The only problem was that the first light rail line in Minneapolis ran along Hiawatha and since it was not an elevated train the traffic lights along its route were completely messed up and switched when the trains went by. With magick, she could change the lights as her car cruised along at near freeway speeds, but now she knew that wouldn't work and she'd likely be stuck at the lights. Just north of the airport, she veered off from 55 onto Highway 62, the Crosstown, and eventually turned north onto Interstate 35W and proceeded into downtown.

Glancing at the address she was glad that Samantha's apartment building was in Minneapolis rather than St. Paul. St. Paul was an older city, and as a result its streets were more irregular than the deliberate grid that criss-crossed its twin. In Minneapolis she usually didn't need directions, just an address, as long as she was in the right general area and kept in mind that streets ran east to west and avenues ran north to south. As she expected, she found the high-rise apartment building easily, parked the stolen police cruiser on the street, and hurried to the front door.

She arrived at the apartment to find the remaining mages gathered in the living room. Jonas and Sofia, the senior members of the Guild, sat on the sofa together, surrounded by Michael, Samantha, Rochelle, and Eric. It was profoundly sobering to realize that they were the only mages left, at least in the Twin Cities.

"Good – you're here," said Michael as Elspeth entered the room. "Do you have any idea where Balzador will be?"

Elspeth took a deep breath and did her best to calm herself. "Slow down a minute," she said softly. "Are you sure that Balzador isn't dead? I saw his body. Jim was still talking to the agents like he was... well... Jim." *Except, of course, Jim would have immobilized the car he thought she was in rather than just blowing it up, which surely would have killed her.*

"With possession the spirit involved usually has access to the host's memories," replied Michael thoughtfully. "His personality

299

would be shifted, though, because those thoughts would be distorted by Balzador's demonic nature. How long were you there after Balzador's body was killed?"

"Moments," she admitted. "I started running for the car when the binding spell let up. I only overheard bits of a conversation – Jim still seemed to recognize the lead agent. Robinson, I think he said the name was. You're right, though. Jim blew up his truck thinking I was in it, and either he hated me from the start and is a fantastic actor or his personality radically shifted in the space of about a minute and half." She sat down, deflated, on the sofa next to Rochelle, who gently laid her hand on her sister's shoulder. "I was so sure it would work!" she exclaimed finally.

"Did he give you any idea where he might be going?" asked Michael again.

"No, but I think I know. He's probably at Aleric's place or one of the other houses of ours that Jim knew about. He might even be at my place, and with magick bound I can't look and see. How on earth do normal people live? This uncertainty is terrible."

"We do have some idea of what he will need to do. He will either be at the site in Rochester in two weeks time to call upon the power of the full moon, or he will seek other victims to sacrifice," said Jonas thoughtfully. "Of course, if the latter is the case, he could perform the ritual anywhere."

"If I were him, I would not wait," commented Sofia. "He will be looking for mages, and not just you, Elspeth."

"Why mages?" asked Samantha.

"Even with the magick of the world bound, the sacrifice of a mage, possibly several, will be needed to call Coronzon unless he wants to wait until the moon is full again and open his circle in Rochester," explained the Italian mage. "Without a full or new moon to assist him, he will need more power to open a new gateway into the Abyss."

"Each of you is thus in grave danger," continued Jonas. "If we move against him as a group, the danger becomes greater.

He will jump at the chance to defeat and sacrifice us all in order to achieve his objectives, and we lack the magick to stop him. Once Coronzon grants him freedom, I believe he will then fulfill what I am sure now is his objective - a full-scale assault upon the Most High and the Archons to tip the cosmic balance in favor of the Dark Lord. This will throw the universe, and possibly many others, into a state of imbalance that could eventually unravel reality as we know it. At the very least, the demons will take this world and reign supreme until the Archons can work out an effective counterattack."

"Which may take several thousand years," added Sofia.

"So we're just totally screwed!" exclaimed Elspeth, fighting back tears. "We don't have any magick. What can we possibly do?"

"As I told you, I have a weapon that may be able to defeat him," said Michael.

"What, like hers?" snapped Rochelle, gesturing to her sister. "That worked well."

"Roach, you're not helping," said Elspeth softly, but with a sharp glare.

"No," replied Michael. "I spoke with Araziel about the current situation. Your grandfather worked with him years ago. At first, I thought that something like Elspeth's dagger would work, but Araziel told me otherwise. The weapon he gave me won't kill Balzador, since that apparently is impossible because Coronzon's magick binds him to the Earth. It will, however, trap him within the blade, unable to act."

"For how long?" asked Rochelle, her eyes softening.

Michael shrugged. "Forever, I guess. He would escape if the blade was broken, but as long as we put it away for safekeeping we'll be safe."

"And our magick will be gone."

"Perhaps," spoke up Jonas, "but I do not think that will be the case. To command magick, Balzador needs a real human body with a nervous system that is capable of resonating with the magical field of the material world. Once his spirit is trapped in Michael's dagger, I believe that the strands of magick he has bound together will be unraveled, and the energy will be returned to its natural place."

"And what if you're wrong?" Rochelle demanded, turning to her teacher.

"If I am wrong, magick will go away," he admitted, "but it is already gone now. Even if it is bound within the weapon, the demons will still be deprived of the power to overrun the world. That is still an improvement over the current state of affairs."

"Of course, to use the weapon we need to find him," pointed out Michael.

"I'll save you the trouble," said a familiar voice from outside in the hallway. The door exploded in a blast of infernal flames, splinters flying everywhere, and Balzador stepped into the room.

The mages leaped to their feet as the demon gestured. A wave of smothering darkness flowed through the room, leaving only Jonas and Sofia still conscious. The demon's eyes widen with surprise as he saw that they were still alive, but he still moved with inhuman speed. Both of the senior mages dove for Michael's dagger, which had fallen out of his hand and lay on the other side of the room, but before they could reach it Balzador drew an odd-looking gun from inside his jacket and fired two quick shots, leaving the two senior mages semiconscious in the center of the room with tranquilizer darts protruding from their sides. "Masters of the Temple," muttered the demon, walking over to where they lay. "If I didn't need the both of you to summon the Dark Lord, those would have been real bullets. But don't worry, you'll be dead soon enough."

With a final effort, Jonas reached once more for the dagger as he lost consciousness, but his hand fell short.

"In here," ordered Balzador. Several more black-clad agents led by Robinson stepped into the room. "I told you that putting tracking devices in our vehicles was a good idea."

"I'm sorry I ever doubted you," replied the agent with a

grin.

Balzador returned his smile. "Put them in the truck. We'll be taking them to the laboratory."

"What are you going to do?" asked Robinson as the other agents began dragging the unconscious mages through the foyer and into the temple.

"Magick," replied the demon. "Don't worry, it'll all make sense once Johnston gets here. Pick up that dagger on the floor and bring it as well. That one tried to attack me with it, and I'll want to examine it further once this situation is under control."

"So you just knocked them all out?" asked Robinson as he picked up Michael's dagger. "I only see two darts."

"I used a spell on the others," explained Balzador dismissively. "Those two, though, are senior members of their organization. They're resistant to magick. Has Dr. Johnston's plane arrived yet?" he asked, quickly changing the subject.

Robinson nodded. "His flight arrived about ten minutes ago. He should be arriving at the lab shortly."

"Good. He'll want to see this. It could give him something to demonstrate at the Congressional hearings next week and keep our budget as high as it needs to be to protect this country. Now come along and help me with the preparations – tomorrow we make history."

XX. Aeon, or Judgment

The Spirit of the Primal Fire
The Elements of Fire and Spirit

Michael slowly came to and looked around. He found himself in a vast room that looked like the inside of a converted warehouse. His hands and feet were bound and he was sitting on a metal folding chair facing an enormous magick circle traced into the floor. Positioned evenly around the circle he saw the other six members of the Guild similarly restrained. Strange devices lined the perimeter of the figure with heavy cables running to the black stone altar that sat in its center, and on the altar he saw a silver chalice and a censor with the sheen of real gold rather than the usual brass. Glancing down at his belt, he saw that his dagger had been taken from him but quickly located it on a cheap folding table behind him that had been set up near what appeared to be the only entrance to the place. Also on the table sat a few other objects, probably Elspeth's crystal and any other magical devices that the mages had been carrying. A heavy electrical whirring sound filled the space, and sunlight tinted slightly red filtered in through skylights high above them. He must have been kept asleep all night and into the following day – but was he seeing the light of sunrise or sunset?

As he looked over his shoulder at the table that held the various magical implements, he heard the door click and watched Jim step into the room. *Balzador*, he reminded himself. The demon was followed through the door by a balding older man in his mid-sixties wearing thick wire-rimmed glasses that gave him a studious look. Balzador was dressed in a black robe, while the older man wore a long white lab coat. "As I was explaining," the demon was saying to the older man as they crossed the room to the circle, "the machinery we have here will allow us to restrain Coronzon once he appears. As you know, the containment system has been under development for some time, and only now do we find ourselves with the opportunity to use it. It will allow us to harness the demon's power and use it to create a most impressive demonstration for your Congressional hearings next week. Even if we can't manage to hold the Dark One indefinitely, we will be able to do so for a long enough time that we should have no problem justifying our budget allocation."

"You've certainly outdone yourself, Agent Warwick," replied the older man, inspecting the equipment. "But why are they here?"

"Unfortunately, summoning the Dark Lord requires the sacrifice of living beings with magical aptitude," replied Balzador, expertly concealing his amusement with the situation and sounding genuinely saddened.

"What?" demanded the older man. "You didn't say anything about this when we last spoke. To waste so many mages…"

Michael tried to speak up, but found that although he was not gagged, it felt like he was unable to formulate words in his mind. Elspeth appeared to be having the same problem, while Rochelle, Eric, and Samantha, along with Jonas and Sophia, who were gagged, were still unconscious.

"We have all the DNA samples we need, in addition to the records of their practices and rituals," said the demon reassuringly. "This won't hinder our research."

"Still, on ethical grounds, it's…"

"Dr. Johnston, surely you understand the value of this experiment," interrupted the demon firmly. "You can't let misguided ethics get in the way of progress, or, for that matter, preserving our funding. Our work is too important."

"James, I'm sorry, but I can't allow this," insisted Johnston. "I'm a scientist, not a murderer. There must be another way."

"Tell that to Elspeth Sprengel's parents – you know, the ones you had assassinated," replied the demon coldly, pointing to the circle of chairs. "That's her over there, all grown up. You and I both know that we need to do what's necessary in order to get the job done."

"Look…" said Johnston haltingly, flustered, "that was a

long time ago. We had no idea what we were dealing with! Knowing what I do now, I would never, under any circumstances, repeat such a terrible crime against…"

Balzador raised his right hand and Johnston immediately stopped talking in mid-sentence, as though in a trance. Michael could see magical energy flowing into the scientist's forehead from the demon's palm. Johnston looked confused for a moment, then shook his head and adjusted his glasses.

"I'll return to the panel and monitor the equipment," he said calmly. "When will you be starting?"

"Soon. Wait for my signal."

Johnston crossed back to the door and closed it behind him as he returned to wherever he had come from. A smile played across Balzador's lips as he gestured in the direction of the circle.

"You bastard!" exclaimed Elspeth, suddenly able to speak. "How can you do this? I loved you!"

"Of course you did, my dear," he replied. "Jim loved you as well up to a point, even though he was also setting you up for recruitment into the magick office and using you to get at your order's research. The problem is that I'm no longer Jim — I'm the demon you betrayed. I see you brought another of those magical daggers, which I would invite you to go ahead and use if I didn't need all of you for the ceremony. I would actually prefer a more magically capable body such as yours, but I can't afford to waste any more mages if this is going to work."

"What are you going to do?" asked Michael.

"Capture Coronzon, just like I told Johnston," replied the demon with a triumphant smile. "As I discovered when I took over this body, the magick office has spent many years and millions of dollars developing these machines, which can hold and stabilize the form of a spiritual entity on the material plane. It means that once Coronzon grants my freedom, all I have to do is throw a switch and the Dark Lord will remain here, his throne vacant for me to assume. It will save me a lot of trouble. Johnston can go ahead with his stupid demonstration after that — I'll be back home, and

307

if Coronzon ever manages to escape he'll find himself displaced. Then maybe I'll imprison *him* on this odious little rock for a few thousand years and see how he likes it."

"I'll see you crushed and defeated, you miserable…" began Elspeth, but Balzador gestured again and she fell silent.

"She's rather tiresome, isn't she?" asked the demon facetiously.

Michael again found himself unable to respond.

Balzador stepped up to the altar. "Charge capacitors," he called out loudly. The whirring sound increased, the pitch rising and the volume reverberating through the chairs and concrete floor. "Cameras on. Activate Tesla coils."

The machine was divided up into four columns, one placed at each of the cardinal directions. As the sound rose, sparks of purple plasma extended out into the room. The effect was physical, but it looked suspiciously like a magical aura. The sparks came together at the cross-quarter points, enclosing the whole circle in a glowing field, and Michael felt the hair on his neck begin to stand on end as static electricity permeated the air.

The demon waited a moment, and then picked up the chalice, walking to each of the four cardinal directions in turn and speaking the words of purification as he traced a circle in the air before each column. "By the salt of earth and the water of the great sea, I purify this place of working." Upon completing his walk around the circle, he returned to the altar and traced an inverted pentagram in the air. "In the name of Typhon, lord of the seas and the deep earth, I purify by water." He then returned the chalice to its place on the altar.

Picking up a small container of incense, he placed some of its contents into the golden censor, which began to fill the area over the altar with thick smoke. He then picked up the censor and walked around the circle once more, tracing crosses over the circles at the quarters and speaking the words of consecration. "By the air and fire that make sweet the world, I consecrate this place of working. " Returning to the altar once more, he traced an inverted

308

pentagram in the air. "In the name of Set, lord of the sun and the boundless sky, I consecrate by fire." He then returned the censor to its place.

He stood silently, connecting with his breath and with the magick of the world that flowed through him. Jim's body did not allow him to use his powers as effortlessly as had his previous form, but he was rapidly becoming more comfortable in it. Michael watched as the energy swirled around the demon, collected over the altar, and slowly began to rotate into a vortex of tangible darkness. As the energy solidified, Balzador spoke the chant.

> *I celebrate the powers of night,*
> *That which vanquishes the light,*
> *This night, Dark One, hear my call*
> *And stand before us all.*

As the energy field spun more rapidly, he raised his arms into the air and intoned the conjuration. "Coronzon, lord of chaos, lord of entropy, lord of dispersion, mighty dragon of death, *telocvovim*, I, Balzador, summon thee from the infernal abyss! Come forth and stand before me, that our agreement may be fulfilled! *Coronzon, zacare ca od zamran, odo cicle qaa, zorge lap zirdo noco Vovin, hoath drilp!*" The smoke from the censor was picked up by the vortex of whirling darkness upon the altar, and the cacophony of the Abyss began to become audible. As the sound rose, Michael thought he heard the click of the door behind him but didn't dare turn his head to look.

"And now it's time for all of you to die," said Balzador, his predator's grin widening. "I'll apologize in advance for not using magick, but I'm not in the mood to contend with resistance to spells." He kept his left hand raised to control the energy of the summoning spell, and with his right pulled a new submachine gun from inside his robe and trained it on the circle.

He never got as far as pulling the trigger.

Instead, his eyes widened and he whirled around viciously,

opening fire in the direction of the door. Michael saw his dagger protruding from the demon's back, and as he twisted his neck to look at the door he saw Daria of all people diving out of the way.

The universe shuddered as the binding spell broke. *Araziel hadn't mentioned that effect*, thought Michael as he suddenly realized he was able to use magick again. *Of course, he hadn't asked the archon about it.* The vortex on the altar began falling apart, scattering shards of blackness throughout the chamber as it collapsed and diminished. Daria managed to get the door open and escape from the room as the wall around the entrance was showered with bullets.

"Stop her!" yelled Balzador, presumably to the agents outside, as he turned back to the circle. "I'll find other magicians next time," he hissed, aiming the machine gun at the bound mages and pulling the trigger back hard.

There was a loud metallic click as the gun jammed.

Looking across the circle, Michael saw Elspeth's gaze fixed on the gun and also noted that the pool of blood at Balzador's feet was getting larger and larger, but the demon appeared not to notice. *How much blood can he lose and still survive?* thought Michael. *Does he think he still has the magick of the world behind him to heal his injuries?* "You troublesome little bitch," muttered Balzador, noting her defiant stare. He threw the useless weapon onto the floor, and moments after he did so Daria raced back into the room accompanied by the other three A.'.A.'. mages. Unfortunately, they were too far from the circle to close the distance before the demon could act. Balzador reached over his shoulder and pulled the dagger out of his back, brandishing it as he charged toward Elspeth.

It was a mistake. From the spray of blood, the dagger must have lodged itself in the demon's heart or aorta such that its presence was the only thing slowing the flow of blood. As Balzador drew back his arm to stab the immobilized mage, he suddenly lost his grip on the dagger and stumbled. As the weapon clattered to the floor, he steeled his mind, summoning the power he had left and willing himself to fight, but the loss of blood was too much for even his demonic magick to overcome. He collapsed to the floor and lost consciousness as the life drained from his physical body. As he fell, the A∴A∴ mages reached the circle and quickly began releasing the Guild mages' bonds.

"I didn't know you could throw a knife, Daria," said Samantha as her instructor untied her hands and feet. She had woken up only minutes ago and was seated on the side of the circle opposite the door. As a result, she had seen the whole fight.

"I'd make a joke about a misspent youth," she replied, "even though I didn't do much besides study back then. One thing I did do was practice throwing knives, and I'm glad my aim is still good."

Rochelle and Eric woke up quickly as they were being untied, but Jonas and Sofia slept right through it, probably because they had been sedated with tranquilizers rather than magick.

As Jim's former body lay still, Michael watched the interplay of spectral light between it and the dagger with his magical vision. Instead of scattering in all directions, the energy of the demon's soul hovered over its deceased physical vessel, constrained to enter another human body by the ancient magick of Coronzon. Like a black hole consuming a star, the dagger began to absorb the light of Balzador's true form, which slowly diminished and then finally disappeared.

"Was that..." began Robyn.

"Balzador," said Samantha, nodding. "The dagger was enchanted to imprison his spirit, and the blood on the blade formed the magical link."

Johnston, Robinson, and the other agents all filed into the room. The scientist practically ran from the door to the circle. "Oh my God!" he exclaimed, honestly frightened. "Are you all right? What happened?"

Michael looked at the old man quizzically, until he realized that demonic magick had clouded everything that had happened, and it was left to him to come up with a convincing explanation. He decided to keep it simple. "He tried to kill us!" Michael exclaimed quickly, indicating Jim's body. "Is that what you train your agents to do?"

"No, of course not!" exclaimed Johnston. "He told me he was going to summon a powerful demon so that we could test our containment system. I had no idea what he was planning. Are the rest of you alright?"

Michael walked across the circle and checked Jonas and Sophia's vital signs. Jonas' eyes flickered open and he looked up sleepily. "Michael?" he said softly. "Where are we?"

"I'm not sure," he replied, "but we won. The dagger worked."

"I can feel the magick flowing back into the world. That's good – as it should be."

"Where *are* we?" asked Michael, turning around and addressing Johnston. "None of us were awake when we were brought in here."

"Downtown Minneapolis," replied the scientist, "on the edge of the warehouse district."

Sophia yawned and opened her eyes. "How did we wind up here?" she asked as she raised her arms and stretched.

"Tranquilizer darts," said Robinson, helping her to her feet. "Sorry about that – Agent Warwick said it was necessary. We used more of the drug to keep you asleep overnight."

"I should have a word with him," said the Italian mage with annoyance in her voice.

"Well…" began the agent awkwardly, gesturing to the body.

"I see," said Sophia. "I suppose, then, that won't be possible."

Jonas had already risen to his feet and was shaking hands with Johnston. "Jonas Votan, Master of the Guild."

"Dr. Cedric Johnston, Director of the CIA Magick Office," replied the scientist.
"I'm pleased to meet you. I understand that your group has made considerable advances in the field of practical magick."

"Indeed," replied the Guildmaster. "We have been

312

elaborating on John Dee's Enochian system for centuries culminating in a magical paradigm that is both simple and effective."

Michael rolled his eyes. Conversations about magick theory with Jonas could go on for hours. He walked over to where Elspeth stood, staring down silently at the lifeless body of her former lover. "I know that he used me," she said slowly, "even before he became Balzador. I still miss him, though."

"I know you do," replied Michael, putting his arm around her shoulders.

"And then there's Johnston. I should pick up the gun and kill him right now. It'll work fine without my Saturn field on it."

"But what would that solve?" asked Michael softly.

"I know," she said with a nod as a single tear ran down her cheek. "That's why I haven't done it. I could see when he was talking with Balzador, and not just from his words. His aura shuddered at the very thought of it – that decision must haunted him every day of his life. All killing him would accomplish is more death and pain. He probably has a family, too."

"Probably," agreed Michael.

"Part of me thinks I'm weak for doing nothing. It's funny – now that my powers are working again I can sense where we are, just a few blocks from Morpheus, where all of this began. That was only two weeks ago."

"It seems like ages," he commented. "So much has happened."

"When I cast the spell at you at the club, the part of me that thinks I'm weak when I don't act was the only part of me that I could hear. I thought that somehow I wouldn't be able to live with myself if I just let you walk away. But in the end it would have been so much wiser – my grandfather would still be alive, I still could have dated Jim, and all I would have had to deal with would have been my own disappointment at being passed over for a place in the Inner Order."

"Balzador still would have struck. He summoned Coronzon before Morpheus, and he would have been a dangerous adversary no matter what happened. But it would have been easier on you, and maybe on all of us."

"I guess what I'm trying to say is that I'm starting to see that the voice in my head that tells me to do something – anything – in response to a situation I find upsetting isn't always right. There's another voice, too, the one that tells me it doesn't matter how I look to everyone else, or what my rank happens to be, or even how I judge myself. When I listen to that voice, there's clarity, not the haze of anger, and it's like the world inside my mind opens up and there's all this space there that wasn't there before."

"And in that space is peace and wisdom and everything else we talk about in our lectures and rituals. The Great Work."

Her eyes sparkled with recognition. "But it's so disconcerting – like standing at the rim of the Grand Canyon and seeing forever in all directions! How do you stand it?"

"Stillness," replied Michael. "It takes time, but that's all there is to it. Just let it go. Concepts get in the way."

She shook her head. "I had no idea."

As he and the other A.'.A.'. mages finished untying everyone, Daria simply walked up to Samantha and hugged her, taking her by surprise as she had never seen her instructor display affection of any kind. "We were so worried about you!" she exclaimed.

"So your scrying stones worked after all?" she asked, still not knowing how the other mages had managed to find them.

"Beautifully," replied her teacher. "Once we found the building it was just a matter of using a couple of talismans to distract the guards and we were able to slip in. The access card for this room was just sitting on a table outside the door – I have a feeling that Balzador was a lot more careless than an actual CIA agent would be, so getting in was easy, and the dagger was sitting right there so I took my shot. The machine gun really shocked me, though. I have one of my protective talismans on and was expecting a spell, and I have to admit this is the first time I've ever been shot at."

"That's one experience I certainly hope to avoid," she

commented.

"It's terrifying!" added Daria with a noticeable shudder. "I'm just lucky that the door is plated with metal and that I wasn't too far into the room to run back out when I saw that Balzador was armed."

"You're also lucky that you didn't miss. I can't tell you how glad I am that you're good at throwing knives."

"That makes two of us. So – can we get out of here? I'm still feeling kind of rattled by the whole thing, and I'm sure I'm not the only one."

"Yes," agreed Jonas. "We can certainly take this conversation somewhere more hospitable."

"I'm going to stay and supervise the cleanup," said Johnston. "But I'll be in touch. Your order's work is fascinating!"

As the mages wandered out of the building and onto the street, the setting sun stared down at them from behind the Minneapolis skyline. Michael put his arm around Samantha as the wind picked up, cool but with a hint of the coming summer. "So is this the life of a practical magician?" she asked, an impish grin drifting across her face.

"Hardly," he deadpanned. "Believe it or not, a lot of the time it's more exciting."

She laughed out loud. "Is that what you tell all your new recruits?"

"Something like that," he said with a chuckle.

XXI. The Universe, or The World

The Great One of the Night of Time
The Element of Earth and the Planet Saturn

The resulting scandal nearly destroyed the Magick Office, forcing Johnston into some clever damage control over the course of the following week. The official explanation was that James Warwick, an otherwise upstanding agent, had suffered a psychotic break after killing a mass murderer with delusions of occult power and proceeded to turn an otherwise well-designed parapsychology experiment into a vehicle for the practice of human sacrifice. Warwick had then been killed by one of the experiment's participants before he could gun down seven bound and unarmed men and women, all slated for some sort of Satanic ceremony. In the interests of national security the events were classified in order to conceal the existence of the Magick Office, but Johnston had a lot of work to do convincing Congress to renew the office's budget for the following year. Fortunately, he and Jonas were able to put together an impressive demonstration of the effectiveness of practical magick and as a result the work of the office was allowed to continue provided nothing so bizarre ever happened again. Johnston also agreed to more extensive psychological testing of his agents to make sure that they all had the requisite mental stability to deal with paranormal phenomena effectively.

"In here, Michael," called Jonas from his study as he heard the front door open.

Michael walked into the room and sat down in one of the chairs opposite his instructor's heavy oak desk. Unlike many of the mages, Jonas favored simple, almost austere woodwork. The desk was large and functional, but without any fanciful scrollwork or decoration. "You wanted to see me?"

"Yes," said the Guildmaster with a sly grin. "Do you like my new paperweight?" He gestured to a piece of what appeared to be a chunk of granite on the desk with a slit hollowed out of the top.

Aside from the slit, the rock looked unremarkable. "I suppose. What's so special about it?"

"Well, it happens to be a holder for this," he explained, taking Michael's dagger from the drawer and placing the point into the slit in the top of the stone. "You even picked a dagger that displays well."

Michael reflexively recoiled to put some distance between him and the weapon. "Is Balzador in there?" he asked trepidly.

"Oh, yes," replied Jonas. "He can hear every word. But you can relax – he is fully contained and can do nothing to either of us."

"You're sure?"

"Positive. You made the dagger, after all – I assume that you trust your own powers and abilities. And Araziel has never failed us. You are completely safe."

Michael breathed a relieved sigh. "So it's over? Really over?"

Jonas' voice was reassuring. "Yes. For all time."

An impish grin crept across Michael's face. "So if I were to tell him how stupid he was for screwing up when he was so close to succeeding, he would hear me?"

The dagger's aura shifted and sparkled momentarily, prompting Michael to involuntarily lean back in his chair as his eyes widened. "Is... is that normal?"

The Guildmaster smiled back mischievously. "It only happens when he's upset, but yes, it's normal. As I said, there is no way that he can hurt you, even if you were holding the weapon. He is completely trapped and will be forever – you and Araziel did your work well."

The dagger sparkled again.

"You're sure there's no way he can get out?" Michael asked again, apprehensively.

"Only if the dagger is physically broken. Even then, he

318

would have to reincarnate as a newborn and start over," replied Jonas. "Needless to say, as Guildmaster I am not about to let that happen and the dagger will be passed on to my successor. In a roundabout way, that brings me to why I wanted to see you." He slid the dagger off to the side of the desk, where it did indeed display nicely, adding a martial edge to the otherwise plain look of the room.

"What's up?"

"We have a problem in the Guild right now with the death of so many senior members in such a short time. Our offices are normally filled on the basis of seniority, and believe it or not, on that basis you are up for a slot on the Supreme Council."

"Our order is that small?" demanded Michael, incredulous.

"The Inner Order is," admitted the Guildmaster. "Remember, with all of the recent deaths we have five slots to fill, and you are the fifth. We have one Inner Order initiate in California, two in Italy, one in England, and you, the most junior member, here in the Midwest. Along with Sofia and I, that fills the Council, assuming everyone accepts. If someone does not, we could wind up with an empty chair, since only Inner Order members and higher can serve."

"Wow," Michael said softly, still amazed. "I had this image of our order as large and international, with mages everywhere. I had no idea that we were down to so few."

"I may have to ask one of you to relocate to Australia as well, since there is a medium-sized group of lower-level initiates there who are now leaderless with the death of poor William," added Jonas, "but I think I may be able to get John to do that – he is the initiate in California, and being a member of one of the Great Families he will not have to worry about finding work."

"That's always nice," commented Michael.

"We are growing, though," continued the Guildmaster. "The latest generation to reach adulthood seems to be much more interested in working collectively within a group structure than

319

was yours or the one before it, and there is considerable interest developing in esotericism and the occult. It looks like we may indeed manage to rebuild our membership within the next twenty years, but right now I need someone to serve on the Council. Will you?"

"Oh, of course, Jonas," said Michael quickly, realizing that he hadn't answered the question. "I'm just surprised. I was only initiated into the Inner Order a month ago!"

"I know," he replied with a sigh, "but sometimes history is made by those who show up, or for that matter those who survive."

"Even though I have to admit that I hoped to serve on the Council someday, this isn't how I imagined it."

"Nor I," agreed Jonas gravely. "We will be holding the installation ceremony as soon as all the Inner Order initiates can travel here, and some of the initial matters we will be discussing are, first of all, how closely we want to collaborate with Samantha's A∴A∴, and secondly, whether or not to lift the ban on Elspeth's entry into the Inner Order. She clearly is a good enough practical magician and she did save all of our lives by jamming Balzador's gun. On the other hand, she also provided him with Liber Iadnamad which allowed him to do what he did, even though she did it because she feared for her life and was lied to. Do you have any thoughts on either of those issues?"

"As far as the A∴A∴ group goes, they seem to be serious and competent even if they're less focused on practical work than we are. From talking with Samantha it sounds like they have some techniques that work differently than ours, so it seems to me that we could learn a lot from each other. Samantha plans to keep studying with you and seeking formal initiation into the Guild while continuing her previous work, and since she has Daria's blessing there it sounds like there isn't any animosity that could get in the way of cooperation."

"That is my opinion as well. Their techniques are different enough that between our two systems I think we may be able to resolve some of the longstanding questions regarding the operation of magical forces. I suspect the idea of working with them will not be controversial, especially given that they did save all of our lives. The decision on Elspeth, however, will not be nearly so simple."

Michael paused, choosing his words carefully. "I think that I saw more maturity from her than I've ever seen up at Johnston's lab. You realize that she was standing in the same room with the man who ordered her family killed years ago with a completely functional machine gun on the floor three feet away from her."

"Yes, and I met with her earlier today. Her presence is surprisingly different, even transformed. I did not expect to see that — but perhaps confronting her past has succeeded where her previous training failed. I felt unexpectedly good about her prospects after the interview."

"I think it had never crossed her mind that Johnston would have regrets about what he did until she heard him talking with Balzador. My opinion is that she's going to turn out just fine, though of course I do have a bit of a soft spot for her and always will."

"Fair enough," said the Guildmaster. "We also should discuss the possibility of working with the Magick Office — I have been in touch with Cedric and I think we might be able to work out some kind of an agreement where he could study the way in which we work magick."

"I heard about your successful Congressional demonstration, but I thought you were opposed to scientific verification," countered Michael. "That's what you've always told me, and it's what you told Samantha, what, a couple weeks ago?"

"Cedric and I have had some conversations that may be changing my opinion on that issue. Bear in mind that this will be under the auspices of a relatively secret government program, and after all nobody tried to ban remote viewing when that became public. It may be that most people just are not interested," explained Jonas. "Besides, the world is changing and the investigation of magick might be just the thing to prompt a new spiritual awakening.

Understand, I am still of two minds about it, but I think it is an issue that should be discussed by the Council."

"I think it's a good thing," said Michael. "After all, both of our organizations believe in the future of magick and believe that it can be used for beneficial ends. Even the situation with Elspeth's parents could have been dealt with in a much more rational way if the Guild and Magick Office had been on speaking terms twenty-five years ago. For us to be fighting each other is silly – magick has more than enough enemies as it is with the skeptical materialists on one side and the religious fanatics on the other."

"That is a true thing," agreed the Guildmaster. "I have always considered you one of my wisest students, you know, and I am realizing that we are reaching the point where it is no longer really proper for you to think of me as a teacher. A senior colleague, perhaps, but your path is rapidly becoming your own."

"What… what do you mean?" asked Michael, taken aback. "You'll always be my teacher. I have so much more to learn – I don't feel ready."

Jonas chuckled. "None of us ever do. A substantial portion of wisdom consists of understanding your own ignorance and limitations. That was why Elspeth had such a hard time comprehending the truth, and why she behaved the way she did. Her conceit and more importantly her raw talent kept her from seeing how much she failed to understand. You're going to be just fine, Michael. I have no doubts."

"I'm glad one of us is convinced."

"We have never spoken of this," said Jonas slowly, "but I know how much you gave up in becoming a magician. Before we invited you into the Guild I spent a great deal of time watching you and your family. We knew that it would be difficult for you, but when I cast the deciding vote I did so because I saw in you great potential for both power and wisdom to emerge. I now can say with all certainty that I made the right choice – and I hope that you feel like you made the right one as well."

Michael shook his head. "I never really had a choice, you

know – I was driven to find the secrets of the universe and I never would have stopped. My parents were spiritual people because they saw that there was more to life than dead materialism. It's ironic, really, that my spiritual progress was the very thing that drove them to reject me. As a magician I've touched the face of divinity again and again, but for all their piety I doubt they'll ever see past their own judgmental worldview. Knowledge scares them – they don't want to see the truth for themselves because they're terrified that they might be wrong, and that would be too much for them to bear. I'm not even angry with them anymore after all these years – I just feel sorry for what they're destined to become living life that way. There's just not much more to say."

"Except to welcome you to the Supreme Council," said the Guildmaster, "and to tell you how proud I am of you and how thankful I am that you once chose to become my student. Looking into the future, I see that you will do great things."

Michael rolled his eyes. "That's what I'm afraid of. I think I've had enough of great things for awhile. Good things would be fine, especially if they aren't hazardous to my life and health."

"Another threat of Balzador's magnitude is unlikely to emerge any time soon, if ever. We have much work ahead of us, but battling demons will be the least of our worries for a long time."

"That's good to hear."

"So are you seeing Samantha tonight?" asked Jonas, changing the subject.

Michael smiled. "Of course. I worry sometimes that we may be moving too fast with everything that's happened, but then again we have a lot in common – as you well know."

The Guildmaster's eyes danced. "Yes, I do. As usual, I find myself thinking how much easier this all could have been if the Council had just listened to me from the beginning."

"Well, I know better than most that you're not always right. You just always get what you want – eventually."

"That I do," agreed Jonas. "I just hope that the things I

want will always be the right things."

"Well, you were right about Samantha being a good Guild mage. I'm amazed at what she's managed to pick up already. Her previous training was quite good, and I'm finding myself a lot more impressed with the A∴A∴ than I once was. I suppose it's not surprising that the order that makes the least public noise is probably the best. At any rate, I really have no idea where this all will lead, but you never know – maybe she and I will wind up starting a new Great Family."

"That would be something," said the Guildmaster, "and I wish you all the happiness in the world."

"I certainly intend to take advantage of that," replied Michael with a wide grin, "at least, until the next crisis. Let's just hope it's a long time off."

000. Epilogue

Ain Soph Aur – Limitless Light

Michael and Samantha lay next to each other on the cool grass that covered the top of the city water reservoir in St. Paul's Highland Park. The huge tank was covered with sod and descended underground, but also rose high above the level of the park and the street as a strangely regular hill with a large flat summit. Hanging out on top of the reservoir at night was theoretically illegal, but concealment spells worked wonders. Besides, the top of the hill was at the wrong angle to be seen from the street so the two of them were not visible to anyone below as long as they did not stand up or walk around.

"So you're on the Supreme Council now," said Samantha.

"At least once the other initiates get here for the installation ceremony. I was completely stunned," admitted Michael. "First to find out how few Inner Order initiates there actually are, and then to realize that I was going to become one of the people who will govern the Guild for decades after being an Inner Order initiate for only a month. It's a lot to process, especially after all that's happened since then."

"I'll bet."

"Then, for Jonas to tell me that I can't really be his student anymore – that was kind of a shock too. He's right, of course. As an Adept I need to be guided by my own conscience and inner light, not by the dictates of a teacher."

"Not only that, but there could be a conflict of interest on the Council or at least it might appear that way."

"We need to meet as equal individuals in order to govern," he agreed. "It's just that he's been my teacher since I was eighteen years old, and he's been more like a father to me than anyone else ever has been. It's not my parents' fault that they are who they are – at least, mostly not their fault – neither of them was born a mage, and so they have no idea what we're like. We need to understand everything. People like them are just looking for spiritual platitudes,

325

not the truth."

"Well, my parents don't really understand my obsession with magick either, but at least they're not fundamentalists. I think on some level they're proud that I've achieved so much – they just don't really understand why anyone would go through what I've gone through just to understand the workings of spiritual forces. Faith is good enough for them."

"I suppose that's the way it is for most people. Just not for us."

They lay there silently for a long time, looking up at the sky. The gentle wind from the southwest was warm with the promise of an early summer, and the full moon illuminated the clouds that speckled the starry field above.

Michael reached out with his mind, extending it to encompass the cloud nearest the ground. He pointed with his index and middle fingers as he visualized a form.

"What are you doing?" asked Samantha, feeling the energy move.

He smiled as the cloud gently twisted and then formed into the rough shape of the letter S. "That's an S for Samantha," he said with a bright smile.

"How do you do that?' she demanded, sitting up and looking down into his eyes.

"It's like the pendulum," he said slowly, "but on a bigger scale. Clouds are soft so they're easier to shape, but instead of focusing on the object you have to focus on the space it occupies. It takes some practice."

"That's the difference, isn't it, between us and everyone else. Most people watching you sculpt a cloud would either dismiss it or run away in terror, but when I see it I ask how it's done. The potential scares them – either the vastness of the universe isn't there or it's something too overwhelming to be believed."

"But the world is stranger than they could even imagine it to be." He reached up and ran his hand through her hair as it fluttered in the night breeze.

326

"I've dated enough unbelievers. Their small-mindedness always trips them up, or at best renders them boring after awhile. You have no idea how refreshing it is to be with someone who actually understands me and shares the greatest passion of my life."

"Oh, I think I have some idea," he replied. "I've dated magicians most of my life, but it's nice being with someone real – not throwing a tantrum and trying to curse me, or not understanding the idea of having to work for a living, or being confused by the idea of saving up money to buy things instead of just ordering them on the spot regardless of the price. The Guild can be such an insular society that it's easy to slip into that sort of righteous narcissism, and I've seen enough silliness along those lines to last a lifetime."

"So we're made for each other!" she said brightly.

"That's a very good thing," he replied warmly.

No fireworks materialized over them as they kissed, but not for lack of energy or intensity between them. Magick was free, flowing through and enlivening all of nature, and the blazing oppressive force that Balzador had wielded like a sword of light in service to darkness now darted between the blades of grass like fireflies, danced among the clouds, and gathered here and there in pools of spectral light visible only to magically attuned senses.

But it was enough.

www.ingramcontent.com/pod-product-compliance
Lightning Source LLC
Chambersburg PA
CBHW032242010726
47494CB00002B/599